PENGUIN BOOKS

Christmas with the Bomb Girls

Daisy

and a

their stories

pub, on the dance floor, in the

happened to them on the bus going into town. It was from
these women, particularly her vibrant mother and Irish
grandmother, that Daisy learnt the art of storytelling.

PENGUIN BOOKS

By the same author

The Bomb Girls

The Code Girls

The Bomb Girls' Secrets

Christmas with the Bomb Girls

DAISY STYLES

PENGUIN BOOKS

PENGUIN BOOKS

UK | USA | Canada | Ireland | Australia
India | New Zealand | South Africa

Penguin Books is part of the Penguin Random House group of companies
whose addresses can be found at global.penguinrandomhouse.com.

First published 2017

001

Copyright © Daisy Styles, 2017

The moral right of the author has been asserted

Set in 12.5/14.75 pt Garamond MT Std
Typeset by Jouve (UK), Milton Keynes
Printed in Great Britain by Clays Ltd, St Ives plc

A CIP catalogue record for this book is available from the British Library

ISBN: 978–1–405–92980–6

www.greenpenguin.co.uk

MIX
Paper from
responsible sources
FSC   FSC® C018179
www.fsc.org

Penguin Random House is committed to a
sustainable future for our business, our readers
and our planet. This book is made from Forest
Stewardship Council® certified paper.

For Clare Marsh, Catherine Wheale and Susie
Stevenson, like the Bomb Girls in my story
our friendship has grown stronger over the years,
regularly watered with tears of laughter and joy.

Prologue

Sweating in the intense heat of a late-summer afternoon, Gladys wiped her brow with the silk scarf she was impatiently trying to shove into her battered suitcase. The thought of being late for the troop-ship that was bound for England made her sweat even more. If she didn't get out of Naples soon, she honestly thought she'd lose her mind. Sitting on the suitcase, she snapped it shut, then noticed she hadn't packed the silky red ball gown she'd regularly worn on stage over the last six months.

How she'd loved the feel of the fabric when she'd worn it for her very first overseas ENSA performance – the slither of silk falling over her slender, tanned body, the deep colour of the fabric that brought out the darkness of her long brunette curls, and the luscious redness of her smiling lips. When she'd sung, swaying to the rhythm of the music she and her fellow musicians played, she had relished the feel of the silk clinging to her hips and breasts, emphasizing her long legs and flat stomach. She'd never felt more vibrant or empowered in her entire life. Catching a glimpse of her wan reflection in the bedroom mirror brought tears to Gladys's eyes; could this be the same girl who had landed in Italy such a short time ago? She'd been brimming with confidence, excitement, curiosity and a determination to bring a smile to every weary serviceman's face. She wasn't just there for fun; Gladys had been on a mission to create happiness wherever she went. ENSA was indeed an accolade in her career, but she also saw it as a duty, her part of the war effort. 'Well, I obviously took that belief one step too far,' she thought cynically to herself. She'd been so starstruck, so green and keen. She simply hadn't been able to believe her big blue eyes when their ship had finally docked in the Bay of Naples. She remembered now that one of the girls had pointed to a plume of dark smoke curling up from a high grey peak that dominated the headland.

'Good God! Is that the latest Jerry bomb drop?' she cried.

The sailors eagerly helping the girls to disembark had guffawed at her naivety.

'It's bloody Vesuvius!' several of them pointed out. 'It's a live volcano – that's why it's smoking.'

Gladys had gaped in amazement; she'd heard about Vesuvius, seen pictures of it in library books, but nothing matched the dramatic reality of it. Her naughty friend Pam, who played the double bass in the All-Girls' ENSA Swing Band, had given Gladys a nudge in the ribs.

'Forget volcanoes, sweetheart. Take a look at all these gorgeous fellas who haven't seen a woman in months!' her best friend had giggled as she slipped her bare arm through Gladys's, and laughing together they'd strutted ashore.

'But that was then,' she remembered mournfully. 'And how very naive I was.'

Lifting the heavy suitcase with an equally heavy heart, Gladys determinedly didn't look back at the red silk ball gown that lay in a crumpled heap on the floor where she'd left it.

1. The Cowshed

Gladys dropped her now even more battered suitcase on the moorland track where she'd stopped to take in deep breaths of clean air. After an arduous sea-trip in a packed troop-ship, followed by a long journey on several packed and smoky trains, she was grateful for the fresh moorland breeze.

'I'm back at the Phoenix,' she muttered dejectedly.

After her surprise appearance in Leeds, where Gladys had emphatically told her parents she'd left ENSA for health reasons, she'd refused to answer any more questions and registered at the local labour exchange, where she had asked to return to her former munitions work at the Phoenix Factory on the Lancashire moors.

'No problem, lovie,' the woman behind the counter had briskly replied. 'Four years into the war and we need more bombs than ever. Churchill's so desperate for more ammo he's now conscripting women of all ages; they'll welcome you back with open arms,' she said as she handed over the forms for Gladys to fill in.

Her father, sitting on one of the benches in the exchange, didn't return his daughter's awkward smile when she announced, 'I'm a Bomb Girl – again!'

Rising, Mr Johnson put on his flat cap, even though the sun was hot outside, then gently drew his daughter's arm through his. 'I'll never understand why you've given up your ENSA posting,' he grumbled as they stepped out into the high street, where sand bags were stacked against shop windows and people hurried by carrying their gas masks and net bags containing small packets of rationed food. 'You were on top of world when you got called up and now you won't even talk about it.'

Gladys's large blue eyes clouded over. 'It just wasn't for me, Dad.'

Mr Johnson snorted dismissively. 'Don't give me that, our Glad!' he protested. 'It were all your dreams come true: playing your alto sax and singing on a stage every day.'

'People change, Dad,' Gladys said as she hurried her grumbling father past a woman pushing an old rusty pram loaded down with coal.

Seeing his precious daughter's troubled eyes brim with tears, Mr Johnson's tender heart contracted. He knew instinctively something had happened to his little girl out there; she certainly wasn't the bright-eyed, shining, talented girl her family and friends had waved off in February. Something had radically altered her former buoyant personality, and, more shocking than that, he hadn't heard Gladys sing once since she'd come back, nor play her saxophone, which had stayed locked in its case under her bed. It was simply incomprehensible to him that his daughter, a born songbird, was now mute. He sighed but said nothing. If her younger brother, Les, had been home, maybe he could have cracked Gladys's hard shell – she'd always responded to his teasing laughter and cheeky questions – but he was at the Front, some-where in northern Europe was the last they'd heard. Maybe returning to the Phoenix would bring a smile back to Gladys's face, Mr Johnson thought. Maybe being with old friends and in familiar places would help ease whatever the pain was that she was suffering.

Picking up her suitcase, Gladys carried on up the track that led to the cowshed that she'd specifically asked to return to when she reregistered at the Phoenix. She wasn't sure with whom she'd be sharing, but it would be comforting to be back in the place where she'd spent so many happy hours. Pushing open the door, she stepped inside and quite spontaneously called out, 'Anybody home?'

Getting no reply, Gladys peered into the bedrooms, which were empty, with the curtains drawn. She looked around in surprise after she had opened them to let in the light. The rooms were dusty, so clearly no-body had been living there, and the wood-burning stove, which had kept them warm through the hard winter, was stone cold. Leaving her case in her old bed-room, Gladys sat on the doorstep and gazed out over the moors, where pheasants cackled and curlews called. Of course Kit and Violet weren't living there any more. Kit had written to tell her that she and Ian had bought a big old farmhouse on the Pennine moors, and Violet was living in the Phoenix's domestic accommodation with her husband, Arthur, and their new baby, Stevie. But why had nobody else been allocated the cowshed as their digs? It was a decent enough place, even if it was a little breezy in the harsh winter months.

Maybe other Bomb Girls preferred the convenience of the on-site factory accommodation to the renovated cowshed.

Gladys glanced back into the main sitting room, which was eerily still. She smiled as she recalled the constant babble of noise she, Kit and Violet used to make as they rushed to clock on at the factory or returned home exhausted after a twelve-hour shift. Kit had been the best at rekindling the wood-burner with whatever she could collect from the moors, and Violet had never wasted time in filling the little kettle for a much-needed brew. There'd been occasional sadness in this place, Gladys remembered, and dark secrets too, which had slowly unfolded over the year as the girls got to know each other. But, oh, there had been so much laughter and joy! Gladys would never forget the first time they'd sung together, and the evening she'd come up with the idea of the Bomb Girls' Swing Band. Neither would she forget dressing Violet on her wedding day or the sight of Kit's son, Billy, toddling around the dining table when he'd finally been reunited with his mother. These women were her best and most beloved friends; along with Maggie, Myrtle and Nora, they were as close to her as family. An overwhelming sense of need brought a lump to Gladys's tense throat; the sooner she could see her friends, touch them and hug them, the better. Leaping to her feet, she quickly closed the door of the cowshed, then retraced her steps, lighter now without her suitcase, down the lane to the Phoenix Bomb Factory.

Kit and Violet were sat around a metal dining table in the noisy canteen, which rang with the strains of the Andrews Sisters' 'Boogie Woogie Bugle Boy'.

'I can never hear that song without thinking of Glad,' Kit said with a heavy sigh. 'Remember how beautiful she looked up on the stage, holding her sax in one hand as she clicked her fingers and swayed her hips. She was a sensation!'

'We weren't so bad either!' cheeky Maggie quipped as she set down her plate of red cabbage, potato pie and mushy peas. 'Even in our overalls we looked good.'

'I preferred wearing our ball gowns,' Nora added as she set down her plate too. 'I've always thought mi bum looked big in mi overalls,' she admitted, with not a trace of embarrassment.

'Really!' Myrtle exclaimed as she took a sip of hot, strong tea. 'There's a war on and you're complaining about having a big bottom!'

Nora smiled her sweet, guileless, gap-toothed grin at the older woman, who'd become more of a mother figure than a friend since the death of Nora's mother, who'd been killed in a bomb attack along with Nora's younger sister.

'I'll never get a fella if I've got a big bum,' Nora joked.

Myrtle rolled her eyes and looked disapproving, but it was hard to hide the love she had for the gawky girl who wore her heart on her sleeve.

9

'Men like something substantial to get hold of,' she said reassuringly.

'What, like the sideboard!' Nora tittered.

As the women around the table burst into raucous laughter, Myrtle appeared momentarily distracted – was she seeing things? But as the tanned, long-legged figure she'd spotted walking through the canteen came closer, she couldn't believe her eyes. Could this really be Gladys, who, when last heard of was on tour with ENSA? As incredulous as she was observant, Myrtle was immediately struck by a physical difference in her dear friend. She was distinctly thinner, and Myrtle saw she'd lost the happy glow in her eyes, and an infectious smile no longer played around her full red lips. Myrtle gave an involuntary shiver; it was as if something had wilfully reined in Gladys's previously wild extrovert character, replacing it with a sadder, older, more sombre woman altogether. What on earth was going on?

As Gladys headed towards her laughing friends, Myrtle was surprised by the unusually cautious smile on her face. Even her voice when she called out 'Hiya!' didn't have the ring of joyful confidence Myrtle so clearly remembered.

The other girls, like Myrtle, were as shocked as she was at the unexpected sight of Gladys, who, they'd imagined, they wouldn't be seeing again for many months, possibly years. Maggie all but choked on a lump of pastry, and Nora just gawped. Violet and Kit were the first on their feet, embracing Gladys in a bear hug that, when combined with those of Nora and Maggie, followed by a discreet kiss on the cheek from Myrtle, all but knocked Gladys off her feet!

'What a surprise!'

'Why didn't you let us know you were coming?'

'How long can you stay?'

'I love your tan!'

'You've lost weight.'

'Sit down, have a cup of tea.'

Barraged with questions, more hugs and mugs of tea, Gladys sank into a vacant chair.

'I came home a few weeks ago ... I'm not going back,' she announced flatly.

Her statement stopped short all the curious chatter.

'NOT going back?' spluttered Maggie, whose secret dream had always been to join Gladys and her ENSA troupe.

'WHY?' cried Nora, whose romantic head was full of images of singing to handsome Desert Rats under palm trees.

Gladys put on a tight bright smile. 'It didn't suit me, all the travelling. I got ill, had to come home, no choice,' she finished firmly.

Kit and Violet exchanged a quick, knowing look. They instinctively sensed that Gladys was holding something back. Between them, they had harsh personal experience of keeping dark secrets for far too long. It had taken Kit almost a year until she'd been forced to open up about her illegitimate son in Ireland, and Violet had lied for nearly the same amount of time about her abusive husband in Coventry. As Maggie opened her pretty mouth to ask yet another question, Myrtle quickly stemmed the young girl's curiosity.

'Let's not be too demanding,' she chided as she re-adjusted her winged, diamanté-tipped glasses. 'Gladys has given you an explanation – we need pry no further.'

Gladys shot Myrtle a grateful look. 'It's wonderful to be back at the Phoenix,' she said with real affection.

'It can't be better than –' Maggie was stopped mid-speech by a fierce glance from Myrtle.

'But the cowshed is empty,' Gladys hurried on. 'Nobody seems to live there.'

'You could live on-site if you don't want to be on your own,' Violet suggested. 'It's convenient for clocking on,' she added with a giggle. 'No running down that wet cobbled lane in the pouring rain.'

'Or you could come and live with us,' Kit said warmly.

'She lives in a big posh house up on't moors,' Maggie chipped in. 'Black-and-white timbered, like summat out of *Wuthering Heights*.'

'With SIX bedrooms and a drive,' Nora elaborated.

Kit laughed off their exaggerated descriptions.

'Glory be to God, it's a big owd heap!' she said in an Irish accent that was softening after months of living in England.

'And glorious views of the Pennines,' Myrtle murmured appreciatively.

'I can't wait to see it,' said Gladys eagerly, then added uncertainly, 'but I think I want to stick with the cowshed. I know it well and I like it there.'

'For sure, if that's what you want,' Kit replied. 'It's only been empty a few months. It's summer too, so not much damp.'

'But do you really want to live there on your own?' Violet asked anxiously.

Faced with the question, Gladys realized she very much wanted to live on her own. There'd be far fewer questions if she was all by herself, and she'd have time to heal her wounds in private.

'I wouldn't mind,' she replied cautiously.

'Maybe me and Nora could move in?' Maggie giggled.

Seeing the look of alarm on Gladys's face, Myrtle quickly intervened. 'Let's give Gladys time to get her breath back, shall we?'

Charmed by the idea of living independently, away from home, Maggie wasn't going to let the idea go.

'Maybe later on,' she said with a wink in Nora's direction. 'Imagine the fun the three of us could get up to.'

Determined to steer the cheeky giggling girls away from the heady idea of cohabiting with her, Gladys said briskly, 'It'll need a good tidy-up.'

'We'll lend a hand,' Violet and Kit said together.

Gladys shook her head. 'You've both got enough to do,' she said firmly. I'll enjoy giving the cowshed a good cleaning and mopping; it'll be like putting my roots down all over again.'

Nora whispered melodramatically, 'Won't you get scared up yon in't dark?'

Thinking of the terrifying nights she'd spent under

canvas, Gladys shrugged as she shook her head. 'There's nothing to be scared of,' she replied, then added under her breath, 'Safer than most places I've been in recently.'

Again, Kit and Violet exchanged a quick, anxious look. The unspoken question that hung in the air between them was: what's happened to our Gladys? As if sensing their anxiety, Gladys pushed back her chair and got to her feet.

'I'd better check in with Mr Featherstone,' she said.

'And Malc too, Love's Young Dream!' Maggie laughed.

'Him and Edna are walking out!' Nora added with a snort.

Myrtle rose to her feet. 'I think it's time these two young things got back to the serious business of building bombs!' she said as she herded the giggling girls out of the canteen.

'I'll pop into the filling shed after I've seen the boss,' Gladys said to Kit and Violet before she too hurried away.

Left alone for a few minutes, Kit and Violet stared into each other's eyes, Kit's dark and thoughtful, Violet's sky-blue and anxious.

Kit was the first to break the silence. 'There's something not quite right.'

Violet nodded. 'She's changed.'

'Something's happened to her,' Kit added knowingly.

'She's keeping something to herself,' said Violet as she lit up a Woodbine, then offered one to Kit. 'I just know it, right *here*,' she said as she tapped the area around her heart.

14

'A secret,' Kit murmured.

A troubled silence descended as they smoked their cigarettes.

'And we know how bad they can be,' said Violet, as they both stubbed out their cigarettes and returned to work in the filling shed.

2. The Phoenix Songbird

Gladys wasn't assigned to the filling shed where she'd previously worked; instead she was despatched to the cordite line. Standing between Nora and Maggie, she listened carefully to their instructions.

'Welcome to the Canary Girls' Department,' Maggie joked.

'Canary . . . ?' Gladys asked.

'Cordite turns your skin yellow and bleaches your hair yellow too,' Maggie added.

Gladys warily looked at the explosive material.

'You have to pack it into them things,' Nora explained, as she nodded towards the bomb cases, which, loaded ninety-nine to a pallet, continuously rolled down the conveyor-belt towards the girls, whose job it was to fill the cases to a specified level. 'Like this,' Nora went on, as she packed the cordite into an empty tube. 'Further down the line they'll be fitted with detonators.'

'Heavens!' Gladys gasped as she stared at the network of rattling conveyor-belts that ran around and above her. 'It's really noisy!' she yelled over the din of the machinery and the relentless music that was belting out of the factory wireless. 'Where do the bomb cases go after we've filled them?'

Keen to show off her knowledge, Maggie added, 'Once they're loaded, they're hooked on to the overhead conveyor-belt.' She nodded at the one clattering above them. 'They're carried round the factory to the packing shed, where they're loaded into ammunition boxes.'

'From there,' Nora chipped in, 'they'll be flown out to our lads working the howitzers on the front line.'

'Mebbe my Les will unload them,' Maggie said wistfully.

Gladys smiled gently at the love-sick girl who had fallen for her handsome brother, Les. 'God keep him safe wherever he is,' she murmured fervently.

Gladys slipped into her new work routine without any complaint, though she really didn't like the yellow stain the cordite left on her long, slender hands, which immediately reacted to the explosive she was working with and broke out in a patch of tiny blisters.

'Your body will get used to the dirty stuff,' Nora assured her. 'It's a common enough reaction.'

Nobody could fail to notice there was one big difference in Gladys these days: she didn't sing at all any more as she worked. Consciously or subconsciously, just about every Bomb Girl sang, hummed, tapped or whistled to *Music While You Work* or *Workers' Playtime*, which rolled out from the factory loudspeakers throughout the entire day. In previous times, Gladys, the Phoenix Songbird, would have raised her beautiful voice and led the singing, sometimes rising from her chair to sway to the music of Joe Loss, Glenn Miller or the Andrews Sisters, the last her absolute favourite. But now Gladys sat mute, concentrating more on her work than on leading the chorus to 'Little Brown Jug' or 'Yours 'Til the Stars Lose Their Glory'. She was sociable enough, always joining in the chatter during their breaks in the canteen, but her friends sorely missed her former radiance. Though Violet and Kit frequently discussed Gladys in private, their free time outside of their working hours gave them hardly a moment to do more than speculate about the changes in their dearest friend.

When she wasn't working her shifts and looking after Billy, Kit – in her new home high up on the Pennines – was busy organizing repair work to their house at Yew Tree Farm, which she'd fallen in love with at first sight. It sat fair and square on the side of a hill facing west. Sections of the house had been cobbled together over the centuries: to the front lay the oldest part, a black-and-white timber structure, whilst the back of the house was built of solid moorland stone.

'Is it too much to take on?' Ian had worried when they'd paid their first visit to the farmhouse in the springtime.

Running after a toddling Billy, Kit had laughed as she replied, 'No! It's grand – I love it.'

Ian had gazed adoringly at his new wife as she scooped up her son, whom Ian had legally adopted. When he thought back to the skinny little Irish girl in threadbare clothes and battered shoes who had walked into his office just over a year ago to seek his help, he simply couldn't believe that the slender young woman with flowing black hair and dark, sparkling eyes was now his wife.

'But there's so much to be done,' he'd pointed out. 'The roof's leaking; every room needs stripping back to the brickwork and redecorating; the windows look as if they've got dry rot – and then there's the garden – it's the size of a field!'

Kit gazed with pleasure at the riotous weeds and old fruit trees that populated the sprawling garden. 'Darlin', you forget I used to dig potatoes for a living. I'll have it dug over in an afternoon,' she promised as she popped Billy on to Ian's shoulders, then kissed her husband on his warm smiling lips. 'I love this place,' she whispered. 'We'll soon make it our own.'

'HOW?' he cried as Billy tugged his hair and pulled it into short spikes. 'You're working factory hours and I'm out of the house almost as long as you are! When will we have time to do all that's necessary to make this rambling old heap into a home?'

'We'll pay proper craftsmen to do the big stuff and the fancy bits we'll do ourselves, together,' she said with a confident smile as she linked her arm through his. 'But we won't be hanging about, Ian,' she added briskly. 'We want a family of our own, and Billy needs brothers and sisters.'

Balancing Billy on his shoulders, Ian briefly took Kit in his arms and held her close. As he did so, he recalled their wedding day, which had unquestionably been the happiest day of his life. As the Bomb Girls' Swing Band had played the wedding march, he'd turned to see his bride walking slowly towards him. Led up the aisle by Edna, her matron of honour, Kit had been a vision in white satin, a long veil obscuring her face, but when he'd lifted it to kiss her full lips, she had looked more beautiful than he'd ever seen her before.

'Pretty Mama!' Billy had gurgled, sitting wriggling impatiently in the congregation between Malc and Mr Featherstone. 'My mama!' Ian had bought the old farmhouse shortly after they'd got back from their brief honeymoon in the Lake District, and when she wasn't on shift work Kit now delighted in restoring their new home to its former glory, cleaning, painting and decorating rooms with Billy at her side was simply a joy. And when she collapsed exhausted into bed beside her husband further joys were there to be had. Both Kit and Ian gloried in their love-making, though Ian had been anxious at first, fearful of bringing back bad memories of her time in Ireland. But Kit soon showed her husband she had no fears whatsoever. She abandoned herself completely to Ian's tender kisses and caresses; in fact, it was more often Kit rather than Ian who suggested they had an early night, so keen was she to make love in their snug new double bed.

Aware of her friends' busy lives, Gladys barely troubled them, seeing them generally at work and catching up with their news in the factory canteen. She enjoyed the peaceful solace of the cowshed, but there were inevitably times when she missed the camaraderie of the old days, so it was a pleasure, one early evening after she'd finished work, to find Edna parked in the despatch yard.

'Hello, lovie!' Edna called in delight when she caught sight of Gladys through the serving hatch of her mobile chip shop.

Gladys hurried towards the middle-aged woman, buxom in her colourful pinafore and turban that just about managed to contain her greying auburn curls.

'Eeh, cock, we've missed you!' Edna declared as she hurried out of the back of her blue van in order to give Gladys a bear hug.

For a few seconds Gladys clung on to Edna, drinking in her warmth and strength. When she reluctantly pulled away, she gazed into Edna's steady green eyes.

'It's good to be back.'

Though shocked by the physical changes in Gladys – her weight loss and the slight ageing in her beautiful face – Edna, like all of Gladys's friends, said nothing.

'Well, then, what's your news?' she asked.

'I decided to come home,' Gladys replied and, from the evasive look in her eyes, Edna knew she'd get no more out of that conversation just now. 'What about you, Edna?'

The older woman's eyes sparkled as she lit up a Woodbine and blew smoke across the sunny yard.

'I'm courtin'!' she announced with a cheeky wink.

Though Maggie and Nora had joked about Edna's love life, Gladys hadn't taken them seriously – she knew too well how prone they were to exaggerate – but, seeing Edna's glowing cheeks and wide smile, she now saw that it must be true.

'Who's the lucky man?' she asked with a teasing smile.

Edna stubbed out her Woodbine and put her hands on her broad hips.

'Bing Crosby!' she joked. 'Actually, he was spoken for, so I settled for Malc, yon factory supervisor!'

Gladys burst out laughing. 'Who would've believed it? As I recall you and Malc were always arguing about something or other.'

'We've had our moments,' Edna chuckled. 'Probably always will!'

'So when did it all start?' Gladys enquired.

'That night at the Savoy,' Edna replied. 'When you got picked up by ENSA. Remember . . . ?'

Seeing Gladys's bright smile fade and her eyes darken, Edna thought to herself, 'Aye, aye, looks like ENSA is at the heart of her troubles.'

'We danced till mi legs were crippled!' Edna continued brightly. 'I 'ad quite a few sherries too, so I wasn't averse to him giving me a goodnight kiss on the cheek,' she confessed. 'In the New Year, round about the time you were getting ready for your first tour, he got in the habit of dropping by the van for a bag of chips.' Edna smiled a soft tender smile that touched Gladys with its gentle sincerity. 'I got used to seeing him, looked forward to it, in fact. We talked about everything: the war, the government, the Allies, family and friends. Then we started talking about each other.' She paused to take a breath. 'He's been married before – she died of breast cancer just before the outbreak of the war.' She sighed then added, 'I think they were very much in love.'

Gladys really didn't want to say anything that might deflate Edna's happiness, but she wondered if Malc had ever got over his wife's death. Fortunately, Edna read her thoughts. 'I asked him outright if he could ever love another woman and he said, dead straight, "Aye, I could love you, Edna Chadderton!" And we've been walking out ever since,' she finished happily.

'Congratulations!' Gladys exclaimed as she gave her friend another hug. 'When's the Big Day?'

'Eh, one thing at a time, our kid!' Edna joked.

The arrival of a gang of factory girls eager for a bag of hot chips brought their conversation to a halt, but, after the flurry of serving and dousing in salt and vinegar, Edna again joined Gladys in the despatch yard, where, after lighting up another Woodbine, she gave her a pat on the shoulder. 'Glad to be home?'

'Oh, yes, so glad.'

'Not what you expected, then?'

Gladys shook her head. 'It was a nightmare,' she confessed.

Sensitive Edna knew when to stop probing. 'Let's hope you get some company soon – we don't want you brooding alone up there for too long. And remember I'm always here for you if you want a bit of a chat.'

'Thanks, Edna,' said Gladys fondly. 'I won't forget that.'

A cheery woman at the front of the queue that was

now forming waved a hand at Edna. 'Come on, kid! We're bloody starving over here!'

'Gotta go,' Edna said as she hurriedly stubbed out her cigarette. 'Pop by for a natter tomorrow night, if you've time.'

'I will,' Gladys promised.

As Edna shovelled crispy hot chips into newspaper bags, she gazed after Gladys's receding figure. 'Something's happened to that girl, over there in them foreign parts,' she thought to herself. 'And, from the look of things, it weren't that good.'

3. Rosa

After a long hard night shift, Gladys made her way through the pearly dawn light to the cowshed, where she fell into a deep sleep that gave her no peace, despite her exhaustion. Images of leering sailors leaning forwards to grab at her red silk dress as she performed on stage filled her dreams.

'No, no!' she muttered wildly as the dream worsened and the sailors stripped the dress off her body, until she stood naked and weeping before them. 'Don't touch me, please don't touch me!' she screamed so loudly she woke herself up with a start.

Shivering and trembling, Gladys stumbled out of bed and headed for the kitchen: she turned on the tap and thirstily gulped down a mug of cold water. Calmed by the sunshine pouring through the window, she decided against going back to bed; she'd had quite enough of nightmares, and a walk on the moors might do her more good than a fretful sleep.

Though still disturbed by the sinister images in her dreams, Gladys felt so much better for being outdoors. The moorland colours were changing: tall fronds of green bracken were turning golden and the heather was losing its luminous lavender hue. But the sun was still strong, warming the rocks and crags she strode past. Taking in deep breaths of pure moorland air, Gladys felt her body respond to the landscape around her. She smiled at hopping bunnies scurrying in her wake and partridges that buzzed low over the terrain where pheasants ratcheted out their raucous call.

'This beats the Mediterranean,' she said out loud. 'This is home.'

Feeling refreshed after stretching her legs and clearing her head, Gladys returned to the cowshed starving hungry. Running up the cobbled path, she wondered what she had in the cupboard for tea: half a tin of spam, some new potatoes given to her by Kit (who'd started her own vegetable garden at Yew Tree Farm), which Gladys hoped she could spin out till the end of the week, and some baked beans. Picking some wild thyme that grew in abundance beside the path, Gladys decided to fry the spam in a bit of fat leftover from a stew she'd cooked a few days before. Hurrying into the cowshed, which nobody ever bothered locking, she dashed to make sure the wood-burner hadn't gone out, topped it up with a few logs, then plonked the little kettle on top for a brew. Busy and preoccupied, she turned to go into the kitchen but stopped dead in her tracks when she saw a slight, dark figure standing behind the front door.

'Wh . . . who are you?' she gasped in shock.

When there was no response, she took a few steps forwards and saw a trembling girl clutching an enormous kit bag. Realizing that the girl might have had the cowshed allocated to her as her digs, she asked gently, 'Have you come to live here?'

When the girl didn't reply, Gladys beckoned with her hand. 'Come and sit down,' she said in a soft voice. 'Sit by the fire,' she added, as she pointed to the old sofa by the wood-burner.

Clutching her kit bag before her like a shield, the girl slowly emerged from the shadows. She was slim and willow-tall with glossy jet-black hair that lay in thick, silky curls around her shoulders, her warm olive skin was enhanced by the late sunlight slanting through the sitting-room window. As she approached Gladys she murmured, 'I, Rosa.'

Gladys smiled as she extended her right hand. 'I'm Gladys.'

'Piacere.'

'Piacere,' Gladys replied as she remembered the Italian she'd picked up in Naples.

Keeping hold of the girl's ice-cold hands, Gladys led Rosa to the sofa, where she obediently sat down.

'Tea?' Gladys suggested.

Rosa nodded. 'Sì, grazie, er, yes, please.'

As Gladys busied herself making the tea, Rosa's large, solemn, almond-shaped eyes roved around the cowshed.

'Is a house for animals, eh?' she asked when Gladys handed her a mug of hot, strong tea.

'WAS for animals,' Gladys replied. 'Now for us, factory workers,' she added slowly.

Over more tea and strong, foreign-smelling cheroots, which Rosa carefully rolled and smoked, the two young women, in pidgin English, began to learn a little about each other. Gladys discovered that Rosa was from Padua, and had somehow managed to travel across Europe. She wondered if it might have been when the Nazis had started to round up the Jews; she couldn't think why else the young girl would have fled her own country. She didn't want to ask the shy stranger directly if that was the case, but Gladys, touring with ENSA way down in the south of the Italy, had heard lots of horrific stories about the persecution of the Jews. Knowing from her own recent experience of how intrusive awkward questions could be, Gladys didn't pursue the matter; if Rosa wanted to talk about her past, it would be better to let her volunteer more information when the time was right.

'How did you get here?' she asked instead.

'I have relatives in Manchester who give me help; they try to teach me the English too,' she added with a blush.

'Your English is good,' Gladys said warmly.

Rosa grimaced. 'I have much to teach, er . . . learn,' she quickly corrected herself. 'I go to' – Rosa struggled to re-call the exact name of the place she had visited – 'exchange of labour.' Gladys smiled at her charming mixed-up words but didn't comment. 'I tell la signora I want to build bombs to kill Germans and she send me here.'

Gladys covered her mouth in an attempt to hide her laughter but it bubbled out of her nevertheless. 'That's so funny!'

'Why funny? I hate Nazi.'

Gladys nodded. 'Me too,' she agreed as she gave Rosa's hand a gentle pat. 'Don't worry, you've come to the right place. That's all we do at the Phoenix: build bombs to kill the enemy. We're all Bomb Girls up here!' she announced.

'Bomb Girls,' Rosa mused with a smile on her face. 'This is good job for me,' she replied happily.

Gladys showed Rosa the two free bedrooms, then left her alone to choose which one she preferred. After warming up the fat in a frying pan, she dropped in slices of pink spam, which she sprinkled with the tangy fresh thyme. As Kit's small new potatoes boiled, Gladys heard Rosa opening and shutting drawers in one of the bedrooms. Relieved that the nervous new girl was settling in, Gladys wondered if Rosa would have had time to sort out her ration cards yet. She hoped so: rationing was getting worse by the week. Even sausages were now rationed and she was grateful for the free wood she could collect from the moors, as coal, gas and electricity were all now rationed too.

'Heck! After the journey she's had the poor kid will be glad of a quiet supper in a safe place a world away from the damn blasted Nazis!'

For such a slender girl Rosa proved to have an enormous appetite, eating all the food that Gladys put in front of her and more besides. Gladys had to dip into the precious rations she'd set aside for the rest of the week, but she did it gladly, pleased to see Rosa eat so heartily.

'Buono,' Rosa said with an appreciative smile.

'Grazie –' She stopped short as she chided herself. 'I *must* speak English,' she said, impatiently scolding herself.

'I speak very bad Italian with lots of mistakes,' Gladys admitted.

'I speak very bad English – with lots of mistakes!' Rosa replied as she lit up one of her cheroots. 'Why you speak Italiano?'

'Oh!' Gladys responded with a start. 'I was in Napoli during the summer.'

Rosa exhaled a cloud of cigarette smoke. 'Perché, er . . . why?'

Gladys could have kicked herself. She spent most of her time trying to avoid talking about Naples, even to her best friends, and yet the first thing she'd told this complete stranger was she'd lived there during the summer.

'Oh, just war work,' she answered as she stood up in order to put the kettle on the stove and, much more importantly, to change the subject. 'Do you know where you'll be working?' Gladys asked.

'I get instructions from il capo, the boss, Mr Feather-stonee.' Rosa pronounced the manager's name as if it was an Italian surname. 'This . . .' she replied, as she drew a piece of paper from her pocket, which she handed to Gladys.

'You've been assigned to the cordite line,' Gladys explained.

To her surprise, Rosa immediately understood cord-ite. 'Explosive,' she said.

Gladys nodded before handing back Rosa's document. 'That's good, you're on the same shift as me – we're both on nights for the rest of the week.'

'We work through night?'

'We work around the clock.' Gladys pointed to her watch as she replied. 'The factory never closes.'

'What time we start?'

'Eight o'clock.' Gladys pointed to the number eight on her wristwatch.

'Tonight?' Rosa gasped.

Gladys smiled as she nodded. 'In four hours' time.'

Clearly panicked, Rosa leapt to her feet. 'I must sleep now, please.'

'Of course,' Gladys agreed. 'Me too.'

Before they went into their separate bedrooms, Rosa sweetly kissed her new friend on the cheek.

'Thank you,' she whispered.

Gladys said with a smile, 'Welcome to the cowshed!'

It was growing dark when the alarm went off. The two bleary-eyed girls struggled out of their beds, then made their way down the lane to the Phoenix, where other women were clocking off from their shifts. Rosa looked bewildered as she watched a sea of tired women walk out of the factory, to be replaced by a wave of fresher ones. Taking Rosa by the arm, Gladys guided her to the stores, where she picked up clean overalls for the newcomer, before taking her to the female changing rooms.

Gladys carefully explained the factory rules for munitions workers. 'No jewellery.'

Rosa held out her hands for Gladys to inspect. 'I have nothing.'

'No earrings?' Gladys asked as she lifted Rosa's wonderful gleaming curls. 'No necklace?'

'Nothing,' Rosa assured her.

Gladys demonstrated how all of Rosa's hair had to be stuffed inside her white cotton turban. It was a struggle, but Rosa finally twirled her thick locks into a pony-tail that she firmly shoved under the turban.

'No hair clips or pins,' Gladys said firmly.

Seeing that Rosa didn't understand, she pointed to a woman removing pins from her own hair.

'Metal is bad with explosives,' Gladys explained.

Though Rosa wasn't fluent in English, she was certainly bright enough to understand the concept.

'Sì, I understand,' she replied, then added with a grin, 'Explosion – BOOM!'

Gladys nodded. 'Exactly – BOOM!'

Just as Rosa was struggling into the big heavy rubber boots that were part of the Bomb Girls' uniform, Kit and Violet came dashing breathlessly into the changing room, followed by giggling Nora and Maggie. They all stopped and stared at the pretty young girl Gladys was helping to dress.

'Hello,' said Gladys, as she introduced Rosa to her smiling friends. 'Meet Rosa – the new Bomb Girl!'

4. Introductions

Everybody was quickly charmed by Rosa's sweet, earnest manner, even on shift work in the middle of the night! Over the loud crashing and clattering of the bombs rattling down the production line, she asked questions about the nature of her work.

'Where go bombs now?'

'Further down the line, they're loaded into ammunition boxes,' Nora said in a very loud voice that could be heard over the thundering roll of the conveyor-belts. Simplifying her language, she added, 'They go to our brave British troops who are fighting the war.'

Rosa nodded respectfully, 'They bomb Nazis.'

Even as she said the words, she remembered what she'd seen on her dangerous journey to England: bombs exploding over cities where innocent children slept; skeletal-thin old men and women being forced to run to waiting trucks where they were herded together like cattle on their way to the abattoir.

'This one's got bloody Hitler's name on it,' Hilda, who was in charge of the line, called out, as she sent another filled bomb on its way around the factory.

Rosa looked incredulously at Hilda. 'You have name on bomb?' she gasped.

'I've got Hitler's name on every sodding bomb I pack with cordite,' Hilda assured her.

Rosa's soft curving mouth twitched and then she began to laugh, so much so that tears streamed down her face.

'Did I say summat funny?' Hilda asked Maggie and Nora, who were staring in some confusion at Rosa, who was trying to catch her breath.

'All bombs are for Führer!' Rosa cried gleefully.

'Well, I'm glad you think it's funny,' Hilda chuckled. 'I don't think I've entertained anybody quite so much since I first hopped into bed with mi 'usband – he thought he'd died and gone to 'eaven!'

Rosa didn't entirely understand Hilda's cryptic humour, but it set Maggie and Nora off laughing.

'Cordite line is very funny place, eh?' Rosa remarked.

'A laf a minute,' Hilda remarked. 'Now can we stop all the nattering and get back to winning the war, ladies?'

The big-hearted women welcomed Rosa into their workplace and into their lives. There was always a mug of tea and a chip butty or a bit of meat pie waiting for her at her friends' favourite table in the canteen. Though Maggie, Nora, Myrtle, Kit and Violet worked in different departments, they always stuck together for a gossip and a catch-up at break times. Clever Rosa was eager to improve her English, which she was starting to speak with a Northern accent, much to the vast amusement of her new friends.

'Say "chip butty" in Italian,' Nora pleaded.

'I say it ten times already, Nora!' she giggled.

'Go on, just for me,' Nora begged.

'Okay, but last time today,' Rosa insisted.

Nora nodded eagerly then waited for the Italian words to spill from Rosa's mouth. 'Panino con patate fritte.'

'It sounds so romantic in Italian,' Nora sighed. 'Patate fritte!' she said, mimicking Rosa's seductive accent.

'Say "meat pie",' Maggie cried.

Rosa thought hard for a moment, then she said, 'Pasticcio di carne. Now we speak English, please,' she said firmly.

'Ignore these two silly girls,' Myrtle advised, as she budged between giggling Nora and Maggie. 'Tell me about yourself, Rosa. What was your life like before you came here?'

'I study art, I paint, I draw,' Rosa replied as she dabbed the air with an imaginary paintbrush.

'Ah, you're an artist,' Myrtle exclaimed in delight.

Rosa blushed as she nodded. 'Sì, well, not proper artist, not yet, but I study art at university but then I have to leave, so not finish my work.'

Awed Nora blurted out, 'I've never met anybody in mi whole life who went to university.'

Ignoring Nora's outburst, Myrtle continued. 'Which university?'

'Padova, a city near Venice,' Rosa replied proudly. 'Galileo, he live there.'

Nora's jaw dropped. 'Who's Galileo when he's at home?'

'A famous scientist who taught in Padova – Padua, we say in English,' Myrtle quickly explained to an over-awed Nora, who looked none the wiser. 'It's an ancient city, near Venice,' Myrtle elaborated.

By this time Nora's big blue eyes were all but rolling out of her head. 'Oooh! Have you been in a gondola?' she gasped.

Rosa nodded. 'Sì, many times.'

Maggie started to giggle. 'Oh, bloody hell,' she cried. 'Our Nora will be thinking that everybody in Italy floats off to work in a gondola!'

'Do stop, you two,' Myrtle scolded as the young girls howled with laughter. 'I want to hear more from Rosa about Galileo.'

'He knew all about the stars, he invented, er . . .' Rosa mimed looking through an eye glass.

'TELESCOPE!' Maggie cried.

'Telescope. Galileo, he study stars,' Rosa replied.

Much impressed, Nora reverently murmured, 'This Galileo fella must have been really, really clever to invent a blinkin' telescope!'

Rosa smiled gently at Nora, whom she loved more with every passing day. 'You are clever, Nora!' she exclaimed. 'You teach me English and you teach me to build bombs too!'

'That's not clever,' Nora said with a dismissive shrug. 'That's just normal.'

Before Nora could take the conversation off in another random direction, Myrtle quickly got a word in edgeways. 'Do you draw or paint now, Rosa?'

Rosa's honey-brown eyes grew wary, 'No,' she said abruptly.

'That's a pity, considering you're an artist,' Nora insisted. 'You must miss it, drawing and sketching and that,' she added vaguely.

'I have no ... how you say, tools,' Rosa said guardedly.

Impressed by Rosa's apparent genius, Nora looked downright disappointed. 'That's a proper shame,' she lamented.

As the hooter sounded out, calling the girls back to work, Maggie stubbed out her cigarette. 'She's not going to get far without owt to paint with, is she?' she said to Nora, who was clearly reluctant to drop the subject.

'I could ask mi dad if he's got any brushes,' Nora innocently offered.

Maggie threw an arm around her friend's shoulders. 'Sweetheart, we're talking brushes for painting pictures, not redecorating the back bedroom!'

Laughing and giggling, with their arms intertwined, Nora and Maggie made their way back to the cordite line, leaving Myrtle shaking her head as she watched them go.

'Silly girls,' she said with great affection.

'Nice girls,' Rosa added with equal affection. 'My friends.'

Rosa met Kit's and Violet's children one sunny afternoon after they'd all finished their shift. At the sight of the babies, Rosa's English went right out of the window. Crouching before Billy, who immediately grabbed hold of her hair, Rosa cooed, 'Oh, che bel ragazzo! Quanto forte un ragazzo!'

Taking beaming baby Stevie in her arms she whispered tenderly, 'Buon giorno, cherubino!'

Rosa was curious about where the babies stayed whilst their mothers worked their shifts.

'Come and see for yourself,' Violet said as she led her to the Phoenix day nursery, which was to the east of the complex, well away from the noise and dirt of the factory. It consisted of various rooms that all opened on to a large partly covered play area, where the babies in the prams could sleep and the older children could play.

'Billy's in here with the toddlers,' Kit said, as her son ran off to play with his friends in the sand pit. 'It's a long day for them, as long as our shifts, in fact, unless someone arrives to pick them up early. They get all their meals here and after their dinner they always have a sleep on these,' she said, pointing out a stack of child-sized metal-and-canvas beds.

'The babies are next door,' Violet added. 'They have their own cots and when they're not sleeping there's a carpeted area where the older ones can roll around with their little friends,' Violet said with an indulgent smile.

'And what about mother who is feeding baby?' Rosa asked.

'I breast-fed Stevie until I had to come back to work, then it was on to the dried baby milk for him – there's no choice,' she said a little sadly. 'But at least I got the chance to breast-feed him – I loved it,' she admitted.

Rosa's face softened as she watched Violet tenderly kiss Stevie on both cheeks before she settled him in his pram.

'Let's go home and see Dada,' she said, as she set off for her home in the nearby domestic quarters.

'She is very good mother,' Rosa observed.

'A wonderful mother,' Kit agreed. 'Though she was a bag of nerves to start with, all fingers and thumbs.' Seeing Rosa's puzzled expression, she added, 'It was difficult at the beginning.'

'Why?' Rosa asked.

'Violet's a nervous woman,' Kit answered thoughtfully. 'Bad things happened to her before she came here.'

'Poverina, poor thing,' Rosa said with genuine compassion. 'How could bad things happen to her? She's an angel.'

Kit shook her head as she answered sadly, 'Believe me, they did.'

It was difficult to get Billy away from his friends, who were now busy eating sand.

'Ugh, no!' Kit cried, wiping sand off Billy's face.

'He looks like you,' Rosa commented. 'Black hair, beautiful big dark eyes and lips like ciliegia, like cherries!' she laughed.

After swinging gurgling Billy around in a circle, Kit popped him into his pram and tucked a blanket over him.

'You must come and see Billy's garden, right up there on the top of the moors,' she said as she pointed through the nursery windows to the high moorland peaks.

Rosa followed her gaze. 'Oh, yes, please, I would like that very much!'

Kit and Ian organized a picnic party for Rosa at Yew Tree Farm.

'It'll give her the opportunity to meet us all outside of work,' Kit said. 'She must think we sleep in our white turbans and overalls!' she joked.

Rosa was charmed by Kit's home. She especially loved the garden, half of which Kit, having persuaded local gardeners to give her their spare seeds and cuttings, had given over to growing fruit and vegetables. Billy had claimed his own little patch too: when Rosa arrived she found him sitting on his tomato plants!

'Your garden, it reminds me of home,' Rosa said wistfully as she scooped the little boy into her arms and kissed him on both chubby cheeks. 'My mother grew zucchini and melanzane.' Rosa quickly translated: 'Aubergines – and big tomatoes – we had cherry trees and peaches.' She stopped short, biting her lip in an attempt to control her emotional memories. As Billy slipped from Rosa's embrace, Kit asked softly, 'Are your parents still in Padova?'

Unable to hold back the tears that seeped from the corner of her honey-brown eyes, Rosa blurted out, 'No, they hiding in the hills, I pray God to watch them.'

Gladys, who was close by and listening in on the conversation, quietly thought to herself, 'So I was right when I thought her family were on the run from the Nazis.'

Only last year Anthony Eden, the foreign secretary, had announced in Parliament that the Nazis were exterminating the Jews, and there'd been footage on the Pathé News of Jews being rounded up and forced to leave their homes.

Thinking how unbearable it would be to be separated from her own family, Kit asked, 'You couldn't stay together?'

'Too many to hide,' Rosa replied. 'We try, but my brother and I, we got taken . . .'

Seeing her friend so upset, Gladys quickly joined Kit. The two women, sat on either side of a sobbing Rosa, knowingly eyed each other, as it was clear the poor girl sat between them had suffered a great deal before she arrived in England.

'You were captured by the Germans?' Kit asked softly.

When Rosa, too upset to speak, just nodded her head, Gladys stroked her bare arm. 'You poor, poor girl,' she murmured.

The arrival of Violet, Arthur and Stevie brought a smile back to Rosa's sad face. Quickly wiping away her tears, she hurried to lift the baby from the pram and show him the vivid orange and yellow dahlias growing in Kit's lovely garden.

All the guests had brought something to contribute to the picnic lunch that they shared in the big kitchen, which had a long wooden table running down the middle. Along one side of the kitchen was an enormous old oak dresser, bright with colourful crockery, and on the other side was a very old black Aga that kept the kitchen warm and the original slop sink that Kit had refused to let Ian rip out.

'It reminds me of home; it's good for me to remember my roots,' she'd insisted.

'But we could have a gleaming new modern sink,' Ian teased.

But Kit was adamant and in the end Ian thanked her for it. On cold nights they bathed Billy in the shallow sink, then they dried him in a warm towel on their laps as they sat in an old Windsor chair in front of the Aga. Kit was serious when she said the sink reminded her of home and how far she'd travelled from those harsh days in Chapelizod and her cruel father's behaviour over Billy. She'd loved Ian McIvor almost from the first moment she'd laid eyes on him, but, after he'd fought a long legal battle to reclaim Billy, she positively adored the man. Even now, preparing a meal with her friends, Kit's eyes wandered around the room in search of her husband, and when their eyes locked for a few seconds the love they had for each other was tangible. Kit's day-dreaming was brought to an abrupt halt by the noisy arrival of Edna and Malc.

'It's not chip butties,' Malc chuckled as he set down a big basket on the table. 'It's a batch of Edna's pies – meat and onion, and cheese and onion – all my ration coupons have gone into yon pies, so you'd best enjoy the buggers!'

'And don't leave them lying around long next to Malc,' Edna joked. 'He'll eat the lot!'

Kit smiled happily at the middle-aged couple, who, between them, never stopped talking and cracking jokes. They too were in love – you could see it in their eyes and smiles, and it made Kit's heart sing to see her friend Edna so content.

As everybody laid their modest contributions on the kitchen table, Rosa produced something they'd never seen before.

'Pizza,' she said.

Everybody stared at the two plates, which held food that looked warm, round, puffy and absolutely mouth-watering.

'They smell delicious,' said Gladys, who'd eaten pizza in Naples. 'It's bread dough,' she explained to her friends. 'Topped with tomatoes, herbs and a bit of cheese.'

'It not so good as pizza we make in Italia,' Rosa explained. 'I no find olive oil, sausage, salami . . .'

Malc guffawed. 'You do surprise me, sweetheart!'

'It looks amazing,' praised Edna.

'Try, please,' Rosa urged.

After everybody had consumed a slice of Rosa's pizza, there was a general murmur of appreciation. Edna was the first to speak. 'Your pizzas, Rosa, are a threat to my chip shop,' she declared. 'I need you to teach me how to make these!'

'Gorgeous!' Malc enthused.

'Is there any more?' Nora asked yearningly.

Rosa laughed and shook her head. 'I make more,' she promised.

'Where does the yeast come from?' Edna asked.

'Yeast?' Rosa puzzled.

'You know, the stuff that makes it puffy,' Edna said, as she used her hands to explain what she meant.

Rosa smiled as she understood Edna's meaning. 'Il lievito – yeast, I get bit from ladies in factory, we share with each other,' Rosa replied.

With his mouth smeared red with tomato sauce, Billy paid Rosa the very best compliment. 'More, more, Rosa pie!' he cried.

Their joint contributions laid enticingly on the oak table brought a smile to everybody's face. Even in the middle of a war that had been raging for four years, they'd brought the very best that their rations could provide. There was Kit's delicious hot soup made from her finest seasonal vegetables; Nora brought some ripe purple plums from her dad's garden; Myrtle had somehow cobbled together a delicious mock-chocolate cake; Maggie had brought along some corned-beef fritters; and then there were Edna's pies and what was left of Rosa' s pizza.

'A feast!' Malc exclaimed.' 'I tell you, it'll be a long time before we eat this well again!'

A happy companionable group sat around the kitchen table, chatting and laughing as they shared their food and passed around jugs of Arthur's raspberry cordial and Malc's home-made beer.

'Careful with that stuff,' Edna warned as Malc poured out his home brew. 'It'll blow your bloody head off!'

'Cheers!' said Malc, as he raised his pint mug. 'Here's to all the happy families!'

Kit and Gladys anxiously watched Rosa, wondering if Malc's completely innocent words might trigger another emotional reaction, and the girl's face indeed clouded over momentarily.

'We are like a family,' Nora commented as she munched her food. 'We stick together and look out for each other.' With tears brimming in her earnest blue eyes, Nora stared adoringly at Myrtle. 'After mi mam and our kid died, I don't know how I would have got by without you all.' Then in all innocence she turned to Rosa and said, 'Have you got any brothers and sisters, Rosa?'

Kit and Gladys held their breath. Only somebody as genuine as Nora could have come out with such a direct but innocent question, but was she inadvertently stepping on a minefield? Both women heaved a sigh of relief as Rosa replied, 'I have brother, older than me, Gabriel.' She reached into her bag and drew out a crumpled black-and-white photograph that was ripped at the edges.

As the photograph was solemnly passed around the table, they all gazed into the face of a beautiful young man with high cheekbones, sweeping, dark hair, almond-shaped brown eyes just like Rosa's and a gentle smile that revealed perfect teeth.

'He's very handsome,' Nora said. 'Nearly as beautiful as his little sister.'

Rosa nodded proudly, 'He very handsome,' she murmured. 'I pray he safe.'

The opportunity Gladys had been carefully waiting

for to ask further questions about Rosa's past was broken by Stevie waking up in his pram and starting to cry for his feed. She sighed – she would have to find another time to gently probe poor Rosa about the family she clearly adored. As Kit helped Violet heat up a bottle of dried milk powder, the rest of the company drifted outside to enjoy the last of the sunshine in the warm garden. Before she left the kitchen, Gladys noticed Rosa looking thoughtful as she picked up a pencil and several pieces of Billy's drawing paper, which she took with her into the garden. Curious, Gladys followed her friend, whom she caught sketching Billy as he played football with Ian. Utterly absorbed in her work, Rosa's hands moved swiftly and easily over the paper as she glanced up and then down again to correct a line or an angle, or to smudge the pencil to create shadows. When she'd finished the football sketch, she turned her eyes towards Malc and Edna, who were sitting on the garden wall, swinging their legs back and forth like teenagers in love, completely unaware of anybody but each other. As Gladys watched Rosa sketch, she suddenly realized that by opening up and talking about the family she loved and missed Rosa had clearly released some inhibitions in herself; it brought a smile to Gladys's face to see her friend more relaxed than she'd ever been previously.

Kit then appeared with a tray loaded with tea things, and Violet handed Stevie to Arthur so she could help pour tea for all the guests. After patting his son's back and winding him, Arthur kissed Stevie on the forehead, then rocked him to sleep in his arms, a sweet image that Rosa also caught on paper.

Just before the party broke up, Malc stood up to make an announcement. Clearing his throat, he said, 'We've got some news for you.' Turning, he took hold of Edna's hand. 'I've asked this lovely woman to marry me and she said yes.'

'Am I daft or not!' Edna joked as she flashed a lovely pearl-and-diamond engagement ring, which she'd managed to keep hidden all afternoon. 'Getting wed at my age!' she laughed.

Violet, Kit, Gladys, Nora and Maggie literally lifted Edna off the ground as they gave her a collective bear hug. 'Congratulations!' they cried, absolutely delighted for their friend.

Myrtle discreetly gave her a kiss on each cheek. 'Wonderful news, dear,' she remarked.

Edna hugged them all in turn, but when it came to Kit she leant over to whisper in her ear. 'I want you to give me away, little lass,' Edna said, as she gave Kit a knowing wink. 'I stood for you, now it's your turn to stand for me.'

Kit stood on her toes so she could reach up and kiss Edna warmly. 'It'll be the biggest pleasure and honour,' she said with a delighted smile.

Before they all went their separate ways, Rosa quietly handed out her sketches. 'For you,' she said shyly to Malc and Edna, who were overwhelmed and thrilled with their portrait. 'And this,' she said to Violet as she gave her the sketch of Stevie in his father's arms, 'is for you, and here I have picture for Kit.'

Kit gazed at Rosa's pencil drawing of her son playing football with Ian. She was quite in awe of how accurately Rosa had captured her son, and how quickly and efficiently she'd worked whilst they all chatted.

'Thank you, you're so talented!' Kit enthused. 'It's so precious that I'm going to frame it to remind me of a perfect day with friends and family.'

Rosa blushed prettily. 'Thank you,' she replied. 'For me is perfect day too.'

Kit exchanged a smile with Gladys; it was the first time since they'd met Rosa that they'd seen such colour in her thin cheeks.

5. The Liberation of Naples

Though Gladys was much happier than she had been on her arrival at the Phoenix, she was still not the Gladys her friends had known and loved before she joined ENSA.

'We miss your singing, dear,' Myrtle had ventured to say one dinner-time when the Andrews Sisters' 'Apple Blossom Time' came lilting out of the canteen radio.

'And the Bomb Girls' Swing Band too – I really miss the fun we had together,' Maggie exclaimed.

'And the music we played, and the excitement of all those competitions, and the applause of the crowd,' Nora added, with real yearning in her voice.

Gladys concentrated hard on stirring her mug of piping hot tea. 'There just aren't enough hours in the working week any more,' she replied limply.

'Nonsense!' Myrtle exclaimed. 'We made time in the past.'

Galvanized by Myrtle, who was usually the soul of diplomacy, Maggie quickly added what they'd all been thinking but had never articulated. 'Music was your life before you left for Italy!'

Maggie, who was walking out with Gladys's younger brother and therefore knew more about Gladys's past than the rest of her friends, courtesy of Les's humorous anecdotes, added, 'He said the two of you used to sing and play all the time when you were at home.'

Gladys fell silent as she recalled those happy days before war broke out, when she and her kid brother would duet upstairs in her bedroom after they'd finished work. Les would play the trumpet he loved so much and she'd be on her saxophone. For hours they'd sing all the popular songs of the day – 'Begin the Beguine', 'Summertime', 'Alexander's Ragtime Band' – until their mother (worried that the neighbours would complain about the noise) banged on the ceiling with the sweeping brush and told them to 'SHUT UP!'

'Whatever you say about lack of time, Glad,' Violet announced robustly, 'you MUST play at Edna's wedding.'

Gladys smothered her dismay. She didn't even want to touch her saxophone, which was still under her bed in Leeds – and as for singing, the very thought made her shudder. Prevaricating, she said, 'Have they set a date?'

'Not exactly,' Violet replied. 'But Edna said she'd like to have a Christmas wedding.'

Gladys gave a sigh of relief, 'Oh, that's ages off,' she retorted.

'No, it's not!' Nora protested. 'We should be rehearsing for Edna's wedding if you ask me,' she added, and she threw Gladys a hurt look.

Gladys gave a chipped, polite smile. 'We've got plenty of time,' she answered airily. Rosa, who knew nothing of Gladys's past history or her astonishing musical talent, watched the exchange with interest; she sensed from Gladys's body language that she was reluctant to be having this conversation and the sooner it was over the better.

'What's she hiding?' Rosa wondered as the factory hooter called them all back to work. 'What changed her life and made her stop singing?'

A few days later Rosa came tearing into the cowshed, where Gladys was washing her hair before they started their afternoon shift.

'GLADEEEES!' she bellowed.

Gladys wiped the soap out of her eyes and smiled – she loved the way Rosa called her 'Gladeeees' when she was really excited.

'The Italians have ... oh, how you call it?' Rosa asked impatiently.

'Surrendered – to the Allies,' Gladys gasped.

'YES, YES, YES!' Grabbing Gladys by the hand, Rosa did a little jig of joy around the kitchen.

'That's brilliant news! We should celebrate with a cuppa before we have to leave to clock on,' said Gladys, and she gave her friend a huge hug before rushing to towel-dry her hair and fill the kettle.

'We drink champagne!' Rosa cried.

'Wouldn't that be nice,' Gladys agreed with a cheeky smile. 'But for the moment we'll have to settle for tea.'

The next morning, eager and still wildly excited, Rosa insisted on going over to the canteen as soon as they woke up. 'I must see the newspapers,' she laughed as she skipped down the cobbled lane to the Phoenix, followed by a yawning Gladys. The daily papers were indeed full of pictures of smiling American soldiers handing out chocolate to little Italian children, soldiers waving American flags. There were pictures too of the heroes of the moment: smiling, handsome Montgomery and General Eisenhower arriving in triumph at the port of Messina. As Rosa, muttering to herself in Italian, pored over every detail, Gladys sleepily flicked through the newspapers. 'Italy surrenders unconditionally . . .' She turned several more pages, then her hand froze in mid-air: gazing out at her from the folds of the newspaper was unquestionably the image of the very man who haunted her dreams. Almost choking, she gasped, 'It's HIM!'

Hearing her cry, Rosa quickly turned towards her friend, who was as white as a sheet. 'Who? Il Duce?' she enquired.

'HIM!' said Gladys, powerless to keep her distress from her friend as she jabbed a trembling finger at an overweight naval officer standing in the background behind stunning Montgomery.

Bewildered, Rosa asked, 'Who, mia cara?'

Trying to collect her raging thoughts, Gladys stammered, 'A . . . a m . . . man I met in Naples.'

Seeing her friend in deep distress, Rosa said, 'Stay here – I will bring tea for you.'

As soon as Rosa turned her back, Gladys screwed the newspaper into a tight ball, which she then hurled into the dustbin. When Rosa appeared with two steaming mugs of tea, she found Gladys quietly weeping. Clutching her hand, Rosa squeezed it. 'Gladyeeees, darling,' she said tenderly. 'You must speak: please tell me why you cry,' she begged.

Gladys focused on Rosa's deep, trusting eyes. She couldn't hold this in any more, and maybe sweet Rosa was the right one to confide in. She had no choice: the photograph of the man she hated most in the world had stirred up such unwelcome thoughts and memories.

'Something happened to me in Naples – something bad,' she blurted out miserably.

Rosa released her friend's arm and, never taking her eyes from her friend's face, calmly lit up one of her cheroots, which she inhaled slowly before she said gently, 'You want tell me more?'

'NO!' Gladys wretchedly exclaimed. Was it not better to bottle up her anguish as she always had in the past? How could an emotional outpouring possibly help? 'I want to wipe it from my mind and never, EVER think about it again.'

Rosa nodded, understanding, but unsure how best she could help her dear friend. For now, all she felt she could do was be there with Gladys in companionable silence as they drank their tea, hoping she would open up and talk more when the time was right.

After they'd finished their tea and the colour had returned a little to Gladys's cheeks, the two of them walked back up the lane to the cowshed, where Gladys slumped on to the sofa. As Rosa stoked the wood-burner, she tried a different approach with Gladys, who was staring at the wall.

'You are clever woman, my friend, you know you cannot' – she paused, searching for the right word – 'wipe away bad thoughts from your mind: the brain is not factory machine that you can switch on and off, like that,' she said as she snapped her fingers. 'Believe me, mia cara, I know these things,' she said. Hoping that sharing her own painful story might help Gladys to confide in her, Rosa started to talk, struggling now and again with the unfamiliar language but determined to reach the troubled woman before her.

'When the Nazis came for the Jews in my city, Gabriel and I took Mama and Papa to friends in the hills near Padova, then we came back.' Rolling a cheroot, she added bitterly. 'That was big mistake.' Before she continued, she lit the cigarette with trembling fingers and inhaled deeply. 'Neighbours betray us and Nazis soon find us.' She paused, forcing herself to recollect the most disturbing of memories.

'They throw us in trucks, old, young, babies, the sick – we whipped and kicked like animals.' Sitting beside Gladys, Rosa stared out of the sitting-room window for a few minutes before continuing. 'Gabriel and I – we know where we going, but not say,' she whispered. 'I see prisoners pushed into the trucks and I see my brother talk to guard.' She shook her head as she recalled the moment with obvious clarity. 'I try listen, I don't know what Gabriel say to guard, but I see him give guard lot of money, then Gabriel he came return in truck, he smile and move me to back of truck, where we stand like this.' Rosa squeezed herself in as if she was being flattened. 'My brother tell me he love me and he tell me to do what he say.' She closed her eyes momentarily to stem the tears. 'No questions, little sister, promise me, mia tesora, *no questions*.' She took a deep, shuddering breath. 'When the trucks move, guard sit by me,' she continued with a glazed expression as if she was reliving the horror of the moment. 'When we turn off main street, guard he push me out the back of the truck, which goes fast. Before I can cry out, I am on ground and truck is driving from me, but I am safe,' she added, still in a state of disbelief at the outcome of the event. 'The last I see of my Gabriel, he smiling at me and then he gone.'

Unable to compose herself a second longer, Rosa crumpled into a heap of helpless sobs. 'Gabriel, he give his life for ME!' she wailed in an agony of guilt and hopelessness. 'Gabriel . . .' she continued to wail like her heart would break in two.

Gladys gathered the distraught girl into her arms, where she rocked her like a child. 'Shssh, shssh,' she soothed. Waiting until Rosa's sobs had subsided, Gladys dared to say, 'Maybe Gabriel escaped too, just like you did?'

'No!' Rosa cried. 'How is possible? He gave all his money to guard for me – to help me. Now he has nothing – no money for . . . what you call, bribe?' she questioned.

Gladys nodded grimly. 'I understand it doesn't look

good for your brother, but you don't know for sure, it's not impossible that he's still alive,' Gladys gently insisted.

'People don't last long in the death camps,' Rosa answered with a shiver of fear. 'Especially without money.'

Gladys, desperate to give Rosa hope, was teary too. 'You mustn't give up, Rosa!' she cried. 'As long as there's hope, there's life.'

'Oh, I wish I could believe that,' Rosa murmured.

Gladys stared into Rosa's beautiful tragic face; she'd known from the first moment she'd met her that here was a woman who had suffered.

'This war is crucifying us – the world is full of pain, degradation and shame,' Gladys murmured as she reached out to stroke Rosa's lovely thick hair. She took a deep breath, understanding it would help both women if she shared her own pain. 'The man in the picture, the one that gave me a fright,' she said slowly, almost in a whisper. 'He raped me.'

Startled, Rosa swung her head round so she could face Gladys, whose bottom lip was trembling as she forced herself to speak for the first time about Captain Miles.

'It was when I was in Naples; the British fleet were in, spirits were high. We were touring the area, entertaining the troops, I was so happy, Rosa – so excited. I loved Italy,' she said with a small smile. 'Even though wherever we went was bombed and blasted, I loved the people, the climate, the language, but most of all I loved singing! Nobody could stop me: I drove the other girls mad, forever bursting into song and jiving around with them.'

Rosa shook her head in disbelief. 'And I have never heard you sing.'

'It was the singing and entertaining that got me into trouble,' Gladys continued darkly. 'One of the naval captains took a fancy to me. It's not unusual for fellas to fall for the ENSA girls – it goes with the job – but this man was different. First of all, he was a senior officer, so he had more licence to move about. He always seemed to be following me; my friends used to tease me: "Uh-oh, here comes lover boy!" But it wasn't like that – he was evil.' Gladys buried her head in her hands.

Seeing Gladys looking drained and white, Rosa sensed her friend had opened up as much as she was able to for now. Taking Gladys's trembling hand in hers, she gave it a reassuring squeeze. 'Leave it, mia cara. I know you have more to say, and I listen when you ready. But I think say enough for now, sì?' Pausing, and noting the relief in Gladys's eyes, she continued gently, 'You home, you safe; now you must think of good things, not bad.'

'I wish I could,' Gladys said yearningly. Gripping Rosa's hand tightly in hers, Gladys said in a weary voice, 'Between us we carry heavy burdens.'

Rosa nodded her head – nobody could deny that.

'The world is falling apart around us,' Gladys continued, now with real passion in her voice. 'But one day, one wonderful day, the war will end, the fighting will stop, and the time will come to build a new and better world,' she added fiercely.

'Please to God,' Rosa murmured as – emotionally exhausted – she lay back on the sofa and closed her eyes. 'We must pray that that day is soon . . .'

Soothed by the glow of the fire, Gladys laid her head on Rosa's shoulder. 'You're right, sweetheart, we can only pray,' she whispered.

It was as if Rosa's outpouring had turned on a tap in her brain. In the days that followed, she started to draw again; using bits of pencil stubs she found in drawers in the cowshed and paper she cadged from Malc's office, Rosa drew everything: Gladys washing her glorious, long, brunette hair in the kitchen sink; Edna's blue mobile shop in the dark despatch yard; Edna leaning against her van; smoking a Woodbine alongside a gang of laughing munitions girls. She drew Nora and Maggie in the canteen; the girls on the cordite line; Myrtle in the despatch shed; and Kit and Violet in the filling shed. The more Rosa drew, the more she realized that drawing assuaged some of the grief and worry she was always holding in, and she found the process not just pleasing but enormously therapeutic.

It was with trepidation that Rosa finally took out the crumpled black-and-white photograph of her brother. Inspired by the drawings she'd already done, she suddenly had an overwhelming urge to try to capture the image of her beloved Gabriel. No matter how much it pained her to look at his dear face, the photograph was already fading and would surely continue to do so, and she knew she had to keep the image of her brother strong and vibrant, so that if he had indeed been killed she would always have a picture of him when he was a handsome young professor, in the prime of his life.

She was on afternoon shifts when she made this decision, which was fortunate, as the light in the early morning, when she started Gabriel's drawing, was at its best.

Sitting in an upright chair by the sitting-room window with the photograph pinned to the wall, she started to sketch her brother's beautiful face: the sweep of his dark hair, the line of his high cheekbones, the distinguished, slightly quizzical eyebrows and long, almost feminine eyelashes. Using only a pencil, and a stubby one at that, she couldn't reproduce quite the liquid golden-brown of Gabriel's eyes, but she caught the smile on his full curving lips. As she worked, Rosa's heart contracted with love.

'Where are you, my darling?' she murmured.

Though tears threatened to overcome her, she furiously forced them back. This was an act of love for her brother, not an excuse to weep and lament. Keeping her eyes focused on the photograph, she worked on until it was finished. Gladys, who'd kept herself scarce so as not to interrupt Rosa whilst she was concentrating so hard, waited until Rosa had laid down her pencil and stretched her hands before she cautiously approached. Genuinely stunned at the quality of her work, she exclaimed, 'Rosa, it's wonderful!'

Rosa smiled at the black-and-white drawing. 'My beautiful brother.'

'We should frame it, Rosa,' Gladys enthused. 'We could hang it on the wall, then we'll always have Gabriel looking at us.'

'Really?' Rosa cried. 'You would not mind?'

'Mind?' Gladys laughed. 'It would be a privilege to have such artistry in the cowshed!'

Rosa walked towards Gladys and hugged her. 'Thank you, mia cara,' she said before tentatively producing the portrait she'd drawn of Gladys whilst she was sleeping. 'This is for you.'

Gladys gazed in delight at the drawing. 'You have such a gift, Rosa! Thank you,' she said as she gave her a kiss. 'I'm going to frame this one too!'

Later on during her tea break at work, Rosa sought out Malc, who, as factory supervisor, could be found in any one of the departments at any time of the day. Eventually after asking her friends where he might be, she tracked him down in the despatch shed. He was deep in conversation with Myrtle, who had a handkerchief to her mouth as if she was trying to stifle the cough that was clearly racking her. Rosa held back until they'd finished their conversation and Myrtle had hurried away. Seeing Rosa hovering, Malc approached her with a worried expression on his face.

'Yon Myrtle's not in a good way – coughing her guts up,' he told Rosa. 'I've sent her home for a lie-down; the sooner she sees the factory doctor, the better.'

Rosa nodded in agreement. She'd overheard a number of women in the factory, who knew Myrtle better than she did, comment on how unwell she looked these days.

Remembering his manners, Malc quickly said, 'What can I do for thee, little lass?'

'I have gift for you,' Rosa said, as she drew the black-and-white drawing she'd made of Edna and the munitions girls from behind her back where she'd been hiding it. 'I did this when Edna not looking, I think you like it,' she added with a shy smile.

A tender smile spread across Malc's face as he took the paper in his hand. 'But it's the spit of my Edna!' he said in astonishment as he scrutinized the drawing. 'Thank you, Rosa, thank you very much. This is un-believably good,' he exclaimed.

After Rosa had gone back to work, Malc's eyes returned to her tender portrait of Edna. 'My word, if you can do this with a stub of a pencil and a sheet of paper, what couldn't you do with a set of oil paints.'

6. Myrtle

As Rosa's English improved, so did her passion for singing popular songs. She loved listening to the wireless that played out on the factory loudspeakers, entertaining the munitions girls throughout the day and into the night. On the cordite line, Maggie, Nora and Rosa sang along to their favourites, and Rosa continued to sing, hum or whistle the catchy refrains even when she was back at the cowshed. Whilst she was washing up or making tea, she'd sing out loud, often getting the words in the wrong order or singing the wrong refrain, which set Gladys's teeth on edge. One evening, as Rosa was washing her smalls in the kitchen sink, she started to sing 'As Time Goes By' from her favourite film, *Casablanca*. Gladys rolled her eyes as Rosa, oblivious to her mistakes, crooned on, but finally, unable to bear it any more, Gladys walked into the kitchen and said, 'You keep missing out the kiss bit.'

'What kiss bit?' Rosa asked.

'A kiss is just a kiss – that bit,' Gladys reminded her.

When Rosa looked blank and shook her head, Gladys quite spontaneously sang the song, emphasizing the section that Rosa always forgot. Rosa listened in rapt delight to Gladys's perfect pitch, and when she'd finished Rosa clapped her hands together, sending bubbles from her washing floating into the air. 'Sing again, oh, please, Gladeeees, sing for me the song again,' she implored.

So Gladys sang the whole song through once more, and this time Rosa joined in and got it word perfect. 'You should sing more, mia cara,' she enthused as they finished the song. 'You have the voice of an angel.'

Gladys brusquely shook her head. 'You know why I'm not keen on all that entertaining stuff any more.'

Determined not to be fobbed off, Rosa wagged her finger at Gladys as if she was a naughty, disobedient child. 'No, no, no!' she chided. 'You tell me to draw my pictures, because you know it helps me, but YOU' – she gave an irritated, dramatic sigh – 'YOU – Gladeeees Johnson, you deny your gift from God.'

'I told you, it got me into trouble,' Gladys insisted crossly.

'But you cannot blame your singing – you were just unlucky. And here you safe!' Rosa exclaimed. 'There are no men here!' she cried. 'Well, there's Mr Featherstonee, and Malc, who loves his Edna, and Arthur, who loves his beautiful wife. What have you to fear here in Pendleton – we are nowhere in the middle,' she concluded with a dramatic wave of her hand.

Gladys couldn't help but smile as she corrected Rosa's English. 'We're in the middle of nowhere,' she said.

Undaunted, Rosa pressed on with her point. 'Essato! Nothing to hurt you here.' Suddenly she gave a low throaty laugh. 'Anyway, I promise I kill anybody who hurt you.'

Seeing the blazing ferocity in her dark eyes, Gladys

was quite sure that Rosa would indeed fight to the death to protect her friend. 'I believe you would!' Gladys laughed.

'So now, sing for me like nightingale,' Rosa pleaded.

'Maybe . . .' Gladys said. 'Just give me time.'

Gladys left the kitchen and Rosa continued with her washing, and, as she rubbed and scrubbed at her smalls in the sink, a wicked smile lit up her thoughtful face. 'From now on,' she thought to herself in Italian, 'I'll sing every song backwards! I'll irritate Gladys so much she'll be forced to sing, even if it's only to correct me!' Checking that the kitchen door was wide open, she started to holler Bing Crosby's popular hit 'Don't Fence Me In'. Making a deliberate mistake that she knew would drive Gladys mad, she crooned, 'Don't put me in fences.' In the next room, Gladys gritted her teeth, then smiled; she was beginning to see that little Rosa with her delicate face and dreamy smile was not a woman to be denied!

Everybody was worried about Myrtle. News of her absence from work quickly got round the factory, and when her friends heard she'd ended up in the Phoenix infirmary they decided to visit her immediately.

'We can't all go,' said thoughtful Kit. 'It would overwhelm her.'

Maggie nodded her agreement. 'You three should go,' she said, gesturing towards Violet, Kit and Gladys. 'You've known her longest. Nora and I will go another time.'

It was tricky arranging a visit around hospital hours, the day nursery and the girls' shifts, but they managed it, and a few days later, when they saw Myrtle lying in her hospital bed, they bitterly regretted that they hadn't come sooner. Under the neatly made hospital sheets Myrtle looked half the woman she had been: her usual trim permed hair looked flat and grey, and she wasn't wearing her signature winged glasses. As Violet, Kit and Gladys approached the bed, they could see Myrtle was dozing; as if sensing their nearness, she stirred and opened her eyes.

'We didn't mean to disturb you, lovie,' Violet whispered.

Breathing heavily and with obvious difficulty, poor Myrtle gazed at her visitors. 'It's so good to see you,' she gasped.

Gladys hurried to take hold of her limp, cold hand. 'Don't exert yourself, darling,' she murmured.

'I've missed you,' Myrtle wheezed as a single tear slipped down her cheek.

The effort of talking brought on a coughing attack, which caused Myrtle great distress. Hacking and spluttering, she struggled to sit up, and, as her friends helped her into an upright position, they couldn't help but notice the bloodied handkerchief underneath Myrtle's pillow. Hearing her patient in distress, the ward sister came swooping towards the women gathered around Myrtle's bed.

'No more than two visitors at a time,' she snapped as she deftly eased the pillows behind Myrtle in order to facilitate her breathing. 'I think that's quite enough for now,' she barked. 'I need to administer medication right away.'

As the girls backed away Myrtle managed a weak, 'Please . . . come back . . . soon.'

'Two at a time!' the sister added as she whisked the curtain around her patient.

Maggie and Nora were the next to visit Myrtle, but the visit devastated poor Nora. 'I can't bear to see her so weak and unlike herself. I miss her bossing me about and teasing me for being so daft,' Nora confessed. 'She's been like a mother to me, advising me when I was in a muddle,' she said as she dabbed her eyes with her usual grubby hankie.

'I know, sweetheart, but you must remember that seeing you upset will upset Myrtle,' Kit pointed out. 'We've got to be strong for her sake.'

Furious with herself for appearing so soft and selfish, Nora exclaimed, 'I know that! I just couldn't stop myself.'

'Then you must only visit when you feel strong,' Violet advised. 'Otherwise you're doing Myrtle no favours.'

Gladys contrived to pop into the infirmary once a day, even if it was for only five minutes. It was easier for her, as she had fewer obligations than Kit or Violet, both of whom had hectic family lives. Gladys always tried to bring something to distract Myrtle from the monotony of hospital life. She took Rosa's black-and-white drawing of herself, which Myrtle was charmed by; she brought some dahlias from Arthur's garden, an oasis of peace and beauty that Arthur had created from a neglected patch of earth just beyond the despatch yard where he grew vegetables, fruit and flowers, which he generously shared with his friends. Kit sent little fruit pies when she had enough ration coupons to buy lard for the pastry, and Edna regularly delivered a little meat-and-potato pasty, which Myrtle relished.

One day when she arrived, Gladys saw Dr Grant beside Myrtle's bed. Seeing them obviously in confidential mode Gladys immediately backed away, but Myrtle weakly called her name.

'It's okay, I'll come back later,' Gladys said as she made to leave.

'I want you to hear what the doctor has to say,' Myrtle told her firmly. Gladys turned to Dr Grant, who nodded in agreement with Myrtle. 'If that's what my patient requests, you may stay,' he reassured Gladys, who quickly sat down in a chair on the other side of the bed, hoping against hope that it was good news that Dr Grant was going to share. But, seeing the set expression on the doctor's face as well as Myrtle's tear-stained one, hope quickly faded. Once Gladys was settled, Dr Grant didn't beat about the bush.

'I'm afraid Myrtle has TB. We hoped it was a severe chest infection – they're fairly common in an explosives factory – but we ran some tests to rule out anything more serious, and I'm so sorry, but Myrtle unquestionably has tuberculosis.'

With tears in her eyes Gladys turned to Myrtle, who after her initial upset looked remarkably calm and resigned.

'I suspected that was the case,' she said bravely, before turning to the doctor to ask, 'How long have I got?'

Dr Grant shrugged his shoulders as he answered honestly: 'Difficult to say, though we're hoping your move to Belmont TB sanatorium up on the moors will improve your condition.'

'When do you intend to send me there?' Myrtle enquired.

'As soon as it can be arranged,' he replied kindly.

After the doctor departed, Gladys struggled to find the right words; this certainly wasn't the time to talk about work or the weather, but neither could she bring herself to talk about the grim reality of Dr Grant's prognosis. Seeing her awkwardness, Myrtle gave Gladys's hand a gentle pat. 'I'm not frightened of dying,' she said quietly. Gripping her hand, Gladys fought back tears. 'I have a strong belief in God,' Myrtle continued. 'His love comforts me and gives me strength to face death, though I shall miss all of you silly cheeky girls,' she said with a shadow of a smile. Seeing Gladys's bottom lip quivering, Myrtle forced a briskness into her voice, 'Now, dear child, do please get me a cup of tea, and see if you can steal a bit of sugar behind Sister's back,' she added with a naughty wink.

After her hospital visit Gladys immediately joined her friends in the canteen, where, choking with emotion, she sat down and broke the bad news. When she'd finished, her friends stared at her with a mixture of shock and incredulity on all their faces, apart from Nora, who was weeping uncontrollably. 'Belmont Sanatorium is where they send folks to die,' she wailed.

Maggie laid an arm around her heart-broken friend,

who buried her face against her shoulder. 'She can't be dying!' Nora sobbed. 'I can't imagine life without Myrtle!'

Rosa, who'd remained quiet out of respect to her friends who'd known Myrtle a lot longer than she had, said softly, 'We must pray for her.'

Gladys nodded in agreement with the sentiment. 'Myrtle has a strong faith – we must pray that what's left of her life is good and pain free.'

'And we must visit her and tell her how much we love her before it's too late,' Nora said, but the very thought brought on another bout of weeping. Utterly heart-broken, she laid her head on the table and abandoned herself to her grief. 'Oh, Myrtle . . .' she wailed.

Everybody in the workplace was saddened by the news, which flew round the factory in no time. All the women who'd worked alongside Myrtle had a soft spot for the upright middle-aged woman who used to be a Sunday-school teacher and played the piano like a professional musician.

'She's so clever and knowledgeable,' one of her colleagues said.

'Always fair, never rude,' another said.

'A hard worker too.'

'Never had a day off work.'

A heavy silence followed, broken only by one of the women saying what they were all thinking.

'My God, she'll be sorely missed.'

7. Flora

Early one autumn morning, Edna drove her little mobile chip shop through the dank mist to visit Kit before she left the house to start her afternoon shift at the Phoenix. As Edna drove, the mist cleared and she was able to stop and admire the majestic view of the high Pennines, where moorland sheep grazed or plaintively bleated as they scampered over the flattened bracken to catch up with one another. It was too chilly for songbirds, but she could hear the buzzing of a partridge's wings as it flew away. The sight of so much natural beauty lifted her spirits but left her feeling guilty when she thought of all those who were suffering on the brutal battlefields of war, not to mention poor Myrtle. Hundreds and thousands of men and women were fighting for the privilege of living at peace in the country they loved. Soldiers who lay dead in mud, RAF pilots lost in deep, watery graves in the Channel and the North Sea, and sailors on minesweepers, weaving their way through deadly seas dotted with German explosives. She sighed as she wiped away her tears. Would the killing ever end? Would it be like the hideous First War, which wiped out 'The Seed of England'?

'Take a hold of yourself, kid!' Edna said sharply to

herself. These weren't the kind of questions you allowed yourself to ask, not if you wanted to stay sane.

Starting up the van's engine again, Edna set off at a brisk pace along the narrow winding road, and, as she approached Kit's rambling old farmhouse, she mischievously switched on the loud chime bells that she used to attract customers. When Billy heard them ringing out, he ran full pelt along the garden path yelling, 'DING! DING!'

Edna brought the van to a halt, then stepped out of it and stood with her arms flung wide open. 'Come on, bonny lad!' she called.

'He loves his godmother,' Kit said fondly as she watched Billy hug Edna.

'And I love my godson,' Edna proudly replied.

'Me do ding-ding,' Billy pleaded.

Edna laughed as he ran up to the van, which she'd left open, knowing how much he liked to scramble inside and explore.

'Here's the ding-ding,' Edna chuckled. 'Go on, press the button.'

Billy banged his little hand on the button that operated the chime bells, then laughed himself silly as they rang out.

'We could be here all day doing this,' Kit warned as she lifted Billy out of the van and headed down the garden path to the front door. 'I don't know about you but I'm dying for a brew.'

'When have you ever known me refuse a cuppa?' Edna joked.

Inside Kit's big kitchen, where Billy's recently washed towelling nappies were drying on a wooden clothes-maiden that hung from the ceiling on metal pulleys, Kit made a pot of tea, whilst Billy ran to his building bricks scattered across the scrubbed stone floor.

'Let's have a cigarette whilst he's playing,' said Kit as she reached for her packet of Woodbines. 'We never seem to have a moment in private, not like the old days when I'd come and visit you every night in the despatch yard.'

'Eeh, we had some heart-to-hearts, didn't we?' Edna reminisced.

'I don't know how I would have got through those dark, horrible times waiting for news from Ireland without you,' Kit confessed.

'It was worth the wait to have this little man by you,' Edna remarked fondly, as she watched Billy build a tower of bricks, then gleefully knock them down.

'Now tell me,' said Kit, wanting to move the conversation to a cheerier topic once they had inevitably shared their sadness over Myrtle, 'have you made any plans for your wedding? It's not long off now, you know.'

Edna pulled down the corners of her wide generous mouth. 'It'll be a small do,' she replied. 'It's not like I've got a big family,' she added with a wistful sigh.

Kit knew exactly what Edna meant by that; leaning across the table, she pressed her friend's hand.

'What wouldn't I give for my daughter to be there on my wedding day,' Edna finally murmured.

Still stroking Edna's hand, Kit wondered how old

the baby girl that Edna's parents had forced her to give up for adoption all those years ago would be now – twenty-seven, twenty-eight years?

As if reading her thoughts, Edna added, 'She'll be old enough to have her own family by now.'

Kit, who'd gone through hell in order to stop her father having Billy adopted, suddenly decided to throw caution to the wind. 'Have you ever thought of trying to trace Flora?' she asked.

Edna smiled sadly. 'Of course! But what right have I to disturb her life and the couple that took her? It would be cruel, not to mention impossible! Even so,' said Edna, as she visibly slumped in the chair, 'there's not a day goes by when I don't think of her: what she's doing; where she's living. Is she married? Has she got children? I'd give my right arm to see her, just the once.'

'You never know, it might not be impossible to trace her – difficult certainly, but you don't know if you don't try,' Kit said thoughtfully. 'I understand what you say about disturbing her life, but maybe there's a way of at least giving her the chance to make contact with you?'

'That's if she wants to,' Edna commented. 'And, anyway, where on earth would I begin?' she added sadly.

'You might try putting an ad in the papers?' Kit suggested.

'Saying what?' Edna gave a mocking laugh. 'Mother seeks daughter, no name known, no place of residence known! And which paper? We don't know if she stayed in this area – she could be living anywhere!'

Regretting she'd even brought up the subject, Kit

was grateful when Billy distracted them. Climbing on to his godmother's knee, he cried, 'Sing, Edde!'

Edna sang every nursery rhyme she could remember until it was time for Kit to take Billy to the Phoenix day nursery.

'I'll give you a lift,' Edna volunteered. 'Come on, love,' she said, as she lifted the little boy into the passenger seat. 'You can play the ding-ding all the way to work!'

As Edna drove Kit and her son along the twisting moorland paths, Kit determined that the subject of finding Edna's daughter was not going to be shoved under the carpet. She'd seen the longing in Edna's eyes; she'd also briefly known the agony of losing her own baby and the ecstasy of being reunited with him. She wanted her dearest friend, Edna, to have that joy, especially on her wedding day.

Later that evening, when she'd finished her shift and got the bus home, Kit found her sleepy husband peacefully reading the *Manchester Evening News* as he toasted himself in front of the warm Aga.

'Darling!' he exclaimed as Kit kissed him before falling exhausted into one of the old Windsor chairs. 'I'll put the kettle on.'

Kit sighed gratefully as she lit up a Woodbine and sank back into the comfy chair. 'How's Billy?' she asked as Ian dropped tea leaves into the big brown tea pot.

'He was tired out when I picked him up after work;

he had a bath and a cup of milk, then he went out like a light.'

'He had a busy morning with Edna,' Kit recalled as she accepted the mug of scalding hot tea from her husband, who sat in the chair opposite her and lit up a Pall Mall.

'Sweetheart . . .' Kit started hesitantly. 'I've had a talk with Edna and I really want to try to track down her daughter, who was adopted shortly after Edna gave birth to her.'

'Catherine Murphy!' Ian chided. 'You are playing with fire.'

Kit leant closer in to squeeze her husband's hand. 'Think how wonderful it would be,' she said. 'Edna and the child she never knew reunited on her wedding day.'

'This is sentimental reasoning,' Ian playfully chided. 'Anyway, first things first: does Malc know about Edna's adopted daughter?'

'I'm sure Edna would have told him,' Kit replied.

Ian held up his fingers as he did a quick calculation. 'You mentioned a while ago that she must be around twenty-seven years old by now. A grown woman, with a life of her own – it would be very wrong to interfere.'

'It's not interfering!' Kit protested. 'What if she's never had the chance to search for her birth mother? Maybe she doesn't even know Edna's name; maybe the parents kept everything a secret from her – that's common with families who adopt.'

'Darling, if that's the case, it's even more important that we're careful. I know you want to help, but the initiative must come from Edna's daughter. It's important from a legal point of view as well as a compassionate one.'

When she heard this, Kit rolled her eyes. 'And there was I, the fool I am, thinking how wonderful it would be for mother and daughter to find each other,' she groaned. 'Sure, I should have known better.'

'The law is there to protect innocent people, my love,' Ian said as he caressed his wife's dark hair, which cascaded in a silky sweep to her slender waist. 'As you say, we don't know what the parents might have told Edna's daughter – you might be opening a can of worms'.

Laying aside her empty mug, Kit rose and, recognizing that she wasn't going to get much further in this, their first discussion about Flora, she smiled seductively as she held out her hand to her husband. 'Come to bed, my darlin',' she murmured.

Ian grinned as he quickly stubbed out his Pall Mall. 'With the greatest of pleasure, Mrs McIvor!'

Oblivious to Kit's fantasy of reuniting mother and daughter, Edna and Malc finally set their wedding date one blustery autumn evening. Edna, as usual, was in her blue van in the despatch yard, serving chips to the last of the Bomb Girls heading off to bed, and to the bleary-eyed ones starting their night shift.

'Eeh! I could stay here all day and all night and still have customers queuing up for chips,' Edna yawned as she closed her serving hatch. 'The Phoenix with its round-the-clock shifts is a regular little gold mine.'

'Sweetheart,' said Malc, as he stowed the salt and vinegar bottles in the van, 'there's more to life than work.'

Edna stopped in her tracks and looked at her fiancé. 'You're right, love, but I've spent all my life working – how else could I have survived on my own?'

'You've done all right for a single woman,' Malc said proudly. 'You've got a thriving chip shop in the centre of town and a little mobile chippy too,' he added with a fond smile.

'Coming up here was a stroke of genius, even if I say so myself,' Edna laughed as she recalled how she'd had an old second-hand van adapted into a mobile chip shop for the specific purpose of travelling up to the Phoenix Factory, high up on the moors. 'Being the hard-headed business woman that I am,' she said with a chuckle, 'I thought to miself, "There's a profit to be had serving chips to them munitions lasses." Well, that was the original idea,' she said as she lit up a Woodbine and handed one to Malc. 'But now, if the truth be told, I come up here for the Bomb Girls themselves. I love them,' she said with tears in her green eyes. 'I love their strength, their humour, their swearing and their down-right cursed determination to win the war and destroy Hitler!'

Malc stared at his wife-to-be, whom he'd seen in many moods but never one quite as fiercely patriotic as this one.

'I've made friends here, and shared secrets too,' Edna continued. 'I just love this factory, and all the brave women who keep clocking on day after day, month after month, year after bloody year, to keep England safe.' She paused to wipe away a tell-tale tear. 'Serving them chips, chatting and laughing, supporting them, believing in them, has made me feel like I'm part of their war effort. I honestly don't know what I'd do without 'em!' she admitted with a watery smile.

'And what would them lasses do without you, my sweetheart?' he murmured, drawing her into his arms. 'What would any of us do without our Edna?' he added as he kissed her full on the mouth. 'Now let's go 'ome and put kettle on!'

Down in Pendleton, in Edna's sitting room, after she'd had a tepid bath to get rid of the smell of lard and chips that was part of her working life, Edna sat drinking cocoa with Malc, who was determined to set their wedding day.

'Christmas!' Edna suggested.

'Churches aren't open on Christmas Day – well, not for weddings,' Malc protested.

'Don't fancy Boxing Day,' Edna mused. 'Always a bit anti-climactic.'

'What's wrong with Christmas Eve?' Malc asked. 'Bing Crosby, White Christmas and all that.'

'Ooh, yes, very romantic,' Edna agreed as she clinked her cocoa mug against his.

'Christmas Eve it is, then,' said Malc.

'And the honeymoon?' Edna giggled like a teenager.

'That's for me to sort out!' Malc answered with a wink.

A few days later, Edna phoned Kit's house, where Ian had had a telephone installed. 'Essential for business purposes,' he'd said with a smile.

'And catching up on the football results from your pal at Old Trafford,' Kit had teased.

When the phone shrilled out, Kit was heading out of the door with Billy in her arms. Grabbing it, she held on to Billy with one hand and the phone with the other.

'I know you'll be in a rush,' Edna said, 'but we've set the wedding date and I want all of my Swing Band Girls – and Rosa too, mustn't leave her out – to meet me in the despatch yard when you can manage it.'

'Leave it with me,' Kit promised.

After she'd dropped off Billy at the nursery, Kit rushed into the canteen, where she and her friends normally met before their shifts began. She found them chatting and laughing as they drank mugs of strong tea.

'NEWS!' she cried, as she joined them and drew a packet of Woodbines from her pocket.

'You're pregnant!' cheeky Maggie guessed.

'No! It's nothing to do with me!' Kit laughed. 'Edna wants us' – she waved collectively at all around the table – 'to meet her in the despatch yard later.'

As the girls eagerly agreed to the plan, Rosa said shyly, 'Perhaps I should not bother Edna?'

All eyes turned on her in surprise.

'Why?' Nora demanded. 'You're part of our crowd; you must come.'

'But you are all Edna's old friends; I am new one,' Rosa tried to explain.

'Don't be daft,' laughed Maggie. 'If you didn't show up, Edna would come looking for you with a rolling pin!'

'Rolling pin?' Rosa asked with a giggle.

Maggie mimed rolling out dough on the canteen table.

'Ah, yes, rolling pin, for pizza!' Rosa exclaimed.

'And for hitting folks who don't turn up when they're asked to,' Maggie added.

'Then I think I must go,' Rosa conceded with a happy smile.

Hours later and feeling a lot less lively than when they'd started their shift, Violet, Kit, Gladys, Nora, Maggie and Rosa gathered around Edna's little blue van in the despatch yard, where Edna handed each of them a bag of sizzling-hot chips.

'Get them down you; you all look worn out,' she said, as she shook salt and vinegar into the open bags of chips.

'It's been a long day,' Gladys yawned. 'But your chips are already making me feel better, Edna,' she added gratefully.

'Mmm, best in town!' Nora announced as she scrunched up the newspaper wrapping and dropped it into a nearby dustbin.

When the girls looked significantly refreshed, Edna

said, 'Well, me and Malc have finally set our wedding date – it's going to be Christmas Eve!'

As her friends warmly congratulated her, Edna quickly came to the point. 'I need help, ladies, I've never been wed before and I don't know, what's the word . . . ?' She snapped her fingers as she tried to remember. 'The protocol! That's it, you know, bride's side, groom's side, and all that organizing stuff.'

Violet and Kit, with recent experience of their own weddings, were the first to make suggestions.

'First things first,' Kit said. 'What are you going to wear on your wedding day?'

'I'm not dressing up as Father Christmas, if that's what you're expecting,' irrepressible Edna joked.

Recalling her own heavenly wedding day, Violet smiled romantically. 'Then there's the guest list and wedding breakfast,' she said. 'Not to mention the flowers and the church.'

'And the honeymoon!' Nora chuckled.

Edna burst out laughing. 'Malc's in charge of the honeymoon.'

'You could have your reception at the Black Bull in town; it's right by the church, so you wouldn't have far to walk in your glad rags if it's snowing,' Maggie suggested.

'Good idea,' Edna said gratefully. 'But the food will be basic, what with rationing.'

'You could park your mobile chippy round the back and we could feast on chips and fritters,' Nora said wistfully.

'It's mi wedding day, lovie, I don't want to be taking mi vows wearing a pinny smelling of chip fat and with mi hair stuffed under a turban!' Edna laughed as she handed round Woodbines to the smokers.

'I'm sure everybody will help with the wedding breakfast,' Maggie said eagerly. 'Our Emily has given me some tips on cooking with rationed food. She's got a great alternative for roast turkey: it's made of sausage meat and herbs, with two parsnips for legs.'

'Won't it look funny?' Nora asked with a puzzled expression.

Maggie nodded. 'Mebbe, but it tastes good, especially with roast potatoes and fresh veg off the allotments.'

Edna smiled gratefully. 'I know your Em's a genius at inventing something out of nothing, but we'll have to make a little go a very long way,' she pointed out.

'I know,' Maggie replied. 'But we can still use our imagination, can't we?'

Seeing her pretty face colour with excitement, Edna nodded. 'We can give it a go – as long as it's an improvement on spam hash or Lord Woolton Pie, I'll be happy.'

'I'd love to help you choose your wedding dress,' said stylish Violet, who knew all the latest wartime fashions and was handy with a sewing machine too.

Kit nodded excitedly. 'We could set a date and have a look round the big Co-op store in Piccadilly; they do everything – hats, suits, frocks and shoes.'

'Don't forget Glad is a genius with make-up,' Maggie reminded everybody. 'Remember how you used to make us all up before we went on stage, Glad?'

Gladys, who'd been relatively quiet up to now, answered with an obliging smile. 'Yes, of course, with pleasure.'

'And I insist on the Bomb Girls' Swing Band playing all the wedding songs,' Edna added excitedly. '"Here Comes the Bride" and "In the Mood", whilst we sign the register, and "Alexander's Ragtime Band" when we leave the church.'

Nora and Maggie literally skipped on the spot with excitement. 'Yes, yes, yes!' they cried gleefully.

Gladys, who was feeling secretly guilty at her reluctance to be involved in any musical activities, reminded her friends that because of poor Myrtle's condition they wouldn't have a pianist. The bubble of happiness that had been growing around the wedding plans suddenly deflated a little.

'Oh, God,' sighed dismayed Violet. 'How could we have forgotten?'

Tears filled Edna's eyes. 'It won't be the same without her,' she murmured.

'She'll be heart-broken not to be there for your big day,' Kit said quietly.

'If she should live that long,' Gladys added sadly.

Rosa, who'd barely spoken until now, was the one to break the long, sad silence. 'I play piano,' she said hesitantly. As her friends turned to her in amazement, she quickly and very self-consciously added, 'I know I not your dear friend, but if I can do something for the wedding, Edna, I be so happy.'

Grateful and very relieved, Edna leant across to kiss

Rosa. 'That's very kind of you, lovie, though I have to warn you about the rehearsals – they'll take up a lot of your spare time.'

Rosa smiled cheerfully. 'I no mind – really.' As she responded, Rosa caught Gladys's eye. 'But I know somebody who will,' she thought to herself.

Oblivious to Gladys's discomfort, Nora beamed at all her friends. 'It'll be just like old times,' she said happily. 'The Bomb Girls' Swing Band are back in business!'

As her friends chatted excitedly, Gladys avoided eye contact with Rosa, who was watching her like a hawk; with a sinking heart Gladys now knew for sure that there would be a revival of the swing band to celebrate Edna's wedding, and that she would have to play whether she liked it or not.

8. Belmont Sanatorium

All of the girls continued to visit Myrtle in the sanatorium, but, again, it was Gladys who spent more time there than anybody. She found her visits oddly peaceful: the steep climb over the moors in blustery autumn gales or on soft golden afternoons, when the sun lingered on the sharp crags and moorland ridges as if it was loath to abandon the world to winter. Gladys took to making a flask of Camp chicory coffee laced with a dash of condensed milk, which she would sip from a little cup as she sat on her favourite boulder, which simultaneously gave her the best views of two counties: the vast sweep of Yorkshire, to the east of the Pennines, and Lancashire, stretching out west towards the glittering Irish Sea.

It was impossible for her thoughts not to fly back to Naples and the views she'd seen there. Even from the wrecked beaches, where bombed-out ships lay prone on their rusty sides like huge abandoned dinosaurs, there'd be scenes that took her breath away. Vesuvius smoking in the far distance; the Isle of Capri shimmering in the heat on a clear day; and the countryside too, especially where they'd set up camp off the busy roads packed with army trucks, jeeps and marching soldiers. She'd seen wild flowers she didn't recognize and songbirds whose names she didn't know, and in the night she'd heard the sound of nightingales warbling melodiously across empty valleys until dawn broke and their song hushed. Lovely memories that were always tarnished by the event that had sent her packing back to England with terror in her heart.

Myrtle looked better for being in the sanatorium: her colour was improving thanks to sitting on the hospital balconies, where she could get the sun on her face or a breeze on her cheeks, but most importantly she was able to inhale pure fresh air. Nevertheless, she had little appetite; the effort of eating exhausted her and often brought on a coughing attack, so she looked thin and her formerly rosy, plump face was sallow and sunken. What she liked best was to lie back in a comfortable chair in the large, communal sitting room and listen to classical music on the wireless: her haggard face visibly relaxed and her eyes grew dreamy and far away, as if she could see something wonderful waiting for her just out of reach. Gladys loved to find her like this, contented and at peace. Often she'd sit with Myrtle on these occasions, holding her friend's limp white hand as they listened to Schubert, Handel, Mozart and Beethoven. One afternoon, as the sun was setting over the moors and the music reached an aching crescendo, Myrtle said quite unexpectedly, 'Tell me if it's none of my business, but I would very much like to understand what's taken the light out of your eyes, my dear child. You are not the same girl we waved off to Italy last year . . .'

Gladys groaned under her breath. 'Bloody Nora's been blabbing!' she thought crossly.

Moving uneasily in her chair, she said, 'It's complicated.'

'Dying's complicated,' Myrtle replied, not unkindly. 'But we all must face it one day.'

Gladys sighed and stood to stare out of the large window that gave a view of the bright orange sun sinking over the dark moors, where she could hear birds calling.

Drawing in a ragged breath, Myrtle added wheezily, 'Did you get into trouble out there?'

Seeing poor Myrtle struggling to get the words out, Gladys felt ashamed of herself. Returning to the chair she'd just vacated, Gladys said simply, 'Yes, that's exactly what happened to me out there, Myrtle, I got into big trouble.' Then she somehow managed to stumble through the shameful sequence of events that had brought her, defeated and depressed, back to England. Myrtle waited until Gladys's trembling hand had stilled before she asked, 'Did you report him?'

Gladys shook her head, then briskly wiped away her tears. 'I didn't tell a soul, I was so ashamed.'

'You poor child,' Myrtle managed to wheeze compassionately. 'You must have yearned to come home, to find sanctuary.'

'I was desperate to get away,' Gladys confessed. 'Plus I was terrified he'd come back and find me and . . . you know, do it again.' Her voice broke as she relived the fear she'd experienced. 'I begged to return to England on the grounds of my poor health; to be honest, it was no lie. I was a bag of nerves, hardly sleeping, not eating.'

Myrtle nodded. 'It was a wise move to get away from him, but if his actions go unreported it will happen again to yet another unsuspecting innocent girl.'

'I thought of that,' Gladys guiltily admitted. 'I sometimes wonder how many other poor girls have been victim to his unwanted approaches.'

Weak as she was, Myrtle was forceful in her response. 'You must stop brooding on the past, Gladys, it's not good for you. You cannot allow a man of violence to destroy your life. He's stolen not only your glorious voice but your radiance too.'

'I swore I'd never sing again,' Gladys confessed. 'I always associate being happy and singing more than I've ever done in my entire life with the start of my troubles.'

'And I understand why you would think that, but, dear girl, it is a very simplistic line to take, rather childish, in fact,' she added with a touch of the old strict Myrtle in her voice. 'You're suggesting that by singing you attract the wrong kind of man, the sort who has only one thing on his mind. Is that correct?'

Feeling a little foolish, Gladys avoided eye contact with Myrtle but gave a brief nod.

'Nobody hurt you or abused you when you were singing up and down the country with the Bomb Girls' Swing Band; nobody hurt you, apart from the once, all the time you were touring with ENSA.'

Again, Gladys gave a brief nod.

'I think you're being superstitious, clinging on to a belief that removing something precious from your life will protect you, when all the time it's destroying you.'

Gladys finally looked up at Myrtle, who by now was clearly struggling for breath and exhausted from the exertion of expressing herself as forcefully as she had needed to. 'Rosa said something very similar,' Gladys admitted.

'And Rosa's right,' Myrtle managed. 'God in his wisdom gave you a wonderful gift . . . use it,' she gasped.

'Please, Myrtle, stop,' Gladys implored, moved beyond words by her dear friend's attempts to help her.

But Myrtle was determined to finish the conversation she'd initiated. 'Let him go to the devil,' she rasped. 'That's where men like him belong. But you're a creature of light – don't go into the darkness, dear child. Sing . . .'

As Myrtle crumpled with sheer exhaustion, Gladys still cursed the odious naval captain who'd almost ruined her life, but her dearest friend, virtually at death's doorstep, had managed to shift something in her and made her see things differently. Suddenly galvanized, she exclaimed, 'You're *so* right, Myrtle! I won't give in to him!'

'Good,' Myrtle wheezed, managing a weak smile. 'Good . . . very good.'

Gladys leant over and kissed her thin, flushed cheek. 'Thank you, Myrtle.'

The older woman smiled wanly. 'You're welcome, dear. Now, if you don't mind, I think I'll rest.'

*

On the bus going home, Gladys realized that she'd never mentioned to Myrtle the other man who had had such an impact on her during her time in Naples and who had been adding to her woes, though for different reasons. Thanks to Myrtle's straight talking, she was finally starting to see beyond just the negative aspects of her ENSA experience; there were undoubtedly wonderful days that sprang to mind, but the truly unforgettable golden day she allowed herself to re-member now was the one on which she'd first met Dr Reggie Lloyd.

Sinking back into that precious memory, she recalled how the troupe had just completed a tour of duty and were taking advantage of the sunshine on their first day off in weeks. She could picture the scene with no diffi-culty at all: after taking it in turns to shower, the girls lay sunbathing in swimsuits and shorts, when they were disturbed by an orderly telling them that a naval doctor would shortly be arriving.

'Tell him to sod off!' cackled one of the cheekier girls. 'We're on the road again tomorrow – we deserve a break.'

'He's been ordered to inoculate the lot of you against smallpox and diphtheria,' the orderly said. 'So be grate-ful for small mercies.'

'Grateful!' the cheeky girl scoffed. 'For having a bloody big needle shoved in mi arm – I don't think so!'

But when Dr Lloyd arrived on his motorbike, all complaints faded. As he switched off the bike's engine and dismounted, not a girl on site failed to notice his muscular body and the shock of dark hair that fell over his mesmerizing silver-blue eyes. He unstrapped his Gladstone medical bag from the back of the bike, and the girl nearest to Gladys moaned softly under her breath, 'God! If he's the doctor, I want to be the nurse!'

Though the temperature was up in the nineties, Dr Lloyd barely broke a sweat as he walked towards his skimpily clad patients, who winked cheekily as they extended their bare arms to him. Washing his hands in a metal bowl of cold water, Dr Lloyd donned a starched white medical coat, then calmly proceeded to inoculate each girl in turn. Exchanging little pleasantries, he worked quietly and efficiently until he came face to face with Gladys. At the sight of her long brunette hair swinging around her slender, tanned shoulders, Dr Lloyd stopped in his tracks, and when their eyes locked they both smiled quite spontaneously, as if they'd known each other before. Gladys's pulse raced, not at the sight of the long needle poised over her arm but at the electricity that she sensed flowing between them. When Reggie touched her damp skin with his cool, tapered fingers, she suppressed a gasp of pleasure.

'This shouldn't hurt,' he said softly.

He was right: Gladys was so wrapped up in the moment she didn't feel a thing.

Aware of his eyes, which he wasn't able to stop sweeping over her chest, amply exposed by her halter-neck swimsuit, Gladys felt a blush rise from her neck to her forehead.

'Ooh, he fancies you!' cried several of the girls as Dr

Lloyd, having finished his task, drove away on his motorbike. Gladys, sunbathing under a tall palm tree, waved away their teasing remarks, but the memory of the doctor's charming smile, his full lips, the dimple in his right cheek and his straight white teeth were firmly imprinted on her memory.

They next met again on board a ship when the ENSA troupe were entertaining a crowd of noisy sailors who wolf-whistled, cheered and joined in every single song they sang. Wearing her red silk dress and swinging to the rhythm of her alto sax, Gladys felt Reggie's eyes on her before she even saw him. Her skin started to tingle when she instinctively sensed he was out there watching her, and when she scanned the crowd their eyes locked just as they had the first time she'd met him. Briefly faltering over the seductive rendition of 'South of the Border' she was singing, Gladys found her knees going weak with desire. Forcing herself to focus on the music, she concluded her act with a foot-tapping rendition of 'Boogie Woogie Bugle Boy' that sent the audience wild. Clapping and cheering, they begged for more, but Gladys bowed her farewell and, blowing kisses, left the stage for the next act, a middle-aged comedian with a penny whistle who wasn't at all well received.

Unfortunately, somebody else also noticed her that night: Captain Tony Miles, the ship's captain, who had a penchant for beautiful, long-legged brunettes. As a happy smiling Gladys left the stage with Reggie's handsome face firmly in her mind, the captain grabbed her by the hand. 'Let me buy you a drink, sweetheart,' he said in a booming commanding voice, which Gladys immediately resented. Shaking off his clammy hand, she tried to move away from him, but he followed her, this time grabbing her by the shoulder as he repeated his request.

'No!' Gladys cried. 'Leave me alone. I'm meeting somebody.'

'Who?' he drawled in a voice that stank of whisky.

To Gladys's delight and astonishment, Reggie stepped in front of her. 'Me,' he confidently announced and, taking Gladys by the hand, he led her away.

'Thank you so much,' Gladys whispered as she hurried after her rescuer. 'The brute was pestering me.'

'I could see that,' Reggie replied with a knowing smile. 'He likes to chase women into submission; he has an outmoded Neanderthal view that the female of the species enjoys the chase,' he said with a sardonic laugh.

Reggie led Gladys to the prow of the ship, which was less crowded and noisy, and, leaning over the railings, they stared out at the lapping waves and the myriad stars in the dark sky. 'This is beautiful,' she sighed. She felt Reggie's eyes on her once more, sweeping over her in the thin red dress that showed every curve and contour of her body. She had an overwhelming urge to reach up and stroke his face, then kiss his lovely curving lips. Staring at each other, they both hesitated, and the trembling moment was lost when a drunken sailor came reeling towards them, asking for a light. In a blink the mood swiftly changed. It would always be so with Reggie, Gladys thought; tantalizingly near, but never really there.

Though unquestionably drawn to each other, there was always something that got in the way of the pair of them getting to know each other, though it was very obvious they both wanted to: Reggie's long, gruelling hours; Gladys's forever travelling up and down the coast entertaining the troops; the fact that when they did snatch a few precious minutes, they would inevitably be interrupted, either by a duty call or by the unfortunate appearance of the wretched Captain Miles, who relentlessly hounded Gladys.

'I don't know how to shake the brute off,' Gladys confessed to a friend one night when she couldn't get to sleep.

'He's the kind of creep that sticks like glue until he gets what he wants,' her friend had remarked. 'If I were you, kiddo, I'd stay right out of his way.'

'I wish to God he'd damn well stay out of mine!' Gladys retorted angrily.

It all changed in the days that followed the captain's vicious attack, Gladys recalled as the lurching bus braked and stopped to collect other bedraggled passengers. As they set off once again through the dark night, Gladys sighed as the precious happy memory faded and in its place came much less welcome ones. She blushed as she remembered how she'd actively avoided places where she might bump into Dr Reggie Lloyd, whom she should have had the guts to say farewell to. But once she'd got official permission to return home, she'd left Naples without making contact with him. Though he'd affected her more than any other man she'd ever met, she was convinced that men like Reggie Lloyd, clever, talented and handsome, wouldn't give her a second look, not when they knew she was damaged goods.

As the bus finally shuddered to a stop outside the Phoenix Factory, Gladys disembarked and, covering her head with a headscarf, she walked slowly and thoughtfully through the pouring rain. Reggie Lloyd was a good man, a man of principle, a man she could have fallen in love with . . . if things had turned out otherwise.

9. Fear in the Sky

On the edge of the solitary moors, the Phoenix fared better than most munitions factories in the Manchester and Liverpool area, many of which were repeatedly bombed by the Luftwaffe. There were rumours everywhere of spies passing on information as to the whereabouts of bomb- and aircraft-making factories, and government propaganda war posters were dotted all over the factory. LOOSE LIPS SINK SHIPS and BE LIKE DAD KEEP MUM warned gossips to be discreet. As the Phoenix's safety officer, Arthur was constantly reminding the workers to keep details about their work and the factory's remote location to themselves. 'We don't want Hitler targeting us,' he regularly told the workers as he walked through the factory, checking the safety equipment. 'Imagine if Gerry got wind of all the munitions factories across Britain and blew the lot sky high – we'd have nothing to send to our brave lads on the front line.'

Maggie, who constantly worried about her soldier boyfriend, Les, said hotly, 'I don't go blabbing to anybody, but I've heard plenty of lasses showing off to fellas in town about building bombs up here on't moors.'

'If I catch them, they'll be reported to the military police just like that!' Arthur said crossly as he snapped his fingers.

Wide-eyed, Maggie looked on the verge of tears. 'They should know when to keep their traps shut!' she cried. 'I wouldn't want to endanger my Les or any other soldiers risking their lives for us.' She gave a long heavy sigh. 'God, not knowing where they're fighting is bad enough, but the thought of them not having enough ammo to fight off the bloody enemy terrifies me.'

Rosa looked up briefly from the shell she was packing. 'I agree,' she said with great conviction. 'The not knowing – as you say – it is the worst.'

Knowing Rosa was referring to her family, her friends quickly glanced at each other; would this be an appropriate time to perhaps probe further into Rosa's past? But when Rosa firmly turned back to her work, they followed her cue and did the same; when the time was right, they were sure Rosa would open up. They didn't know anybody who didn't live in fear these days: mothers worried sick about sons, sweethearts parted, and everyone living in dread of that fateful knock on the door.

Keeping up with the momentum of the shells relentlessly rolling towards them on the conveyor-belt, Maggie continued, 'Every time I hear news on the wireless of a massive attack in northern France or Belgium, I wonder, could Les be there? Or have they gained enemy territory and moved on?'

Gladys, working beside Maggie, gave her a reassuring pat on the hand. 'Our Les has his wits about him,' she said. 'Remember he was the only prisoner that escaped the German round-up last year?' As Gladys withdrew her hand, Maggie's eyes widened when she saw how raw and even blistered in places it was. 'Isn't that painful?' she asked, as she nodded at Gladys's inflamed skin.

'More itchy than painful,' Gladys replied, looking ruefully down at her hands. 'I thought I'd get used to it – after all I did work with explosives in the filling shed – but I never had a reaction like this.'

'Cordite's a bugger!' Nora declared. 'First it bleaches your hair, then it turns you as yellow as a banana! But I've not seen a reaction like that before, Glad.'

Gladys gave Nora a rueful smile. 'Hopefully it'll go away soon.'

As Tommy Dorsey and his orchestra blared out from the factory loudspeakers, the girls gave up on their conversation and tapped their feet as they hummed along to 'On the Sunny Side of the Street'. In the filling shed, Arthur, pushing a trolley before him, also whistled along to the popular tune as he collected trays, each containing twenty-five filled cases, from the workers' benches. As he passed his wife's bench, Arthur bent to give her a gentle kiss on the cheek.

'Less of your canoodling!' an older woman chided as she gave blushing Violet a cheeky wink. 'Leave that till you're in private.'

Before Arthur moved on to the next bench, Violet quickly whispered, 'How was Stevie when you dropped him off this morning?'

Arthur smiled fondly; his wife's initial nervousness had grown into a full-blown, all-consuming love for her son; she quite simply adored Stevie, who had her enormous violet-blue eyes and his father's silky blond hair.

'He was fine,' Arthur assured her. 'All smiles and giggles. As soon as I set him down on the play mat, he grabbed another kiddie's toy and started chewing it.'

'Little monkey,' she said fondly. 'I'll pick him up as soon as I've finished my shift.'

Arthur grinned as he moved on. 'If you can get him away from that nursery he loves so much.'

'He loves his mum a lot more!' Violet laughed, as she turned back to the shell she was filling with mucky grey explosive.

As Tommy Dorsey was replaced by Joe Loss, the shrill sound of a siren caused consternation amongst the workers.

'Isn't that the signal to evacuate the factory?' one of the women asked nervously.

Arthur's face was grim. He knew exactly what it was. 'Christ!' he thought to himself. 'I only hope this is a practice, and that there aren't enemy planes in the area!'

Keeping his voice as calm and moderated as possible, he called out, 'Into the shelters, ladies, right away.' The shock amongst the women was palpable. 'Surely it's just a false alarm, you know, one of them practice evacuation exercises the management love to try out on us?' Maggie half-joked.

Ignoring her flippant question, Arthur continued to usher the workers in his care out of the factory. Hearing the women grumbling about having to go outside into the cold, Arthur put on his firmest safety manager's voice, calling out with increased urgency, 'Come on, don't hang about. Everyone out!' he yelled, hoping against hope that young Maggie was right and it would just turn out to be a safety practice.

As the siren continued to shrill out, women around the plant frantically grabbed their coats and gas masks, and in a steady stream made their way to the air-raid shelters built some distance away from the main factory site. As soon as she was safely out of the filling shed, a white-faced Violet left her friends to hurry over to her husband, who was marshalling workers across the yard to safety.

'What's happening, Arthur?' she demanded.

Knowing how nervy his wife was and how worried she'd be about little Stevie, Arthur summoned up his most reassuring voice. 'Probably something and nothing,' he said as he steered her back towards her friends. 'It might be just a precaution, sweetheart, but we have to go through the hoops. We'll be back inside in no time.'

'I don't want to go into the air-raid shelter without Stevie,' Violet protested loudly.

Aware that one overwrought woman, even if she was his wife, could spread panic like wild fire, Arthur hurried up to Kit, with whom he locked eyes. 'Look after Vi, will you, sweetheart? I've got to get back to the factory and clear the site,' he said urgently as he placed Violet's hand in Kit's. 'She's anxious about our Stevie.'

Kit nodded. God; she was worried sick about her own boy too. But knowing Arthur had a vital job to do, she said briskly, 'You'd better get off.' Then, turning to Violet, who was on the edge of tears, she added with a forced smile, 'They say the best air-raid shelter on the entire site is right next to the nursery block; Stevie and Billy will be safe and sound there till we get the all-clear, then we can go and pick them up.' She squeezed her friend's hand, hoping to God that she was right.

Violet nodded as she took in Kit's reassuring information. 'You're right,' she said. 'They're probably a lot safer with matron than we'll be where we're going.' She was still deathly pale, but she stuck with Kit as she reluctantly followed her into the air-raid shelter.

Back inside the factory, Arthur ushered more frightened women to safety, overhearing some of their nervous comments as he did so.

'There are no barrage balloons to hide the site from enemy planes,' one woman cried as she ran by.

'The site's camouflaged,' the breathless woman beside her replied.

'And what the hell's the point of that if the bloody Luftwaffe are flying so low they can see the lace on our knickers!' her friend scoffed.

Exasperated by loiterers who were holding up the evacuation, Arthur began to lose patience. 'Come along now,' he shouted, but his voice was beginning to be drowned out by a noise that was getting louder all the time – a noise that sounded increasingly like a low-flying plane. Cupping his hands to his mouth, he yelled, 'GET THE HELL OUT OF HERE – NOWWW!'

Also hearing the plane, the remaining women ran screaming to the safety of the factory shelters, leaving Arthur shielding his eyes to gaze up into the sky.

'JESUS!' he gasped.

From behind a bank of cloud he saw what looked like the tail of a German Messerschmitt. With his heart hammering against his ribcage, Arthur watched the plane fly east over the moors. Was it heading home or was it heading for the Phoenix? Were there more fighter planes behind this one? Was it possible the Germans had somehow got wind of the Phoenix's location? His frantic thoughts were disturbed by the sound of sobbing, and turning he saw a lone woman crouching in the open doorway that led into the packing shed.

'What the hell are you playing at?' Arthur cried angrily. 'You should be in the bloody shelters!'

'Sorry, sorry,' the old woman gibbered in terror. 'I can't go in them shelters – please don't make me go, *please*,' she begged hysterically.

With the plane almost overhead, tight-lipped Arthur simply said to the distressed woman, 'It's too late for that now anyway.'

In the shelter where Kit and Violet, along with Maggie, Nora and Rosa, nervously crouched, every single woman around them held her breath as the terrifying noise overhead grew ever closer and ever louder. As the deafening roar of the engine drummed in their ears, Kit crossed herself and prayed, 'Hail Mary, full of grace, the Lord is with thee, blessed art thou among women.'

With her eyes shut tight, Violet also prayed under her breath, tears running down her cheeks, 'Please, God, look after my baby, please, God, look after my son.'

Inside the packing shed, Arthur positioned himself and the weeping old woman against a solid supporting wall. Expecting her to run off in a panic, he said firmly, 'Don't move from here unless I tell you to.' Seeing her trembling and shaking in fear, he added, 'Hopefully the plane will pass over.'

'Holy Mother of God, I hope so,' she whispered.

Holding his breath, Arthur crouched down by the open door to watch the plane's progress. As it cruised over the dense moorland terrain, it showed no sign of being on a bombing mission.

'Has it missed us?' the woman gasped.

'I don't think he's even seen us,' Arthur replied incredulously.

Squinting, Arthur caught his breath, however, when he did see the unmistakable sight of the plane's bomb hatch slowly unfolding. As if it was happening in slow motion, he watched as the pilot offloaded what must have been his spare bombs over the desolate moorland terrain. 'Sweet Jesus!' he gasped as the bombs plummeted to earth, right on target for the domestic quarters, which housed the infirmary and the day nursery. Every part of Arthur's body turned to ice. 'NOOOO!' he bellowed as, regardless of his own safety, he rushed to the open door, from where he watched the bombs explode. Falling to his knees, he sobbed out loud, 'Spare my son, please, God, spare my Stevie.'

Inside the shelter, the terrified women gazed at each other, incredulous.

'Have they flown over?' Nora gasped as the sound of the Messerschmitt's engine receded slightly.

'God be praised,' Rosa murmured.

No sooner were the words out of her mouth than they heard the bombs explode, causing the ground beneath them to shake. The terrified women gripped each other for support.

'Christ! It's missed us but it's hit some other poor buggers nearby,' one woman murmured.

Violet, half mad with fear, leapt to her feet. 'STEVIE!' she screamed hysterically.

Fighting off her friends, who were trying to hold her down, she kicked and punched her way free, then ran sobbing towards the door, which she flung open.

'STEVIE!' she yelled. 'STEVIE!'

Through the open door of the packing shed, Arthur watched in horror as his wife erupted from the air-raid shelter and like a thing demented ran screaming across the yard. Horrified by the agonized expression on her face, he bellowed, 'STOP, VIOLET! STOP! You must wait for the all-clear.'

Before he could take a step towards his wife, Arthur heard a dull thud behind him, followed by a thundering, rumbling noise as the building started to collapse. As hundreds of tons of debris engulfed him, the last thing Arthur saw before he sank unconscious to the ground was his wife running towards the blazing domestic quarters.

When Arthur came round, it was dark, and, grunting with pain, he made a frantic effort to free himself, but realized with horror that he was hemmed in on all sides. Straining to turn his head, he saw that the brick-work and machinery that had fallen on top of him from the floor above had landed on the old woman too. Groping, he reached out to her; feeling his way up her motionless body, Arthur tentatively touched her temple in order to find a pulse, but all he felt was a warm flow of blood trickling over his fingers.

Realizing the poor woman could not be saved, he shuddered. 'So how the hell did I survive that?' he wondered.

With images of Violet's agonized face in his mind, Arthur struggled to free his feet, which were trapped under a heavy door that had missed the old woman but landed on top of him, protecting him to a large extent from the tumbling masonry. Trapped in the darkness and half crazed with fear, Arthur frantically shouted for help as he wriggled and twisted to free himself, but soon he started to gasp from the smoke and dust. Straining to breathe, Arthur realized that he could die buried under half the Phoenix Factory, never knowing whether his wife and son were dead or alive. As drowsiness weak-ened him, images of Violet floated into his mind: Violet the first time he'd laid eyes on her – terrified of men, she'd been nervous of his attention, but his love and patience had won through in the end. He'd courted her in his allotment garden in the summertime; he remem-bered how the sun had caught her long, silky hair, turning it silver-bright, and her eyes had shone as blue as the bluebells that grew wild on the moors. How he loved her, body and soul! The birth of their son completed their happiness; he knew it was Violet's total devotion to her baby that had sent her running recklessly in the direction of the Phoenix's domestic quarters. She would always unquestionably have put her life before that of her beloved son. 'Oh, Vi,' he murmured as tears pricked his eyes. 'Please, my love, stay safe.'

Small flickering flames flaring up in the darkness snapped him out of his drowsy reverie. He was fearful that the factory might soon be ablaze and there'd be no escape; he gasped for air as smoke engulfed the chamber in which he was imprisoned. As the fetid smoke curled down his throat, Arthur was startled by the sensation of cold water trickling from above.

'Somebody's trying to put out the fire!' he realized. 'Somebody's up there!'

Too hoarse to yell, he frantically searched around in the darkness for a weapon, and, finding a long metal stick that had once belonged to a piece of machinery, he began to bang it hard against the wall.

'HELP! HELP!' he croaked weakly.

The water that had started as a trickle was now flowing fast down the wall, soaking his clothes and lodging in a muddy pool underneath him. Freezing cold and shivering, Arthur continued to bash the metal stick and then suddenly he was conscious of a muffled voice behind the debris.

'Anybody there?'

Arthur tried to shout but all that came out of his throat was a hoarse croak. 'HELP! HELP!'

'Hang on, mate!' somebody called out to him. 'We'll have you out soon.'

Holding his breath, Arthur listened intently to the distant scratching sounds, which were coming steadily closer. 'Oh, God,' he prayed. 'Let me live, please let me live to see my wife and son again.'

There was a loud scraping noise above him as rescuers removed wreckage and a slit of light entered the dark chamber.

'HERE!' Arthur screamed. 'I'M HERE! HELP!'

Flooded with gratitude, Arthur watched the firemen slowly but steadily burn away metal and machinery, until they had cleared a hole big enough to drag him through. Grabbing hold of the fire crew pulling him to safety, Arthur sobbed with relief.

'Well done, pal,' one of the fire crew said as they hauled Arthur to his feet. 'Anybody else down there with you?'

Arthur nodded. 'A woman,' he told them. 'She's lying under the rubble, but she's gone,' he added grimly.

As some of the rescue workers attempted to locate the dead woman, the ambulance driver guided Arthur through the choking debris to a door that hung from its shattered hinges. 'Come on, we need to get you to hospital; you've lost a lot of blood,' he said.

For the first time Arthur realized he'd been wounded; looking down, he saw a huge tear in his thigh from which blood was pumping. Nevertheless he resisted his help. 'No,' he gasped. 'I need to find my wife and son.'

'Leave that to the rescue workers,' the driver advised as he firmly led Arthur to the back of his vehicle. 'Sorry, pal, you're going nowhere but Manchester Royal Infirmary,' he said as he settled Arthur on to a stretcher and slammed the doors shut behind him.

When the women heard the all-clear, they staggered out of the shelters. Cold and stiff after sitting tense and hunched for so long, they gazed at the piles of dusty debris that lay scattered across their pathway.

'VIOLET!' Kit called as she looked distractedly around the factory yard for her friend.

As the police arrived to guide the women to safety, Kit grabbed hold of Gladys's arm.

'I'm not leaving until I've found Billy,' she whispered fiercely.

Gladys nodded. 'We've got to find Violet too.'

Kit nodded as she replied, 'She'll have gone to the nursery, for sure.'

'Keep down and follow me,' Gladys said in a whisper as she slipped under the cordon the police had erected.

Crouching low, Gladys and Kit ran hell for leather towards the nursery, which was situated at the far end of the domestic quarters. Surrounded by a large play area, they were relieved to see it was surprisingly intact, though there were no children or staff in sight. Frantic now to find Violet and the children, they painstakingly searched the pram shed, the laundry, the little cloakroom where the kiddies hung up their gingham overalls, even the outdoor privy that the staff used.

'Oh, God!' Kit cried in despair. 'They've got to be somewhere.'

It was in the empty garden that they finally spotted Violet, who hardly seemed to notice their arrival. Ashen faced, she was casting wildly about. 'Where are they?' she cried in anguish. 'Where have they taken the children?'

As all three women stared at each other in misery, the sound of children's voices, as sweet as music to their ears, came floating through the air. Turning in the direction of the babbling voices, they saw the staff emerging from the nursery air-raid shelter, which was mercifully obscured by a bank of trees and overgrown bushes. They cradled the babies and led the toddlers, who were desperate to run around and play after being cooped up so long. At the sight of little Billy's sweet, smiling face, Kit's legs almost gave way with relief. Rushing to embrace their children, whom they clung on to for dear life, Violet and Kit sobbed with relief as they smothered them with kisses. Violet, hugging Stevie like she'd never let him go, cried, 'Oh, my darling! You're safe, Mummy's got you.'

The fire and ambulance crews arrived as Violet and Kit, still holding their babies, left the nursery area along with Gladys. As they walked out on to the factory road, Ian came roaring up in his Ford Anglia. Seeing them, he slammed on the brakes and leapt out of the car. 'Kit! Billy!' he cried, embracing them in the circle of his arms and fighting off tears. 'Oh, thank God!' he half-sobbed with relief. 'I heard about the bombing on the news; all the roads were blocked by police barricades. I thought, I thought . . .' His voice broke as he expressed his terror. 'I thought I might have lost you both.'

'We're alive, thank God, we're all alive!' Kit cried as she leant against her husband's warm chest and wept.

Looking round at the shattered buildings that the bomb had hit, Ian's face whitened. 'Christ!' he murmured. 'It's nothing short of a miracle that the nursery missed the blast.'

'When we heard the plane flying over, we thought we were safe, but seconds later the bombs exploded,' Kit said, then, as the full horror hit her, she buried her head in her hands. 'I don't think I've ever been so terrified in my life. All I could think of was Billy, my little boy,' she wept.

Laying a strong arm around his wife's slender waist, Ian led her away from the disaster site. 'Come on, my darling, let's get you home.'

Carrying Billy, Ian opened the car door for Kit, Violet and Gladys, but Violet held back.

'I can't come with you,' she announced. 'I've got to find my Arthur.'

Kit shook her head. 'You can't go back to the factory, Vi – it's not safe.'

'I can't leave until I know where he is,' Violet said with tears in her eyes. 'Please look after Stevie till I get back,' she said as she handed her baby to Gladys.

'We'll keep him safe at Yew Tree Farm,' Kit called after Violet, who, having secured the safety of her son, would now know no peace until she found her husband.

10. The Search

Violet got a lift off an obliging policeman who was driving into Manchester. After she was dropped off at the Royal Infirmary, she ran into the entrance hall, where she suddenly stopped dead in her tracks. This was déjà vu: she'd been in this exact spot before and recently too. Just before their wedding, Arthur had discovered defective fuses in the filling shed, and in a delicate, deadly operation he'd removed them to an explosion pit, which was situated a safe distance from the Phoenix, in order to detonate them. Unfortunately, one of the fuses had blown up in Arthur's handsome face, causing facial injuries and damage to his right eye. What condition would she find her husband in now? Violet thought as she rushed to the front desk, where a frantic receptionist was trying to deal with a noisy crowd of anxious relatives all yelling questions at her, most of which she couldn't answer. Following their example, Violet pushed and shoved her way to the front of the queue, where she made her enquiries. The receptionist scanned a long list on her desk. 'He's in theatre; he'll be taken to a post-surgical ward, but as of now I don't know exactly which one,' she said quickly, turning to the next person and thereby dismissing Violet, who stood pole-axed with shock.

'Why is my husband having surgery?' she cried, but nobody heard her or cared to listen. Violet made her way to a nearby bench on which she slumped down. She'd seen Arthur in the factory as she was running across the yard to the nursery – what had happened to him? she thought frantically. Scanning the crowded entrance hall, she was surprised to see Mr Featherstone talking to a group of women who appeared to have minor injuries, judging by the dressings they were wearing. 'MR FEATHERSTONE!' she called as she ran towards him.

The factory manager looked concerned when he saw Violet. 'Mrs Leadbetter,' he said. 'How is your husband?'

Violet shook her head. 'I'm waiting for him to come out of theatre,' she replied. 'Do you know what happened to him?' she asked nervously.

Mr Featherstone caught her arm and walked her away from the group so they could speak in private.

'The back wall of the factory collapsed,' he explained. 'Arthur was trapped under the rubble.'

'Why was he in there anyway?' Violet cried.

'He was doing his job: protecting a poor woman, who was found dead under the rubble by the rescue workers. It's a miracle your husband survived, Mrs Leadbetter.'

Violet stared desolately into the middle distance; before he'd been appointed safety officer at the Phoenix, Arthur had been working with explosives in active service. Whilst dismantling a German booby-trap bomb, he'd lost fingers on both of his hands, which meant he could no longer serve in the army.

'I know my Arthur's a hero,' she thought to herself. 'But I wish to God he wasn't *quite* such a hero.'

Violet had no idea how long she sat there, dazed and terrified, praying that her brave husband would be alive and well. She jumped when she felt a hand on her shoulder. 'I've just been directed over here to speak to you,' a tired-looking nurse told her. 'Are you Mrs Leadbetter?'

Violet leapt to her feet. 'Yes! My husband?' she cried. 'Where is he?'

'He's on Ward D4.'

'Can I see him?' Violet begged.

The nurse nodded as she set off across the hall. 'You can, but only briefly,' she replied as Violet almost ran to keep up with her hurrying footsteps. 'He's just come out of theatre, so I suggest you keep your visit short and say nothing that might agitate him.'

Violet softly wept when she saw Arthur, whose broken leg was in traction and stuck out at an odd angle in the air. He had an oxygen mask over his face, which was scarred with deep cuts and dark bruises, and his breathing was laboured. 'My poor darling,' Violet whispered as she took his hand in hers and kissed his fingertips. 'Five minutes,' said the nurse. 'Then I really need to check his wounds.'

Murmuring his name and stroking his limp blond hair away from a gash on his forehead, Violet stayed until she was asked to leave. 'Goodnight,' she said as she reluctantly left his bedside. 'I love you, Arthur. God bless.'

It was far too late to catch any buses back to Pendleton, so Violet asked the weary nurse on the reception desk if she could briefly use her phone to get a lift home. She was grateful to Ian when he arrived half an hour later and drove her home through the dark night to the warmth of Yew Tree Farm. As soon as she was indoors, Kit beckoned to Violet, and after laying a finger on her lips she silently led her upstairs to the spare bedroom, where Stevie lay fast slept in Billy's old baby cot.

'Awwwww.' Violet let out a long slow smile of happiness as she gazed in adoration at Stevie's peaceful, contented face.

After gently rearranging the soft blanket that covered her son, she followed Kit downstairs, where Ian was already brewing tea in a big brown pot.

'Oh, thank you,' Violet said with a grateful smile, wrapping her cold hands around the mug of hot, strong tea he offered her. 'I could really do with this,' she assured her friends as she drank deeply, then reached for her cigarettes.

After telling her friends all that she knew about Arthur's condition, Violet anxiously asked, 'How have the boys been?'

'Fine,' Kit replied. 'Ian and I bathed both of them down here, in the big sink, then dried them on the rug in front of the Aga. They had a whale of a time,' she giggled.

'Stevie kicked his little legs in the air and Billy blew

kisses on his tummy,' Ian recalled. 'They laughed themselves silly.'

'I still have Billy's feeding bottle and some dried milk,' Kit added. 'Stevie had a good feed before bedtime, then fell fast asleep in Ian's arms.'

'Thanks so much,' Violet said as she gazed from Ian to Kit. 'It would have been a nightmare taking Stevie to the hospital. I was there for hours,' she said with a yawn. 'But I would never have rested if I hadn't seen my Arthur.' Her eyes filled with tears. 'I wonder how the poor man is now?'

'They've probably settled him for the night,' Ian assured her.

'You should get some sleep too, sweetheart,' Kit urged. 'You've got a long day ahead of you tomorrow.'

11. Visiting Hours

Violet woke up in the pearly dawn light to the sound of birds twittering sleepily on the moors outside her window. Wriggling her toes to familiarize herself with where she was, Violet thought first of Arthur. Had he slept well? Was he in pain? When she heard Stevie's first little coos and gurgles as he too awoke to a new day, she leapt out of bed and lifted him into her arms.

'Hello, my sweet,' she murmured as she gently laid him on the bed to change his damp nappy. When he was snuggled up in a clean one, she climbed back into bed, where she lay down with Stevie beside her. As he continued to burble and chatter, Violet drank in the beauty of his perfect skin and chubby little limbs; even after a day as dark as yesterday, when they had all but lost a husband and a father, Violet could not help but glory in the joy of being Stevie's mother. A loud squawk followed by little pattering footsteps on the stairs announced that Billy was on his way to see his friend Stevie.

Over breakfast, tea and toast and Kit's mouth-wateringly juicy wild blackberry jam, Kit said, 'Ian and I want you to know that you and Stevie can stay here with us at Yew Tree Farm for as long as you like.'

'Oh, Kit, you're so kind!' Violet cried with tears in her eyes.

'I was talking with the rescue workers yesterday,' Ian continued. 'They said the domestic site has taken the biggest hit, virtually razed to the ground.' More tears came to Violet's eyes as she thought of her home smashed to smithereens. 'Of course they'll rebuild it as quickly as possible,' Ian hastily added. 'But for the moment this is your home, and Arthur's too once he's been discharged,' he said generously.

'I can't tell you just how grateful I am,' Violet said as she handed Kit a Woodbine.

'We've always stuck together, both in good and bad times,' Kit reminded her with a warm smile.

'And this is hard indeed,' murmured Violet.

As the little boys rolled around on the kitchen floor, giggling and squeaking, Ian told Violet that the plane that had caused such havoc to the Phoenix had been traced. 'It was on its way back to Germany after a bombing-raid over Liverpool,' he said. 'Apparently the pilot dumped his unused bombs on the moors.'

Violet's eyes opened wide in shock. 'So it wasn't an actual attack?'

'Apparently not, though it damn well felt like it,' Kit said with a rueful laugh.

'It's common practice for German pilots to dump unused bombs in desolate places,' Ian explained. 'It lightens the load for their return flight home,' he added.

'How very convenient for the Germans!' Violet scoffed as she inhaled her Woodbine.

After a rather long breakfast, Violet took Stevie back upstairs to play with Billy until it was time to catch the bus into Manchester. Before leaving, Violet buried her face in Stevie's soft blond curls. 'Goodbye, Mummy's little angel, be good for your aunt Kit.'

Arthur was conscious when she arrived for afternoon visiting time.

'He's very weak,' the sister explained. 'Do your best not to overtire him.'

With her heart fluttering in her ribcage, Violet hurried down the long ward to Arthur's bed. 'Darling!' she cried when she saw him propped up on his pillows with his tractioned leg still stuck in the air at an awkward angle.

'Sweetheart,' he murmured weakly, as she sat on the chair beside his bed and clutched his hand in hers. 'How's Stevie?' he asked weakly.

'He's fine,' she answered with a bright smile. 'All the children were safe and sound in the nursery air-raid shelter,' she added.

'You were silly, running off like that,' he scolded.

Violet blushed as she remembered her wild, reckless run across the despatch yard to the day nursery. She'd barely heeded her husband's voice in her crazy panic to find her baby.

'I had to find Stevie,' she said guiltily. 'I was out of my mind with fear.'

Arthur squeezed her hand again. 'I know, but you could have got yourself killed.'

'You nearly got yourself killed too, my sweetheart,' she reminded him with a smile. 'Typical you, always putting others before yourself.'

'The woman I helped,' he whispered as he choked up. 'She died.'

'I know, but you did what you could and almost lost your own life in the process. I sometimes wish you weren't always such a hero, Arthur Leadbetter! There'll be nothing left of you if you carry on being a safety office. First you lose your poor fingers,' she said as she tenderly kissed his damaged hands. 'Then a bomb goes off in your handsome face, and now this!' she said with a smile as she stared at his injured leg. 'You're my brave wounded soldier, and I'm very proud of you.'

An orderly came along, noisily rattling a trolley around the ward; she poured tea from an urn for Arthur and craftily slipped Violet a cup too. 'Don't let sister see you drinking it, but you look in need of a cuppa,' she said with a kind wink.

As Violet helped Arthur drink his tea, she told him about the devastated domestic site, but, seeing his face crease with anxiety, she quickly added, 'Don't go worrying yourself, lovie, it'll be rebuilt by the time you're discharged; until then Stevie and me have been invited to stay with Ian and Kit for as long as we like.'

Arthur smiled with relief, 'They're good kind people,' he said gratefully.

'They've given us one of the bedrooms. Stevie sleeps in Billy's old baby cot and I have a bed by the window. I look right out on to the moors – it's lovely,' she told him.

'I bet Stevie loves playing with Billy,' Arthur said with a grin.

'For a little lad, he knows what he wants,' Violet

laughed. 'He's only to see Billy with a toy or a piece of toast and he squeals till he gets it too.'

'We'd better teach him some manners before he gets kicked out of Yew Tree Farm,' Arthur joked.

Seeing him getting tired, Violet put aside his teacup, then sat beside the bed as he drifted off to sleep. She stayed by her husband's side, holding his hand until the visitors' bell clanged and she, along with the other friends and relatives, was ushered out of the ward.

Violet got back to Yew Tree Farm just in time to bath Stevie and put him to bed. As he snuggled down in his borrowed cot, Violet sang 'Golden Slumbers' to him until he fell fast asleep. Tiptoeing in order not to disturb Stevie, she looked around the room, which Kit had decorated in a pretty, flowery wallpaper. She wondered sadly if there was anything left of their home. The domestic site had been hastily thrown up to house munitions workers and their families, but they'd been a place to call their own. Violet recalled how Arthur had arrived home every Friday with a bouquet from his allotment behind the despatch yard – spring blossoms, followed by summer blooms, followed by autumn flowers. She remembered the last bouquet he'd brought: a bunch of big, floppy, late chrysanthemums that she'd last seen on the kitchen windowsill before she walked out of the house with Stevie. She sighed. It had been a humble dwelling, but it was the place where she'd first shared a double bed with her husband, and Stevie had been born there. It made her sad to think of it in ruins, but at least they were alive, not like the poor woman Arthur had tried to save, who lost her life under a pile of rubble.

12. The Phoenix Rises

In the weeks that followed the bombing, Violet, Stevie, Kit and Billy were a surprisingly happy little group, loving their unexpected time together, even if it was in difficult circumstances. The boys, though different in age, bonded as they played together and shared their mealtimes, whilst Kit and Violet, who had always been close, grew even closer as they cared for their children and cooked and cleaned side by side in Kit's big old farm kitchen. At the end of the day, after Violet had returned from visiting her husband in hospital and the babies were fast asleep, the two women sat together beside the cosy Aga, smoking Woodbines as the bitter autumn wind whistled across the dark moors outside.

'It's just like old times,' Kit said with a nostalgic smile. 'Remember, when we all lived together in the cowshed?'

Violet nodded. 'Goodness,' she recalled. 'How we got ourselves tied up in knots keeping secrets from each other.'

Kit leant closer and added in a low voice, 'I've got another secret,' she confided. 'I really want to help find Edna's daughter, Flora.'

Violet gasped in astonishment. 'How on earth can you do that?'

Kit's shoulders slumped as she expressed her

disappointment. 'It turns out to be much more compli-cated than I thought,' she confessed glumly. 'Ian said that even if we could trace Flora, which might be impossible, we have no right legal right to approach her, so it's hopeless.'

'Oh . . .' Violet's deflated voice expressed her own disappointment.

'He said,' Kit continued, 'that the only thing we can do is keep an eye on the adverts in the local and national papers.'

Violet's brow crinkled in confusion. 'How's an ad in the paper going to help?'

'People sometimes advertise when they're searching for their birth parent,' Kit explained. 'I've seen a few – though not Flora's, unfortunately.' As she spoke, Kit stood up and walked over to the highly polished oak sideboard, where she picked up several newspaper clip-pings, which she handed over to Violet who read them out loud: 'Ronald Pemberton living in Tonge Moor, Bolton, born 1923, searching for birth mother, whose name might be McManus, originally from the Old Trafford area of Manchester.' Violet glanced up at Kit. 'It is a bit of a long shot,' she remarked.

Kit shrugged as she lit up another Woodbine. 'I know, but it's all we can do – chances are that Flora knows nothing at all about Edna, nor being adopted either.'

'Hmm,' Violet muttered thoughtfully to herself. 'But what if her adoptive parents have died and Flora's found her birth certificate with her real mother's name on it? You do hear of these things.'

'Maybe,' Kit replied with a wistful smile.

'You mustn't give up, Kit – keep on trying,' Violet urged. 'Just imagine how happy Edna would be if her lost daughter walked back into her life.'

With work suspended until the Phoenix was safe for the workers, Rosa had a brainwave. When she heard from Violet that children were not allowed on the ward at visiting time, she thought of a way of helping Arthur, who was desperately missing his little boy.

'I'll do drawings of Stevie which you can take to hospital for Arthur,' she told a delighted Violet.

'That's a wonderful idea,' Violet cried. 'It will definitely cheer him up.'

Rosa wasted no time in visiting Yew Tree Farm, where, using sheets of paper ripped from a writing pad, she drew black-and-white images with a stubby pencil: Stevie fast asleep in his cot with his arms thrown back in abandon; Stevie reaching out to grab Kit's tabby cat; Stevie hungrily drinking milk from his bottle – lots of tender images that delighted Arthur and momentarily brought his boy closer to him. When Violet passed on her husband's grateful words of thanks, Rosa smiled. 'I am the one to thank Arthur,' she remarked. 'Now my hands feel empty without a pencil – I want to draw everything I see!'

Two weeks after the bombing, the front part of the factory, which had survived the explosion, was passed as safe by an inspector and the munitions girls returned to work.

'I can't believe we're back,' Nora said as they all clocked on.

'It felt like a holiday to start with,' Maggie admitted. 'But then I started to miss all of my friends, plus I was worried sick that Les's infantry wouldn't have enough bombs to fight Jerry!'

'The Phoenix doesn't exist just to send ammo to your boyfriend!' Nora teased.

'Maybe not, but I often mark my bombs with a kiss for Les or a cheeky message like "This one's for you, Adolf!"'

'You're mad!' Nora joked.

'Like as not,' Maggie giggled. 'But it helps to pass the time of day.'

'Welcome back to the Phoenix!' Malc exclaimed as the girls trooped up to their workbenches. 'Come on, lasses,' he urged. 'We've got to make up for lost time – we don't want the enemy to think they're winning the war.'

'Don't worry,' a woman in the filling shed scoffed. 'We'll have bombs flying out of here by this time next week.'

As the bomb line started to roll, the women combined to work harder than ever; it was their duty to keep the men with the Howitzers on the front line well stocked with ammunition, and if it meant working overtime to meet their quota, they'd do it for love of King and Country.

The Phoenix nursery didn't reopen at the same time as the factory. 'We're in the process of rebuilding the domestic units,' Mr Featherstone explained to the mothers. 'We can't have you and your babies tramping through a building site. You'll just have to arrange alternative child care for the time being,' he advised.

Violet and Kit developed a plan that suited both them and their children: they worked alternate weeks, so one of them could be at Yew Tree Farm minding the babies whilst the other went out to work. They felt guilty when they knew how hard the other munitions girls were working, but, like Kit said, they couldn't possibly take their babies into the factory and there was nobody else to mind them. Knowing how anxious Violet was about leaving Stevie, Kit had a quiet word with her friend. 'You don't need to worry when you're away from Stevie,' she assured Violet. 'He's perfectly safe with me, sweetheart.'

Violet blushed. 'I'd trust you with my life, Kit,' she responded. 'I know Stevie couldn't be in a safer place, it's just that I . . .' Her voice faded away in embarrassment.

'You don't have to explain,' Kit said gently. 'You love him so much you can't stop worrying about him. You did have a fright – it's not surprising you feel that way.'

Violet nodded her head before blurting out, 'But it's not healthy, Kit! I don't know any other mother who worries so much about her baby. I don't want Stevie growing up soft and mollycoddled.'

'You'll worry less as Stevie grows older,' Kit told her. 'It's just because he's so little and precious, and because of the troubling times we're living in.'

Violet stared at her friend with her wonderful wide blue eyes. 'I never imagined I could feel such love,' she confessed. 'I thought I couldn't love anybody more than my Arthur, but when Stevie was born I felt possessed by such a fierce protective love, a bit like a lioness with her cub,' she added with a shy smile.

'There's nothing wrong with that!' Kit cried. 'Look how hard I fought to get my son back. I'm sure all mothers have that feeling from time to time –' She stopped short, as she was interrupted by a loud squawk from the cat. 'Except when my cheeky little monkey chases the cat around the room and pulls her tail!' Kit laughed.

Back at work, Rosa got into the habit of sketching her friends and other women in the canteen, smoking, eating, laughing and chatting as they relaxed during their tea break. Eager to extend her repertoire, in her free time she moved out of the canteen in order to draw images of Bomb Girls at work in the filling shed, on the cordite line and in the packing shed, loading bombs into wooden boxes. Seeing her around so often, Rosa's fellow workers lost their inhibitions as they became accustomed to her presence, and this easy familiarity enabled Rosa to catch images that had an individual style all of their own.

'Make sure you keep 'em safe,' Malc said as he admired Rosa's most recent sketches, of women lining up beside Edna's mobile chippy on a frosty night with a new moon shining silver light down on to the yard. 'They're a record of your time here, like a diary,' he observed. 'But I tell you what, kid,' he added with a chuckle, 'I'm going to get you a proper artist's sketch-pad – them little scrappy bits of paper don't do proper justice to your artistry.'

Rosa laughed at what she thought was a preposterous

idea. 'And where you get artist's sketch-pad? They rationed too, no?'

Malc winked as he tapped the side of his nose. 'Leave that to me, lass,' he replied. 'Least said, soonest mended!'

True to his word, Malc showed up a week later with a proper sketch-pad and some coloured pencils. 'There you go,' he said with a pleased smile. 'Let's see what you can do with that lot.'

It was during the second week back at work that Gladys's allergic condition really flared up. It got to the point where her hands itched so much she scratched them until they bled.

'You not go on like this,' Rosa protested as she smoothed cream into her friend's hands before they went to bed. 'You must see doctor.'

With all the local tragic events that had recently taken place at home and the exciting progress of the Allies in Italy, the last thing Gladys wanted to do was to stop building bombs. 'This isn't the time to be slacking and fussing over chapped hands – I want to work, and that's that, Rosa,' she staunchly protested.

But in the end, she was forced to report to Dr Grant, the Phoenix doctor, when her wounds became infected. He'd been brought out of retirement to take charge of the small Phoenix Infirmary and was shocked at the condition of Gladys's raw, red hands.

'You have a chronic condition, young lady,' he pronounced after he'd completed his examination. 'It looks like a serious allergic reaction to cordite.'

'But I've worked with explosives before,' Gladys pointed out. 'And never suffered a reaction as bad as this one.'

'It's perfectly clear cordite doesn't suit you,' he pronounced. 'You're going to have to take at least two weeks off work if you're ever going to give your skin a chance to heal.'

Gladys was yet again indignant at the prospect of being taken off the bomb line. 'I won't stop work!' she exclaimed.

'You have no choice, my dear. Being away from raw explosives is the only way to ease your condition,' the doctor insisted.

'Surely I can wear gloves?' Gladys pleaded.

Dr Grant shook his head firmly. 'Cordite gets everywhere – you need a complete break from a toxic explosive environment; come back in two weeks,' he said, as he firmly ushered her out of the surgery door.

Feeling guilty about not pulling her weight, and wondering what on earth she would do with herself for two weeks, Gladys returned to the cowshed, where Rosa had made a pastry-based pizza, as there was no yeast to be had. The improvised pizza, topped with tinned tomatoes, a scratching of cheese and some wild thyme picked on the moors, was so delicious it briefly cheered Gladys up, but, as she wiped pastry crumbs from her lips, she grumbled to Rosa about the doctor's decision to lay her off work.

'I'll go mad staying at home all day!' she declared. 'Not to mention how bad I'll feel, sitting twiddling my thumbs whilst all my friends are slaving away putting in extra hours for the war effort,' she told Rosa, who hummed to herself as she cleared away the dirty dishes. Recognizing the tune, Gladys looked at her incredulously. 'Surely it's too early for "Jingle Bells"!' she exclaimed.

Rosa giggled. 'Nora teach me tune, so I know by Christmas.'

'She might have taught you the tune, but not the words – you've got them all wrong, *again*!' Gladys remarked as irrepressible Rosa incorrectly warbled, 'Oh, jingling bells, jingling bells, all the jingling way.'

Seeing Gladys shaking her head, Rosa protested, 'Okay, so teach me the right words!'

After Gladys sang the correct words in her wonderful, lilting voice, Rosa clapped her hands in sheer delight. 'The Bomb Girl Nightingale!'

Gladys pulled down the corners of her mouth as she said, 'I suppose I could go around the factory singing to my pals – at least it would give me something to do during my damned sick leave.'

'No, no, no!' Rosa chided as she wagged her finger at her friend. 'Stay away from explosive – do what the doctor say, mia cara.'

Gladys looked thoughtful as she put a kettle full of water on top of the crackling wood-burning stove. 'You know, I've been thinking about asking the staff at Belmont Sanatorium if I could help nurse Myrtle: that would be a good way to spend my time when I'm off work.'

The two women exchanged a sad look. All the rest

and fresh air hadn't done anything to improve Myrtle's condition, and the bombing of the Phoenix had severely shocked the sick woman. Even though her friends regularly visited her, they all knew that Myrtle, in a hospital that was chronically short staffed, spent most of her days lying in bed waiting for death to claim her. Rosa reached out to hug Gladys. 'That a wonderful idea.'

Gladys gave a shy smile. 'Do you think they'll have me?' she asked doubtfully.

'Certo! Of course,' Rosa replied robustly. 'And poor Myrtle will be very happy.'

It was round about this time that Kit started feeling sick in the morning. Recalling her pregnancy with Billy, she vividly remembered how ill she'd been in the first months with him – so ill that she'd been forced to confide in her sister, who'd begged her not to let on to their father. 'He'll kill you if he finds out you're expecting a babby!' she'd said in a terrified whisper. 'He'll tear you limb from limb.' Knowing her father as she did, Kit never doubted her sister's words, so she'd suffered in silence until her body could keep her secret no longer and her belly swelled out under her ragged pinafore. Putting bad memories aside, Kit surveyed her comparatively flat stomach as she examined herself in the wardrobe mirror. Sometimes she couldn't believe that the woman looking back at her with flowing, waist-length black hair, huge dark eyes brimming with contentment and a slender body that showed no sign of the bag of bones she had been on her arrival in England was Kitty Murphy from Chapelizoid, Dublin.

Even in a time of war, love and happiness had transformed her into a beauty – not that Kit ever described herself as such, but her husband assured her she was at least once a day and Billy always called her 'Pretty Mummy' every time he kissed her. Examining her small, firm breasts, Kit recalled how tender and swollen they'd become when she was pregnant with Billy; a sudden tingling sensation made her acutely aware that she could be repeating the whole process over again, but this time with Ian as the father of her child. Instead of a man who'd raped her, she would have a husband to love and care for her, a wonderful man who had already taken Billy as his own son and given him a name he could be proud of. She smiled secretively as she slipped a silk underskirt over her naked body and started to dress. In the weeks after the terrible explosion at the Phoenix, she and Ian had been even more passionate in their love-making; the fear of losing each other had accelerated their joy in one another and they'd made love more often than ever before. It would be surprising if she wasn't pregnant, Kit thought with amusement to herself; she'd hardly been able to keep her hands off Ian, and he'd obviously felt the same way too. For the time being, Kit decided, as she hurried downstairs to help Violet with the children, she wouldn't mention anything to her husband; she'd wait to see if she missed another period, and then, when she was sure, she'd break the good news.

13. Gladys and Myrtle

Gladys wasted no time in arranging a meeting with the matron of Belmont Sanatorium, who eagerly accepted Gladys as a volunteer.

'With Myrtle bed-bound these days, it would be company for her to have you close by,' she said gratefully.

And so Gladys became a daily visitor to the sanatorium. Striding the three miles over the moors, Gladys enjoyed the bracing wind on those cold, damp days, and the smile on Myrtle's thin, pale face that greeted her as she breezed in smelling of fresh air made the long walk, often in the rain, worthwhile. The sight of Gladys reading to Myrtle became a familiar one to the staff; Gladys sang to her as she brushed her now entirely grey hair, helped her use a bed pan and fed her, though most of the time Myrtle was too weak even to eat, but she tried her best just to please Gladys.

'It doesn't feel as awkward as having the nurses wash me,' Myrtle whispered gratefully as Gladys gently soaped her back and shoulders. 'I hope you don't mind, dear?' she asked with a shy apologetic smile.

'Of course I don't mind!' Gladys exclaimed as she settled Myrtle back on her pillows, which she'd plumped up. 'It's a privilege, and I enjoy spending time with you,' she added tenderly.

Seeing the tears well in Myrtle's tired eyes, she added with a cheerful smile, 'Now how about a nice cup of tea?'

As Gladys hurried off to make it, Myrtle admired the girl's long, brunette hair swinging around her slender shoulders and the sway of her shapely hips. 'Ah, to be young,' she sighed.

Tears stung her eyes as she recalled happier times when Gladys had been driven by her vision of an all girls' swing band, which, by sheer force of will, she'd brought to fruition, with Myrtle, the oldest by far, playing the piano. They'd been wonderful days. Even with a war raging and rationing getting ever harsher, she had never been happier in her life.

'How we used to laugh!' Myrtle said as she and Gladys drank their tea.

Gladys smiled as she remembered too. 'We would never have got anywhere without you,' she said appreciatively.

'Nonsense,' Myrtle remonstrated. 'We all brought our different talents.'

'You really helped Nora with her trombone playing; it was you who gave her the confidence to play,' Gladys reminded Myrtle.

'Poor child,' Myrtle sighed as she remembered how she'd taken Nora under her wing after the tragic death of the girl's mother. 'Promise you'll keep an eye on Nora when I'm gone,' she asked softly. 'She's as innocent as a babe and needs so much mothering.'

Gladys's eyes filled with tears; the thought of Myrtle

considering her own death was unbearable. Seeing her sad, Myrtle reached for her hand. 'As I've told you before, I have no fear of death; in fact I welcome the Lord coming for me.'

'Please, don't say things like that,' Gladys begged as she fought back more tears.

'I need to talk about it, if you don't mind, Gladys?'

Taking a deep breath to steady herself, Gladys nodded.

'I have no family,' Myrtle started. 'I lived alone before war broke out, in Harrogate.' Taking a deep ragged breath, Myrtle continued. 'I'd like you to sell my house when I die and share the proceeds among all of you girls, Rosa included, as you really are like the family I never had.'

At this point Gladys could no longer hold back her tears. 'Oh, Myrtle, no!' she cried.

'You would be doing me a huge favour, not to mention putting my mind at rest,' Myrtle assured her. 'I shall write all this down in my will of course, as long as I have your permission to act on my behalf?'

'I'll do my best,' Gladys promised.

'Oh, and I'd like you to share all my jewellery amongst the girls,' Myrtle added with a wry smile. 'Jewellery was always my one luxury, and I hope it will always remind you of me.'

Gladys smiled as she recalled Myrtle's wonderful collection of pearls, necklaces, earrings, brooches and bracelets. 'We don't need jewellery to remind us of you,' she assured her friend, who by this time was weak and pale with exhaustion. 'But it's a lovely thought, Myrtle – I'm sure the girls would treasure any gift from you.'

'Good, so that's all agreed,' said Myrtle as she closed her eyes and sank back on to her pillows. 'Now dear, before you go would you mind reading me another chapter of *Jane Eyre*? It sends me off to sleep nicely.'

Gladys took the bookmark out of the page where she'd stopped reading the night before and continued with the story of the lonely governess struggling to make a living on the wild Yorkshire moors. As she read, she saw Myrtle's eyelids droop with fatigue and within five minutes she was sleeping peacefully. Closing the book, Gladys bent to kiss her friend goodnight and as she did so she wondered how many days would be left before the Lord came to claim His faithful servant.

14. Romance

When Maggie and Gladys heard that Les was coming home on leave, they were both happy for very different reasons. Maggie couldn't wait to hold her boyfriend in her arms, to kiss and cuddle him as she'd dreamt of doing every night since he left. Whilst Gladys, though obviously excited for herself, was also deeply relieved that Les had at last got leave, as her highly strung mother had been making herself ill worrying about her son. Gladys was also looking forward to having time on her own with Les: she needed to talk to him about the changes at work and what she should do next. Knowing she wouldn't have five minutes' peace with Les when Maggie was around, Gladys hoped they'd be able to have some time to themselves when they were alone in the cowshed. So she reacted with some surprise when Maggie asked if she could utilize the spare room in the cowshed whilst Les was on leave.

'Why?' Gladys asked bluntly.

Maggie coloured before she blurted out, 'I don't want to spend all my time with Les at home with Mam watching our every move.'

Gladys bristled. 'So what do you plan on doing alone in the cowshed?' she asked sharply.

'Don't go getting all suspicious,' Maggie replied

hotly. 'Les is only here for a few days, and I don't want it spent in my house talking about how terrible the war is and how bad rationing is getting.'

Gladys appreciated what Maggie was saying, but she knew Maggie too well; she was always the one who would turn the situation to her advantage. Determined not to be manipulated, Gladys added, 'I'll check it's okay with Rosa; after all, she lives in the cowshed too.'

Maggie looked sulky. 'I know you don't want me there because you don't trust me to be on my own with your brother,' she muttered mutinously.

'Stop being so judgemental, Maggie,' Gladys exclaimed. 'I want our Les to have a good time whilst he's on leave – God knows he deserves it after serving so long on the front line – but I also hope he'll spend time at home with Mum and Dad, who worry themselves sick when he's away.'

'I'll see that he does,' Maggie replied in a proprietorial manner that irritated Gladys.

'Good,' said Gladys, before adding, 'I'd better go – Myrtle's expecting me this morning.'

Maggie watched Gladys disappear over the misty moors. Cross as she was with her friend, she couldn't help but admire her tall, slender body and the swing of her glorious, dark hair. Turning towards the Phoenix, Maggie thought to herself, 'I don't care what anybody says: I want Les all to myself for at least some of the time he's home on leave.'

Gladys, striding over the heather that now lay dull and flat under her feet, scowled irritably. Maggie was a little minx! She never stopped going on about how gorgeous Les was, and who was she, Les's devoted sister, to argue with that? There was nothing wrong with their having a serious kiss and cuddle in private, but, knowing Maggie as she did, Gladys doubted how strong her willpower was. What would happen if Maggie fell pregnant? Her parents would blame Les, Maggie would be disgraced, and her own parents would be devastated. Gladys kicked a pebble out of her way, and her scowl deepened. But who was she to judge anybody? On those balmy nights in the Bay of Naples, singing under the stars with Dr Lloyd's eyes burning into her, she'd felt her body go limp with desire. Her girlfriends in the ENSA troupe fell in and out of love every other week, but she'd remained unaffected by the eager sailors' amorous advances. Only one man had turned her head; but, waiting like the good little girl that she was for Dr Lloyd to make the first move, Gladys had missed her chance altogether. 'I should have been more forthright,' she chided herself, then laughed out loud at the irony. 'Just like Maggie!'

The war put everybody's emotions into a whirl: fear, insecurity, longing, passion and desperation conflicted with each other and former values suddenly seemed empty. What was the point of 'saving yourself for marriage', as the old saying went, when your lover might be blown to bits in an air attack or shot by the enemy? No wonder there were so many war brides, suddenly married with a baby in their arms. Maybe a baby was the best you could hope to be left with when you'd lost the one you loved? Making love was natural, but the consequences of one passionate moment could be disastrous, and that's what she was worried about when it came to leaving Maggie on her own for too long with Les.

It was a relief to reach the sanatorium, though she was soon alarmed to find poor Myrtle gasping for breath. 'She's had a bad night, poor soul,' the nurse on duty told Gladys. 'She'll be happy you're here,' she added with a smile.

Gladys quickly sat down on the chair beside Myrtle's bed. 'Poor darling,' she murmured, as she took her friend's cold hand and gently stroked it. Too breathless to answer, Myrtle turned her dark-brown eyes on Gladys, who could see the fear there. 'I'm here, lovie, shssh, don't worry,' she whispered.

When Myrtle was calmer, Gladys sat and chatted to her in as normal a voice as she could muster, telling her of everyday occurrences, which always comforted and amused the older woman. 'So Les is coming home and Maggie's counting down the days,' she said. 'Of course, Nora's nose is out of joint because she's not got a fella.' Myrtle smiled knowingly as she listened to Gladys; she knew exactly how fed up gauche Nora would be – no matter how hard she tried to find a boyfriend, no man seemed interested in the raw-boned, pale-faced, freckled girl with big teeth.

'Poor girl,' Myrtle wheezed.

Myrtle's spasms of acute breathlessness terrified Gladys more than she would ever let on. There were times when she thought she'd lose her, but, thank God, so far she'd managed to soothe and assure her through the attacks. Not that Myrtle's breathing was improving; if anything, it was rapidly deteriorating, and Gladys dreaded the day when no matter how hard she and the nursing staff worked to alleviate her symptoms, Myrtle would no longer be able to draw breath. Banishing the terrible thought from her mind, Gladys suggested they have a cup of tea, which they drank in peaceful contentment.

'How are your hands healing?' Myrtle enquired with some effort.

Gladys held her hands up for her friend to examine. 'It's taking time,' she said with a grimace at the red skin, which, though no longer oozing, nevertheless looked raw and painful. 'I feel so guilty not working but' – she gave Myrtle a cheeky smile – 'if I was on the cordite line, I wouldn't be here drinking tea with you.'

'And for that I am most grateful,' Myrtle said with a faint shadow of a smile.

Les returned on a packed troop-train and immediately went home to Leeds, where he was welcomed with great joy and celebrations. Gladys held back until Les had hugged and kissed his sobbing mum before throwing herself into his arms. 'Glad, oh, Glad, am I happy to see you,' he murmured, rocking his sister in his arms and kissing her cheek. After releasing Gladys from his bear hug, Les turned to his father, who was moved to tears by the sight of his son, who looked a lot thinner than when they'd last seen him.

'Son,' Mr Johnson said as they embraced. 'Good to have you home.'

'Good to be home, Dad – now, where's our tea?' laughed irrepressible Les. 'I'm bloody starving.'

Mrs Johnson, who'd been saving ration coupons for months, laid on a spread for a warrior's return: sandwiches with meat and fish paste, jelly and stewed apples, corned-beef rissoles and a potato-and-onion flan, which Les demolished in no time.

'Delicious, Ma,' he said contentedly, as he leant back in his chair and lit up a Capstan. 'I've not eaten so well since I last sat round this table with you,' he assured his mother, who glowed pink with happiness. After they'd finished tea, Mr Johnson volunteered to wash up.

'Mebbe you two young uns can play us some music,' he said with a meaningful look at his daughter. 'Just like you used to do in the old days, before you both went away.'

Gladys went upstairs to her bedroom, where her alto sax lay where she'd left it, under the bed in its case, untouched since her return from Naples. Les, who'd collected his trumpet from his own bedroom, looked surprised when he saw Gladys standing empty-handed. 'What's up, our Glad?'

In answer, she gave him an awkward shrug. 'Don't fancy it these days,' she said dismissively.

Taking her by the hand, Les guided his sister to her single bed, where he firmly sat her down. 'What's up?' he demanded. 'Out with it, our kid.'

Knowing Les would never take no for an answer,

141

Gladys kept her voice as quiet as possible. 'Music got me into trouble in Naples.'

Les visibly stiffened. 'A fella?' he asked sharply.

Fighting back tears, Gladys nodded.

'Did he try to, you know . . . ?'

Knowing Les would kill anybody who so much as laid a finger on her, Gladys carefully downplayed the event. 'He tried to,' she lied.

Gladys shuddered; she really didn't want to take this conversation any further. 'Anyway,' she said abruptly, 'the whole thing put me off playing.'

But Les was not to be fobbed off. 'How could playing the alto sax get you into trouble?' he persisted.

Gladys sighed as she rolled her eyes to the ceiling. 'The man who' – she searched for an appropriate word – 'bothered me first saw me performing on stage, and after that he wouldn't leave me alone.'

Balling his fists, Les leapt to his feet. 'I wish I could get mi hands on the bastard, I'd smash his face in!' he snarled.

Gladys smiled. It would have given her the sweetest pleasure to see Captain Miles with a bruised and bloody face; as it was he'd got away scot free. She was just, Gladys was sure, another woman in a long list of many.

Forcing himself to calm down, Les sat down on the bed, where he slipped a strong arm around Gladys's drooping shoulders. 'You can't let a man like that take away your natural talents.'

'That's exactly what my friend Myrtle said,' she retorted.

'Come on,' Les coaxed, as he moved away from her to pick up his trumpet. 'Remember this?'

After blowing into the mouthpiece and readjusting the valves, Les played their old favourites: Judy Garland's 'Somewhere Over the Rainbow', followed by Bing Crosby's 'You are My Sunshine' and Gracie Fields's 'Sing as We Go'. It was physically impossible for Gladys to sit primly on the bed whilst her brother's music filled the room, and, though not yet ready to reach for her alto sax, Gladys sang the lyrics, clicking her fingers and swaying to the rhythm of the music whilst Les's fingers flew over his trumpet, which he'd played since he was a child in the Salvation Army. When they had finished, they both fell breathless on to the bed, which sagged under their joint weight.

'It's good to hear you sing again, Glad,' Mr Johnson said as he tapped gently on the bedroom door. 'I've waited a long time but I knew if anybody could get you going, it'd be our Les,' he added with a happy, knowing smile.

'So we'll do it again soon, eh, Sis?' Les teased, as he pulled Gladys to her feet and spun her round as if they were jiving.

Dizzy and giddy, Gladys laughed as she replied, 'All right – if you say so!'

Les returned to Pendleton with Gladys, who, on the bus journey over the moors, spoke of her concerns about Maggie.

'She's young and impetuous – and mad about you,' she started.

'Who could resist me?' Les teased as he gave her a saucy wink.

'You're going to have to take responsibility, Les,' Gladys replied. 'Maggie's a hot-headed girl who might finish up doing something she'll regret.'

Les sighed. 'God, my battalion's not seen hide nor hair of a female in months. Some of the chaps go crazy for a woman out there; they even sleep with prostitutes when they get the chance, and suffer the consequences,' he added darkly.

Gladys gulped uncomfortably. She was now beginning to regret she'd brought up this touchy, sensitive subject. 'I sympathize, Les, I really do, we're all human,' she said hurriedly. 'All I'm saying is don't return to the Front leaving the girl you love in the family way.'

Seeing his sister's flushed, earnest face, Les took hold of her hand and squeezed it hard. 'I'll do my best,' he promised. 'But if Maggie turns those big baby blue eyes on me, I'll struggle.'

'And so will Maggie if she finds herself pregnant in a month's time,' Gladys concluded.

When Maggie saw Les waiting for her outside the factory gates, she all but flew into his arms. 'Les! Les! Oh, Les!' she cried as he swung her around in a wide circle before giving her a long, lingering kiss on the lips.

'Good to see you, sweetheart!'

Burying her flushed face against his warm chest, Maggie was in ecstasy. 'Did you miss me, darling?' she murmured into his ear.

'Course I did, every day and all night,' he murmured back.

As the young couple strode away with eyes only for each other, Rosa caught sight of Nora's sad, wistful face. Slipping an arm through hers, Rosa said confidently, 'Your turn will come soon, my sweet.'

'It's a long time coming,' Nora replied with tears in her eyes. 'I think I'll finish up a spinster, living with mi dad till I'm an old lady.'

'Ridiculous!' Rosa scolded. 'A young man out there will come looking for you one day.'

'He might come looking, but when he sees how plain and stupid I am,' poor Nora lamented, 'he might turn around and walk right away.'

'Silly girl!' Rosa said fondly. 'Come home to the cow-shed and have a cup of tea with Gladys and me,' she urged.

After Nora had downed several cups of tea and smoked some of Rosa's strong cheroots, Gladys suggested that she visit Myrtle with her. 'I know she'd love to see you.'

Nora blushed as she avoided eye contact with her friend. 'I can't, Glad,' she muttered. 'I can't bear to see her gasping for breath, and in so much pain. I love her so much,' she said as she burst into floods of tears.

'I understand, it's hard, but you're like a daughter to Myrtle and she misses you.'

Nora's eyes opened wide in disbelief. 'You know, I've never thought about it like that,' she confessed.

'Come and see her soon,' Gladys begged. 'She's not got long.'

Nora stubbed out her smoking cheroot as she replied, 'It's time I stopped thinking of myself,' she said bravely. 'I'll come and see her on my next day off,' she promised.

Whilst Les was staying overnight with his sister in the cowshed, he decided to do a few odd jobs for her. When Maggie returned from her shift, she found Les stripped down to the waist, sawing a plank of wood, which he intended to use as a shelf in the kitchen. Maggie's heart skipped a beat at the sight of his strong chest and muscular arms; and the scent of his skin, warm and with a slightly salty sweaty tang, made her heart race. Wrapping her arms around his neck, she stood on her tiptoes in order to reach his lips and kiss him lingeringly. Feeling her curvy body pressed against his, Les returned the kiss, exploring Maggie's mouth with his tongue.

Knowing that Rosa was at work and Gladys at the sanatorium, Maggie wriggled out of her coat and cardigan, then led Les into the spare bedroom, where, aroused and hot with desire, Maggie pulled him on to the bed. Feeling her beneath the thin cotton blouse she was wearing, Les slowly undid the buttons so he could see the soft curve of Maggie's shoulders and the swell of her full breasts, which peeped seductively from her brassiere. 'Christ!' he gasped as he buried his face against her chest. 'You're so beautiful.'

Wild with desire, Maggie reached for the buckle on Les's trousers. 'I've missed you, darling, I want you so much,' she muttered as she hoisted him on to her body.

'God, you have no idea how much I want you too,' he said with a yearning groan.

Lost in a sensual world of their own, where all their sensations clamoured for sweet fulfilment, Maggie would definitely have succumbed and so would Les had not his sister's words rung in his ears: 'You're going to have to take responsibility, Les.' Though he didn't want to heed them, not at a moment like this, with Maggie half naked in his arms, he knew he had to or he'd never be able to look Gladys in the eye again. 'Sweetheart,' he moaned in a husky voice as he lifted his weight off Maggie, 'we can't do this.'

Maggie's eyes flew wide open. 'We can,' she cried. 'I bought some condoms off a married woman I work with. It's safe, Les,' she begged as she ran her hands through his hair, 'Please . . .'

With a superhuman effort Les pulled himself away from Maggie. 'Sweetheart, I love you too much,' he sighed.

Frustrated and humiliated, Maggie scrambled into an upright position and quickly fumbled with the buttons on her blouse. 'Why don't you just admit the truth – you don't fancy me – it's as simple as that!'

Les whirled round, the colour flaring in his cheeks. 'Maggie! How could you even think that?' he exclaimed.

'Easily, Les, look what you've just turned down.'

Clearly eager to get away, Maggie threw on her clothes and grabbed her coat.

'Don't leave like this,' Les pleaded. 'You must understand, I want to protect you, sweetheart –' He got no further. Flaming with anger, Maggie pushed her way past him and all but ran out of the cowshed, slamming the door hard on her way out. Devastated, Les slumped into the nearest chair. 'So much for doing the right thing!' he fumed.

About an hour later, as Les was in two minds about whether to walk down the hill into Pendleton in order to talk sense into Maggie, Nora came in supporting Gladys, who was sobbing her heart out. Stunned by the sight of his wretched sister and fearing the worst, Les rushed forwards. 'Sweetheart, Glad! Is it Mum?' he gasped.

Gladys shook her head as she rested her hot, wet face against his strong shoulder. Desperate to find out what had upset Gladys so much, Les turned beseeching eyes on Nora, who simply said, 'Myrtle died an hour ago.'

As Les soothed his sobbing sister, Nora, oddly calm and composed, made a pot of strong tea, which she poured into mugs and handed round. After a few sips of the tea, Gladys started to breathe more normally. 'I don't know what's the matter with me,' she confessed. 'I've known for months that Myrtle was dying – she was quite prepared for it – but seeing her so still, so cold, knowing I'd never see her again, talk to her, laugh with her.' Tears welled up afresh in her eyes. 'It was wonderful that Nora was with her at the end, though.'

'I'm so glad you made me go,' Nora admitted. 'You know how scared I was, but the moment I saw her face I didn't fear anything at all. She was just my Myrtle.'

Laying aside her hot tea, Nora lit up a Woodbine, which Les and Gladys refused. 'I'll always treasure that time with her before she slipped away, and the relief of seeing her not having to fight for every breath,' she said as she gave a deep shuddering sigh. 'Finally at peace.'

'One thing's for sure,' Gladys said, wiping away her tears with Les's proffered hankie. 'If ever a soul went straight to their maker, it'll be our darling Myrtle's.'

15. Farewell

The very next day Les waited outside the Phoenix, having been told by Rosa what time Maggie would clock off work. His heart constricted with sadness when he saw his girlfriend's normally smiling happy face red and blotchy from crying. Disentangling herself from Nora, who was holding her arm, Maggie hung back as Les waited for the crowd of girls to pass. Expecting at least a smack across the face from Maggie, he approached tentatively. 'I just wanted to say how very sorry I am for upsetting you,' he said humbly.

Looking up at him with her big blue eyes brimming with tears, Maggie's bottom lip trembled like an upset child's. 'I'm sorry I lost mi temper,' she blurted out as she ran into his arms and hung on to him for dear life. 'I love you so much, Les. I'd do anything, *anything* for you.'

Burying his face in her tumbling auburn curls, Les tried to steady his voice, 'Darling, I want you more than anything in the world, but I want to do the right thing by my future wife-to-be.' Pulling slowly away from Maggie, he gazed deep into her eyes. 'Maggie Yates, love of my life, will you marry me?'

For perhaps the first time ever, Maggie was speechless, which gave Les the opportunity to reach into his pocket for the tiny black leather box he'd concealed there. Flipping open the lid, he murmured, 'I know it's not a big flashy diamond, but it's given with all my love and devotion.' Les took hold of Maggie's finger, stained yellow with cordite, and slipped the engagement ring on to it.

With tears of utter joy streaming down her face, Maggie looked from her new engagement ring to Les and back again. 'Speak, for God's sake!' he cried. 'You being quiet is even worse than you shouting at me!'

'YES! YES! I will marry you!' Maggie yelped as her voice came back. 'It's the most beautiful ring in the world,' she added as she jumped into his arms and wrapped her legs tightly around his waist. 'YESSS! I want to be your wife, Leslie Johnson.'

Locked in each other's arms, kissing and squeezing each other tight, the young couple finally came up for air. 'I was going to give it you last night,' Les confessed.

'And I went and ruined your romantic proposal,' Maggie said guiltily.

'What I was trying to say, before you . . .'

Seeing her fiancé looking embarrassed, Maggie completed the sentence for him. 'Buggered off in a paddy!'

Grinning, Les nodded. 'What I was going to say was, as much as I adore your gorgeous body and can't wait to make it my own, I really want to do things properly. I've been brought up the old-fashioned way, so you'll have to like it – or lump it!' he ended with a chuckle.

Laying her head trustingly against his warm shoulder, Maggie murmured softly, 'If you can wait, I can too, though, like you just said, the wait will probably kill us both, but it's all in a good cause!' She reached up to kiss his lips and stroke his handsome, smiling face. 'The trouble is, you're too bloody good-looking for your own good.'

'Then I'll cover mi head with a bucket next time I'm home on leave,' he teased. 'And you can wear one too – that should keep us both safe.'

Swinging giggling Maggie round and round, Les laughed with happiness. 'I love you, Maggie Yates, my beautiful wife-to-be!'

The Bomb Girls' Swing Band finally reunited for Myrtle's funeral. In the Phoenix chapel, where they'd practised for all their successful big-band numbers only the year before, the girls, including Rosa (who was inseparable from her friends these days), gathered one bleak November evening, but there was no joy in their meeting.

'It's not the same without her,' Nora sighed.

Maggie, who had been highly emotional since Les's departure back to the front line, brusquely wiped away a few tears. 'She was so clever and patient.'

'And funny too,' Gladys added.

'And long-suffering, putting up with us lot,' Violet said with a fond smile.

'And she played like a real professional,' Kit said wistfully.

'What're we going to do without her?' Nora asked. 'Nothing will sound right without a piano.'

As her voice trailed sadly away, Rosa reminded them, 'I play the piano.'

All eyes turned to Rosa and she blushed in embarrassment. 'My mother make me take piano lessons until I sixteen.'

Maggie blurted out, 'You're an artist AND a pianist too!'

Rosa shrugged. 'My mother an artist and a pianist,' she replied modestly. 'I just did what I was told.'

'So could you play with us?' Kit asked.

'With pleasure,' Rosa replied. 'If you don't mind me taking Myrtle's place,' she added anxiously.

Gladys, whose discomfort and anxiety about performing in public had eased considerably since her conversations with both Myrtle and Les, said eagerly, 'We'd be grateful.'

'It won't be fancy classical stuff, though,' Maggie warned. 'We'll play all of Myrtle's favourites.'

'Though she did like "Greensleeves",' Nora chipped in. 'That's a classic, in't it?'

'Let's see what the piano sounds like,' Rosa said as she approached the old upright.

'Myrtle always complained that it was like getting blood out of a stone,' Kit laughed.

Rosa sat down before the instrument, flexed her small delicate fingers and then played a rippling chord along the keys. Looking up, she smiled ruefully. 'It out of tune – but if Myrtle made it work so can I,' she said determinedly.

'The piano in Pendleton church where the funeral

will be held is much better than that old thing,' Violet assured her.

'So,' Rosa said as she surveyed her friends, 'we start?'

Gladys, who hadn't had time to go home and pick up her alto sax, for which she was secretly very grateful, was perfectly content accompanying Maggie and Nora on a borrowed trumpet. As her lips settled around the mouthpiece, Gladys felt the return of the familiar thrill of excitement that always used to come with her playing; or was it Myrtle, looking down from heaven and blessing her for freeing herself from a superstition? Whatever it was, Gladys couldn't help but smile. 'This is for you, my darling Myrtle,' she said to herself as she ran her fingers up and down the valves and the music flowed. Kit, who hadn't played the drums since she'd got married, tried to remember how to play the old dusty set that belonged to the chapel, and Violet smiled happily as she trilled up and down on her precious clarinet. Rosa accompanied them beautifully on the ancient piano, and, after playing for a good half-hour, the former Swing Girls' expressions changed from gloom and sadness to pleasure.

'I'd forgotten how good it can be,' Maggie enthused.

'Remember those great days in the dance halls?' Nora reminded her friends.

Violet grimaced as she recalled the nightmare competition in Stockport, when her husband had dragged her screaming off the stage and driven her, still screaming, back to their family home in Wolverhampton. 'Not

ALL of them were great days,' she reminded her friend with a rueful smile.

Dreamy-eyed Nora reminisced, 'Going to London to play with Joe Loss at the Savoy Hotel. I've still got the posh pink soap I stole from the ladies',' she added with a cheeky smile.

'Without Myrtle we'd have got nowhere; she was such a trooper,' Violet remarked.

'So come on, ladies,' Gladys urged. 'Let's pick the best songs we can for her funeral service.'

After some heated discussions, they agreed on three of Myrtle's favourites: 'When the Saints Go Marching In' and 'Abide with Me', as well as 'Greensleeves' when the coffin was carried out for burial.

'How are we going to get through the service without breaking down?' Violet asked.

Surprisingly, it was Nora who came back with a firm reply. 'We'll do it for Myrtle – she would have kept a stiff upper lip if it was any of us – and we'll do the same for her.'

With Myrtle gone and her role as carer ended, Gladys was at a loose end. Two weeks off work had turned to four weeks, after which there was no sign of improvement in her irritated skin condition. When Myrtle was dying, Gladys had been grateful to have extra time with her friend, but now she was alone, bored and desperately missing Myrtle, she longed to rejoin her friends on the Phoenix bomb line. At least they were doing something worthwhile for their country, which, even after four long years of war, looked unlikely to achieve peace any time soon. Plus, if she were on the cordite line (even with bleeding hands), she'd have the camaraderie of all the brave women around her. Left to her own devices, Gladys felt useless, unproductive and downright depressed.

Rosa, at her wits' end with Gladys moping about, suggested she went home for a few days. 'Visit from you will cheer your parents, now your brother back with regiment.'

Gladys smiled mischievously. 'I could even take his fiancée along with me?' she teased.

'No, mia cara!' shocked Rosa exclaimed. 'It is for your brother to introduce Maggie to the family – not you!'

'Only joking,' Gladys chuckled. 'God knows what they'll make of Maggie. One thing's for sure: neither Mum nor Dad, nor anybody else, will get a word in edgeways with Miss Yates around.'

Gladys took Rosa's advice and made arrangements with her mum to go home, but before she got the bus over the moors to Leeds she collected Myrtle's belongings from the sanatorium: these included copies of the letters she had sent to her solicitor in Harrogate and a set of keys. As Gladys slipped them into Myrtle's small suitcase, which smelt of lavender water and talcum powder, she thought of her friend's last request: she had asked Gladys to be her executor and had instructed her solicitor in Harrogate accordingly. It felt too soon after Myrtle's death to be even considering these things, but, thought Gladys, with all this spare time on her hands, shouldn't she be doing something useful and productive for her late friend? There was nothing to stop her getting the train over to Harrogate, where she could introduce herself to Myrtle's solicitor and discuss with him the possibility of putting Myrtle's house on the market. After all, the sale of the house would have a big financial impact on all of the girls' lives, which was what Myrtle had planned; it was her responsibility to work not only for Myrtle but for her friends too.

As Gladys left Pendleton, Arthur finally returned home. After such a long stay in hospital, he was simply ecstatic to be back where he belonged, at home with his family. Malc and Violet drove over to Manchester Royal Infirmary to pick up the invalid, who, though massively underweight and on crutches, hopped into the car with a big smile on his face.

'Oh, my God!' he cried as he embraced Violet. 'I'm thrilled to see the back of that place!'

'They looked after you well, sweetheart,' Violet gently reminded him.

'I know, and I'm grateful, they did a great job stitching me up, but I'm longing to go home,' Arthur admitted with a tell-tale tear in his eye.

'You've got a brand-new home to go home to,' Malc said as he set off driving. 'My God, you wouldn't believe how quickly they worked on rebuilding the domestic quarters; must have been priority orders from the top,' he added with a knowing wink.

Edna was waiting with Stevie for Arthur's return, and, after dropping Arthur off, Malc and Edna discreetly left the family in peace. Like Edna said, 'They'll need a bit of privacy.'

As Violet clung to her husband, whose handsome face was scarred by the masonry that had landed on top of him, wide-eyed Stevie started to cry. Holding out his arms to his mother, he sobbed until she picked him up and gave him a hug too. 'It's all right, sweetheart, Daddy's home now.' Stevie looked nervously at the stranger who was his father, then fiercely wrapped his arms around Violet and buried his face in her neck.

'Best not to overwhelm him,' sensitive Arthur advised. 'He's obviously forgotten who I am; it'll take him time to get used to having me around again.'

Violet gave Stevie his bottle, then settled the yawning baby in his pram. Returning to her husband's side, she leant her head against his shoulder and softly murmured, 'It was good to be able to stay at Kit's house, especially at the beginning when I was visiting you all the time, but after a while I missed our little family and most of all I missed you, my love.'

Arthur gently stroked her beautiful silky blonde hair. 'You know I can't go back to work at the Phoenix until I get the all-clear from the doctor?'

Violet nodded. 'It'll be nice for you to spend some time at home with Stevie, though I wish I could be here with you both,' she added a little enviously.

'I'm sure once Stevie's got used to having me around he'll settle down in no time,' Arthur said confidently.

Violet gave a cheeky giggle. 'Seeing as I'll be the only worker in the family,' she teased, 'I look forward to coming home and finding my tea on the table.'

Arthur groaned. 'Don't ask me to do anything creative with an ounce of lard and a tin of spam!' he joked.

Violet nuzzled his cheek. 'I've made potato hash and pickled red cabbage for our tea tonight,' she said proudly. 'And I got some baking apples from Kit's garden, so we can have apple pie for pudding.'

With a look of compete adoration, Arthur gazed into his wife's beautiful face. 'I've missed you so much, Violet. Lying in that hospital bed, day after day I could think of nothing but how much I loved you and Stevie.' Hearing his tender words, Violet's eyes filled with tears. 'Without you there's nothing,' he whispered as he leant to kiss her soft pink lips.

'Don't say that, sweetheart!' Violet exclaimed. 'Please God, we have a long life before us, with more babies,' she added with a wistful smile. 'And when the war's over, we'll save up and buy ourselves a house, with our own garden, where you can grow fruit and vegetables.'

Lifting her golden curls to his lips, Arthur smiled too. 'A house of our own,' he mused dreamily. 'I say Amen to that.'

Gladys spent a few days with her parents, who enjoyed her company, but then, anxious to complete Myrtle's business before the funeral took place, Gladys took a train to Harrogate, where, after a long walk across the windy common, she found Myrtle's little house tucked away in a side street. Feeling like an intruder, Gladys cautiously opened the front door and stepped inside. Shivering with cold, she realized the place had obviously not been lived in for a very long time. Gladys walked around the house, which Myrtle had left neat and tidy. There was an old-fashioned candlestick phone with a separate mouthpiece on a dusty wooden table in the hall, beside which stood a sepia photograph in a large ornate frame. It showed a laughing little girl sitting on her mother's lap. Though the photograph must have been taken over forty years ago, the child was unquestionably Myrtle. Her hair in those days was dark and lay in fat ringlets around her bonny face; her mother was in a long skirt and a lace blouse buttoned up almost to her chin. The woman was struggling to keep her irrepressible offspring on her knee. Gladys smiled in wonder – could the mischievous child really be prim Myrtle? There were more pictures of Myrtle dotted around the sitting room: with her mother on a windy promenade; as a bridesmaid; as the schoolgirl wearing a smart blazer with a trim boater; and as a young pianist sitting upright at a concert piano. When Gladys saw a black-and-white photograph of Myrtle's parents on their wedding day, she wondered why there were no photographs of her with her father. When she saw a sepia photograph of him in military uniform, with the words '1916, the Somme' at the bottom, Gladys assumed that Myrtle's father, like so many millions of other young men, never came home and she grew up an only precious child with a doting mother.

Feeling more of an intruder than ever, Gladys crept up the dark stairs to Myrtle's bedroom, which was at the back of the house, overlooking the wildly over-grown garden. Gladys stroked the mauve sateen eiderdown that covered the single bed, which Myrtle must have slept in for most of her life. There was a pic-ture of the Good Shepherd above it and on the other side of the room there was a large dressing table with three bevelled mirrors. Gladys sat on the padded velvet stool and gazed into the mirror that Myrtle must have gazed into a thousand times. 'I hope you don't think I'm snooping, dear friend,' Gladys said as she nervously slid open the small drawers that ran down both sides of the dressing table. She smiled when she saw Myrtle's jewellery, and with tears in her eyes she recalled her words, 'Jewellery has always been my weakness.'

There were necklaces, brooches and earrings, includ-ing a number of diamanté pieces; a three-strand necklace of pearls with matching drop earrings in a pretty, heart-shaped leather box; a solid silver bangle; and, best of all, a gold charm bracelet with a heart-shaped lock with Myrtle's initials engraved on it. Gladys gripped the bracelet in her hand as she fought back tears; these things were so precious and personal they totally overwhelmed her. She glanced into the mirror – was she imagining that Myrtle was watching over her?

When she unclenched her hand from around the bracelet, Gladys gasped in delight: on close examina-tion she saw that every one of the little glittering charms was a perfectly crafted musical instrument. A trumpet, saxophone, violin, flute, a little drum and a piano! Enchanted, Gladys put the bracelet on her wrist and jiggled it just for the pleasure of hearing the charms tinkle together. Remembering Myrtle's instructions to share all of the jewellery amongst the girls, Gladys swallowed her grief. Following Myrtles' instructions, she carefully placed the leather box containing the pearl necklace and earrings, which Myrtle had specified were for Nora, into her handbag along with the precious bracelets, necklaces, brooches and earrings. Snapping the clasp of her handbag shut, Gladys turned to go, but as she did so her eyes fell on a cut-glass crystal perfume sprayer. She squeezed it and deeply inhaled: it was Myrtle's characteristic fragrance, crisp and sharp Lily of the Valley. The fresh intensity of the fragrance immediately summoned up Myrtle, making Gladys shiver as if she'd just entered the room. Laying the bottle in her bag alongside the jewellery, Gladys returned downstairs, where she stood at the door and surveyed what had been Myrtle's home. How different life must have been once Myrtle was conscripted. Taken away from her cosy middle-class home, thrown into a bomb-making factory with hundreds of noisy women, sharing communal lavatories and bathrooms, working all the hours that God sent and living off rationed food – how had a genteel, very private person like Myrtle ever adapted? But she had – she'd given her all to the war effort, and miraculously she'd joined a band of riotous young women who had set their hearts on becoming a swing band. 'My God . . .' Gladys said out loud. The qualities she brought to the table with her: manners, knowledge, tolerance, compassion, maturity, a penetrating sense of humour and, last and most precious of all, her skill at the piano. As Gladys closed the door on the cold, empty house, she whispered, 'Thank you, Myrtle, for putting up with us and,' she added as she blew a kiss down the empty hallway, 'for all your wonderful gifts. They will help us feel close to you every single day.'

A few days later, just before the funeral, Gladys joined her friends in the canteen.

'Oi, missis!' Maggie bawled. 'You're supposed to be on sick leave.'

'I'm sick of sick leave,' Gladys joked as she plonked her mug of canteen tea on the table around which all her friends were gathered. 'Wish I was back at work with all of you,' she admitted.

'You must be mad, not with the state of your hands,' Kit exclaimed as she closely examined them. 'They don't look much improved,' she added bluntly.

Gladys grimaced. 'I don't know what I'll do if I can't come back here.'

'You could rejoin ENSA,' Nora suggested in all innocence.

Gladys quickly changed the subject by tipping all of Myrtle's jewellery on to the table. There was a pause as the girls goggled at the glittering pile.

'Where did it all come from?' Violet cried in amazement.

'It's Myrtle's. She asked me to collect it from her home in Harrogate and share it out amongst all of us, her friends,' Gladys explained.

Gladys purposefully didn't mention that the proceeds from Myrtle's house sale would eventually be distributed among them all, as the solicitor had told her that the sale might take a while, there being a war on and money short. She didn't want to make an announcement and raise everybody's hopes if that were the case.

'Myrtle wanted each of us to have some of her jewellery to remember her by, so pick what you like,' Gladys said. 'But, first, I have to give this to you, Nora: Myrtle's specific instructions,' she added with a smile.

Nora gaped at the heart-shaped leather jewellery box for several seconds before she vehemently shook her head. 'No, that's too posh for me.'

'Myrtle thought otherwise,' Gladys said firmly, as she dropped the gift on to Nora's lap. 'Go on, open it,' she urged.

Nora nervously eased open the clasp, then gazed in utter wonder at the pearls lying on white satin inside the box. 'Oh, my God!' she gasped in shock. 'I've never worn pearls in my life.'

'There's always a first time for everything,' giggled Maggie, as she draped the three strands of pearls around Nora's neck. Even in her grubby white overalls, Nora looked stunning: the creaminess of the pearls brought out the delicacy of her fair complexion and enhanced the glow of her red hair. 'Earrings too!' Maggie exclaimed.

The girls carefully chose their own individual pieces:

Kit asked if she could have Myrtle's second set of pearls, the ones she wore for all their concerts, her 'Pendleton Pearls', as Kit called them. Maggie loved the diamanté jewellery, and Violet was charmed by the old-fashioned brooches. Gladys asked if she could have the charm bracelet, and at everybody's insistence Rosa took the solid silver bangle.

'It feels wrong,' Rosa protested. 'I didn't know Myrtle like you did.'

'Never mind that. Myrtle included you in all her plans – you were one of her girls,' Gladys said staunchly.

'Now we'll all have something of Myrtle's to wear for her funeral,' Nora said as she dreamily felt the coolness of her new pearls under her fingers.

As the hooter went calling them all back to work, Kit said with a laugh, 'For the love of God, take off your jewellery – here comes Malc!'

Though Myrtle's funeral was heart-breaking, the fact that she'd asked (in her will) to be buried in Pendleton rather than Harrogate spoke multitudes.

'She wants to be near us,' Nora wept as they gathered around the freshly dug hole into which the coffin was slowly lowered.

'Dust thou art and unto dust thou shalt return,' the vicar mournfully recited from his prayer book.

Before they departed, each of the girls dropped a clod of earth into the grave and blew a kiss. 'Goodbye, Myrtle, we'll never forget you,' they each murmured in turn.

*

Though many Bomb Girls had lined the route that the cortège took, bowing their heads in respect and sometimes crossing themselves, not many were able to take time off work for the simple wake, which Edna and Gladys had set up in the cowshed. Even Myrtle's closest friends had to rush back to work, and quite suddenly Gladys found herself alone in the cowshed, surrounded by cold cups of tea and empty plates. Feeling unbearably sad, she stepped outside to breathe in the damp autumn air. Pulling her cardigan tightly around her body, Gladys gazed up at the stars that came and went as storm clouds scudded overhead. Sighing miserably, Gladys said out loud, 'I can't go on like this. I've GOT to get back to work or I'll just go mad!'

16. The Phoenix Artist

Apart from occasionally supplying Rosa with some quality cartridge paper and proper artist's pencils and crayons, Malc was also Rosa's greatest fan. Her artistry delighted him; her skilful accuracy and use of colour were impressive enough, but what Malc most admired was the sensitivity of Rosa's work: the way she could create an image of a woman, in a clattering bomb factory with conveyor-belts trundling overhead and all around, whilst the woman in the centre of the picture remained intent and focused on filling shells. Or a group of women at their ease, heads thrown back, laughing as they relaxed and smoked during their break in a crowded canteen. Or a woman in the packing shed, open to the bitter moorland weather, loading heavy explosives into wooden crates, totally concentrated on despatching artillery to regiments on the front line. Sometimes just looking at Rosa's drawing brought tears to Malc's eyes. 'She's just got it,' Edna remarked. 'No fuss, no bother, just quiet, intense observation; it's like she's lost herself in her work.'

Malc nodded in agreement with his fiancée. 'I've seen her around the building even when she's not working; she just turns up early with her sketch-pad and pencils and sets to – nobody takes any notice,' he laughed. 'It's not like anybody's posing for her or show-ing off; they take her for granted, as if she was part of the furniture!' he chuckled. 'And she captures the lasses, always natural like – dirty and grubby, smoking fags, laughing themselves silly, bone weary, but always working, always building bombs.'

'Does Mr Featherstone know he's got a talented art-ist in his factory?' Edna asked.

Malc shook his head as he stubbed out his cigarette in readiness for helping Edna shut up her van for the night.

'It might be worth a mention,' Edna remarked. 'He might sub her a few pencils himself,' she joked.

Rosa kept her sketch-book in Malc's office; it was a convenient arrangement she'd made with him so she could quickly pick up her work and continue with it whenever she had a free moment. One evening, with-out consulting Rosa, Malc presented the sketch-book to Mr Featherstone.

'Thought you'd like to know we've got our very own Phoenix artist!' he proudly announced.

Stunned, Mr Featherstone gazed in astonishment at Rosa's work. 'They're very impressive,' he commented as he polished his glasses, then popped them back on to get an even better look. 'Who's the artist?'

'Rosa Falco, on't cordite line,' Malc told him.

'The pretty little Italian lass!' gasped Mr Feather-stone, who remembered interviewing her when she had arrived at the Phoenix, hardly able to speak a word of English.

'Aye, before she arrived here she trained as an artist at a proper Italian university,' Malc replied. 'She's right bloody talented if you ask me,' he added with an even prouder ring in his voice.

The next morning Mr Featherstone came hurrying across the factory floor to find Malc, who was busy in the despatch shed. 'Can I have a word?' he asked.

Malc nodded and both men hurried into Malc's office, where they could actually hear themselves speak over the sound of the rattling machinery. 'I mentioned your news to my wife over our tea last night,' Mr Featherstone started. 'She's a bit of an artist herself; there's nothing she doesn't know about the local art world,' he added rather self-importantly. 'Anyway,' he continued, 'Mrs Featherstone told me about an exhibition due to be launched at a little art gallery in Salford.'

Malc's eyes were beginning to glaze over; he knew from years of experience that Mr Featherstone could witter on for England about his wife, and right now he had a despatch that urgently needed loading. Just as he was about to make his excuses, Mr Featherstone got to the point. 'It's called "Women at War" and I think little Rosa Falco's drawings would sit very nicely there.'

Malc did a startled double-take. 'Where?' he asked, making it evident that he hadn't been listening.

'I've just told you, Salford Art Gallery,' Mr Featherstone said shortly. 'There's a prize for the winner, money, I think,' he added vaguely. 'If she likes the idea, Mrs Featherstone and I will personally deliver young Rosa and her work to the gallery.'

It was at this point that Malc's eyes opened wide; later he indignantly told Edna, there was no way he was going to allow his own little prodigy to be driven to the art gallery by Mr Featherstone and his wife. 'I told him straight, if anybody's driving Rosa to the gallery it'll be me and my fiancée – thank you very much! What I didn't say to Featherstone was, you and your bloody missis are not taking the credit for our Rosa's work.'

Edna laughed at Malc's outraged expression. 'He was only trying to be helpful,' she pointed out.

'Mebbe but it's me that's been keeping my eye on the lass, helping out wherever I could.'

'You mean buying black-market artist's material for your little pet!' Edna chuckled.

'All in a good cause,' Malc replied with a wink. 'No, Edna, love. If anybody's introducing Rosa to the local art world, it'll be me and thee!'

'You'd better let Rosa know what's going on, then,' Edna advised. 'She'll be in for a shock.'

Rosa was more surprised than shocked when she heard Malc's news. 'The sketches – they are nothing special,' she protested.

'Let's see what the gallery says, shall we,' Malc said as he and Edna chatted to her later that day.

'They're looking for pictures of women at war, and your drawings are all about that,' Edna pointed out. 'It's worth driving over to Salford with a few of your best sketches, just to see what response you get, eh?'

Rosa smiled; who could resist Edna's warm persuasiveness and Malc's enthusiasm? 'You very kind friends,' she conceded. 'It would be nice to go with you, if you have time?'

'We'll make the bloody time!' Malc answered robustly.

'And you, Mr Malc, you naughty man, stealing my drawings,' Rosa chided as she wagged her finger at a grinning Malc.

'I knew if I asked you'd just say no,' he chuckled knowingly.

'Is true,' Rosa admitted. 'I never think of these things.'

'Good job somebody round here's got a few bloody brain cells!' Malc joked. 'Right, back to work, young lady, and in between filling shells can you find ten minutes to knock off a few more drawings!'

It was several days later before they could all spare a few hours to drive over to Salford; in fact, it was the day of Gladys's third appointment with Dr Grant at the Phoenix Infirmary. Knowing how desperate Gladys was about getting back to work, Rosa suggested that she should cancel the gallery visit and go with Gladys instead.

'He's got to sign me off this time; it's been over a month now,' Gladys said with forced breeziness. 'I'm sure it'll be fine. Off you go – you mustn't keep Malc and Edna waiting.'

Gladys waved the excited little party off, then made her way up to the factory, bypassing it as she headed for the newly rebuilt domestic quarters and the infirmary. After a very close examination of both hands, Dr Grant sat back in his chair and stared at Gladys, who knew before he even opened his mouth what he was going to say. 'It's bad news,' he declared. Gladys's heart sank; she knew her hands weren't much better than they had been, but they weren't any worse either. 'Considering you've had so much time off and have avoided any contact with cordite, there's little sign of improvement. I'm afraid, young lady . . .'

Gladys stopped listening. What was she going to do now? Her mind drifted back to when she'd first been conscripted to the Phoenix Factory; after all the fuss she'd made about leaving Leeds and the band she played with at the Locarno dance hall, Gladys had loved her time in Pendleton. She certainly didn't love the dirty work, but God, how she loved her workmates and the camaraderie they shared, day in and day out. And now she was being forced to leave. Was her life going to be nothing but a series of farewells? She'd left ENSA and now the Phoenix. Where would she go next?

'But,' she said as she glared at her wretched hands, 'they're much better than they were.'

'Time off has helped,' the doctor agreed. 'But just from looking at your skin I can see the condition would immediately flare up again.'

Almost at screaming point, Gladys burst into tears. 'Don't you understand? The Phoenix is my life – I love it – I don't want to be sent away!' she pleaded as tears fell from her lovely blue eyes.

Dr Grant shuffled uncomfortably. 'Dear child, I'm simply trying to protect your health, not send you away. I could sign you off right now but you'd be back here in less than a week, I can promise you.'

'But I never had this condition in the filling shed; it's only the cordite line that brings it on,' she cried, repeating something she said on every visit to the surgery.

'It's a build-up of both,' he told her firmly. 'All I can say is, with those hands of yours, working with explosives is quite out of the question.'

When Gladys left the doctor's surgery, she was still crying. 'This is the end of the road for me,' she thought to herself as she walked home. 'I'd better pack my bags and say my goodbyes right away – no point in dragging it out. My Phoenix days are over.'

With Manchester and Liverpool being regularly targeted by the enemy, precious artworks had been removed to safety, but there were temporary rolling exhibitions, and the gallery, nothing really but an old shop in Salford, was one such. The curator was busy hanging pictures when they arrived, and there was a big sign in the window announcing the 'Women at War' exhibition.

'Looks like we've come to the right place,' said Malc as he and Edna helped Rosa unload her work from his car. 'Right, then,' he continued as he strode towards the shop. 'Best foot forward.'

Once they were in the exhibition space, Rosa did most of the talking. The gallery owner was charmed by her sketches and accepted them with great enthusiasm. 'It's wonderful that word is getting around,' he told them. 'I'm hoping we'll have an interesting, eclectic set of works to show to the public.'

Malc picked up one of the pamphlets lying on a bench by the door. 'I see there's prizes?' he said curiously.

'Fifty pounds for the first prize,' the owner replied. 'That should help any struggling artist, not with foreign travel, unfortunately,' he quickly added. 'Sadly that's out of the question these days, though there's nothing like the works of the great masters to broaden the mind.'

'I hope the Raphaels and Tintorettos, and all other masterpieces, are locked away from thieving Nazis,' Rosa said heatedly.

The gallery owner turned to her and said, 'We hear terrible things about priceless works of art being stolen by German officers. God, they must have had a field day when they invaded Paris,' he said with a small groan.

Rosa's brow crinkled with fury. 'Nazis destroy all they touch!' she fumed.

Seeing the conversation was taking a turn for the worse, Edna asked in a cheerful voice, 'So when does the exhibition open?'

'Any time now,' the owner replied. 'Work's coming in all the time . . .' His eyes lingered over Rosa's sketches ranged on the table before him. 'I must say, Miss Falco, your images of women at war really are most insightful.'

Rosa almost skipped into Malc's car, where, in the back seat, she hugged Edna. 'Thank you, thank you, this is very exciting!' she cried as she clutched Edna's hand and squeezed it hard.

Malc, in the driver's seat, turned on the ignition and they cruised slowly through the bombed streets of

Salford, past shattered mills and rows of tenement blocks reduced to heaps of rubble. 'Look at the kiddies picking through the wreckage,' Edna exclaimed. 'Poor little mites.'

'Odds on they're looking for bits of scrap metal to sell to the rag-and-bone man,' Malc remarked.

'Who is this rag-and-bone person?' Rosa asked.

'They're fellas that go around the area with a hand-cart, looking for rubbish to trade in for a few coppers,' Edna explained. 'You sometimes hear them calling down the back streets. "Any old iron! Any old iron!"'

'You won't hear 'em up on't moors,' Malc chuckled as they made their way home. 'There's nowt up there for them bar a few wild birds and a clump o' heather!'

Rosa asked Malc and Edna if they'd like to pop into the cowshed when they dropped her off. 'I make you brew,' she said, using one of Edna's favourite expressions.

'Much as I'm gagging for a cuppa, lovie, I've got to get back to the shop and set up my stall for my customers,' Edna replied as she gave the excited girl a farewell kiss.

Feeling happy and light-hearted, Rosa almost glided into the cowshed, where there was no sign of Gladys in the kitchen or sitting room. 'Gladeeees!' she called.

'In here,' came a low reply.

With her heart sinking, Rosa hurried into Gladys's bedroom, where she found her friend lying miserably on her narrow single bed.

'Mia cara!' Rosa said softly as she sat down on the bed and stroked Gladys's limp hands.

'I'm leaving the Phoenix, Rosa.'

Stricken Rosa put her hand to her mouth. 'NO! That's not possible.'

'It's more than possible,' Gladys retorted as she dragged herself upright. 'There's nothing here for me with these damn hands!' she raged.

'Come, my sweet,' Rosa urged as she held out a hand to Gladys. 'Let me make you tea.'

Gladys followed her friend into the sitting room, where Rosa busied herself with boiling water and stoking the wood-burner with fresh logs.

'I suppose I'll just go back home and find work in Leeds,' Gladys said, as she gratefully took the mug of hot tea that Rosa proffered.

'No! You cannot leave me!' Rosa exclaimed. 'You my best friend, Gladys, you and the girls here, you are my family, you cannot leave me,' she wailed as she burst into tears.

Seeing poor Rosa so upset took Gladys's mind off her own misfortunes. 'I'm so sorry, sweetheart, it's not like I want to leave you or this place, where I've been so happy. I've racked my brains over and over trying to think what I could do in order to remain at the Phoenix. I even begged to go back to the filling shed, where I worked without any problem before I joined ENSA, but Dr Grant's adamant: he said explosive material is bad for my health,' she sighed as she stared into the fire that crackled cheerily and warmed the room. 'I wish Myrtle was here – oh, what wouldn't I give for her sound advice right now,' she said as she felt fresh tears sting her eyes.

Rosa's eyes widened at Gladys's words. 'MYRTLE!' she exclaimed.

Gladys looked alarmed. 'What about her?'

'You loved nursing, mia cara?' Rosa enquired.

Looking puzzled by her obvious question, Gladys replied, 'You know I loved it, but I loved Myrtle, so it was no hardship.'

'But you did the things the nurses do?' Rosa enquired with a calculating look in her big, dark eyes.

'Yes,' Gladys answered. 'In the end, the nursing staff, encouraged by the matron, let me do everything for Myrtle; they trusted me to look after her and she preferred me to nurse her rather than strangers, no matter how well intentioned they were.'

Rosa sprang to her feet and started mumbling in Italian. 'Allora, ecco la risposta al tuo problema!'

'What?' cried Gladys who had no idea what she was going on about. 'Speak English, for God's sake!'

'Here is the answer to your problem!' Rosa announced.

'What?' Gladys said again.

'Think!' Rosa exclaimed, patting the side of her head.

Frustrated almost beyond words, Gladys raised her voice: 'WHAT are you talking about?'

'My Gladeeees, you must be a nurse! You must train as nurse!'

Gladys's jaw literally dropped wide open.

'You would be perfetto!' Rosa exclaimed.

'ME? A NURSE?' Gladys almost choked.

'That is what you have been, a nurse,' Rosa pointed out.

'But that was for Myrtle,' Gladys reminded her.

'So now you do for others,' Rosa said with a gentle smile. 'Myrtle has blessed you – this is her advice.'

The hairs on the back of Gladys's neck stood on end and she felt goose bumps on her skin. 'Oh, my God!' she gasped as she buried her face in her hands. 'I can almost feel her beside me,' she whispered.

'She is here, for sure,' Rosa said with simple faith.

Gladys took her fingers away from her face and stared at the scudding clouds outside the window. It was true that she had enjoyed the experience of nursing; apart from the pleasure she'd had from being with Myrtle right up until the end, she had liked the ordered atmosphere of the sanatorium and the conscientious care of the staff. Taking hold of Rosa's hand, she kissed it. 'I'll go and see Dr Grant tomorrow – and this time,' she laughed joyfully, 'it won't be about my bloody hands!'

As the girls had their sparse tea of fish paste on toast with a grilled tomato on top, Gladys apologized for not asking about Rosa's gallery visit earlier. 'I'm sorry, I forgot about it after the doctor dropped his bombshell.'

Rosa shrugged as she bit into her hot toast. 'You had much on mind.' After she'd munched her mouthful, she told Gladys about the gallery owner's reaction to her drawings, then she surprised Gladys by saying, 'You remember the relatives I stayed with in Manchester?'

Gladys nodded as she recalled the conversation they'd had some months ago. 'Yes, you said they helped you when you first arrived, after your escape.'

'I feel bad that I do not visit them,' Rosa admitted. 'Always there is so much to do here at Phoenix,' she said with a smile. 'But now is a good time to meet; maybe they will enjoy to see my work in Salford?' she said a little uncertainly.

'I'm sure they will be very proud of you,' Gladys assured her modest friend. 'In fact, we're ALL proud of you, Rosa, our little Phoenix artist!'

17. The New Girl

The next day, Gladys wasted no time in seeing Dr Grant at the Phoenix Infirmary. After she'd explained her intentions, the doctor was truly astonished. 'You *really* want to train as a nurse?' he asked.

'Yes, I think I do, but I've no idea how to go about it,' Gladys admitted.

'Well, you could start right here,' he said. 'Most of our trained nurses have been deployed to field hospitals – an extra pair of hands would be a godsend. Here we nurse the sick and wounded from the factory in two small wards, one male, the other female; children are usually admitted on to the women's ward, which we also use as a maternity unit.'

A smile lit up Gladys's rather tense face. 'Start here, at the Phoenix?' she asked incredulously. 'That would be perfect – I wouldn't have to leave – I could stay!' she exclaimed as she broke into a laugh.

'I warn you, Gladys, you'll be thrown in at the deep end; we have no choice but to train nurses on the hoof these days,' Dr Grant explained with an apologetic smile.

Gladys's smile faded. 'How will I know what to do? Who will teach me?' she asked nervously.

'It's myself and the ward sisters; there isn't time for the intensive-theory courses we used to provide. Any lectures you do attend will be in your own time off,' Dr Grant replied. 'To be blunt, it's a case of getting stuck in. You'll find out soon enough if you have a real vocation,' he assured her. 'Our two ward sisters are notoriously overworked and consequently fairly impatient,' Dr Grant warned. 'One of them will be your assigned nurse: stick to her like glue – watch and learn, Gladys.'

With everything happening so quickly, Gladys began to panic. 'B-b-but isn't there something I should read first?' she babbled.

'You can read as much medical information as you want, but believe me there's nothing like first-hand experience on the wards,' Dr Grant replied. 'I don't think your hands will trouble you too much in a hospital environment,' he added with a grin. 'We don't deal with raw explosives!' he teased.

In a daze, Gladys left the infirmary; it had all happened so quickly. What if she wasn't a bright learner? Would they throw her out at the end of her first week? Excited, elated and nervous, Gladys shook her head as she muttered to herself, 'Singer, Dancer, Bomb Girl – and now a Nurse!' Then another thought hit her: if she was training to be a nurse, would she be able to stay on in the cowshed, or was it only for munitions workers? Hurrying over to the Phoenix, she knocked nervously on Mr Featherstone's door, which was flung open by the imposing figure of Marjorie, Mr Featherstone's secretary, who protected her boss like a Rottweiler protects a bone. 'Yes?' she snapped. After Gladys explained her situation, Marjorie shut the door in her face then reopened it ten minutes later, 'He'll see you now, but only for five minutes.'

After hearing what Gladys had to say, Mr Featherstone looked doubtful; Gladys's heart fluttered – would he ask her to leave the cowshed? Should she have even come here and blurted out the truth? She could have kept her circumstances a secret, but then somebody would inevitably see her in her nurse's uniform and there would be questions asked. Bomb Girls didn't normally go to work in a starched white uniform and a winged starched cap!

'There are only two of us in a three-bedroomed accommodation,' she quickly informed Mr Featherstone.

'We'd normally install you in the nurses' quarters,' he told Gladys. 'But they got blown up in the recent explosion, so you might as well as stay put for now. Of course, we'll be sorry to lose you off the bomb line, but needs must in these hard, dark times,' he concluded gloomily.

Too restless even to consider going back home to the cowshed, Gladys all but skipped out on to the misty moors; she couldn't believe her luck. She'd been accepted to train as a nurse at the little Phoenix hospital, and she could stay in the cowshed with Rosa too. She could never have dreamt of a better outcome. Singing loudly, she stopped in her tracks and smiled. 'You're singing, Gladys Johnson,' she laughed at herself. 'You're singing because you're happy and there's a big new world waiting for you.'

Still singing, Gladys struck out for Yew Tree Farm, where she hoped to find Kit. Luckily Kit was on afternoon shift, so she was in with Billy, but she looked unusually pale and wan when she opened the front door to her friend. 'Come in,' she cried when she saw Gladys on the front doorstep. Desperate as she was to talk to somebody about her new appointment, Gladys couldn't ignore how poorly Kit looked.

'Are you sick?' she asked as she scooped squealing Billy into her arms and kissed him on both dimpled red cheeks.

'I'm pregnant,' Kit said with a weak smile.

Gladys was so shocked she almost dropped the child in her arms. 'Pregnant? Really?' she gasped.

Kit grimaced as she replied, 'Really, really, if being sick all morning has anything to do with it. Come on,' she urged, 'I'll put the kettle on, but if you'll excuse me I won't make a brew – the smell of tea turns my stomach,' she admitted.

'I'll do it,' Gladys said as she popped Billy back on his feet, and he promptly ran off to chase the cat. 'Does Ian know the good news?'

'How could he not?' Kit chuckled. 'With breasts as big and tender as mine, plus the morning sickness, he couldn't fail to notice.'

'He'll make a wonderful father,' Gladys said as she popped tea leaves into the pot and poured boiling water on top of them.

'He's already a wonderful father to Billy; there could be none better,' Kit assured Gladys. 'He's so caring and loving – I couldn't be luckier.'

Gladys gave Kit a glass of cold water whilst she filled

a mug with strong tea and then added a splash of condensed milk.

'You know something,' Kit continued, 'this pregnancy couldn't be more different from my first, with Billy. I was as sick as this but trying to hide it from mi da. I was genuinely starving; it's a miracle that Billy was born so healthy; all that I lived on for nine months was spuds and cabbage. Look at me now, safe and warm in a lovely home.' She sighed with contentment. 'I never fail to thank God for his blessings.'

Tall, slender Gladys leant over to kiss small slight Kit. 'You deserve every blessing,' she said with real love. 'The family and the home that you've created here are a joy to all who visit. Now listen,' Gladys said excitedly, 'I've got news too!'

After Gladys had told her about her visit to Dr Grant, Kit clapped her hands. 'Nurse Gladys Johnson!' she cried excitedly.

'But . . .' said anxious Gladys. 'There has to be more to becoming a nurse than wanting to stay on at the Phoenix just so I can be near my friends,' she said with a guilty giggle. 'I mean, nursing is a vocation; it's not about where you live.'

'Don't be so hard on yourself; it's not like you haven't nursed before,' Kit said, reiterating what Rosa had previously said to Gladys. 'You know, to a fair extent, what you're doing.'

'It's still scary,' Gladys confessed. 'The thought of not being a volunteer but a real trainee nurse. Plus Dr Grant gave me a fright when he said there was no time for proper training these days – it's all a bit sink or swim,' she added with a nervous laugh.

Kit gave Gladys a reassuring pat on the arm. 'Take it a day at a time, sweetheart, and see how you get on: that's my advice. Try not to worry about what's round the corner – you'll find out soon enough if it's the job for you – and one thing's for sure,' Kit said as she burst out laughing, 'you won't be working with cordite in the Phoenix Infirmary!'

On the bus home, with Kit and Billy sitting beside her on the back seat, Gladys remembered about Kit's efforts to find Flora, and asked if she'd made any progress since they'd last chatted about it. Kit shook her head. 'We've given up, to be honest; what with me expecting and working long shifts and looking after Billy, there's not much time left over to work my way through long lists of personal ads,' she admitted. 'I'd do it if I thought there was any real hope, but the chances of her getting in touch . . . I suppose we've given up for the time being,' she confessed.

Gladys couldn't argue with how demanding not to mention exhausting Kit's day was, but nevertheless she couldn't hide her disappointment. 'It would have been nice for Edna,' she said wistfully.

Kit nodded as she cuddled Billy on her knee. 'That's what motivated me in the first place,' she said as she nuzzled her little boy's cheek. 'The thought that a child of mine was somewhere out there and I couldn't reach them would drive me mad.' She smiled up at Gladys as she added, 'Remember how hard Ian and I worked on tracking down Billy after he'd been smuggled out of the convent?'

'I remember seeing your face when you came back from Ireland without Billy,' Gladys replied. 'I thought you'd never get over the disappointment.'

'I swear I wouldn't have – that's what makes my heart ache for Edna. She's had no contact with her child, now a woman, since she gave birth to her. They could pass in the street and they wouldn't even know each other,' she said with a heavy sigh.

When the bus lumbered to a halt at the Phoenix, the girls went their separate ways: Kit to the nursery, which had recently reopened, and then on to the factory, where she would clock on for her afternoon shift in the filling shed. After getting a good-luck hug from Kit, Gladys made her way to the cowshed, where she anxiously prepared for her first day at the Phoenix Infirmary.

The following morning Gladys reported for duty at 7 a.m.; she was met by her assigned nurse, who briskly issued the new trainee with a uniform.

'I'm Sister Atkins,' she barked. 'Don't leave my sight.'

Gladys fastened the buttons on the simple white dress, which had a starched collar and cuffs, then she bundled her thick brunette hair under the starched white cap, which she pinned firmly on to her head with hair grips. Gladys smiled as she recalled how taboo clips and grips were on the cordite line: one small metal clip could spark off an explosion. Luckily things were different in the hospital: otherwise, she'd have hair drifting out of her cap and would certainly get a ticking off from the strict ward sister.

'Patients who work at the Phoenix site are admitted into the infirmary, where we treat them as best we can and assess their needs,' Sister Atkins explained as she all but ran down the echoing corridor to the men's ward. 'Dr Grant assesses them, and if he's happy that we can meet their nursing-care requirements, the patient is admitted. If, however,' she said as she flung open the heavy double doors to the ward, 'Dr Grant considers their requirements too sophisticated for us – we are after all a very small cottage hospital – then the patient will be transferred by ambulance to Manchester Royal.'

After tying clean aprons around their waists, they entered the ward, where Gladys was relieved to see there were only three patients: one man had his arm in a splint; another was linked up to an oxygen tank; and the third man was fast asleep. 'On my morning round I take my patients' pulse, temperature and blood pressure, and write a record on the clip chart hanging at the end of their bed. You'll be doing that several times a day, Johnson, so watch and assist.'

Feeling she was all fingers and thumbs, Gladys took a thermometer from its container, then, as she shook it prior to popping it into her patient's mouth, she had a sudden vivid memory of Myrtle, with her mouth wide open, patiently waiting for Gladys to take her temperature. 'This is no different,' Gladys reassured herself, and the thought gave her confidence; if what she'd done in the sanatorium was good enough for her dear dying friend, she hoped it would be good enough for the sick gentlemen in her care too. Boosted by the thought, Gladys watched the sister like a hawk; she was swift yet efficient, and she didn't bark at her patients like she barked at the nurses. There was a tenderness in her movements that impressed Gladys, and she made a note to try to emulate that in her own work.

After being frog-marched to the women's ward, where Gladys yet again assisted Sister Atkins in taking their pulse, blood pressure and temperature, she followed the sister into the sluice room, where together they emptied and sterilized bedpans. After this it was time to dispense the women's medication, and before Gladys knew it dinner had arrived from the Phoenix canteen in great metal vats that kept the food relatively warm. After she and the sister had served dinner to their patients, they had to assist them to the toilet, then beds had to be remade, whilst some patients required bed baths before afternoon-visiting time. Sister was strict about the number of visitors: no more than two and no children. Whilst patients were busy with their visitors Gladys watched Sister restock the supply cupboard and reorder a long list of medication that would have to be signed off by Dr Grant.

By the end of her long, twelve-hour shift, Gladys's hands were red raw with washing and scouring, but at least they weren't bleeding, and she'd got through the day without doing anything too disastrous. After being on her feet virtually all day, Gladys was longing for a hot bath and several cups of tea. As she was soaking in the bath later that night, Rosa returned home and without any hesitation pulled up a chair beside the bathtub so she could hear all about Gladys's first day as a nurse.

'Exhausting, but I loved it,' Gladys told her friend with a smile. 'The only time I left my assigned nurse was to go to the toilet!'

'I hope so too!' Rosa chuckled. 'Will you go to medical lectures?' she asked.

'Dr Grant told me that we can attend lectures only in our off-duty time.'

'It very demanding work,' Rosa said gravely.

'No more than working on the cordite line, except nobody regularly gives birth on the cordite line,' Gladys replied with a giggle.

At the end of the first week, Gladys had learnt a lot more about nursing than filling in charts and scouring bedpans; whilst shadowing Sister Atkins, she'd spent time with patients, comforting, supporting and reassuring them that they would get better and return home to their families, which is essentially all they yearned for. She'd learnt to sterilize wounds, change bandages, and remove a splint and plaster of Paris; she'd taken so many pulses, temperatures and blood pressures she was almost doing it in her sleep! Her back ached with stripping and remaking beds, and bundling up endless bags of laundry, but she was so happy to be busy and useful again. Under Sister's beady-eyed guidance, she'd administered medication, and on her third day on the women's ward she'd even helped deliver a baby! The mother was a woman whom Gladys recognized from her time in the filling shed; she'd gone into premature labour and had been rushed to the infirmary by Malc, who gratefully offloaded his patient to Gladys and Sister Atkins.

'Bloody hell!' he murmured to Gladys as he got the moaning young woman into a wheelchair. 'I'd rather you than me, cock!'

To begin with, Gladys felt not unlike Malc, terrified. The woman's pain seemed unbearable, but, after getting her into bed and closing the curtains around her, Gladys did everything Sister Atkins instructed and she watched her every experienced move. It was wonderful to see how the sister quickly calmed the patient, how she got her breathing under control and helped her through the worst of the contractions. When another patient called out for help, Sister Atkins looked Gladys firmly in the eye and said, 'Over to you, Nurse Johnson: monitor her breathing exactly as you saw me do – I'll be back.' And with that she abruptly disappeared.

Left on her own for the first time since she'd started her training, Gladys felt panicked: why hadn't Sister sent her to the other patient, who probably only wanted a drink of water? Why leave her with a woman just about to give birth? A hot hand gripping her own banished all further questions – she had to get on with the job!

'I want to push,' the woman moaned.

'Good, that's good,' Gladys said in a voice that she didn't even recognize as her own. Remembering what Sister had said to the patient only ten minutes earlier, she quickly added, 'Try to hold on till the next contraction.'

As the poor woman wrestled with the urge to push, Sister Atkins came breezing back and quickly assessed the situation. 'Well done, Nurse,' she said briskly.

'NOW!' cried the woman, and within a quarter of an hour her baby was born, and Sister Atkins was instructing Gladys on how to clean off the birth fluids and tie the umbilical cord. It was uplifting to hand the clean, swaddled baby to the mother, who clasped her new daughter to her breast. 'Thank you, Nurse,' she said with a grateful smile. 'Can you believe this is my fourth?' Gladys almost swayed with shock: heavens, if this was an experienced mother delivering her fourth child, how hard must it be for a new mother with her first baby?

By the end of the week, though weary and foot sore, Gladys could hardly believe how much she'd learnt by just shadowing Sister Atkins, who, as the week wore on, became less brusque with the new girl. She actually praised Gladys on her observation and the attention she gave to those in her care. 'Emotional support and understanding are vital in the nursing profession; it's our responsibility to make our patients as comfortable and relaxed as they can be in the circumstances.'

Patients' smiles and kind, welcoming words when she walked into the wards made Gladys sure she was doing the right thing; she had so much to learn, but she was confident that she'd made the right decision; and, though her training was unquestionably going to be tough and challenging, she was certain that Trainee Nurse Gladys Johnson was exactly where she belonged.

18. 'Women at War' Exhibition

A few days before the opening of the exhibition in Salford, Rosa went along to the gallery with Malc and Edna, who had gone to the expense of having her drawings framed. Malc was now in the process of hanging them on the gallery wall alongside other artists' work.

'It's fascinating to see pictures of so many different examples of women at work,' said Edna as she carefully examined each of the exhibits in turn.

There were images of Land Girls: one hot and sweaty as she dug up potatoes in a ploughed field; another leading a huge, gentle cart-horse along a farm track of thick, churned-up mud. There were portraits of women driving Red Cross trucks, nurses on the front line, at the casualty-clearing stations, administering first aid; there were images of women on high scaffolding riveting together parts of planes, and girls in munitions factories building bombs and artillery. 'None of them is as good as our Rosa's drawings,' Malc said in a very loud whisper, which the gallery owner couldn't help but overhear.

'Shssh!' hissed Edna as she gave her fiancé a sharp dig in the ribs.

'Well – it's true!' Malc said indignantly. 'She's the best of the lot.'

'I know,' Edna whispered a reply. 'But we don't have to broadcast it, do we?'

Rosa was particularly fascinated by a series of oil paintings titled 'Ferry Girls'. 'Who are these Ferry Girls?' she asked her friends.

'They're lasses who transport planes from one airfield to another,' Malc explained. 'The RAF can't spare their pilots for the job, so they brought in female pilots to fly replacement Spitfires, Hurricanes, Whitleys, Hawkers, or what have you, to airfields around the country.'

Rosa's dark eyes widened. 'Dio!' she exclaimed. 'They are brave women!'

'Indeed they are. The RAF are going through fighter planes like I go through a bag of Edna's chips!' Malc joked. 'I don't know what they'd do without the Ferry Girls; it's dangerous too – quite a few have been shot down by enemy fire.'

By this time Rosa was staring intently at the artist's brushwork. 'They're beautiful,' she said. 'Squadron Leader Roger Carrington.' She read aloud the artist's name in the corner of his paintings. 'He's very good,' she said admiringly.

Malc, who was inordinately proud of their very own Phoenix artist, stalwartly repeated that her work was unquestionably the best, which made Rosa blush. 'We all very different, Malc,' she said modestly.

Before they headed back home, Rosa popped a letter in the post. 'I invite my relatives in Manchester to my exhibition; I really want them to see my drawings,' she told her friends, as they drove slowly home over the misty moors in Malc's ancient Rover (fuelled, Edna was sure, with black-market petrol!).

'I've never understood how you ever managed to make contact with them in the first place?' Edna asked.

'My relatives in England; they visit my family in Padova when I was young. Gabriel had address from my parents; he give to the people who smuggle me out of Germany.' Rosa sighed heavily. 'My brother think of everyone . . . except himself.'

'He must love you very much, Rosa,' Edna said softly.

'He does!' Rosa exclaimed emotionally. 'More than his own life.'

Not wanting to upset Rosa by asking too many questions about her brother, Edna continued, 'Your relatives must have got the surprise of their life when you turned up on their doorstep in Manchester?'

'They are VERY surprised,' Rosa replied. 'But they took me in, just like other Jews took them in at start of the war. Manchester people, they are so kind to me,' she said with a grateful smile.

'Weren't you frightened out of your wits when you arrived in England?' Edna asked.

'Not frightened – very sad,' Rosa admitted. 'I wanted to learn English – I wanted to give something – pay back with war work.'

'So the Labour Exchange sent you to't Phoenix to be a Bomb Girl,' Malc chuckled.

'I said to Mr Featherstonee, my English not so good. He say, "You don't need English to build bombs, lass!"'

Rosa said in a perfect imitation of the dour Northern factory boss.

Malc nodded. 'Just a determination to bomb the buggery out of Germany!'

When Malc dropped her off outside the cowshed, Rosa thanked her friends for helping her.

'Don't fret,' joked Malc. 'We'll take our commission fee when you're rich and famous!'

In the end, Rosa went to the opening of the 'Women at War' exhibition on her own. All of her friends were working, even Edna (who was committed to driving her mobile chip shop to the Phoenix that night), so Rosa, with nervous butterflies fluttering in her tummy, took a bus into Salford, then walked in the pouring rain to the gallery, which was packed with eager visitors. Though it was wet and damp outside, it was warm and steamy inside the gallery, where people jostled against each other in order to view the exhibits. Breathing in, Rosa made her way slowly around the room, and was excited to hear comments about her own work.

'Rosa Falco has a fine eye for detail,' one man boomed as she slipped by.

'And a delicate use of shading,' the woman beside him observed. 'Her depiction of the woman at work is quite profound,' she added, as they moved on to the next painting, leaving Rosa standing before an image of Nora and Maggie she'd drawn only weeks ago. They were laughing, as usual, as if sharing a joke, their white overalls and turbans contrasting starkly with the darkness of the factory building and the metallic conveyor-belts that ran alongside them. Rosa smiled at the image of her friends, whom she'd sketched so quickly that they were hardly aware it had happened. When she'd shown them the drawing, done in dark pencil tones, Maggie had grimaced. 'We look a bloody mess!' she'd laughed. 'You could have told us what you were up to, then we could at least have put on a bit of lipstick and rouge.'

'That would spoil it!' Rosa had cried. 'I wanted you normal, as you are when you work.'

'Well, I wouldn't buy owt like that to hang up in my front room,' Nora giggled. 'It's too realistic for my liking. Now, if it were flowers and little birdies, that'd be a whole different story.'

Rosa gave a groan as she shook her head. 'Flowers and little birdies I do not do!' she protested.

Suddenly there was a gap in the crowd around her and Rosa spotted her aunt and uncle admiring her paintings on the opposite wall. 'ROSA!' her aunt cried, as she rushed forward to embrace her niece. 'Mia cara, you look wonderful,' she exclaimed when she saw the physical change in the girl that had left Manchester as thin as a rake.

'You have been eating well,' her uncle joked.

'Yes, and the work too is good,' Rosa replied as she embraced her uncle.

'It must be,' her uncle enthused. 'Otherwise you

could never have created such amazing images,' he said, pointing to her drawings. 'They are superb, Rosa!'.

'You have great talent, child,' her aunt added. 'So like your dear mother; she would have been so proud to see your work exhibited.'

Rosa blinked away a tear and replied to her aunt in Italian. 'Thank you. I owe so much to Mama, even though I used to protest at how strict she was and how she would never compromise with second best. She gave me the best training; I wish with all my heart I could tell her that now,' she said with a wistful sigh.

'Your work is a testament to your mother's artistry and determination, Rosa,' her aunt assured her, also reverting to their native language. 'It's a true gift that you can paint these brave women so intent on working for their country.'

Rosa smiled and nodded in agreement with her aunt. 'They really are wonderful women. I don't think I've ever met better.'

After they'd done the round of all the exhibits, Rosa accompanied her relatives outside, where they walked to the nearest public house. 'Let's have a little chat,' her uncle suggested as he ordered whisky for them all. 'So how are you, child?' he asked Rosa as he passed round a small jug of hot water that his wife used to dilute the strong liquor.

Still speaking in Italian, Rosa replied, 'I'm happy, Zio. I love the munitions factory; I have marvellous friends; and, now I'm drawing, life is better than I could ever have hoped for,' she concluded with a smile, which quickly faded when she saw the look her aunt and uncle exchanged. 'What is it?' she asked sharply. 'You have news of Gabriel?'

Her aunt awkwardly busied herself with a packet of cigarettes, leaving her uncle to answer the question. 'No, we have had no news of Gabriel since you left us, Rosa; otherwise, be assured we would have got a message to you immediately.'

Seeing their grim expressions, Rosa held her breath.

'It is the prolonged silence that concerns us,' her aunt added. 'Not that we expect to hear directly from Gabriel if he's in a prison camp, and it is not uncommon to hear news from the Underground workers, with whom we have close ties, as you know from your own experience, Rosa,' she reminded her niece.

Clutching at straws, Rosa said in a frantic voice, 'He may be ill! He may have been removed to another camp.' Tears bubbled up unbidden in Rosa's dark brown eyes as she imagined her cherished brother crawling with disease, malnourished and wearing rags, being transported in filthy packed trains from one camp to another in the middle of winter. 'He could be frightened and alone, on the run, in hiding,' she frantically added.

Her aunt and uncle nodded in agreement with her. 'He could be any of those things,' her uncle said. 'We can only hope and pray for good news.'

Rosa buried her face in her trembling hands. What had she been thinking of? Only ten minutes ago she had been glowing with happiness and pride; now here she was, imagining her beloved brother dead of typhoid or cholera, or shot through the head as he tried to escape. Her two worlds – that of the Phoenix and that of the death camps – collided at such a speed she could barely breathe. 'I should be doing something,' she said urgently.

'You're doing everything you can, child,' her aunt pointed out.

'Oh, yes!' Rosa scoffed in self-disgust. 'Painting women at work! I should be fighting to free my brother, just like he did everything to free me – I should be fighting for HIM!' she raged at herself.

Seeing his niece was about to lose control, her uncle covered her hands with his. 'The worst thing you can do, Rosa, is panic; we do what we've always done: we wait and, as your aunt says, we pray.'

'I'm sorry, Uncle,' Rosa whispered. 'I'm angry at you for speaking the truth. Forgive me,' she begged as he handed her a clean white handkerchief and she mopped away her tears.

'Stay strong, Rosa,' he said firmly.

'We will pass on any information, be assured of that,' her aunt promised before they said goodnight and parted ways.

Back at work, Violet was the first to notice how quiet Rosa had become over the course of the next few days. 'I think she's stopped sketching too,' she whispered to Kit during their tea break in the canteen. Kit's gaze drifted over to Rosa, who was queuing up at the canteen counter for a mug of tea and a round of bread and marg.

'She does look pale,' Kit remarked. 'Have you talked to Gladys about her?'

Violet shook her head. 'It's difficult to catch Gladys now that she's working at the infirmary.'

As Rosa approached their table, Kit said in a hurried whisper, 'Let's try and see Gladys later, when we pick up the kiddies from nursery.'

When they'd finished their shifts, Violet and Kit hurried over to the domestic quarters, where they hovered around the infirmary entrance, keen to get a glimpse of Gladys. They finally saw her through a window: looking smart in her uniform, she was smiling as she pushed a hospital trolley loaded with a tea urn. Waving frantically through the window, they caught Gladys's attention and she sneaked outside to speak to them. 'What's the matter?' Gladys asked her friends as she glanced nervously over her shoulder to check that Sister wasn't on her tail.

Not having time to beat about the bush, Kit blurted out, 'There's something wrong with Rosa.'

'She's definitely not herself,' Violet said urgently.

'I agree with you,' Gladys replied. 'She hasn't been herself since the exhibition opened in Salford.'

'That surprises me,' Kit remarked. 'She was so thrilled and excited to start with.'

'She isn't any more,' Gladys told her friends. 'She seems to have gone off drawing too.'

'We noticed that,' Violet said grimly.

'We can't force her to draw,' Kit pointed out.

'We thought, seeing as you're living with her, you might be able to have a word with her,' Violet said.

Gladys nodded. 'I'll try,' she promised. 'Though with our different shifts, we hardly see each other these days, but I'll make a point of talking to her.'

'Thanks, Glad,' Kit said gratefully. 'We'll try talking to her too, but she might open up more to you, especially if you can get her in a quiet moment on her own.'

A loud cry made Gladys jump. 'Johnson! Your patients are in need of a hot drink – see to it, Nurse.'

'Sorry, Sister,' Gladys apologized. As she turned to go, she quickly said to her friends, 'I'll talk to Rosa just as soon as I can.'

Gladys managed to talk to Rosa a few days later; by leaving work promptly and rushing home, she caught Rosa before she left for her shift. 'This makes a nice change,' said Gladys, as she put the kettle on the crackling wood-burner, then flopped down beside her friend on the old battered sofa. 'What's your news, sweetheart?' she asked in apparent innocence.

Rosa shrugged. 'Nothing much.'

'Nothing much!' Gladys echoed her words with a laugh. 'You've got an exhibition on in Salford and you call that nothing much! You might come first out of all those talented artists and win a prize – you could be famous!'

'What is the point?' Rosa asked in a flat empty voice. 'I've lost interest, Gladeeees, that's the truth.'

'I don't believe you,' Gladys said bluntly.

With a scowl on her face, Rosa continued, 'It seems pathetic to fuss over a few pencil drawings, when men and women are dying in death camps all over Germany.' Rosa seethed as she lit up one of her cheroots. 'I want to do more than bloody draw!' she added scathingly.

'You're doing more than your bit,' Gladys pointed out. 'Working on the cordite line, building bombs for soldiers at the Front.'

'I wish it was ME on the front line,' Rosa cried angrily. 'I wish somebody would give me a bomb or a rifle to shoot the Nazis!'

As Gladys handed Rosa a mug of tea, she could see tears spilling from her friend's eyes. 'We're all working hard to bring about peace, Rosa.'

'But we are no nearer to it!' Rosa cried. 'Four years, we fight the Germans, four years, and they still are winning.'

'Not true, Rosa!' Gladys protested. 'We defeated them in North Africa, and the Allies are making steady progress through Italy; we'll get there, especially now that Mussolini is out of the way.'

Rosa's shoulders slumped. 'And how many men and women have died?'

Abandoning her mug of tea, Rosa put her face in her hands and sobbed. Feeling sorry for her friend, who was so clearly racked by misery, Gladys sat down beside her again and put an arm about her shaking shoulders. 'It's so unlike you to be defeatist, sweetheart. What's happened? What's changed you?'

'Gabriel . . .' Rosa wailed as she abandoned herself to grief. 'Gabriel . . .' she repeated with such yearning and heartbreak in her voice it made Gladys cry too.

'Have you had bad news?' Gladys asked as she frantically tried to grasp what was upsetting her dear friend so much. 'Is he dead?' she whispered as she clung on to Rosa.

'Nobody knows, nobody hear from him in months!' Rosa cried. 'My uncle said even the Underground workers who got me out hear nothing from Gabriel. It doesn't look good, Gladys. Oh, WHY didn't he escape with me? WHY did he stay and let me go?' she cried, as she subsided into floods of tears all over again.

Gladys waited until Rosa's sobs had subsided before she spoke, and when she did it was with infinite tenderness. 'You know exactly why Gabriel stayed, sweetheart.'

Rosa nodded. 'I know . . . he gave me freedom, but, Dio,' she raged, 'sometimes I wish I had given it to him.'

Gladys took a deep breath to steady her nerves. 'You're right: your brother did sacrifice himself for you, but only because he loved you so much, Rosa – he knew that you would make the best of your freedom, which you have done.' As Rosa turned to her friend with eyes full of sadness, Gladys continued. 'Think how proud Gabriel would be to walk into the Salford gallery and see your pictures hanging on the wall. He would know better than anybody how well your mother taught you to draw, how hard she tutored you in order to pass on her learning.'

Rosa gave a shadow of a smile. 'He know, for sure. I always complain to him about my mother,' she confessed with a bleak smile. 'He always positive; when I think of it now, I see he pushed me hard, just like Mama.'

'So be positive for Gabriel: create for him, celebrate for him – and thank him, wherever he may be on God's earth, for the precious gift of freedom he gave you.'

A long thoughtful silence followed Gladys's passionate outburst; then suddenly Rosa stubbed out her smoking cheroot and rose to her feet. Reaching down, she kissed Gladys on both cheeks and headed for the door.

'Hey, where are you going?' Gladys, suddenly anxious that she'd overstepped the mark and had upset Rosa, called after her.

'I will do as you say, Gladeeees, I will draw for my brother, Gabriel!' Rosa replied with a strong ring of determination in her voice.

'Make him proud of you,' Gladys said as she choked back tears.

'Oh, I will,' Rosa retorted with a brave smile. 'Dio, I will!'

19. Trainee Nurse

Gladys was rather nervous when Sister Atkins told her she had to report to Dr Grant's office before she started her morning round. 'Is there a problem?' she asked anxiously.

'You'll soon find out,' Sister Atkins replied as she relieved Gladys of the thermometer she was holding. 'Off you go – don't leave the man waiting.'

'Come along in,' the doctor called when Gladys gave a nervous little knock on his door. 'Morning, Nurse Johnson,' he said cheerily when she walked in. 'Take a seat,' he added, indicating the chair across the desk from him.

Perched anxiously on the chair, Gladys said, 'I hope everything's all right, Doctor?'

Grant beamed at the lovely trainee, whose blue eyes were wide with concern and curiosity. 'Couldn't be better,' he replied. 'Sister Atkins has been singing your praises.'

Gladys was so surprised by his statement that she burst out laughing. 'That's the very last thing I expected to hear you say,' she chuckled.

'Words of praise don't come easily to Sister Atkins's lips; she's a hard taskmaster and a perfectionist to boot. We've had a few trainees leave in floods of tears, but you, young lady, I'm delighted to say, have weathered the storm.'

'I've loved every minute,' Gladys retorted with an eager smile. 'And I've especially loved shadowing Nurse Atkins: she *is* a perfectionist,' she said reverently. 'It's surprising how much you can pick up if you stick to somebody like glue!'

'You were assigned to an excellent teacher,' Dr Grant agreed. 'Sister Atkins and I are both in agreement that you would now benefit from a short stint in a big teaching hospital.'

'Goodness,' Gladys gasped. 'I feel like I'm only just getting my feet under the table.'

'We don't want you to get too comfortable,' the doctor laughed good-naturedly.

Assuming she'd be heading for Manchester Royal Infirmary or the hospital in Salford, Gladys was stunned when Dr Grant said, 'You'll start at St Thomas' Teaching Hospital in London on Monday.'

Gladys couldn't believe she was hearing correctly; for all her struggle to stay in a close, familiar community, she was now being sent nearly two hundred miles south – to London!

'You don't look pleased,' the doctor commented.

'I'd prefer to remain in the North,' Gladys confessed.

'I know it's a big jump, but the timing's good for us,' Dr Grant explained. 'The trainee we recently sent to St Thomas' is returning here to do further work, which frees up a space for you – it's a straightforward swap,' he concluded.

Sister Atkins was more excited than Gladys about the transfer. 'You'll do well, and you'll come back with far more knowledge than you had when you left.' Seeing Gladys's anxious face, she gave her a brisk pat on the back. 'Cheer up, Nurse, it's not for long, and you'll learn so much. Now I suggest you finish your final shift on Saturday afternoon, which will give you time to prepare for your journey south on Sunday. We'll also provide you with return train tickets; we don't want to lose you on the way, do we?' she joked.

Gladys was sad to say goodbye to her patients, and they were sad to see her go. 'You're bound to break someone's heart down South with those beautiful eyes of yours,' one of the gentlemen said to her.

'I'm going to advance my training,' Gladys assured him. 'Not fall in love.'

'I've heard that before,' the patient teased.

'Come on,' Gladys laughed. 'Time for your bed bath – and no more cheek – or I won't scrub your back!'

In the few hours they had together on Saturday after Gladys had finished work, Rosa helped her friend pack her suitcase. 'I won't need much,' Gladys said. 'Sturdy shoes, underwear, warm coat, make-up, nylons, one precious pair,' she laughed as she carefully wrapped them in tissue paper so they wouldn't snag. 'I won't even have to bother with my uniform: Sister Atkins told me that St Thomas' provide their own.'

'But you'll need clothes to go out in – surely you

won't be working all of the time,' Rosa exclaimed in shock.

'If St Thomas' is anything like the Phoenix Infirmary, I'll be fit for nothing at the end of the day but bed; the last thing on my mind will be going out on the town. Anyway, I'm sure it'll be dangerous: bombs falling all the time and wardens rushing everybody into air-raid shelters.'

Rosa's pretty face darkened. 'Take care, darling. I want you back in one piece and as soon as possible.'

'I'll take care, promise,' Gladys said as she hugged her anxious friend. 'And I'll get back just as soon as they let me go. I'll be homesick for you and our cosy cowshed.'

Early the next day, Rosa insisted on accompanying Gladys to Clitheroe Railway Station.

'Please,' Gladys implored as Rosa, looking like a lovely child with her lustrous dark hair draped untidily around her shoulders, helped her with her case. 'I can do this on my own; please go back to bed. You'll be clocking on soon, and you need your sleep.'

'No, mia cara!' Rosa said stubbornly. 'I accompany you.'

When it came to it, Gladys was actually very glad that she had somebody she loved to wave her off; the thought of returning to London brought back a rush of memories that Rosa's sweet, smiling, hopeful face might help to dissipate.

'Arrivederci, Gladeeees,' she cried as the train pulled out of the station in a great big wheezy blast of smoke. 'Good luck!'

*

The local train stopped in Manchester, where Gladys caught one bound for London that stopped at every major town they passed through to pick up and drop off passengers, mostly troops being mobilized. As the noisy steam train puffed and wheezed its sooty way to the South, soldiers and sailors stood shoulder to shoulder in the crowded corridors and squeezed into overcrowded carriages, where one poor lad climbed into the netted luggage rack and promptly fell asleep. Gazing at the tired men, some of whom were hardly more than boys, Gladys's heart ached for them. They looked so tired and grimy; the younger ones, slumped against anything they could find, gazed dully out of the window, whilst the older ones constantly smoked cigarettes as they bantered cheerfully amongst themselves. Nobody could ignore a beautiful young woman like Gladys, who took all their cheeky comments in good heart and shared her packed lunch with them.

'It's only meat-paste sandwiches,' she said apologetically, but the way the food was so rapidly consumed suggested the soldiers hadn't had anything fresh in a long time.

The last time Gladys had been in London was with the Bomb Girls' Swing Band, when they'd all stayed at the Savoy and had been in such high spirits. This arrival late at night couldn't have been more different. Even though she was optimistic about her new nursing career, there was no doubting the depression and fear that walking through the bomb-torn streets of the blasted city brought on: barrage balloons floated high over a London that was literally crushed by relentless bombing-raids. The bus she took rumbled by shattered office and tenement blocks; holes gaped like open black mouths in the fractured ground; and the air stank of leaking sewers. When she arrived at St Thomas', Gladys's spirits didn't lift at all: the hospital, wrapped in an inky darkness, looked formidable, and Gladys had no idea where and to whom she should report her arrival. A nurse in a dark cape, pulled around her to keep off the damp mist rising from the river, kindly stopped in front of a bewildered Gladys, who stood on Westminster Bridge wondering which way to go. 'Can I help you, love?' the breathless nurse asked.

'I'm trying to find the nurses' quarters,' Gladys explained.

'Follow me – I'm on my way there myself,' she said as she led Gladys across the road to a tall, narrow house that looked empty. 'They've got the blinds down,' the nurse explained. 'Don't worry: it ain't as empty as it looks.'

She was right; once Gladys entered the building, there were nurses, in various forms of disarray, dashing around everywhere. 'Register at the office, where you'll be allocated a bed and food tickets,' Gladys's new friend informed her, before she dashed off to her own dormitory. Feeling unbelievably weary, Gladys signed in and, almost too tired to eat, drank a mug of tea and ate some bread and marg before heading to her own dorm, where, after a quick wash and a change of clothes, she stumbled to her bed and fell into the deepest sleep.

It seemed like she'd only just closed her eyes when

suddenly she was woken by the loudest explosion she'd ever heard. Thinking she was having a nightmare, Gladys buried her head deeper under her blankets, but a voice yelling 'Everybody out!', followed by a shrieking siren, forced Gladys to open her eyes and grope her way out of bed.

'What's going on?' she mumbled blearily.

As the ground quaked and trembled beneath her feet, Gladys had to clutch her bed to stop herself from losing her balance.

'Into the shelters!' yelled a woman's voice.

As the sleeping women staggered to their feet, Gladys followed blindly in their wake, not having a clue where she was going or what she should take.

'Grab your gas mask, love,' a girl beside her said. 'And a dressing gown too: it's bloody freezing down in the shelters.'

Yawning and rubbing her eyes, Gladys mumbled, 'Can't we just stay here?'

'You could do, if you want to meet your maker,' the girl replied. 'I wouldn't risk it myself.'

Feeling rather pathetic for asking such a stupid question, Gladys obediently followed the girls, who were herded by traffic wardens into the nearest Underground station, which was quickly filling up with local families holding tired, frightened children and furiously wailing babies. 'Find a spot and park yourself,' the friendly girl advised. 'I'm Ethel, by the way.'

Gladys clung close to Ethel, who seemed to know her way around. 'I'm Gladys, just arrived.'

'Poor you, what a bugger of a night to arrive,' Ethel commiserated. 'Keep down, sweetheart,' she warned as another explosion went off.

'That sounded close,' said Gladys with a shudder of terror.

'Jerry seems to like bombing anything near the River Thames, bastard! We get it a lot,' Ethel said as she lit up a Woodbine, then offered one to Gladys, who politely declined.

'Is it like this every night?' Gladys anxiously asked.

'Can be – we get a run of them, until Jerry turns his attention elsewhere, but he always comes back, like a bad penny!' she joked.

Feeling like her eyelids were as heavy as lead, Gladys wondered how anybody could remain as cheerful as Ethel, who, in between the ear-shattering explosions, chatted to her neighbours and cracked jokes until the all-clear siren went off. Then, staggering to their feet, they left the shelter of the Underground and emerged, blinking and shivering in the cold morning light. 'Innit gorgeous, bombs or not?' Ethel mused as she pointed towards the rising sun turning the Thames crimson-red. 'I wouldn't bother going back to bed, Gladys,' Ethel advised as they re-entered the nurses' quarters. 'If you're on a morning shift, you'll be expected on the wards by seven.'

Gladys nodded and thanked Ethel for all her help.

'Anytime, my sweetheart,' Ethel replied as she blew her a goodbye kiss.

After changing out of her nightdress, Gladys washed

in the communal bathroom, where she threw cold water on to her face in an attempt to wake herself up. 'I look like the living dead!' she groaned as she brushed her hair and cleaned her teeth, then set off for her first day shift at St Thomas'.

Nothing could have prepared Gladys for the days that followed. After being given a much smarter uniform than she was used to, she and the other trainees were addressed by a nurse who made Sister Atkins sound like an archangel. Gladys and another girl were assigned to the amputees' ward, which was crowded with soldiers suffering from severe wounds. The ward sister quickly told Gladys and her colleague that the men would have originally been treated at casualty clearing stations at the Front. 'Our first job is to clean them up in order to assess the extent of their wounds,' she explained. 'You'll work alongside an experienced senior nurse, whom you'll learn from and co-operate with. Off you go.'

Assigned to a Staff Nurse Andrews, Gladys donned a clean apron, which within an hour was covered in blood and pus. Moving along the line of beds ranged on both sides of the ward, the nurses bathed their patients' wounds and removed their filthy dressings. When it came to changing her first stinking gangrenous dressings, Gladys actually thought she might faint. 'Take a break, Nurse,' Andrews said sharply. 'And breathe through your mouth; you smell less that way.'

Covering her mouth, Gladys hurried into the staff toilets, where she was violently sick. Washing her face and wiping her mouth, she fought back tears; these poor men, lying limp on their hospital beds, had been through hell; wounded by enemy fire, they'd been shipped home like cattle and now they were waiting patiently for somebody to clean them up and get them better. It was enough to make anybody weep, the resignation in their eyes, combined with their sadness and fatigue. How much had these men gone through before a stray bullet hit them, shattering bone, ravaging tender flesh? 'At least I'm alive,' she'd heard a few say. Not like the friends they'd left behind on the battlefield. Just thinking of their brave selflessness made Gladys grit her teeth; if these soldiers could bear the pain, she could damn well do what was expected of her – and do it to the very best of her ability.

'All right, Johnson?' the senior nurse enquired.

Gladys nodded. 'I'm fine, thank you.' Turning to her patients, Gladys said with her most radiant, heart-stopping smile, 'Who's next, gentlemen?'

'Over here, sweetheart, come and bat those big blue eyes at me and I'll forget all about the pain,' a cheeky soldier joked.

Gladys turned towards the soldier, whose amputated hand was oozing noxious yellow pus. Maintaining a stiff upper lip, Gladys did as she'd been advised; she breathed through her mouth and with infinite care she gently unwound the man's bandages and washed clean his festering wound.

Gladys never knew how she got through that first week on the amputees' ward, nor how many clean aprons she replaced for the bloodied ones she left in the sluice room. The days were a blur of gangrenous images, surgical dressings, tea trolleys, meal trolleys, record charts, thermometers, bedpans and once a trip to the morgue, pushing the body of a soldier no more than a boy who had died of blood poisoning in the night. Her shifts never seemed to end; when wounded soldiers from the Front were dropped off by the Red Cross, the nurses on duty were expected to work until they dropped. When Gladys finally slumped on to her bed (deranged by lack of sleep), there was little hope of rest. Sirens shrilled out almost every night, and, though she would willingly have stayed in her bed, even risked a bomb falling on her, she was dragged complaining into the Underground, where she learnt to sleep with her eyes open.

It was on one such night, slumped in the dirty, dusty, packed Underground shelter, that the all-clear sounded as usual around dawn. Gladys dragged herself to her feet, wondering whether she'd have time to snatch a round of hot toast and some tea before she started her shift. She trudged along the line of yawning people exiting the Underground in various states of disarray. Wishing she'd grabbed her nurse's cape instead of her grubby dressing gown, Gladys pressed herself into the surging crowd, hoping nobody would comment on her nightwear. As she did so, she was passed by a tall, dark-haired man in a stained white doctor's coat who was mounting the Underground steps two at a time. There was something familiar about the ease with which he moved, the way his black hair curled at the base of his neck and the attractive slant of his strong broad shoulders. Involuntarily Gladys's skin prickled and her pulse raced. Surely it couldn't be him? Reggie Lloyd couldn't possibly be back in England? Shaking her head, as if she was delirious, Gladys returned to the nurses' quarters to prepare for work, but her hands trembled as she dressed. Just the sight of a tall, dark, elegant doctor in a white coat had reduced her to pulp. Was she EVER going to get over Dr Reggie Lloyd?

20. St Thomas' Training Hospital

Thanks to Ethel's help, Gladys was becoming used to the stresses and strains of London life and being attacked by German Messerschmitts almost every night. Ethel, a born-and-bred Londoner, took events in her stride; familiar with frequent German air-raids since the start of the war four years ago, she was matter-of-fact about getting into the Underground shelter as soon as the sirens sounded. She always remembered her gas mask and her packet of Woodbines, and she kept up her own spirits and those of her neighbours by singing, chatting and joking all through the night. 'I don't know how you keep it up,' Gladys yawned as Ethel burst into yet another rendition of 'It's a Long Way to Tipperary'.

'You get used to it, sweetheart,' she retorted as she gave Gladys a dig in the ribs. 'Our lucky night,' she added. 'The WVS ladies are joining us, so we're sure to get a cuppa or, better still, a nice bowl of soup and a piece of bread.' Gladys followed Ethel's gaze and saw the Women's Voluntary Services ladies set up their tea stall in order to raise the spirits of the weary souls destined to another night of rough sleeping.

Ethel couldn't advise Gladys on her daily workload – she was on orthopaedics, whilst Gladys was on a male surgical ward – so generally their paths inside the hospital didn't cross very much. Luckily, Staff Nurse Andrews was a fine professional to work alongside, and she had the grace not to bark at Gladys when things went wrong. One of Gladys's regular duties was to assist Andrews in prepping amputees for theatre; sometimes Gladys had the gruesome task of having to shave various parts of the men's bodies, which she initially found mortifyingly embarrassing. However, as time went by, she became accustomed to the task, as she did to so many other onerous duties. There were two well-designed theatre suites with teams of surgeons operating on wounded soldiers around the clock. As Gladys wheeled one groaning patient after another back to the ward, she was always aware that when these poor men were back on their feet they'd be returned to the battlefield, where the whole ghastly business would start all over again. The waste of life and the agonizing suffering the troops endured made Gladys endlessly sad, and she yearned for the day when peace was declared and the bloodshed would stop.

There was quite a frisson among the nurses when they encountered any of the good-looking young doctors who manned the operating theatres. There was also fierce competition as to who should escort their patients to theatre, which was the best place to eye up the new doctors. Luckily for Gladys, she and Staff Nurse Andrews didn't need to compete: Andrews was married and had eyes only for her sailor husband, so it was Gladys who wheeled sedated patients on a trolley to theatre. One afternoon, feeling bleary-eyed with fatigue after yet another sleepless night in the

Underground shelter, Gladys made her way to theatre, not knowing that Dr Reggie Lloyd was awaiting his first patient of the day. He too had had a tough night in the air-raid shelter, but like the true professional he was, Reggie was focused on his work and on the poor buggers recently arrived from the casualty clearing stations on the front line. God! He thought he'd seen some grim sights in his working life in Naples, when he was serving with the British Naval Fleet, but the injured men he operated on day after day after day were in some cases quite literally shot to bits. As he tied his sterilized gown around his waist and started to scrub up, he firmly centred his thoughts on the cases awaiting him and the medical procedures expected of him. As the pretty blonde theatre sister he'd been dating for a few months tied a mask around his face, Reggie winked at her, then turned to receive his patient, presently being wheeled in by a nurse he'd not seen before. Tall and slender with gorgeous legs and a sway to her hips that even a nurse's uniform couldn't disguise, Reggie was sure he recognized her. When he saw a lock of dark brunette hair escape from her starched white cap to settle on her shoulders, he was certain the nurse was no other than Gladys Johnson – the woman whom he'd first seen singing on stage in a slinky red dance dress.

He'd asked a couple of friends if they knew anything about her sudden disappearance, but nobody seemed to know any more than he did. 'It was all very odd,' Reggie thought to himself, feeling again the pain and hurt of her departure, and the rumours that had reached him about Captain Miles. Shocked to see her here, he managed to pull himself together as he cast a final look at Gladys's trim backside before the doors of the operating theatre closed behind her. It seemed she hadn't recognized him, so he had a little more time to gather his thoughts before he saw her again.

Reggie did indeed see Gladys several more times as she dropped off patients before hurrying back to her ward – once he thought she had recognized him, but an anaesthetist treating his patient got between them and when he looked again she'd gone.

As for Gladys, she was beginning to think she was seeing things: first she imagined she saw Dr Lloyd leaving the Underground shelter early one morning; now she was convinced she'd seen him in theatre. The handsome face that had looked so familiar was hidden behind a surgeon's mask, so she couldn't be sure. But his stunning blue eyes, which were staring hard at her, were clearly visible, and hard to mistake. Gladys began to dread delivering and picking up her patients from theatre – what would she say if it really was him and he approached her? How could she explain why she'd run away? God only knew what he must think of her! Little flirt, typical ENSA girl, out for a good time.

It was only when Reggie called the ward and Gladys picked up the phone and recognized his deep, smooth voice that she knew for sure that he was indeed one of the doctors in the operating theatre. Reggie, on the other end of the line, hadn't a clue which nurse he was speaking to; he was merely phoning the ward to request that a patient be collected from the recovery room. Breaking into a sweat, Gladys half muffled the phone as she answered, 'Yes, right away.'

In a panic, Gladys hurried out of the nurses' station to ask Staff Nurse Andrews if she would be kind enough to pick up the patient, but she refused. 'That's your job,' she said curtly.

Gladys's heart sank. She didn't want to see Reggie, especially not like this, blood-stained and weary. But duty called: her patient had to be collected. And hopefully, she rapidly reasoned, by the time she arrived Reggie would surely be back at work in the operating theatre. Keeping her head bowed, Gladys scuttled into the recovery room, where she found her patient semiconscious on a trolley. Grabbing the trolley, she quickly pushed it towards the double doors when a familiar male voice behind her called out, 'Let me help you, Nurse.'

'Oh, no!' thought Gladys. 'It's him!'

In a blind panic she rather ungracefully bolted for the doors, but Reggie sprang forward to heave them open, and when he turned he was face to face with Gladys. Blushing furiously and completely lost for words, she could only stare at him.

'Are you working on D4?'

Completely tongue-tied, Gladys could only gulp and nod.

'Men's surgery?' he asked.

Wishing he'd stop asking questions, she blurted out, 'Yes, I'm a trainee on the ward.'

'I thought I recognized a back view of you the other

day,' he commented, which made Gladys blush even more as she recalled how he used to compliment her on her shapely backside. His eyes swept up and down her soiled uniform. 'How long have you been a nurse?'

'I, er, oh, not long,' she flustered. 'I started my training in a small hospital up North; they sent me down here to widen my experience,' she said, knowing full well she was babbling.

Intrigued at her change of career, Reggie couldn't stop himself from asking, 'Are you enjoying it?'

'Yes, yes . . .' she answered directly. 'Very much.'

Gladys's patient groaning in pain as he regained consciousness mercifully interrupted their conversation. 'If you'll excuse me,' she gasped as she all but ran back to the ward, where she completed the rest of her duties in a daze.

When her shift was over, Gladys hurried back to the nurses' dormitory, where she sat on the side of her bed pretending to read a magazine, but all the time thinking about Reggie Lloyd. She truly believed when she left Naples she would never see him again, but fate had drawn them together in the most bizarre twist of circumstances. If it hadn't been for her allergic reaction to cordite, she'd never be retraining as a nurse. As the night wore on, Gladys reasoned that she was making a mountain out of a molehill; so they had a brief romance, but it didn't amount to anything more than a kiss and a cuddle.

He was without doubt one of the most handsome young men she'd ever seen; she was sure there'd be nurses lining the hospital corridors to date him. Why would he hold a flame for her, she asked herself, when he was surrounded by eager young women? Anyway, she reasoned as she blushed with shame, he'd probably heard Captain Miles bragging to his chums in the officers' mess about his conquest. 'That brunette saxophonist, she couldn't get enough of it!' she could almost hear him say. Feeling sick at the thought of the odious officer gossiping about her, Gladys was sure that none of his pals would have suspected that Miles had forced himself on her. 'My God! What must Reggie have thought if he heard Captain Miles boasting about her in the bar?' Only nights before the rape, she'd been in his arms, kissing him as they stood on board his ship, watching the smoke curling up from Vesuvius. No wonder Reggie had been so cold with her when she bumped into him in theatre. Thank God her stint at St Thomas' was a short one; she'd soon be back in Pendleton, miles away from London, safe and sound in the cowshed with her own darling Rosa.

Just as Gladys was brushing her teeth in readiness for bed, the air-raid siren shrilled out.

'Christ! Would you bloody believe it?' cried Ethel as they both grabbed their nurses' capes and gas masks. 'Here we go again.'

Halfway through the evening, with babies bawling all around them and an old man in slippers playing an accordion, Ethel turned to Gladys and said, 'What's up with you, gel? You've got a face on you like concrete.'

'I'm tired,' Gladys said, which was true.

'And . . . ?'

'I bumped into an old boyfriend.'

'Oooooh! And where was that, then?'

'The hospital,' Gladys said bleakly. 'It's not like I go anywhere else.'

'Where in the hospital? The emergency department?' Ethel joked.

'The operating theatre,' Gladys retorted.

'Oooh, I hope the poor bugger pulled through?' irrepressible Ethel joked.

'He's not a patient, he's a doctor; I met him in another hospital, somewhere else,' she prevaricated. The last thing she wanted was to tell gossipy Ethel that she used to be an entertainer with ENSA – she'd never hear the end of it!

Ethel paused mid-drag of her fag. 'A bleeding doctor!' she exclaimed. 'Aren't we the lucky one?'

'It was awkward,' Gladys confessed.

'I'd like a bit of awkward with a doctor!' Ethel tittered.

Gladys groaned under her breath; why had she even bothered to tell Ethel about Reggie? Then, to her surprise, Ethel all but echoed her own words. 'Forget him, sweetheart. From what I know about doctors, and I speak from experience,' she added with a saucy wink, 'he'll have nurses queuing round the block for him. You might be a good-looker, darlin', but best to let the bugger go.'

Gladys smiled sadly. 'Don't worry, Ethel – we both let each other go a long time ago.'

Gladys didn't see Reggie for another week; then, one

afternoon as they were both hurrying along a hospital corridor, they literally walked slap into each other. Gladys felt like she'd been punched in the stomach when she saw him, and he felt his knees go weak. Before she shot off like a startled rabbit, Reggie blurted out, 'I was sorry I never got a chance to say goodbye to you before you left Naples.'

'It was a bit rushed,' she said quickly.

'But the ENSA troupe stayed and you left,' he said pointedly.

'Yes, I had to, a new posting,' she lied, and from the look in his piercing blue eyes she knew he didn't believe her.

'So nothing to do with Captain Miles?' said Reggie, rashly grasping the bull by the horns.

Gladys's paled. So he did know she'd been involved with the vile captain – but did he know the truth or just idle gossip? Playing for time, she said sharply, 'Why would you ask that?'

'Just something I heard,' he told her.

Gladys's eyes filled with tears. Oh, what had he heard? That she was a little tart? An easy lay? Wishing the earth would open up and swallow her whole, she struggled hard to stop herself from bursting into tears. She'd left ENSA and hidden herself away in the Phoenix Factory specifically to get away from humiliating conversations like this one. Just hearing the captain's wretched name brought back unbidden a string of nightmare memories: his mouth over hers, pushing her struggling against a tree, him gripping her hands tightly behind her back as he ripped at her clothes, walking away from her whistling as she lay weeping on the ground where he'd left her. Feeling like she was going to make an even bigger fool of herself if she didn't immediately get away, Gladys dodged around Reggie. 'If you'll excuse me. I've got to get back to my ward.'

Seeing her anguished face, and struck by the thought that perhaps such anguish indicated a more complicated story than the one he'd imagined, Reggie gently caught her arm. 'Gladys!' he cried. 'Can't we spend some time together, you know, catch up?'

Seeing the bewildered look in his eyes, Gladys suddenly felt sorry for Reggie; it wasn't his fault Captain Miles had raped her – why was she making him suffer?

'Could we meet tomorrow, just for a drink?' he asked quickly. 'When we've both finished work?'

Gladys's heart skipped a beat – should she? Wouldn't it be best to just leave it? She'd be gone soon anyway. But, as she gazed into his handsome face, she heard herself saying, 'All right, ring me on the ward when you're finished in theatre; we could perhaps go for a walk,' she replied.

'Yes,' he said with a relieved smile. 'I'll ring you tomorrow.'

But tomorrow never came. A truckload of wounded soldiers fresh from the Front arrived that afternoon, and when Reggie phoned to say he was free Gladys had no choice but to tell him that she couldn't leave the ward. 'How about later?' he suggested. 'We could go for a drink.'

Thinking she'd be free by the evening, Gladys agreed

to meet Reggie at the entrance to the hospital at nine o'clock. 'That should give me enough time to tidy myself up before I meet him,' she thought to herself. But back in the nurses' dormitory, just as she was making herself up in the communal bathroom, the wretched air-raid siren went off and there was no alternative but to grab her nurse's cape and gas mask and follow the line of nurses into the Underground shelter, where Gladys slumped on the ground and promptly burst into tears of sheer frustration. Even the sight of the kindly WVS ladies handing out mugs of tea and meat-paste sandwiches didn't raise her spirits. For the first time since Gladys had arrived at St Thomas', she was overcome by homesickness. What wouldn't she give to be back in the cowshed with Rosa and her dear friends; how she missed their strength and humour and most of all their love. Feeling utterly wretched, Gladys pulled her nurse's cape around herself and tried to sleep. 'Hopefully Reggie will understand why I didn't show up,' she thought to herself as she dropped off.

Reggie, who'd been standing at the hospital entrance waiting for Gladys, also heard the air-raid siren. 'Bugger!' he fumed. If ever a couple were fated not to meet, it had to be him and Gladys; everything seemed to conspire against them whenever they made any kind of arrangement.

'Come along, sir,' the night porter said as he urged people to safety. 'Jerry's back. Get yourself into the shelter right away.'

Stubbing out his cigarette, Reggie joined the line of

people hurrying into the Underground, which was packed with local families and staff from St Thomas'. Walking around the WVS ladies, Reggie looked for somewhere to sit and his eyes landed on Gladys curled up on the dirty floor with her cape pulled around her. Reggie's heart contracted when he saw her long, beautiful brunette hair tumbled around her pale, tired face. There were grubby smudges on her cheeks from the tears she'd shed, and her full lips were parted as she breathed softly in her sleep. Moving quietly so as not to disturb her, Reggie removed his warm overcoat, which he tucked around Gladys, then he settled down beside her, raising her gently so she wasn't sleeping on the floor. He propped her against his shoulder, then he too fell asleep. The all-clear siren woke them both with a jolt. Gladys blinked in disbelief when she saw Reggie beside her. 'How did you get here?' she mumbled blearily.

'Same way as you, I suppose,' he replied with a yawn. 'I thought you'd be more comfortable leaning against me than lying on the filthy floor.'

The air-raid warden interrupted their conversation. 'Everybody out – Jerry's gone home and so should you,' he yelled.

Out in the bleak, raw, dawn light, Reggie suggested they should find some breakfast. In a nearby crowded Lyons Café, he bought tea and toast for both of them. 'I have to admit,' he confessed as he set the food down before Gladys, 'I never expected to see you in a nurse's uniform.'

Wrapping her hands around the mug of tea he

offered, Gladys said with a shrug, 'ENSA life, all that travelling, it just didn't suit me.'

Remembering Gladys in her performing role, beautiful, talented, radiant – and obviously having the time of her life, Reggie simply didn't believe her. He'd heard the rumours about Captain Miles, and knew he was a renowned Lothario; from the way Gladys had reacted to his rather abrupt question when they'd bumped into each other in the hospital corridor, clearly these rumours were true – or at least partially. But, remembering now the look of intense anguish on Gladys's face when he'd mentioned Miles's name, something about the whole thing didn't sit easily with him – something irked. He vividly recalled Gladys's deep dislike of the lecherous captain; Reggie had never had the impression that she was mad about Miles – quite the opposite, in fact. He'd seen the look on her face when Miles flirted with her; to Reggie it was clear she had detested the man. He knew in his gut something bad had happened to her, something so bad she'd had to run away, but she clearly wasn't going to tell him the truth, even though he'd asked her several times. He shrugged; he wasn't going to push it if she wasn't ready.

After telling Reggie that her training period at St Thomas' would finish at the end of the week, he suggested, she thought out of politeness, that they should meet up for a drink on her last night. Having agreed a time and a place, they bade each other a rather formal goodbye and hurried off to their different places of work – Reggie feeling hurt that she clearly didn't trust him enough to tell him the truth and Gladys rather regretting that she'd made yet another date with persuasive Dr Lloyd.

The next two nights saw no air-attacks, which was a blessed relief; apart from the fact that Gladys could sleep in her own bed, it also gave her time to catch up with some little jobs that had been neglected. Standing in her dressing gown in the nurses' laundry, she washed and rinsed a pile of underwear, which she hung on a large clothes-horse to dry. Just as she was finishing her task, Ethel walked in with a puzzled expression on her face. 'They said I'd find you here,' she exclaimed as she lit up a Woodbine. 'What was the name of the doctor fella you was moping on about the other night?'

Gladys looked surprised but answered her question. 'Dr Lloyd, Reggie Lloyd.'

'Tall, gorgeous, big-blue eyes, always in theatre?' Ethel persisted.

Gladys was suddenly cautious; she really didn't want another in-depth conversation with Ethel about Reggie. 'Yes, I suppose so,' she answered casually.

'I was dead right to tell you to forget him,' Ethel said before she paused to take a deep drag on her cigarette. The hairs on the back of Gladys's neck began to prickle.

'What's all this about, Ethel?'

'He's only walking out with one of the theatre sisters,' Ethel told her. 'You know, the posh blonde one who thinks she's a notch above everybody else?'

Gladys stared at her. 'Are you sure?' she asked sharply. 'Could it be silly hospital gossip?' she added.

'No gossip, my sweetheart – heard her talking about love's young dream with mi own ears,' Ethel continued. 'I was dropping something off in theatre and she was chatting with another nurse – she said she was head over heels with Dr Lloyd and had been since he first asked her out three months ago.'

Gladys's pulse began to race; she *knew* he would have a girlfriend! And for God's sake, she fumed, why the hell not? He was handsome, charming, talented, a catch for any woman. So why was he messing about with her? Rekindling some faded love affair for old times' sake or much, much worse, after all the gossip he'd heard about her behaviour in Naples, did he think she was an easy lay and he'd pick up where Captain Miles left off? With blood pounding in her temples, Gladys railed furiously at herself, 'You fool! You stupid idiot!' She should never have got involved with Reggie all over again. Well it was too late now; yet again she'd made a bloody fool of herself, and she had only herself to blame. Picking up her belongs, she headed towards the door. 'Thanks for letting me know, Ethel.'

'You're welcome, love. Always listen to your auntie Ethel – she knows all about what's going on in this place.'

Gladys didn't go to meet Reggie, who waited for her for over half an hour in the pouring rain. Eventually – wet and angry at being snubbed by a woman who kept bewitching him with her sparkling blue eyes – Reggie walked away determined that he was going to put Gladys Johnson once and for all out of his mind.

21. 'The Winner is . . .'

When Rosa was invited to the award ceremony at the exhibition, she once again had to go to the Salford art gallery by herself. Her relatives in Manchester had the flu; Gladys was in London; and Edna and Malc would be in the despatch yard in Edna's mobile chip shop, serving food to hungry Bomb Girls coming off their shifts. Rosa could have invited Nora and Maggie, but she thought they'd feel awkward and out of place in an art gallery; for sure, Nora would. Everywhere she went was too posh for her! And Rosa thought it would be unkind to invite Maggie without Nora, so she let the matter lie. When it came to it, she rather liked the idea of going on her own: she could take a last look at all the artwork before the exhibition was dismantled and perhaps meet the other artists, with whom she'd barely had a chance to chat.

After she'd finished her early-morning shift, Rosa hurried home to the cowshed, where she had lived alone since Gladys departure to St Thomas'. Running a rather tepid bath, Rosa soaked away the smell of explosives that seemed forever to cling to her body. After she'd washed her hair, she sat in front of the crackling wood-burner and, wrapped in a thick towel, she dried and brushed her long hair until it shone like dark mahogany. Working on a bomb line removed much of the women's femininity: out of necessity, their hair was banished into a turban, all jewellery was banned, and hair grips and clips were strictly taboo. Suddenly, with her hair swinging in long, silky curls around her shoulders, Rosa wanted to pamper herself; she wanted just for a few hours to feel like a woman.

After changing into her underwear, Rosa found her only pair of nylons, which she attached to the clips of her suspender belt, then she searched through her meagre wardrobe trying to find something to wear. Staring at her second-hand tweed skirts and cardigans, Rosa sighed. She had a pretty pale-pink silk blouse, but none of her skirts did it any justice. Wondering if Gladys might have something she could wear, Rosa looked inside her wardrobe, where a black pleated skirt immediately caught her eye. Feeling a bit guilty, but knowing that Gladys wouldn't mind her borrowing it, Rosa slipped into the skirt, which perfectly complemented her pink blouse and also brought out the glossy sheen in her dark hair. She added the lovely solid-silver bangle that Myrtle had left her, and, after appraising herself in the small mirror in the bathroom, she grabbed her hat, coat and bag, and set off down the hill to Pendleton to catch the bus into Salford.

It was pitch dark by the time Rosa hopped off the bus and hurried towards the gallery, where all the blackout blinds were pulled down tight. She blinked when she stepped out of the gloom and into the illuminated gallery, where the vibrant colours from all the exhibits lit up the room with jewel-like hues. 'Lovely to see you again, Miss Falco,' the owner of the gallery said as he approached with a tray on which were fluted glasses of sweet sherry. 'Do help yourself.'

'Thank you,' Rosa replied, taking a full glass.

'Your pieces have proved to be very popular,' the owner enthused. 'We've had some offers, if you'd like to sell any of them.'

Rosa gazed fondly at her sketches of the Bomb Girls and shook her head. 'I have to ask my friends for permission to sell,' she answered shyly.

'Of course,' he retorted. 'Now, if you'll excuse me, I can see the reporter from the *Manchester Guardian* has just arrived,' the owner said excitedly and dashed off to greet her.

Sipping her sherry, Rosa was drawn to the paintings of women assembling fighter planes in a vast hangar; yet again she admired Roger Carrington's brushwork and his use of colour. 'He's good,' Rosa mused. 'In fact, he's very good, quite a talent.' The female workers were dressed not unlike the Bomb Girls, but instead of working at ground level they were high up on scaffolding or perched precariously on ladders, putting together sections of planes that were ten times the size of themselves. Rosa jumped and spilt her sherry as a voice directly behind her said, 'Hard work, eh?'

'Ooooh!' she gasped as she wiped the sticky sherry off Gladys's pleated skirt. 'You startled me,' she said, and turned to face a tall man wearing an RAF uniform.

'I'm so sorry,' he exclaimed as he took a clean hankie from his pocket and helped her mop up the sherry. 'I'm such a big clumsy oaf!'

Rosa gazed up into the stranger's handsome face, which was dominated by a shock of tawny brown hair that fell in a fringe above his commanding hazel eyes. In the second that their eyes locked, Rosa felt a blush rising from her neck; willing it to go away, she took a deep breath, only to feel the wretched blush spreading to her cheeks, which started to glow a pretty pink.

'Pleased to meet you,' he added as a hasty after-thought.

Feeling thoroughly flustered, Rosa quickly introduced herself: 'I am Rosa Falco.'

The smiling man, who had a charming spatter of freckles across his tanned cheeks, gripped her hand and exclaimed, 'ROSA FALCO! I love your work!'

Rosa gulped as she felt the blush spreading even further into her hairline. What on earth was the matter with her? Trembling and dithering like a schoolgirl at everything this rather loud extrovert man said to her.

'Delighted to make your acquaintance, Rosa!' As he pumped her hand and grinned at her, Rosa mumbled, 'And what is your name, sir?'

'That's me,' he replied, pointing at the pictures on the wall. 'They're mine.'

Now it was Rosa's turn to exclaim in delight, 'You're Roger Carrington!' she cried. 'I love your work too!'

After Roger had found her another sherry, which trembling Rosa could hardly hold still, they found a narrow bench on which they perched and stared at each other.

'I've only just arrived,' he told her. 'The RAF couldn't spare me,' he added ruefully. 'I'm stationed in Norfolk – we don't get much time off these days, but when I did I came straight up here. Bloody hell!' he chuckled. 'Couldn't be more different to flat old Norfolk – all hills and valleys, much colder too.'

Rosa gazed at him in wonder; he was the most open, direct, unembarrassed, confident person she had ever met in her life. His body seemed to exude warmth: it was as if the sun poured out of him, she thought, as she stared, mesmerized by the flecks of gold in his eyes. Sitting closer as more and more people crowded around the exhibits, Rosa discovered that Roger Carrington was in fact Squadron Leader Carrington stationed near King's Lynn in faraway Norfolk. She listened in rapt fascination as he talked about his experience of painting the women in his pictures.

'I was sent to Lincoln to pick up a Lancaster, an aeroplane,' he added, when he saw the crinkle of confusion on her brow. 'They're bally beauties!' he raved. 'Four engines, paddle-bladed propellers, huge bomb base,' he added dreamily.

Rosa grinned; she hadn't the faintest idea what Roger was talking about, but it didn't matter – she could have listened to him describing Lancaster bombers till the sun rose.

Seeing her indulgent expression, Roger quickly gathered his thoughts. 'Anyway, that's how I came to meet these amazing women. Ironically, they were building the same bally planes that we fly and regularly blow up!' He gave a rueful laugh, which revealed his strong white teeth and the dimples in his softly tanned cheeks. 'They were up on ladders, as you can see, so tough, so determined. I loved them all, even the older ladies, who ticked me off for being a reckless pilot!'

Roger's eyes locked with Rosa's. 'She's utterly beautiful,' he thought; she had the most wonderful hair, which floated in a mass of silky darkness around her perfect, heart-shaped face; her dark, almond-shaped eyes were alight with excitement; and her full, pouting, pink lips were slightly parted, as if she was holding her breath. Tearing his eyes away from her, Roger asked, 'Where did you find your models, Rosa?'

Tingling at the caressing way in which he said her name, Rosa replied, 'They are my friends – Bomb Girls from the munitions factory where I work.' Winking, she added, 'Secret location. "Loose lips sink ships,"' she said, quoting the Phoenix posters that she saw every day, warning the work force against gossiping to strangers.

'My lips are sealed,' he replied with mock solemnity. Staring at a black-and-white sketch of Maggie and Nora titled 'Cordite Girls', he commented, 'I see you prefer pencil to paint?'

'No,' she answered. 'It was all I had to start with – sometimes I use coloured pencils.'

'I think your work is delightful,' he said with unashamed enthusiasm. 'I love the way you've caught the women totally absorbed in their work.'

'They get used to me being around them,' Rosa giggled. 'Really, after time they don't see me, which is what I want.'

He nodded. 'Know what you mean — always best to catch your models absorbed in their work or truly relaxing at their leisure.' As a hush fell upon the room, Roger gave her a gentle nudge. 'Oh-oh, looks like the judges have come to a decision and there's going to be an announcement,' he whispered.

Rosa's stomach flipped, and this time it wasn't because of Roger Carrington sitting close by her side. She loved her work and was proud of it; she dreaded it being judged by strangers who couldn't possibly know the hardships of bomb building or the stark conditions munitions girls endured in the factory environment.

'It's time to announce the winners, ladies and gentlemen,' the gallery owner called out. 'The judges have chosen their top three artists, so starting at Number Three, I have an envelope here for Squadron Leader Roger Carrington from RAF Norfolk.' Looking genuinely surprised, Roger stepped forward to receive his prize money; then, after shaking the gallery owner firmly by the hand, he quickly returned to Rosa, who by this time had lit up one of her cheroots. 'Want one?' she asked. Roger shook his head as he drew out a packet of Pall Mall.

'Second prize goes to Dorothy Chesterton, who unfortunately can't be here tonight due to work commitments,' the gallery owner announced. 'So, ladies and gentlemen, on to the winner. The first prize goes to a very talented young lady — Rosa Falco.'

As people around her started to applaud and smile in approval, Rosa, weak with shock, involuntarily slumped against Roger, who removed the smoking cheroot from her trembling hands and gave her a pat on the back before helping her to her feet. 'Off you go, old girl,' he urged.

Blushing furiously, Rosa received her prize-winning envelope, which contained fifty pounds. She felt it would be rude and careless just to bow and walk away without saying something; she wanted to thank these good people and the gallery owner who'd displayed her work. 'Thank you, ladies and gentlemen, thank you, sir, for your services here in your gallery,' she started nervously. 'I am an Italian Jew who escaped the Nazis. England and the English welcomed me. The women I paint' – she pointed at the images of her friends looking down on her like guardian angels – 'they are Bomb Girls who work so hard to help win this terrible war; I love them very much, they are my inspiration,' she concluded abruptly, and, with tears stinging her eyes, Rosa returned to her seat, where Roger was waiting for her.

'Well done, that was beautifully put,' he said warmly. 'So what are you going to spend your winnings on – a new hat?' he joked.

Rosa peered in disbelief at the money peeping out of the envelope. 'I will give this to the brave men and women who saved me from the death camp,' she said starkly as she stared up at him with tears filling her eyes.

Without stopping to think if he wasn't behaving just

a little bit inappropriately with a woman whom he'd only just met, Squadron Leader Roger Carrington swept Rosa into his arms and hugged her. Rosa could happily have stayed pressed against his warm chest, but when she saw people dispersing into the night and the gallery owner collecting empty glasses and clearing the overflowing ashtrays, she rather reluctantly left the warmth of his embrace in order to search for her hat and coat.

As they walked down the dark empty streets, Rosa shyly asked, 'Tell me, Mr Carrington, how will you spend the money you win?'

'Probably buy black-market petrol to get me back to Norfolk – that's how I got here in the first place. Paid a chap to fill up my tank, so I could drive up to see my work exhibited,' he laughed.

'I hope the long journey you made was worth it?' she said self-consciously.

'It was worth it, all right,' Roger answered with a broad smile. 'I met you,' he said with unconcealed delight. Stopping by an old Morgan sports car, he added, 'Want a lift?'

Rosa halted uncertainly. 'But . . . you have to drive far tonight?'

Roger shook his head. 'It would be hard driving nearly two hundred miles in the dark without any headlights on,' he told her. 'I'll book into a B & B in town after I've dropped you off. Just point the way, and I promise I won't ask any awkward questions about secret factory locations,' he said with a knowing wink as he opened the rusty old door and helped Rosa into the passenger seat.

As they roared out into the open countryside, which was pitch dark with only a few faint stars to guide them along the narrow moorland roads, Rosa felt breathless with joy. The car was small and cramped, and she had no choice but to sit close to Roger, whose RAF flying jacket smelt of tangy soap and cigarettes. The smell was so enticing she had to stop herself from burying her face in his leather jacket, and when she sneaked a peep at him, intent on driving along the inky roads, she had to stop herself from running a hand through his thick, tawny hair. 'God, what's happening to me?' she thought again. 'I'm a complete mess.'

Forcing herself to think straight, she asked Roger about his work. 'I have a lot of dedicated men under me and a team of superb officers; we fly out on bombing-raids most nights and regularly lose good men and planes in the process. It's tough, but it has to be done.'

Though daunted by the thought of his flying into enemy territory, Rosa asked in as steady a voice as she could muster, 'You love flying very much, I think?'

Accelerating past a herd of sheep which scuttled away into the darkness, Roger answered with a cheer-ful laugh. 'You bet! It's the best thing in the world.'

'Don't you get frightened?'

'Terrified,' he confessed. 'But adrenaline takes over when you see Jerry heading straight for you.'

Imagining the scene too vividly, Rosa quickly changed the subject to something a little more cheer-ful. 'Do you have family?'

'Yes. They live in a big, draughty house full of dogs

near Oxford. How about your family?' he asked. 'Where are they?'

Rosa stared at the rain that was now spattering the car windows. 'I don't know,' she answered flatly.

'Damn!' he exclaimed as he slammed the handbrake on and stopped the car in order to apologize profusely. 'How bloody crass of me. I'm so sorry, forgive me,' he begged.

Rosa shrugged as she replied, 'There is nothing to forgive.'

After she'd told him of how she'd been parted from her family, Roger lit up a Pall Mall for both of them. 'My heart aches for you,' he said with genuine emotion. In an easy silence, they sat smoking and staring at the stars, then Roger reluctantly started up the engine. 'If I leave the old lady for too long she cools down, and then I might finish up pushing her all the way back to your digs,' he joked.

Luckily, the 'old lady' leapt into life and they made it to the cowshed, where Rosa quickly stoked up the wood-burner, whilst Roger admired her unique accommodation. 'This is amazing,' he enthused. 'Snug and cosy, and right on the moors – it must be wonderful in the daylight, when you can see the hills and the wildlife.'

Rosa nodded as she boiled milk for cocoa. 'I love this place – it is a good home for me.'

'Do you have it all to yourself?' he asked.

'I share with my best friend; she is nursing in London for a while.'

When the cocoa was made, they sat side by side on

the old battered sofa with their feet toasting by the crackling wood-burner. 'I never expected anything like this,' Roger chuckled as he cuddled closer to Rosa, who certainly didn't move away from him. They sat talking and smoking for well over an hour; then Roger reluctantly dragged himself to his feet. 'You need to get some shut-eye, or you'll be useless on the bomb line tomorrow,' he joked.

'You too must rest before you drive tomorrow,' she said anxiously, as they stood rather awkwardly in the open doorway. 'Please, be careful, Roger,' she added softly.

'I will, I promise,' he said, as he fastened his leather flying jacket and wound a long, woolly scarf around his neck. Then, to her delight, he leant in to kiss her on both cheeks, where his lips lingered before he forced himself to draw apart from her.

'Goodbye, beautiful Rosa!' he said with a flourishing bow, which made her laugh. 'Promise you will write to a poor pilot stuck in the middle of nowhere?' he implored with a charming smile.

'My English is not so good,' she answered with a blush.

'Rightio, better idea!' he exclaimed. 'We'll send drawings to each other: little postcard drawings of our lives in different parts of England.'

'Yes!' she cried in delight. 'But please, no pictures of you in dangerous places – I will worry,' she said before she could stop.

'I promise I won't worry you,' he said tenderly.

Blowing a kiss over his shoulder, he walked towards his rusty old Morgan, which, after he cranked it up, slowly shuddered into life. 'Goodbye, sweet Rosa!' Roger called as he leapt aboard and released the handbrake.

'Goodbye!' she called back as the car lurched forward and Roger, still waving farewell, disappeared from view.

Rosa waited until the noise of the engine had completely disappeared; then she went back into the cowshed, where she lay on her bed wondering if she'd just dreamt about spending an evening with handsome Squadron Leader Roger Carrington.

22. Mr Snowman

Gladys's return to the Phoenix on a bleak late-autumn evening sparked off a rush of excitement. 'Now that we're back together we should cheer each other up and start making plans for Christmas. Wouldn't it be nice if we could all celebrate Christmas together at Yew Tree Farm?' Kit said excitedly.

'Will you be able to manage, Kit, what with you being pregnant and having a toddler to look after too?' Nora asked solicitously.

'I'll be fine – nearly over the morning sickness,' Kit replied as she affectionately patted her tummy.

'It'll be Stevie's very first Christmas,' said Violet with a dreamy smile. 'My little boy's first Christmas, imagine that.'

Her friends gathered around the canteen table exchanged an indulgent smile; there was no more doting, besotted mother than Violet.

'It'll be nice for us to be together and share the cooking,' Maggie said eagerly. 'Though I haven't heard whether Les will get leave.' Her eyes strayed to Gladys, who had so far not involved herself in the conversation.

'I don't think I can leave mi dad on his own,' Nora fretted. 'Since Mam and our kid died, he gets over-emotional at any kind of celebration.'

'Well, then, bring him too,' Kit exclaimed. 'The more the merrier.'

'Will your husband like so many people in his house?' Rosa enquired.

'My friends are Ian's friends. The offer's there,' Kit continued. 'Though it's probably too early to make plans, a lot could happen before Christmas,' she prophesized in all innocence.

'Yeah, we might win the war!' Nora said drolly.

'Or we could be on night shift all over Christmas,' Maggie groaned.

'Actually,' Kit quickly added, 'there's something else on my mind.'

Her friends turned to stare at her earnest face.

'You're not having twins?' incorrigible Maggie teased.

'Will you be quiet, Maggie Yates, and give the woman a chance to speak?' Violet chided her with a smile.

'It's just,' Kit started, 'we mustn't forget in all the excitement that Christmas will be a special time for Edna too.'

'Forget!' hooted Maggie. 'You must be joking. Every time Malc walks past the cordite line, he gives us the latest countdown to their wedding day. I think the poor fella's nervous,' Maggie added with a cheeky wink. 'You know, their first night.'

'But Malc, he was married before now, yes?' Rosa asked.

Maggie waved her hand dismissively. 'That's as may be,' she said in a low voice. 'But it must be years since he did, well, you know what,' she giggled.

'Oooh, Mags, you are a tinker!' Nora squealed.

As all the girls tittered, Rosa cast a glance in Gladys's direction – what on earth was the matter with her? She'd arrived back from London subdued and with- drawn. At first Rosa had put it down to exhaustion; the journey from London to Pendleton had taken nearly all day, and Gladys told her she'd barely had anything to eat or drink. But, as the days went by and Gladys returned to work at the Phoenix Infirmary, a place where she'd formerly been very happy, and there was still no significant improvement in her spirits, Rosa really began to worry.

One night as she was sleeping she thought she heard Gladys crying softly in the next room; unable to bear the sound of her weeping, Rosa rushed to her friend's bedside. 'Mia cara, Gladeeees, darling,' she murmured softly as she clutched Gladys's hand. 'Talk to me, please,' she implored.

Gladys shook her head. 'Not now, Rosa, not now,' she begged.

'You sick? I get you something?' Rosa fretted.

With her lovely, dark brunette hair fanned out on her pillow, Gladys whispered, 'I'm not ill, just so sad. I'll be fine, I just need time.'

Rosa had no choice but to wait until Gladys was ready to talk to her, but it wasn't easy, especially when the other girls passed comment on Gladys's subdued mood.

'She's not been right since she went to London,' Nora commented.

'Them bloody Southerners!' Maggie joked. Seeing Kit's

247

and Violet's disapproving looks, she quickly moderated her tone. 'It obviously doesn't suit her being away from us, that's all I was trying to say, like,' she quickly added.

'It's not fair,' Kit exclaimed. 'Just as she was getting back to normal after leaving ENSA, then this goes and happens.'

'I wonder what did happen down there in London?' Nora murmured darkly.

'Nowt good from the look of things,' Maggie replied.

'Don't forget how badly Gladys took Myrtle's death,' Violet reminded the group.

'We all did,' choked Nora, who cried every time anybody mentioned Myrtle by name.

'It makes no sense; she was excited about her training,' Rosa reminded everybody. 'She could not wait to get started.'

'She's come back looking terrible,' Nora fretted. 'She's lost weight; she doesn't eat; she's quiet, no chatting and laughing these days.'

'Also I hear poor girl weeping in the night,' Rosa informed the group in a whisper.

'Oh, dear,' murmured Violet. 'Something really is wrong.'

Sweet-natured Nora refused to be despondent. 'She'll buck up now she's back with us,' she said positively.

Rosa smiled at Nora's genuine earnestness. She really was one of the kindest souls on earth; she hoped Nora's optimism was justified, but her instincts told her that the pain Gladys had returned home with would take a long time to go away.

Kit amused her friends by telling them about Billy's exciting days at the day nursery. 'The staff have been making Christmas decorations with the children. I keep telling Billy that Father Christmas isn't coming for a long time, but it makes no difference.' She burst out laughing as she added, 'He says he wants a big red nose, just like Rudolph's!'

'Stevie seems to like Arthur singing carols to him at bedtime,' Violet said, as she lit up another cigarette before the hooter called them all back to work. '"Silent Night" gets him off to sleep in no time,' she added fondly.

A few days later the first spatter of snow fell over the moors, and the children in the Phoenix nursery watched in wonder as it drifted by the window and settled like a white blanket over the garden. With an excited smile on her face, the matron turned to the children. 'Shall we build a snowman?' she whispered.

Billy's face lit up. 'Snowman! YEAHH!' he cried, heading for the door.

Matron, who had a soft spot for the irrepressible little boy with his wide smile and laughing eyes, called out loudly, 'Coats on first, children.'

After struggling into their coats, the giggling children ran outside, where, with Matron's help, they busily rolled snow to make a snowman. Matron popped a woolly bobble hat on the snowman's head. 'Now we need some little stones for his eyes and some twigs for his mouth and nose.' The children scattered across the garden, where Billy kicked a ball that had been left out in the snow. 'Ball!' he gurgled as he ran after it, waving his hands in the air.

'Get the ball,' Matron laughed as she helped the other toddlers roll a snowball.

Billy chased the ball, which rolled away, so he stopped beside a bush and tried to break off some twigs, but when the freezing cold wood wouldn't bend Billy hunkered down to see if there were any twigs down below. Scraping away the snow, he found no twigs but something else instead.

'What have you found, Billy?' Matron asked as she approached the little boy.

'Ball!' he cried in delight as he pointed at a large, dark metal object, half of which was buried in the ground, whilst the upper part stood out starkly against the newly fallen snow.

'Ball!' cried Billy as he started to roll the 'ball' out of its hiding place. 'Play ball?' he asked.

Matron smothered a gasp as she recognized what the 'ball' actually was. 'Not now, darling,' she said, then with lightning speed she picked up Billy and ran across the garden shouting, 'Inside children, inside – right away.'

Once inside the building, Matron instructed her staff in a quiet but very tense voice to get all the children out of the nursery straight away. Seeing fear on their faces, she said with added urgency, 'Evacuate the nursery immediately.'

As babies were wheeled away in their prams and toddlers filed out in an orderly line, Matron grabbed the telephone on her desk and in a trembling voice asked to be put through to Mr Leadbetter, the safety officer. Arthur was in fact sitting at his desk chatting with his wife, who was on her break. They were having a friendly argument about what Stevie would most like for Christmas. 'A teddy bear!' Violet had laughed in delight.

Arthur shook his head as he teased her. 'He's a little lad; he'd prefer a toy car.'

The shrill ring of the phone interrupted their conversation. 'Safety officer, speaking,' Arthur said into the mouthpiece.

His blood ran to ice as he heard the by now almost hysterical matron gasp, 'I think we've found an unexploded bomb in the nursery garden! Please come quickly.'

Arthur's heart skipped a beat as he leapt to his feet. 'Where are the children?'

'I've evacuated the nursery,' Matron answered quickly. 'My staff are with the children. I told them to get as far away from the building as possible,' she added breathlessly.

'I suggest you do the same right away,' Arthur advised as he put down the phone and quickly dialled the fire brigade.

'Arthur,' Violet said when she saw her husband's face drain of colour. 'What is it, what's happened?'

'The matron thinks she's found an unexploded bomb in the nursery garden.'

'Hello, hello,' a male voice on the other end of the phone boomed.

Turning away from Violet, Arthur spoke in curt

professional mode. 'We need all the emergency services at the Phoenix domestic site right away – there's a possible unexploded bomb in the nursery garden.' As he continued to give orders in a clipped urgent voice, he didn't see Violet, directly behind his back, bolt out of the office.

With Arthur's words ringing in her head, Violet ran like a thing possessed out of the factory. She didn't follow the main road to the domestic site, which ironically the children from the nursery, led by the carers, were marching along in the other direction. Instead, she took the shortcut across the despatch yard that most of the working mothers usually took. 'Stevie,' she panted as she ran. 'Stevie – wait for Mummy, sweetheart, Stevie, Mummy's coming, Stevie wait for me!'

Inside the factory, Tommy Dorsey replaced Joe Loss and his orchestra on the radio loudspeaker, which suddenly went dead and was replaced by the shrill sound of a siren going off. 'Isn't that the signal to evacuate the factory?' one of the women called out to Malc.

'It is indeed – everybody out!' he bellowed.

'What's going on?' a nervous woman asked.

'I don't know yet – let's just do as we're told and get out of the building. Come on, ladies,' Malc said in his loudest but calmest voice. 'Let's be having you.'

As the bomb-making machinery cranked to a slow halt and the bombs on the overhead conveyor-belt swayed precariously above them, the munitions workers, casting anxious glances at each other, hurried out of the factory. 'Get yourselves as far away from the site as possible,' Malc urged, as they filed by. Rosa, Nora and Maggie spotted Kit amongst the surging crowd of women.

'Where's Violet?' they called out to Kit.

'I don't know,' Kit called back. 'I didn't see her come back from her break.'

Afraid that they'd hold up the line by turning back to search for Violet, Malc quickly said, 'I'll nip back and have a look for her,' he promised. 'Just as soon as you lot are off the site.'

After following the strict rules of safety protocol, Arthur slammed down the phone and turned around to find his wife had gone. 'Violet?' he called as he left the office and rushed into the corridor, where there was no sign of her. 'Maybe she's gone back to the filling shed?' he thought to himself. But she couldn't have gone there, he realized; the building was being evacuated. Then he remembered the last thing he'd said to her: 'There's an unexploded bomb in the nursery garden.' With piercing terrifying clarity, he knew exactly where his wife would have gone. 'Oh, Christ!' Though his legs felt like they'd turned to water and would give way beneath him, Arthur ran across the despatch yard taking the same shortcut that his wife had used just minutes earlier. 'VIOLET!' he bellowed. 'VIOLET!' His blood ran cold when he recalled that he'd never told his wife that the matron had evacuated the children to safety. Feeling like his lungs would explode, he ran faster than he'd ever run in his life. 'VIOLET!' he yelled as he finally reached the nursery garden, where toys were strewn in the snow.

As a blinding flash went off, Arthur moved like a man in slow motion. 'VIOLET!' he heard himself scream as the bomb exploded and flying debris mushroomed around him.

Matron, with her staff and the children in their charge, heard the explosion too. Safe on the road between the factory and the open moors, the adults exchanged terrified glances. 'Thank God, we got out,' murmured Matron as she crossed herself. The sound of shrieking sirens followed by the sight of police cars, ambulances and the fire services brought a smile of relief to all their faces. The children clapped their hands in excitement and started to make 'Nee-Naw' noises like the police cars.

'Well done, ma'am,' a senior officer said to Matron when he saw them all safe and sound. 'Keep on moving – the further away from here you are the better.'

When the munitions workers heard the ear-shattering explosion, there was a general cry of fear.

'It came from the domestic quarters,' Kit said in terror.

'Are the bloody Germans attacking us again?' Nora panicked.

'Impossible! There've been no planes flying over,' Maggie, who was calmer, pointed out.

'But it did sound like a bomb going off,' Kit said anxiously.

'And we still don't know where the hell Violet's got to,' Nora fretted.

Standing in the freezing cold on the moors with snow falling, the munitions workers were getting impatient.

'What's going on Mr Featherstone?' they called out, as he approached with Malc by his side. Seeing the women's fearful expressions, the manager came straight to the point. 'A bomb has gone off in the Phoenix nursery garden,' he started. A number of women, including Kit, cried out when they heard this. 'Don't worry,' Mr Featherstone called loudly over the commotion. 'Matron got all the children out in good time; they're alive and well,' he assured his workers.

'Where are the poor little buggers?' one desperate mother called out.

'We've had a message from the rescue crew: Matron and her staff are with the children on the edge of the moors, just off the main road to the factory.'

Without waiting for permission to leave, mothers with children in the nursery set off running.

'I'm going to get Billy,' Kit cried. 'If you see Violet before I do, tell her I've gone to get the children,' she called over her shoulder.

Seeing the shivering women standing before him, Mr Featherstone quickly finished, 'I advise you all to go home and get warm; we'll send out word when the factory's safe to return to.'

Rosa suggested that Maggie and Nora should come back to the cowshed with her, but Nora was desperate to see her dad, who would be worrying himself sick about her. Maggie accompanied her friend into town, leaving Rosa to walk home wondering anxiously about Gladys in the Phoenix Infirmary.

The fire and ambulance crew caught up with Arthur, who was gasping for breath after his frantic dash to the nursery; taking in the devastated children's playground where blasted toys were strewn everywhere, and shrubs and trees wrenched from their roots lay burning where they'd fallen in the snow, the fire officer murmured, 'Thank Christ they got the kids out.'

'Check there's nobody on the site,' Arthur warned.

'And go easy,' the fire officer added. 'There might be another bomb.'

As the crews split up to search the premises, Arthur's attention was claimed by a mangled pram, which had been blown sideways and still had a single wheel spinning inexorably round and round. The sound drew him towards the pram, which he recognized as Stevie's; the very pram they'd saved all their money and their coupons for, the one Violet laughingly claimed her son sat in like a royal prince when she wheeled him to nursery every day. Though Arthur knew all the children were safe, his son's name slipped from his lips, 'Stevie?' There was no response, nothing but the creaking of the slow-turning wheel. And then he saw her: she was lying motionless beside the upturned pram, on her side, her arms reaching out, her face covered by her glorious silky blonde hair. 'VIOLET!' Arthur began to wail. 'VIOLET!' he screamed. As he moved towards his wife's body, which was covered in dust and blood, the ambulance team intercepted him.

'Leave this with us, pal,' they said gently, but Arthur fought them off like an animal about to be caged.

'Get off me!' he bellowed as he punched blindly at anybody who touched him. Falling to his knees, he sobbed as he turned to gaze at the prone body on the ground. 'She must have been running to Stevie's pram when the bomb went off,' he gasped, as sobs ripped through his body. 'She was trying to save our son!' Arthur buried his face in his hands. 'It's all my fault,' he cried. 'It's my fault,' he repeated.

As his cries became hysterical, his scream echoed out over the decimated site where his precious wife had lost her life. 'Sweet Jesus Christ – IT'S ALL MY FAULT!'

23. The Worst News

Some hours after the explosion Mr Featherstone called Malc into his office, where he was told about Violet. 'Arthur found her; they say she died searching for their baby,' Mr Featherstone said as he wiped tears away from his eyes.

'Oh, my God!' Malc gasped as he slumped into the nearest chair.

'The rescue workers think that the bomb that killed Violet must have been dropped at the same time as the one that devastated the Phoenix only a few months ago,' Mr Featherstone added.

'It must have just sat where it landed until one of the kiddies found it. Matron said the child who discovered it thought it was a ball and rolled it towards her, which probably activated it once it was disturbed.'

'It's a blooming miracle the child's alive,' Malc exclaimed.

'Matron said it was Kit's little lad, Billy, who found it,' Mr Featherstone told him.

Lost in the horror of it all, Malc could only groan in disbelief. 'Oh, God . . .'

'Arthur's been taken to Manchester Royal.' Seeing Malc's look of terror, he quickly added, 'He's okay – well, no injuries, but he had to be heavily sedated, the shock, you know,' he said limply.

Suddenly galvanized, Malc rose from his chair, 'I'll go and see the poor bugger right away,' he announced.

'They might not let you see him,' Mr Featherstone warned.

Malc turned to him with a face set like concrete. 'Just let them bloody try and stop me!' was all he said before he turned and left the room.

A quarter of an hour later Malc was driving Edna in his old Rover (fuelled by black-market petrol) to Manchester Infirmary. Still in shock, Edna was weeping quietly into her handkerchief. 'The poor kid, so young, so beautiful and happier than I've ever seen her.'

Though Malc felt like weeping too, he was trying hard to focus on what lay ahead. Gripping Edna's trembling hand in his, he said, 'We've got to think of the living, sweetheart. Arthur and Stevie are going to need us more than ever before.'

Edna nodded and stifled her tears, and when her breathing returned to normal she lit up two cigarettes, one of which she handed to Malc. 'You're right: we've got to do our best for Violet's family,' she said with a catch in her voice.

Luckily, visiting time hadn't quite ended, so they were allowed to see Arthur, though the sister did say to them, with a firm glint in her eye, 'Mr Leadbetter is in a state of severe shock; please don't overtire him.' When they arrived at Arthur's bedside, they thought he was asleep, but, hearing their footsteps, his eyes fluttered open. 'Malc! Edna!' he cried, looking utterly wretched. 'Have you seen Stevie?'

'Don't worry, he's fine,' Edna quickly assured the

stricken man, though in truth she hadn't a clue where Stevie was.

'Thank God for that,' Arthur sighed, then his eyes drifted off and for seconds he just stared at the wall opposite his bed. 'She ran off after Stevie when she heard about the bomb,' he murmured as if he was talking to himself. Tears rolled uncontrolled down his cheeks. 'I never told her Stevie was safe with Matron – that's why she went to look for him,' he sobbed. 'If only I'd told her, if only I'd thought,' he wailed in an agony of guilt. 'It's all my fault!'

Seeing her patient in distress, the ward sister hurried over to the visitors, who were frantically trying to soothe Arthur. They were allowed to spend another ten minutes with him, and they reassured him over and over again that it wasn't his fault in the slightest, but a tragic accident.

Eventually Edna reluctantly turned to Malc and said, 'I think we'd better go – the poor man is exhausted.' But she promised tearfully that they'd be back very soon, that they were all here for him, and always would be.

Before they could even say their farewells, the sister quickly whisked the curtains around Arthur's bed; yet his agonized cries followed them out into the corridor. '*I should have told her. It's all my fault.*'

When Gladys and her colleagues saw flames licking the air near the nursery, they had wondered if they should evacuate the infirmary, but the rescue workers – after putting out the fire and thoroughly examining the infirmary – assured them it was safe. In a lather of anxiety, Gladys wondered where her friends were. The shock of the explosion had blown away her former lethargy: all she wanted now was to make sure the people she loved were safe. When her shift finally finished, she leapt on to her old rickety bike and cycled furiously to the cowshed, where she found a white-faced Rosa waiting for her. 'Thank God!' Gladys cried as she rushed to her friend and they clung on to each other for dear life. 'I've been worried sick,' Gladys admitted.

'We were sent home,' Rosa explained as she hugged Gladys tightly.

Agitated and anxious, Gladys began to pace the room. 'What about the others?'

'They fine,' Rosa assured her. 'We left factory together, but not Violet; we don't know where she go.'

'Didn't you check?' Gladys asked sharply.

'Malc stop us from going back to factory,' Rosa explained. 'We think Violet with Arthur.'

Gladys gave a little smile, 'Well, he's the safety officer, so she'll be fine.'

At Yew Tree Farm, Kit was worried sick about Violet. When she'd arrived on the moors where the matron and her staff were guarding their precious little flock, Violet wasn't there as she'd been expecting.

'Where's Stevie mum?' Kit asked Matron, who shook her head.

'She hasn't shown up so far; perhaps you'd be kind enough to take charge of Stevie for the time being.'

'Of course,' said Kit as she took Violet's son in one arm and held on to Billy with her spare hand.

Once home, she and Ian bathed the babies, then between them they fed Billy a boiled egg and soldiers, whilst Stevie ravenously sucked on his bottle of warm milk. 'He must be wondering what's happened to his mama, poor child,' Kit said, as she sat by the Aga with Stevie on her knee. 'Where could she be, Ian?' Kit fretted. 'Do you think we ought to drive over to the domestic site just in case she's there?'

'Darling,' he reasoned, 'the domestic site is right next door to the nursery; they must have been evacuated by now – that's if it's still standing,' he added grimly.

'How will either of them know where Stevie is?' Kit continued to fret.

'Hopefully Arthur or Violet will have heard from one of the girls that you picked up Stevie and they'll come looking for him here,' Ian replied.

Billy waved his bread soldiers in the air and burbled, 'Ball! Play ball!'

'Where did you find a ball, sweetheart?' Ian asked curiously.

'Play ball in snow,' Billy babbled.

Little knowing what a lucky escape Billy had had, both of his parents looked at one another and smiled. 'Well, for all of today's drama, Billy seems to have had a good time,' Ian chuckled.

About an hour later, there was a loud knock on their front door. When Ian opened it, he knew from the grim expressions on Malc's and Edna's faces that something was badly wrong.

'Can we come in?' Malc asked abruptly.

Ian held the door wide open for the couple, who hurried into the kitchen, where Edna exclaimed with relief when she saw Stevie wrapped in a warm shawl in Kit's arms. 'Thank God he's safe with you!'

'Where's Violet?' Kit immediately asked. 'Have you seen or heard from her? We don't know where she is.'

Edna's eyes strayed to Malc. 'We've got bad news,' she said.

Seeing Kit go pale, Edna reached out for the baby in her arms. 'Violet's dead,' she said almost in a whisper.

Seeing his wife sway, Ian grabbed Kit and led her to one of the chairs by the Aga. Edna quickly filled up a glass with tap water, which she handed to Ian, who pressed it to his wife's lips.

'What happened?' he asked.

'She were running to't nursery when the bomb went off,' Malc said in tremulous voice. 'She were trying to find the little lad,' he added as he reached for his handkerchief to wipe away the tears that seeped from the corner of his eyes.

'Holy Mother of God,' Kit gasped. 'Violet, my Vi, dead!' she sobbed. 'I should have gone back inside and looked for her,' Kit cried guiltily. 'Why did you stop me Malc?' she wailed.

'It would have been too late, lovie; she'd have left the factory by then,' Malc told her sadly.

'I can't believe she died like that,' Ian said as he too bit back tears. 'How's Arthur?' he asked.

'We've just left him at the infirmary; he's out of his mind,' Edna replied as she rocked Stevie back and forth. 'They've sedated him, but he just keeps blaming himself, keeps saying if only he'd told her Stevie was safe she'd never have run off on her own.'

Shocked beyond words, Ian slumped into the chair beside his wife's. 'How's the poor fella ever going to get over a tragedy like this?'

'And as for Stevie, God help the poor little mite,' Edna said as she kissed the top of the sleeping baby's head.

'At least he's safe,' Malc added gratefully.

'And that's all Violet ever wanted,' Edna sighed.

After several strong cups of tea, which Ian laced with brandy, Kit put Stevie to bed in the room he'd shared with his mother such a short time ago. When she came back downstairs, she'd made a decision which she shared with the group. 'Stevie's got to know us of late; he should stay here until Arthur's well enough to take him home.'

Ian nodded. 'He'll be lost and confused without either his mother or his father, but we'll do our best till Arthur can manage.'

'Arthur will be relieved to hear that,' Edna said.

'The tragic irony is that Violet died trying to save her baby, who was safe the whole time,' Ian said mournfully.

Malc slowly rose to his feet. 'Come on, lass,' he said as he held out his hand to Edna. 'We've got to go and break the bad news to the other lasses now.'

As Ian showed Malc to the front door, Kit whispered to Edna with tears in her eyes, 'Life will never be the same again. Violet was a ray of joy – the world will be so much poorer without her.'

For the second time that night, Edna and Malc broke the tragic news, this time to Gladys and Rosa, who were utterly pole-axed. As the three women clung to each other and wailed with grief, Malc went outside, where he smoked several cigarettes in rapid succession. The snow had stopped falling and the stars twinkled in an icy-cold sky; a new moon sailed out from behind a tissue of cloud and gently illuminated the moors, from where owls hooted. It had been without doubt one of the worst days of his life. 'And it's still not over,' Malc muttered to himself. They'd yet to tell Maggie and Nora, who would be devastated. They were living through a time of war; loss of life was, whether you liked it or not, commonplace, but this particular loss of life – sweet beautiful Violet who after so many years of hardship had found a man she could love and trust – was particularly hard to take. And then their joy of having Stevie, who Violet loved with such a passion that she had risked her life trying to find him. Malc gave a weary sigh as he stubbed out a cigarette; the impact her passing would have upon the lives of those she'd left behind was immense: Arthur widowed, Stevie motherless, her friends bereft – a light had gone out, never to be replaced.

The Phoenix Factory was soon declared safe for production, and the Bomb Girls returned to their work, albeit with one of their number gone. It was a personal loss to anybody who had encountered lovely, delicate Violet, who everybody mourned. They mourned for her husband, and they grieved for her baby, who would grow up without the love of a mother who all but worshipped him. These were hard sad times, but life had to go on; as one of the women in the despatch shed said, 'The Germans aren't going to stop the war whilst we're grieving.'

After an extensive search for further undetonated bombs, workmen were allowed on the site to start rebuilding the nursery, which was urgently needed by munitions mothers who'd farmed their babies out to friends and relatives. Pregnant Kit had more than enough to do with two babies on her hands, and, given the tragic circumstances, Mr Featherstone gave her extended compassionate leave to look after Stevie until Arthur, who was mentally in an extremely fragile state and still needing hospital treatment, was fit to look after his son himself.

Once the infirmary had released Violet's body for burial, funeral arrangements had to be made, but, though Arthur was consulted, he was in such a state of shock nothing seemed to penetrate his profound grief. Yet again it was left to Malc and Edna to try to support the heart-broken widower, who couldn't stop blaming himself for his wife's death.

'All this blaming business isn't helping at all,' Edna said as she and Malc sat outside Arthur's ward waiting for the bell to ring for visiting time. 'It's getting him nowhere – it's the future he's got to look to now.'

'I don't know,' said Malc with a heartfelt sigh. 'I can't seem to get through to him at all.'

'He'll have to make some decisions about the funeral,' Edna insisted.

'Just do what you think Violet would have wanted,' Arthur told Edna and Malc half an hour later. As he stared hollow-eyed and vacant at them, Edna wondered if he was losing the will to live.

'He's GOT to see Stevie,' she told Malc when they were leaving the hospital. 'Seeing his son might be the only thing that helps him.'

The battle-axe of a sister allowed them to bring the little boy on to the ward, but she warned them that if he started to cry she'd have to ask them to leave. 'He's bound to bloody cry,' Malc seethed. 'That's what babbies do!'

Holding the struggling baby in her arms, Edna whispered, 'The sight of Stevie might bring a bit of life back to him.'

'Let's hope so,' said Malc as they walked towards Arthur, who was sitting in the hospital chair beside his bed. Staring vacantly out of the window, he looked thin and unkempt; he needed a shave and his blond hair was unwashed and untidy. He bore little resemblance to the handsome man that Violet had adored, but Stevie had no trouble recognizing him. Throwing out his arms, he smiled and gurgled at his father, who glanced up and gazed at his son in wonder.

'Stevie?' he said, his voice quivering with emotion.

As the child wriggled to reach his father, Edna quickly handed him over. 'He's missed you so much,' she told Arthur.

'Stevie, Stevie,' Arthur cried, as tears coursed down his thin face. 'I've missed you too.' Kissing his son's pale blond hair, which was exactly the same colour as Violet's, he sobbed as if his heart would break, 'Oh, little man . . . what are we going to do without her?'

Seeing poor Arthur racked with grief and terrified the sister would swoop down and ask them to leave, Malc laid an arm around his friend's shaking shoulders. 'You have to be strong for Stevie now, pal; he needs you more than ever.'

Arthur nodded as he wiped away his tears. 'I know you're right,' he said as he stroked Stevie's soft silky skin. 'Who's been looking after the little lad?'

'We told you,' Edna reminded him gently. 'He's been staying with Kit and Ian at Yew Tree Farm; he loves Billy.'

Arthur looked blank. 'Billy?' he asked as he tried to focus on the world outside the hospital.

'Kit's son,' Edna explained.

Dropping his voice, Arthur anxiously asked, 'Does Stevie cry for Violet?'

Edna wished she could lie but she couldn't. 'Kit says he cries the most at night-time; he needs his daddy,' she added gently but firmly.

Looking down at his son, now yawning widely, Arthur murmured, 'He's so like Violet . . . she died trying to find him,' he added with a catch in his voice. 'She loved him so much.'

Seeing the sister looming, Edna quickly said, 'We've got to go.'

As Arthur reluctantly handed his son back to her, he said beseechingly, 'Please bring him back soon.'

'I will,' Edna replied. 'I promise.'

There was no doubting that Stevie's visits to the infirmary helped Arthur's slow and very painful recovery. The sight and sound of his little boy brought a smile to his lined face and colour to his sunken cheeks. And when the day of the funeral dawned, Arthur carried Stevie down the aisle of the church to the front pew, beside which Violet's coffin stood. As the vicar who had married Violet and Arthur, and baptized their first-born, now said prayers for the dead, then committed Violet's body to a grave in the churchyard, there was not a dry eye in the congregation. It took all of Arthur's strength not to throw himself into the dark grave where his wife lay. The only thing that prevented him from following her was the son she'd left behind. Holding Stevie tightly, Arthur made a promise by the graveside.

'I'll look after our child, my darling. I'll give him all the love you would have given him, and I'll tell him how much you loved him every single day. I'll never forget you, my darling. Rest in peace, my Vi.'

Weak with grief, Arthur turned to Malc, who was standing close by. 'I need to go home,' he murmured as tears coursed down his anguished face. 'It's time we were a family again.'

24. Riding the Storm

The days that followed Violet's heart-breaking funeral were dark, as mid-winter approached and the world seemed drained of light. Dark in mood too: Arthur's desperate need to be with his son urged him to request an immediate discharge from hospital.

'I'm needed at home now,' he told the doctors, who were concerned about his mental stability. Malc, who picked Arthur up, was also concerned about his friend's state of mind.

'Sure you're up to this?' he asked cautiously as he drove Arthur back to the domestic quarters, which, after the bomb blast, had been hastily repaired in order to rehouse the workers.

'I'm not sure about anything these days,' Arthur admitted. 'One thing I do know is Violet won't be at peace until she knows I'm home looking after her boy.'

'I only hope you're not tempting fate by coming home too soon,' Malc fretted.

'It's got to be done,' Arthur retorted. 'I need to get back to work and I need to be with my son,' he added as he blinked tears from his eyes. 'I have to try and get back to normal, Malc. Violet wouldn't want it otherwise.'

'Don't go overdoing it,' Malc advised. 'Edna's prepared

enough food for a fortnight, so you don't need to worry about shopping and cooking, and Kit's drawn up a rota for one of the lasses to take Stevie to nursery and collect him every day until you get yourself organized.'

'Those Bomb Girls,' Arthur murmured. 'Violet always said her friends were angels: now I see exactly what she means. They'd do anything for one another.'

'It's true, they would,' Malc assured him with a proud smile.

As Malc pulled up outside Arthur's home, he couldn't help but see Arthur's face drop: last time he was here, Malc thought as he helped his friend out of the car, Violet, Arthur and Stevie had been a happy little unit with hopes for the future. Wiping the depressing thought from his mind, Malc steered Arthur into the house, which Edna had mopped and polished until it was shining bright; there was a mouth-watering smell of baking coming from the oven.

'Potato pie!' Edna announced as she hugged Arthur. 'Look who we've got to welcome you home!'

Kit had arrived earlier with Stevie, who waved his little podgy hands at his father. Arthur swooped him up into the air. 'WHEEEE!' he cried. 'Dada's home.'

They sat around the crackling fire drinking tea and, though they tried hard to find easy, harmless subjects to talk about, an awkward silence fell, which eventually Arthur filled. 'I keep thinking she'll walk in,' he said with a catch in his voice. 'She was so beautiful; she filled the place with laughter.' His eyes drifted to the photographs on the mantelpiece: Violet on her wedding day, radiant with flowers in her hair, and another of Violet just after Stevie was born, smiling ecstatically with her new baby in her arms.

'It'll take time, lovie,' Edna said softly.

'We'll do everything we can to help,' Kit promised.

Arthur buried his face in Stevie's curls. 'We'll have to be brave soldiers,' he said to the little boy on his lap. 'We mustn't let Mama down.'

Though she'd thought of Roger Carrington more than once since his departure, Rosa had certainly not had time with all the traumatic events taking place even to think of sending him a postcard drawing, so when she received one from him she was delighted.

Gladys, who was polishing her work shoes, looked up when she heard Rosa gasp after opening a brown envelope.

'It's from a friend,' Rosa replied as a tell-tale blush bloomed on her cheeks.

'A man?' Gladys asked with a teasing smile.

Rosa nodded. 'I met him at the art gallery in Salford – look,' she said proudly, as she showed Gladys a beautiful little postcard drawing from Roger.

'It's amazing,' Gladys said as she admired the small but perfectly accurate black-and-white sketch of a fighter plane, underneath which he'd written in tiny writing: 'My delight, my Spitfire. Rog x'.

'Have you sent him a drawing?' Gladys asked.

'No!' shocked Rosa exclaimed. 'Drawing pictures has not been my priority in these sad days.'

'Well, you should think about it now,' Gladys said as she put on her polished shoes and fastened the laces. 'He obviously likes you, if he's gone to all that trouble for you,' she said as she nodded at Roger's picture.

'I like him,' Rosa admitted with a small smile. 'He talks so much and laughs so loudly. He got third prize in the painting competition,' she said, recalling the happy evening they had spent together.

'And you got first prize!' Gladys exclaimed. 'Violet told me.' There was a sudden catch in her voice as she remembered one of the last conversations she'd had with Violet. 'She told me you'd won fifty pounds . . .' Her voice trailed away as she kept her head down, apparently concentrating hard on lacing her shoes, but Rosa knew Gladys was hiding her tears.

'Violet was so excited when I won,' Rosa said with a sad sigh. 'She said I should buy lots of new clothes.'

Gladys stood up and reached for her coat. 'Typical Violet: she was always the first to wear the latest fashions. Will you treat yourself?' she asked as she did up her coat buttons.

Rosa shook her head. 'I've sent the money to my relatives in Manchester,' she replied. 'I want them to help others like me,' she explained.

'Good for you, Rosa,' Gladys said as she headed for the door. 'I still think you should make time to do a quick sketch for that fella of yours, even if it's just the rusty old wood-burner,' she joked. 'See you later, sweetheart,' she called over her shoulder.

Rosa watched Gladys through the window as she

tried to cycle to work in the teeth of a bitter north-easterly wind that was blasting the moors. Since Violet's traumatic death, Gladys had been less withdrawn, but Rosa longed to know what had happened in London that had made her so sad on her return. Sighing, she turned back into the room, where the first thing she saw was the crackling wood-burner. Smiling to herself, she grabbed a slip of writing paper and a pencil, then she quickly started to sketch; if she was lucky, she'd just have time to post her drawing to Roger before she clocked on for work.

A few days later, Kit finally got to talk to her friends about something that had been troubling her since the explosion. 'Please don't take this the wrong way,' she started as they all gathered around their favourite table in the canteen for a short tea break. 'Now may not be the right time to talk about it, what with all the sadness around us, but nevertheless I'm going to say it.' Taking a breath, she added, 'I'm really worried about Edna not getting the sort of wedding she deserves.'

The girls looked across the table at one another; if truth be told, since Violet's death, Edna's wedding had not been at the forefront of their minds, which made them all feel a little guilty.

'She's booked the church for the service,' Maggie said quickly to cover her unease.

'And she told me that the Black Bull in town are doing the reception,' Nora added.

'I know,' Kit agreed. 'But she's not bought a wedding

outfit, plus we've not agreed on the music and the hymns, which we would have done in the past – and, worse still, she doesn't even talk about it,' Kit pointed out. 'We've not done anything with her like she encouraged me and Violet to do on our wedding days.'

'I suppose she's just not got the heart for it,' Gladys said sadly.

'That's exactly why we should push her into thinking of herself,' Kit urged. 'Knowing Edna, she'll be assuming it's not appropriate to make a fuss at this time of mourning.'

Rosa smiled compassionately. 'Edna, she always puts others before herself.'

'Nevertheless, Kit's right,' Gladys said. 'We're Edna's friends; we should be encouraging her to plan her big day. She's waited long enough for it to come round.'

'We could talk to her tonight when she's parked up in the despatch yard,' Nora said, now eager to make up for lost time.

'We'll get her talking about the wedding, then we'll see how she's feeling,' Maggie added with a cunning wink.

'I'm sorry, I can't come,' Kit said apologetically. 'I'll be at home with Billy.'

'Don't worry, we can talk to Edna,' Gladys assured her.

'Whatever happens,' Kit said in a resonating loud voice, 'don't take *no* for an answer!'

Edna, always the one for a laugh and a chat, looked distinctly down in the mouth when her friends turned up after they'd clocked off from their shift.

'Try and be subtle, our kid,' Maggie whispered to Nora, who'd been fretting about Edna all day. 'Let her do the talking.'

Her words were wasted on impetuous Nora, who immediately blabbed, 'We've been thinking about your wedding, Edna!'

Looking like she didn't want to engage in the conversation, Edna agitatedly wiped down her little counter and rearranged the salt and vinegar bottles several times. 'I haven't had a minute,' she said quickly. 'What with Arthur coming home, and now I hear little Stevie's got a tummy bug – it never seems to end.'

Rosa gently caught hold of her hand. 'Come, mia cara, let's smoke a cigarette,' she suggested.

Edna rather reluctantly stepped out of her mobile chip shop and joined the smokers in the despatch yard. 'I won't have one of your smelly fags,' she said to Rosa with her old cheek. 'I'll stick with mi Woodies.'

As the mood lightened a little, Gladys said, 'I bet you've not had time to sort out an outfit for the wedding?'

Edna rolled her eyes. 'I thought I'd wear mi best suit; Malc ses he doesn't mind.'

'But wouldn't it be nice to surprise him?' Maggie suggested with a glint in her eyes.

Spurred on, Nora added, 'Imagine you in a bonny frock and a hat – and nice shoes; Malc would be dead proud.'

'So would I!' Edna exclaimed. 'But there isn't time. Anyway, it doesn't matter,' she said as she stubbed out her cigarette. 'Worse things happen at sea.'

Before she could dash back inside the van, Gladys said, 'Kit and I could come into town with you the day after tomorrow, when we change our shift rotas.' Seeing Edna hesitate, Gladys ploughed on. 'Come on, it'll be a laugh – we can get our dinner at Lyons, make a day of it,' she said persuasively.

'I'll have to see if Arthur can spare me,' Edna said guiltily. 'I promised I'd make tea for him on Saturday.'

'Don't be daft!' Maggie laughed. 'I can do that. I know my cooking's not up to yours but I can make a cracking mince-and-onion pie. I've saved up a few weeks' rations for him, and I'd be glad to help.'

'So that's that, then,' Gladys concluded. 'We'll get the bus as soon as Kit and I have finished work, okay?'

Edna flushed with a sudden unexpected sense of excitement. 'If you say so,' she said gratefully.

The girls' trip into Manchester was a tonic; all of them had known Violet well and just being able to talk about her openly and naturally seemed briefly to bring her back.

'I remember when she lent me her coat,' Kit recalled fondly. 'It was on our first walk down to the Phoenix and it was pouring down. I'd got an old rag of a coat and Violet, who owned two smart coats, without any fuss or bother draped one of them over my shoulders. When I protested she just laughed and said, 'Come on, Kit, I can't wear two coats at once!'

One of Gladys's most treasured memories was of the night Violet showed them her silver clarinet. 'She told us her mother had taught her to play as a little girl; she played a tune for us, maybe it was "Greensleeves", I don't exactly recall, but she played with such sadness and longing it brought tears to our eyes,' Gladys confessed.

'I best remember her walking out of Arthur's allotment garden last summer: she was carrying a huge bouquet of larkspur, delphiniums and lilies, and she looked like a bride, even though she was still wearing her Bomb Girl uniform,' Edna reminisced with a sigh. 'She was so very beautiful.'

After they'd got off the bus and found a nice table in a Lyons Corner House, Edna wagged her finger at her friends, who were enjoying cheese flan and mashed potatoes. 'Now remember, Violet had the best fashion sense of the lot of us; when she got dressed up she looked like a model,' she said with a fond smile. 'For her sake we must keep up her high standards and not let the side down.'

All three women gazed at each other for several seconds. 'It's good to talk about her – it feels like she's keeping an eye on us,' Kit said with an emotional catch in her voice.

Edna winked. 'If we're clothes shopping, I suspect Violet will be watching our every move!'

So with Violet's high standards in mind, the three friends entered the big Co-operative store in Piccadilly. 'Let's start with your dress first,' Gladys suggested.

Edna nodded as she replied with a happy smile, 'You know what, I'm beginning to enjoy myself.'

In the ladies' wear department the three women

'Ooohed' and 'Ahhed' over lace, silk and satin tea dresses.

'Don't forget about "Fashion on the Ration"!' Edna reminded them as she checked the prices on the sales tags.

Kit and Gladys, who had previously made a plan, exchanged conspiratorial winks.

'Don't let "Fashion on the Ration" ruin your big day, sweetheart,' Kit said as she looked down at her tummy and smiled. 'I won't be using my clothing coupons so you can add them to yours.'

'You can have mine too,' Gladys added. 'I bought loads of stuff in London before I joined ENSA.'

Before Edna could open her mouth to protest, both of her friends laughed as they gently nudged her.

'Go on, splash out!' Kit urged.

'Spoil yourself for a change,' Gladys laughed.

Getting more and more excited as they walked along racks of coats and smart suits, Edna finally decided she was going to try on a vivid royal-blue wool coat with big deep pockets and a red velvet hat with a brim that set off her grey-and-red hair. When she walked out of the changing room, Kit and Gladys gasped in delight. 'You look like a film star!' they exclaimed.

'I feel like a film star,' Edna said as she stood in front of the full-length mirror to examine her reflection. 'You don't think the hat's too much?' she asked as she anxiously scrutinized the grey hair growing at her temples.

'No!' Gladys cried. 'The hat is gorgeous, glamorous and very festive too.'

'A perfect hat for a Christmas wedding,' Kit agreed.

Edna turned slowly so she could check the back view of the coat. 'Do you think my bottom looks a bit too big in this coat?' she fretted.

'Don't be daft!' Kit laughed. 'It's a perfect fit, and it'll keep you warm.' She started to giggle as she added, 'If it snows, you'll need a pair of wellies!'

Edna grimaced. 'I am not wearing wellies on my wedding day, but I do fancy a pair of them posh tie-up brogues with little heels.'

'OOH!' Gladys teased. 'There's no holding you back now, Edna!'

By the end of the afternoon, Edna had everything she wanted. The black leather heeled brogues she finally chose were high enough to give her a bit of height and a swing to her walk, which offset the fine woollen coat.

'Thank you so much,' she said as they returned to the Lyons Corner House they'd started off in for a pot of tea and a toasted tea-cake. 'I'd never have chosen so well without you girls helping me – and donating all your clothing coupons too.' Taking a deep drink of tea from her cup, Edna asked, 'So, what will you two be wearing on my wedding day?'

'Seeing as I have the important job of giving you away, I'm going to wear my honeymoon suit,' Kit started. 'You know, the smart black barathea with the short skirt?' she reminded her friends, who nodded in approval. 'It still fits, just,' Kit quickly added. 'I'm going to brighten it up with a spray of flowers.'

Edna turned to Gladys. 'What about you, Glad?'

'I'll wear one of my best silk tea dresses underneath my mother's fur coat and, like Kit, I'll try and get a spray of flowers from somewhere, even if they're artificial,' Gladys replied.

'Flowers might well be a problem in mid-winter,' Edna said as she winked at her friends. 'Malc said he's going to get me a bouquet, though where he thinks he'll find roses in December don't ask me!'

'Knowing Malc, he'll move heaven and earth to keep his promise,' Kit said with a knowing smile.

By the time they'd got off the bus in Pendleton, Edna had agreed on the hymns and the music that Kit and Gladys had suggested on the way home: 'Here Comes the Bride', 'Jerusalem' and 'Alexander's Ragtime Band'.

'Well, thanks to you two lasses I'm sorted,' Edna said gratefully. 'All I've got to do is show up, looking like a radiant bride' she joked.

'You'll knock Malc's socks off in your new outfit,' Gladys promised.

'Now you can look forward to your wedding day without any worries,' Kit added.

'Apart from mi husband getting arrested for trying to buy a dozen red roses on the black market, I've nothing at all to worry about!' Edna chuckled.

Before Edna kissed her friends goodbye, she said quietly, 'And we'll try to make it as good a day as possible for Arthur and young Stevie; it's bound to bring back a load of memories for poor Arthur.'

Kit sighed. 'So many bad things have happened to him here he must feel cursed.'

Edna dropped her voice. 'He said to me and Malc the other night that Pendleton's not the right place for him any more.'

Kit and Gladys gasped. 'Do you think he might leave us?'

Edna shrugged. 'Who knows, lovie? He's got a lot of love here, but every one of you Bomb Girls must remind him of the woman he's lost. We'll just have to wait and see, and support him in whatever he decides to do.'

After waving farewell to Gladys and Edna, who happily walked the short distance home with her shopping bags, Kit waited in the town square for Ian to pick her up in his car. When he drove up with Billy in the back seat, Kit could see from the expression on her husband's face that something had happened. Suddenly anxious, she said, 'What is it, Ian? What's wrong?'

It was only after she'd climbed into the front seat and Ian had pulled into the traffic that he answered.

'There's an ad in the *Manchester Evening News* – in the personal column.'

25. A Wild Goose Chase?

Kit must have read, then reread, the advert Ian had cut out from the *Manchester Guardian* over a dozen times.

> I am trying to contact a Mrs Chadderton, aged around 43 years, living in the Clitheroe/Pendleton area of Lancashire. If you know of her, or of any of her family, please get in touch. Thank you. Replies to Box 515, c/o *Manchester Evening News*.

'It's got to be her, Ian!' she exclaimed as she brewed tea, then lit up a Woodbine.

'Ye-ess,' he said cautiously. 'But it could be a debt-collector or a blackmailer,' he pointed out. 'We don't want to raise Edna's hopes, then put her in touch with a crook.'

'No!' cried Kit. 'That would be awful, but, then again, we can't let this opportunity slip by, can we?'

As Billy tugged at Ian's hand and called 'Dada! Dada!', Ian bent to lift the giggling little boy into his arms. 'No, I don't think we can pass it by, but it's our duty to protect Edna; we should be the first to question the advertiser, and only if we think she really might be Edna's daughter can we introduce them.'

Kit nodded in complete agreement with her clever, cautious husband. 'So please, darling, can you send a note to the box number before you leave for the Phoenix tomorrow?' Ian asked as he headed upstairs to put sleepy Billy to bed.

The following morning Kit found it difficult to pen a delicate reply with Billy careering around, so she waited until he was quietly playing with his building bricks before she settled down to write.

To whom it may concern,

I know of a Mrs Chadderton in the Pendleton area; she is alive and of the age you mention. Before I impart further information, I should like to meet you in person at your earliest convenience. Please reply through the personal column in the Manchester Evening News.

Signing her name, she addressed the note to Box 515 at the *Manchester Evening News*. After posting the reply on her way to work Kit felt quite tense; she would have given anything to talk to Violet, to open her heart to her friend, who was always sensitive and compassionate about other people's problems. But that was impossible. Kit would never be able to share a secret with her beloved friend again, and the knowledge of that left Kit feeling lonely and bereft. She could talk to Gladys, who'd known Kit almost as long as Violet had, but their working hours never coincided these days, and Kit couldn't go knocking on the infirmary door, asking for ten minutes alone with Nurse Johnson. Feeling sad, Kit entered the filling shed, where she and Violet had worked side by side for so long, laughing and joking, singing along to the radio, moaning about how tired they were, yawning through the long night shifts, both of them longing to get home to cuddle their babies. She was roused from her reverie when she saw Arthur walking along the line of benches. 'Arthur!' she cried. 'How are you?'

'I already feel better for being back in here,' he admitted as his eyes gazed wistfully at the bench where his wife used to sit.

Kit, who instinctively knew what he was thinking, smiled sympathetically. Fortunately, one of the older women spotted Arthur and called out, 'Oi! Have you come to bother us, buggerlugs?'

Arthur grinned as he made his way over to the cheeky woman, whose determinedly upbeat manner brought a smile to his face. 'I thought I'd better keep an eye on you lot,' he joked back.

As Kit watched Arthur, she marvelled at him; he was a tough man, all right, facing the workforce who were grieving for Violet too. Maybe his return would help both him and the workers. Kit sincerely hoped so.

Ian and Kit didn't have long to wait for a reply from Box 515. A few days later, there was a response to their ad in the personal column of the *Manchester Evening News*.

'Am available to meet,' Kit read in suppressed excitement. 'Suggest Manchester Town Hall, this coming Friday, at five o'clock.'

Kit handed Ian the paper. 'If I left Billy at the nursery after work, I could hop on a bus and meet you in Manchester,' Kit said quickly.

'Isn't it a bit of a rush for you, sweetheart?'

'I don't mind – the sooner we can see the mystery advertiser, the better,' she said with a nervous smile.

'Okay,' he answered, then, knowing his wife as well as he did, he added, 'Don't go getting your hopes up, missy.'

'I'll try not to,' she promised.

With the arrangements made, Kit began to feel weak and shaky; this was what she had wanted, but the thought of going through with such an extraordinary meeting made her feel quite sick. What questions could she actually ask the stranger? She racked her brains trying to recall all the details Edna had told her about parting with her daughter.

'I had a baby too,' Edna had confessed, almost a year ago now, she recalled. 'A daughter, a beautiful little girl. I called her Flora. At six weeks she was taken from me, adopted by a rich childless couple in Penrith. I tried to find her again, but there was no Flora Chadderton on any adoption records. The father was a local lad, Edward Pilkington; we'd been courting since our school days. We only did it the once, just before he went off to the war, the First War, that is. Eddie never knew he had a daughter; he died at Passchendaele, blown up in a German rocket attack.'

'Oh, my God!' thought Kit. 'If I get this wrong, Edna will never forgive me.'

By Friday lunchtime, Kit was a nervous wreck. 'What's up?' Maggie asked when Kit pushed away her mushy peas and corned-beef hash dinner.

'I just can't stomach it,' Kit groaned.

286

'You've got to keep your strength up now you're eating for two,' said Nora, who always ate like a horse.

'I'll be all right – I'll get a slice of bread and marg,' Kit assured her as she slipped from the table and nipped into the ladies' toilets. 'Oh, if only I could clock off now and get the whole business over and done with,' she thought to herself as she washed her hot face in cold water.

The sight of Ian, tall and handsome in his warm tweed overcoat, standing outside his office waiting for her, instantly calmed Kit down. 'Let's pray this isn't a wild goose chase,' he said as he drew her arm through his and pulled her close to keep her warm.

As they crossed Albert Square, Kit was struck by a sudden thought. 'How will we know who we're looking for?' she cried.

Ian smiled. 'Somebody will be looking for us, so hopefully we'll catch sight of each other.'

Kit groaned. 'Oh, I hope so. I can't go through this again – my stomach's in knots.'

Ian patted Kit's hand as they walked towards Manchester Town Hall's impressive Victorian entrance, but as they did so it started to rain.

'Oh, no!' Kit cried as the rain obscured her vision.

Sheltered from the rain, they stood in the entrance, peering from left to right and back again. Feeling rather silly, Kit muttered, 'We must look like owls!'

'Shssh!' Ian warned as a tall woman approached them.

Gripping her handbag, the woman said nervously,

'I'm the person who requested information in the *Manchester Evening News*, Box 515.'

Ian nodded. 'We responded to your ad,' he said quietly. 'You're seeking information about a Mrs Chadderton?'

Before the woman could reply, a man running out of the rain pushed past them. 'Perhaps we should find somewhere quieter?' Ian suggested.

The woman pointed to a pub on the corner. 'Would that be convenient?'

After they'd found a quiet table in a corner and Ian had bought the ladies sherry and himself a half pint of bitter, they all sat staring awkwardly at each other. Kit tried her best not to stare at the nervous woman, whose hand visibly trembled as she reached for her sherry glass. There was no doubting she had the same red curly hair as Edna, but now they were in the pub Kit could see she also had her mother's green eyes. Feeling sudden pressure on her arm, she realized that Ian was trying to draw her attention.

'If you can start by telling us what you know,' Ian suggested. 'I'm a solicitor,' he added. 'I'll take notes, if you don't mind?'

The woman nodded and then started. 'I'm Flora Forester, Forester's my married name,' she quickly added. 'My maiden name, my adoptive parents' name, is Hardman. I grew up in Penrith and only recently found out, after the death of my mother, that I'd been adopted as a baby.'

'May I ask how old you are, Mrs Forester?' Ian politely asked.

'I'm twenty-seven years old. I was born in 1916,' she replied. Kit caught her breath – she was exactly the right age.

'I have my birth certificate here,' Mrs Forester added, and she handed it to Ian and Kit, who read it carefully; Kit's eyes widened and her pulse started to race. 'Oh, my God!' she thought. 'It's all here!'

Edna's name; the father's name, Edward Pilkington; name of child, Flora; and her date of birth – all signed and sealed by the county registrar. Holding her breath, she waited for Ian to take the lead.

'I'll have to make further checks,' Ian said smoothly. 'May I keep your birth certificate in order to do so?'

'Yes, yes, of course,' Flora replied. 'But when can I see my mother?' she implored.

'If everything is in order, you should be able to make contact soon,' Ian replied.

Feeling Kit fidgeting beside him, Ian, under the cover of the table, pressed her knee to stop her from speaking. 'Here's my card,' he said to Flora. 'Ring me at my office in two days' time.'

Looking slightly deflated, Flora rose. 'Two days isn't long in a lifetime,' she said, then after saying goodbye she left the pub.

'I was terrified you were going to start telling her all about Edna,' Ian said to Kit, who looked like she was going to burst with excitement.

'I felt like it when I saw the birth certificate; she even looks like Edna!' Kit cried.

'I thought so too,' Ian agreed.

'But you're sticking to the rule book?' Kit said.

'Yes,' Ian responded in a firm voice. 'I have to check that the birth certificate is one hundred per cent legitimate. I have to be absolutely certain that Flora Forester is Edna's daughter before I even think of arranging a meeting.'

'I know, you're right,' Kit agreed. 'But, oh!' she cried as a shiver of excitement went down her spine. 'I just can't wait to see the two of them reunited.'

After conducting his checks at Somerset House, Ian was quite satisfied that Flora's birth certificate was in order, so when she phoned two days later they arranged a time and a date when Flora could come to his office to finally meet her mother.

26. Night School

Gladys was happy to be back in the Phoenix Infirmary, where, after her intensive training at St Thomas', she felt so much more confident and assured.

'Well, you seem to have learnt a lot down South,' Sister Atkins said, as she watched Gladys deftly remove a line of stitches from a patient's arm, then, after sterilizing the wound, neatly change the dressing – all the time chatting easily to the nervous patient, who visibly relaxed under her care.

'It was non-stop down there,' Gladys told her. 'What with the air-raids most nights and the shifts never ending, I barely got any sleep. But,' she added with a bright smile, 'my goodness, I learnt *so* much.'

'I knew you would benefit from the experience of working in a big, busy teaching hospital,' Sister Atkins replied. 'It's good to have you back, Nurse Johnson.' As Gladys hurried off to the sluice room, Sister Atkins noted a new maturity in her trainee. 'She'll go far if she carries on like this,' she thought to herself.

Dr Grant had recommended that Gladys should attend some lectures at Manchester Royal Infirmary. 'They're by a number of visiting doctors and surgeons who've been asked to deliver lectures to trainee nurses. I know you have to attend in your own time, but I think you would benefit from them, and it will build on your St Thomas' experience.'

'My St Thomas' experience,' Gladys thought ruefully to herself. 'Little do you know, dear Dr Grant, that it consisted of a lot more than nursing wounded troops fresh from the front line.'

Gladys was keen to learn more, and after the long gruelling hours in a London hospital an extra couple of hours at the end of her shift at the Phoenix wasn't so bad. After she'd read through the leaflet that Dr Grant gave her, Gladys decided she'd try to attend a couple of lectures that were on post-surgical procedures, something she was considering pursuing once she'd got her basic qualification. Violet's death had had an immense impact on all her friends; the far-reaching effect on Gladys was a determination to care and nurse the victims of war to the very best of her ability. She had lost two beloved friends in a very short space of time; her personal memorial to them would be dedication to her new vocation.

After finishing her shift, Gladys changed out of her uniform – the nursing staff were strictly forbidden to wear their uniforms outside the hospital for fear of cross-infection – and set off for the bus stop next to the Phoenix's main gates. As she stood in the dark waiting for the bus, she jumped in shock as she felt a tap on her shoulder.

'Where've you been all my life?' a familiar smoker's voice whispered behind her.

'Malc!' Gladys exclaimed.

'We all miss you on the cordite line, Glad,' he said. 'How's nursing suiting you?'

'I LOVE it!' Gladys replied. 'In fact, I'm on my way to a lecture at Manchester Royal right now,' she told him.

'Do they give lectures on building bigger bombs to drop on Jerry?' he joked. 'Cos if they do, I'll send my cheeky Bomb Girls along with you for a bit of further education.'

'I don't think they need any teaching, Malc,' she laughed. 'Anyway, tell me, how are your wedding plans going?' Gladys asked.

'All going smoothly since you lasses took my Edna into town to get herself dolled up,' he replied with a grateful smile.

'Not long now,' Gladys retorted.

'Don't talk about it,' he groaned. 'I've still not tracked down a bouquet for Edna; bloody roses at this time of the year in these parts, even courtesy of the black market, are as rare as soddin' hen's teeth!'

'I'm sure you'll manage somehow, Malc, you *always* do!'

An hour later, Gladys arrived at Manchester Royal, where she followed the porter to a small lecture theatre. 'In there, Miss,' he said.

Gladys enjoyed the lecture, which concentrated on monitoring vital health signs and managing acute pain post-operatively. Because of her recent nursing experience at St Thomas', she was aware of some practices, but it was invaluable to learn of more. As she left, Gladys checked the title of another lecture scheduled for the end of the week; when she saw it was on post-op complications, she made up her mind to attend it. 'The more I can build up my knowledge, the better a nurse I'll be,' she thought to herself as she left the hospital.

Arriving home late, she found a yawning Rosa filling a heavy stone hot-water bottle.

'You are late,' said Rosa as she topped up the kettle. which she popped on top of the wood-burning stove.

Rosa gazed fondly at her tired but excited friend after Gladys had explained where she'd spent her evening. 'You love nursing so very much, mia cara,' she remarked.

'I *really* do,' Gladys assured her. 'I was telling Malc earlier how much I enjoyed it. I'm glad Dr Grant packed me off to London; it really was a good experience – well, most of the time,' she admitted to Rose for the first time.

'Oh . . . ?' Rosa asked, unsure how far to probe.

'I met up with a doctor . . . who I knew from Naples,' Gladys volunteered.

Rosa's eyes widened in horror. 'Dio! Not that *bad bastard*?' she said, using the words she'd picked up on the factory floor and pronouncing them with a strong Northern accent, which was so out of keeping with her exotic Mediterranean looks.

Gladys shook her head. 'No! Not him, thank God!' she exclaimed as she gratefully accepted the mug of cocoa Rosa handed to her. 'Someone *else*, ' she said, emphasizing the word for Rosa's benefit. 'I liked him very much, but we parted on bad terms. I was shocked sideways to see him at St Thomas',' she told Rosa.

'More than shocked,' Rosa thought to herself as she recalled how often she'd heard Gladys crying herself to sleep most nights after her return home.

'We kept arranging to see each other, but it never worked out,' Gladys said with a shrug. 'Then I found out he already had a girlfriend anyway, so I stood him up.'

Rosa sighed. 'Forget doctors,' she cried. 'They bring you bad luck, my Gladeeees.'

'Cheers to that!' Gladys laughed as she waved her mug of cocoa in the air. 'Leave him to his London girlfriend!'

Though she was dog-tired by the end of the week, Gladys was still keen to attend the next lecture at Manchester Royal. This time she didn't need directions but went straight along to the lecture theatre, where she stopped dead in her tracks. A piece of paper pinned to the door told her she'd come to the right place – POST-SURGICAL COMPLICATIONS – but her heart almost rose up into her throat when she saw who was delivering the lecture: DR R. LLOYD.

'What's HE doing here?' Gladys thought angrily, and then the next question that raced through her mind was: should she stay or should she go?

Hurrying into the ladies' toilets, Gladys locked herself in a cubicle, where she frantically tried to collect her thoughts. Was she really going to spend the rest of her life running away from Reggie Lloyd or was she going to behave professionally? He was a doctor; she was a trainee nurse; it looked like their paths might occasionally overlap – they certainly had so far, she thought grimly. He was delivering a lecture on a subject that she was interested in and also planned to specialize in; she could sit there and take notes or she could run off back to Pendleton. Throwing back her shoulders, Gladys decided to stay; even if the wretched man showed up with his glamorous girlfriend, she hadn't come all this way on a dark night after a long shift only to go all the way home again. She was Nurse Johnson – and she was damn well staying for Dr Lloyd's lecture, girlfriend breathing over his shoulder or not! Taking a deep breath, she left the ladies' and entered the lecture room, which was half full of chattering nurses. Hurrying to a seat at the back, Gladys sat down, took out her pencil and note pad and waited for the lecture to begin.

Five minutes later, tall, handsome Dr Lloyd appeared in a white coat carrying a sheaf of notes, which he carefully placed on the dais in front of him. He was tired, having spent a long day on the wards with his trainee surgeons, who he'd travelled up from London to supervise. He'd been asked by the senior registrar if he would kindly deliver a lecture before he took the train back to London, and Reggie, though exhausted, had agreed. It was tough on trainee nurses these days; after being thrown in at the deep end, they hardly had any opportunity to attend lectures or do anything other than practical work. It was the least he could do. He had half wondered if he would bump into Gladys Johnson whilst he was in Manchester – she was a trainee nurse after all, with an irritating habit of always running away without any explanation, he'd reminded himself.

When he spotted her at the back of the lecture hall, he wasn't as stunned as he had been when he'd seen her in the operating theatre at St Thomas'. Unfortunately, nobody, not even he, who'd been let down by her too many times, could fail to miss that mass of wonderful long, rich, brunette hair. Turning his attention to his notes, Dr Lloyd began his lecture, whilst Gladys, pencil poised, drank in every detail of his face: his sweeping, dark hair with the tantalizing mop that always landed on his eyebrows, causing him to flick it impatiently away, only for it to slide back down again. As he continued in a low, soft voice, Gladys started to take notes – after all, that's what she was there for, she told herself. As before, she found that she was excited and stimulated by the content of the lecture; it made her long to be back working in post-operative wards.

At the end of the lecture the trainee nurses gathered up their belongings and filed out of the theatre; as Gladys passed Reggie, who was still at the dais collecting together his notes, he called out to her in a cheery doctor's voice, 'Goodnight Nurse Johnson.'

Blushing to the roots of her hair, Gladys nevertheless managed to summon up her cheery nurse's voice: 'Goodnight, Doctor.'

Reggie couldn't resist watching the sway of her shapely hips as she left the room along with the other nurses, and before he could stop himself, because he knew he really should know better, he grabbed his notes and hurried after Gladys, who was all but running out of the hospital.

'Gladys!' he called before she disappeared out of the door. 'Stop!'

Reluctantly she stopped and turned. 'WHY does he insist on chasing after me?' she thought furiously.

Seeing the resentment in her startling blue eyes, Reggie hesitated. 'I just thought we might have that drink you promised me?' he said challengingly. 'Seeing as you missed the last one,' he couldn't stop himself from adding rather pointedly.

Gladys gave an overdramatic sweeping glance around the hospital entrance hall. 'Would that be with your girlfriend, or have you left her at St Thomas'?'

Reggie's mouth fell open as the penny dropped. So was that why she'd stood him up on her last night in London?

'Actually, I haven't got a girlfriend any more,' he answered.

'You had the last time I saw you,' she added sharply.

'Nooooo,' he replied slowly. 'I called it off just after I met you.'

Gladys's jaw dropped; was he telling the truth?

'Just out of curiosity, is that why you stood me up, Gladys? Because you thought I was two-timing you?' he asked, looking her straight in the eye.

Caught on the back foot, Gladys blushed to the roots of her glossy brown hair. Flustered, and knowing it was all so much more complicated than that, she simply didn't know what to say.

Seeing her discomfort, Reggie continued, 'So how about that drink? I'm leaving on the eleven o'clock train from Piccadilly, so that doesn't give you very much time for bolting,' he said cryptically.

Trying to ignore his flippant comments, which made her feel like an overwrought, slightly hysterical school-girl, Gladys said brusquely, 'There's a pub across the way. I can't stay long – I've got to catch the last bus home.'

Reggie raised his eyebrows; her invitation was as warm as coming home to an igloo.

In the pub, Reggie bought a pint for himself and a port for Gladys, who seemed intent on avoiding eye contact with him.

'Cheers,' he said, raising his glass.

'Cheers,' she said, keeping hers on the table.

As they'd already got off to a bad start, Reggie decided he had nothing to lose by coming straight to the point. 'I know what happened, Gladys.'

She turned to him with a startled movement. 'What do you know?'

'About Captain Miles.' Seeing her eyes grow wide in fear, he took her hand. 'No need to run off,' he assured her. 'He's been court-martialled,' he added solemnly.

'*What?*' she gasped as the colour drained from her face.

'I heard the story from an old school pal of mine who served as a naval officer with Miles; he was the one who told me that Miles had been reported for indecent behaviour.'

Gladys was so shocked she could hardly catch her breath.

'He's always had a reputation as a ladies' man,' Reg added.

'That's putting it bloody mildly,' she exploded.

'He went a step too far, though; a plucky young WREN serving in the Admiralty reported him for rape.'

'She went to the police?' Gladys spluttered incredulously.

'She took it right to the top,' Reggie assured her. 'Report has it that Miles denied it emphatically, said she was a little flirt, but somehow she had evidence: a witness who'd seen Miles driving her off and, fearing the worst, had followed; as luck would have it, he vouched for her and Miles was promptly court-martialled.'

'My God!' Gladys cried. 'What a brave woman to go public like that!'

'Course it's all been kept hush-hush – bad for public morale to have this sort of thing in the papers – and the woman's name has been kept secret to protect her.'

With a trembling hand, Gladys picked up her wine glass and downed almost all of the rich fortifying port. Reggie took a deep drink from his pint pot of beer then said softly, 'That's what happened to you, isn't it, Gladys?' When she didn't answer, he added, 'I remember seeing him hound you; I knew he wouldn't stop. I'd seen him do it too many times before. He always bragged that he got what he wanted.'

'Oh, he got what he wanted, all right,' Gladys seethed.

The anger in her bubbled up like a suppressed volcanic eruption – it came bursting out of the very core of her. 'He's an animal!' she raged. 'He ruined me – he took away my life and made me feel like dirt.'

Still holding her hand, Reggie squeezed it hard. 'Is that why you ran away without any explanation?'

Gladys slowly nodded her head as she desperately tried to squeeze back tears that were threatening to overwhelm her.

'I told nobody – I couldn't even speak the words. I wanted to get as far away from him as possible, even if it meant leaving ENSA, which I loved,' she finally admitted.

Reggie balled his fist, which he slammed down hard on the table, causing the landlord to scowl at him. 'I could kill the bastard!' he cried.

'He's had his comeuppance,' Gladys said with real satisfaction. 'I pray to God he never lives it down.'

Recalling that shameful, degrading time, Gladys turned her deep, dark-blue eyes on the man beside her. 'I'm sorry, Reggie. I didn't want to leave without saying goodbye, but I just couldn't face you. I thought you might have heard what he'd done – as you say, Miles was a bragger. I couldn't bear even to look you in the face for fear of what you might think of me.'

'I *knew* there had to be an explanation as to why you slunk away like a thief in the night,' Reggie declared.

Taking a shuddering breath, she blurted out the truth. 'I . . . I thought you'd be disgusted by me.'

'Darling!' he exclaimed, catching her in his arms.

'My poor precious darling. How could you ever think you'd disgust me?'

'I was raped – I was tainted,' she sobbed as she leant against him.

'But it wasn't your fault,' Reggie protested. 'You were the innocent victim of an accomplished predator. Miles was a past master at persecuting women.'

Warm in the circle of his arms, Gladys raised her beautiful, tear-stained face to his and whispered uncertainly, 'You were happy with me in Naples, weren't you, Reggie?'

'Happier than I've ever been in my entire life,' he whispered back, then kissed her soft, trembling lips.

The same giddy sensation she remembered from his first kiss under the Italian stars drenched Gladys, and she felt weightless, as if she was floating into a new world bursting with exploding stars. Worried that they might get thrown out of the pub by the landlord, who was looking at them suspiciously, Reggie pulled Gladys to her feet and led her outside. In the cold, wintry, inky darkness, they fell into each other's arms and kissed until they had to stop to draw breath.

'Oh, my God, I remember those kisses, Nurse Johnson.'

Clinging to him, Gladys had to be assured one more time that this was really happening. 'Tell me again that you really don't think that I'm a ... a whore?' she blurted out the word that had haunted her for months and months.

'Darling, it's the very last thing I would ever think

about you. The first time I laid eyes on you, I was struck by your sweet freshness, your love of life, not to mention your gorgeous legs!' he teased. 'But then when you opened your mouth and sang on stage, I literally went weak at the knees!' he confessed. 'What happened to you was unpardonable – I hope the bastard rots in hell for it, but it doesn't take away from *you*, my dearest girl.'

After kissing her hard on the lips, Reggie murmured into her ear, 'I *really, really* don't have a girlfriend in London,' then he added as he gazed into her radiant face, 'unless you would agree to take up that vacant position?'

Gladys couldn't stop smiling. 'If only we'd talked sooner,' she groaned as she snuggled closer to Reggie, who smelt of hospital disinfectant and tangy soap.

Reggie smiled ruefully. 'God only knows I tried, but it was like courting a jack rabbit: you were off and running every time I broached the subject. Mind you, at the time, I didn't know any more than rumours about Miles,' he reminded himself. 'It's only recently that his dirty deeds have come to light.'

'He should face the firing squad,' Gladys said through gritted teeth.

'I'd happily fire the first bullet,' Reggie said. 'Anyway, let's forget about him,' he continued as he tenderly swept his fingers across her high cheekbones. 'So now, my darling, now that we have an understanding, please, dearest Gladys, can we pick up where we left off?'

Gladys couldn't stop herself from bursting out laughing. 'Not quite! I'm in Manchester and you're in

London,' she pointed out. 'It'll be a very different court-ship from the one we enjoyed in sunny Naples.'

'So what?' he said robustly. 'There's a war on – most young lovers are separated by distance these days; lucky I've not been posted to the Middle East.'

Gladys smiled – compared with the Middle East, London was no distance away. 'We can write,' she said eagerly.

'Often!' he teased.

'Maybe even speak on the phone if I can sneak into Sister's office and use her phone when she's not there,' Gladys giggled.

'And we can meet!' Reggie cried as he picked her up in his arms and swung her round in the air before he safely deposited her back on the ground and kissed her long and lingeringly. 'My sweetest, darling girl,' he said in a rush of emotion as he buried his lips one more time in her glorious hair. 'We can't be parted for long, other-wise I'll lose my mind!'

'Oh, Reggie,' Gladys said in a rush of guilt. 'I'm so, so sorry for all the misunderstandings.'

'The misunderstandings I now understand!' he said jovially. 'They're all gone!' he said, as if by magic he was throwing them away. 'They've disappeared on the breeze – along with the girlfriend,' he chuckled.

Even though he was teasing her, Gladys couldn't stop herself from asking, 'When did you really stop seeing her?'

'I told you, sweetheart, it was over the minute I saw you in theatre,' he replied with a grin. 'I decided I pre-ferred brunettes to blondes.'

As Gladys's bus loomed into sight, Gladys threw her arms around Reggie and kissed him passionately. 'Write my darling, please write to me.'

Clinging to her, Reggie kissed her for the last time. 'I promise,' he said. 'Oh, God, this is so hard,' he sighed.

'Now we've found each other we've got to say good-bye,' she whispered, in tears again.

The bus conductor's gruff voice startled them from their caresses. 'Are yer gettin' the buzz or not?' he snapped.

Gladys reluctantly tore herself away from Reggie.

'Bye, my darling,' he said as he ushered her on to the bus's platform, then stepped back as it pulled away.

'Goodnight, my love,' Gladys called out as darkness engulfed Reggie and he disappeared from sight.

'Goodnight, my one true love,' she said to herself, taking a seat and travelling home in a dream of incredulous happiness.

27. The Best News

It proved difficult to work out a subtle plan that would bring Flora and Edna together.

'I don't think it's right to say straight out, "We've found your daughter,"' Kit fretted. 'The shock would be too much; it might even kill Edna!'

'I think that's highly unlikely, darling,' Ian said as they smoked their final cigarette before retiring to bed for the night. 'She's as strong as a horse!'

'How do you think we should play it?' Kit asked anxiously. 'All Edna knows is we're going into Manchester tomorrow to do a bit of extra shopping for her wedding.'

'Well,' said Ian, 'I suggest that as soon as you get off the bus in Manchester you tell her you have to pop into my office to pick something up. Our meeting with Flora is at noon, so plan to get a bus that will get you into Piccadilly around then.'

Kit nodded and started to breathe more easily. 'I can do that,' she said confidently.

'And the rest is between them,' Ian concluded.

As Kit brushed her waist-length, lustrous, raven black hair in their bedroom, Ian came up behind her and put his hands gently on her tummy. 'How's my little baby?' he asked softly.

'Quiet for now,' she answered, laying her small hands over his. 'But that will change in the New Year, when the baby starts kicking,' she told him.

'Will I be able to feel it?' he asked incredulously.

'Yes, of course,' she assured him. 'You'll be able to see him turning too as he gets older,' she added.

Ian's eyes widened. 'Do you think we're having a boy?' he gasped.

'I haven't a clue!' Kit laughed. 'I only say "he" because of Billy. One thing's for sure,' she joked. 'It'll be one or the other.'

'What would you really like, Catherine?' Ian asked. 'Go on, be honest.'

'As long as it's healthy, I really don't mind,' Kit started, then blurted out, 'I'd love a little girl.'

'A daughter,' Ian said with a dreamy look in his eyes.

'You're getting all soppy, Mr McIvor,' she teased.

'I'm so happy, darling,' he said as he pulled her into his arms. 'With all the tragedies surrounding us these days, I realize more than ever how precious life is and how lucky I am to have you.'

Taking Ian's hand, Kit led her husband to bed. As they fell into each other's arms, Kit reached up to kiss her husband's lips. 'I love you so much,' she murmured as she abandoned herself to his caresses.

The next day, Edna chatted merrily on the bus all the way into Manchester. 'I can't think of anything else I need, apart from a pair of nylons and maybe some soft leather gloves,' she said with a smile. 'I only wish Malc would let on where we're going for our honeymoon. I don't know whether to pack for a hike up Scafell mountain or a fishing trip up the Nile!' she joked.

'You can't go far – you've only got a few days off, like the rest of us,' Kit reminded her.

'I feel sorry for all those poor buggers working at the Phoenix over Christmas,' Edna remarked. 'Mr Churchill can't stop production just for festive fun – though thank God it's not me that's working,' she said with relief.

'I feel sorry for all the troops serving their country who can't be home with their families this Christmas,' Kit said with a sad sigh. 'Imagine how they must feel? Stuck in muddy trenches, or on freezing-cold U-boats, or flying night-raids over Germany – there can't be much to celebrate in those conditions.'

'I can never take in the sacrifices them lads are making for all of us here at home,' Edna said with a catch in her throat. 'We'll never really know how much they've gone through, or have yet to go through,' she said emotionally.

As the bus rumbled past Victoria Station, Edna made a positive attempt to change the mood. 'What do you think your Billy would like for Christmas?' she asked.

'A reindeer!' Kit laughed. 'Or an elephant – that's what he said the other day.'

When the bus pulled up at Piccadilly, Edna turned towards the Lyons Corner House. 'Let's start the day's shopping with a pot of tea,' she said eagerly.

Kit took a deep breath, then she said as lightly as she could manage, 'Do you mind if we pop into Ian's office first?'

'No,' Edna replied cheerily. 'Mebbe he'll offer us a cuppa!'

As they accompanied Ian's secretary to his office, Kit felt light-headed. What if Flora didn't turn up? What if Edna thought she and Ian had overstepped the mark, interfering in her private life? Before she could think of another problem, the door swung open and there was Flora, sitting upright on a chair beside Ian's desk. Kit held back so Edna could walk in first. She stopped short when she saw the young woman with the curly red hair and trembling smile.

Ian came from behind his desk. 'Edna,' he said gently, 'I'd like to introduce you to your daughter, Flora Forester.'

Edna's stout legs literally went from underneath her. Before she crumpled to the floor, Ian grabbed her under the arms and guided her to a chair. Kit handed her a glass of water, but Edna pushed it away in order to gaze at Flora sitting opposite her. Time stood still as Edna drank in every detail of the lovely young woman . . . Here was the baby that had been taken from her, now an adult. What years had she missed? How many events in a young girl's unfolding life had she not witnessed? As both women tried to contain their teeming emotions, Kit remained discreetly in the background, moved beyond words.

Ian continued in a formal voice, 'Mrs Forester placed

an ad in the *Manchester Evening News* – that was how we found her.' He turned towards Flora, who explained further.

'I found my birth certificate after my mother had died. I had no idea I was adopted.'

Leaning forward in her chair, Edna grasped her hands and asked curiously, 'Did you grow up in Penrith?'

'Yes, I did,' Flora answered. 'My parents were good to me. They were both old, which is why I think they adopted me, because it was too late for them to have children.' She gazed into Edna's brimming green eyes. 'I always wondered where I got my green eyes from, and now I know,' she blurted out.

In a blink Edna was on her feet. All self-control gone, she rushed to her daughter, who was taller than her, and, weeping, gathered her into her arms. 'Oh, my little Flora, my little girl!'

As the women fell on each other with tears coursing down their cheeks, Ian nodded towards the door. Taking his cue, Kit slipped out of the office, followed by Ian, who quickly wiped tears from his own eyes. 'I thought we should give them a moment together,' he said.

'I'm going to put the kettle on,' Kit said firmly as she headed towards the tiny office kitchen.

'I wish there were something a little stronger than tea,' Ian said as he helped Kit lay the tray.

'When I think of my joy at finding Billy when he was still a baby, I just wonder how Edna is feeling after twenty-seven years of separation,' Kit said with more tears in her eyes.

'Knowing Edna, one thing's for sure: she'll be desperately in need of a brew and a cigarette,' Ian said.

When they returned to the office, Edna and Flora were sitting side by side, holding hands and smiling. 'I've just been telling our Flora,' Edna started then stopped as she added, 'Listen to me! I only met the child ten minutes ago and she's already one of the family!' she laughed.

'You were telling me about my father, Edward Pilkington,' Flora reminded her.

'Oh, aye,' said Edna as she gratefully took the cup of tea and cigarette that Ian offered her. 'A proper bonny lad, though you must remember you got your looks from me,' she joked. 'We, you know, got carried away just before he went away, and you were the result.' Edna laid down the cup and saucer as memories overwhelmed her. 'I never wanted to part with you, sweetheart. I loved you more than I can ever describe, but it wasn't to be,' she said with a long sigh. 'I was sixteen years old and I had no sway over my parents, who were strict Methodists; they insisted that you were put up for adoption. It just about broke my heart, but there was nothing I could do about it. I had you for six weeks, then you were gone; I cried for months.'

Flora gave Edna's hand a firm squeeze. 'I always knew there was something not quite right. My parents looked after me well. I had a good education too, passed my Eleven-plus and went to the local grammar school.'

'The first brainy one in a long line of numbskulls!' Edna chuckled.

'But when I found my birth certificate whilst I was clearing out the house, something just clicked in my brain. I knew that, come what may, I had to find you. I had to know who I really was,' Flora explained.

After nearly an hour of non-stop talking, Ian said apologetically, 'I'm going to have to ask you ladies to leave – I have a client due any minute.'

'Of course,' cried Edna, leaping to her feet. 'We could carry on talking at the Lyons Corner House over the road?' she suggested to Flora, who reluctantly shook her head.

'I can't tell you how much I'd love that, but I've got to get the train home,' she said mournfully.

'You're going back to Penrith?' Edna gasped, as if she was frightened of losing her daughter all over again.

'I'm afraid I have to,' Flora explained. 'I've been staying in digs whilst I've been in Manchester, but now I really have to go home to my little girls, who my husband has been taking care of.'

Edna's eyes opened wide in wonder. 'You have children?' she cried.

'Catherine and Marilyn,' Flora told her proudly.

'Now I've got even more family to meet!' she cried joyfully. 'Just imagine,' she laughed as she turned to a smiling Kit. 'I'm a grandmother!'

Outside the office, waiting for the taxi that Ian had called to take Flora to Victoria Station, Edna clung to her daughter. 'Please, will you come back soon?' she begged.

'Yes,' Flora promised. 'Next time I come to see you, may I bring my daughters to meet you?'

'Yes, oh, yes, please!' Edna cried. 'Bring anything that's yours, cat, dog, goldfish, hubby – I'll welcome all with wide-open arms,' she enthused.

'What would you like me to call you?' Flora asked solemnly.

'What did you call the woman who adopted you?' Edna asked.

'Mother.'

A slow smile spread across Edna's radiant face, 'Then you can call me Mum,' she said with tears of happiness in her eyes. 'Mum will do for me.'

With promises to meet up soon, mother and daughter waved each other goodbye, then Edna quite literally slumped against the nearest wall. 'Oh, my God, did I just dream all of that, Kit?' she asked in a dazed voice.

'No, sweetheart, it really happened,' said Kit, linking her arm through Edna's and supporting her as they walked into Piccadilly. 'You have a daughter who's finally found her mum!'

Edna wrote to her daughter almost as soon as she got home, urging her to come and visit. 'We've got to make up for lost time,' she wrote with tears in her eyes. 'Bring the whole family and stay as long as you like.'

Flora quickly wrote back, promising to bring her little girls at the weekend, but not her husband, who'd been on a short leave from the army and had unfortunately returned to his regiment.

Malc had never seen his fiancée so radiant nor so

energetic. 'Oh, lovie,' she said as she hugged him with excitement. 'There's so much I want to share with them.'

Malc squeezed her tight, 'Don't rush it, sweetheart, one thing at a time, eh?' he cautioned.

'You're right,' she agreed. 'Mustn't overwhelm the poor child, but just imagine, Malc, I have my daughter back after all these years.'

'I hope she likes me,' Malc said cautiously. 'Did you tell her you were getting wed?'

'I most certainly did,' Edna replied. 'I even asked her to the wedding.'

'It would a nice touch if she came,' Malc said, as he gazed at Edna's happy, smiling face. 'It would make your day.'

Seeing her fiancé suddenly uncharacteristically nervous, Edna sensed Malc might be wondering where he might fit in, now that Edna had a family. 'He'll be worrying about the new pecking order,' she thought with sensitive insight. Cuddling up to the man she loved, she gave him a kiss, then whispered reassuringly, '*You'll* make my day, sweetheart.'

Suddenly, after what seemed like an eternity of pain and grieving, excitement was in the air. As Edna waited for her daughter's visit with her grandchildren, Gladys and Rosa were virtually dancing around the cowshed on the days they received missives in the post from their boyfriends.

'I don't know how he does it,' Gladys sighed as she clutched Reggie's most recent letter to her chest. 'He's working every hour God sends, but he still manages to write to me nearly every day.'

'I hope you do the same for him?' Rosa laughed.

'I try,' Gladys giggled. 'And what about you?' she teased. 'Are you sending Roger little drawings every day?'

'I try,' Rosa mimicked her friend and they both burst out laughing.

'Oh, Rosa,' Gladys said guiltily. 'Is it wrong to feel so happy?'

'Gladeeees! Don't be silly,' Rosa chided. 'You have waited a long time to be happy, certo.'

'Yes, but being so happy makes me feel very guilty,' she admitted. 'I have only to visualize my brother Les's dear face and all my happiness disappears.'

Gladys stopped short – she could have kicked herself as she saw Rosa's smile fade at the mention of her brother. Given Rosa's brother's possible circumstances, it was without doubt a stupid, crass thing to say. Desperate not to pop Rosa's small bubble of happiness, she quickly asked, 'But you must be keen to see Roger Carrington?'

'Of course,' Rosa replied with a philosophical shrug. 'But who knows? We must live each day we are given.'

'Like Violet and Myrtle did,' Gladys recalled. 'And now Edna has a new family, it's wonderful – I've never seen her happier.'

Rosa nodded as she said profoundly, 'Each in our way, we must live life to the full.'

28. Two Little Bridesmaids

Catherine and Marilyn couldn't believe that their new nana in Pendleton had a chip shop, and Edna couldn't believe that she had two beautiful little granddaughters.

'Granny in Penrith has gone to heaven,' Catherine told Edna, who stared in rapt adoration at the little girl's mass of fiery red hair, big hazel eyes and charming snub nose scattered with freckles.

'I hope she'll be happy with Jesus,' Edna said sincerely.

Tall Marilyn, who had sky-blue eyes and a straight blonde bob, chipped in, 'Grandad went to heaven a long time ago, so he'll be looking after Granny now,' she assured her new nana.

'Will you die soon?' Catherine asked cheerfully.

Edna swallowed a laugh. The child was asking a serious question, but Flora and Malc, who'd just met his fiancée's daughter, were bursting with suppressed giggles.

'I bloody hope not!' snorted Malc behind his hand. 'We're about to get wed.'

'I want to get to know you two little chicks and your mummy a bit more before I go to heaven,' Edna replied. 'And I want to teach you how to make the best chips in Lancashire!' she added, and, unable to stop herself, she scooped up the girls and settled them on her lap. 'Now I've a big favour to ask you two.'

Catherine and Marilyn looked at her expectantly. 'I'm going to marry Malc,' she said, pointing to her fiancé, who suddenly looked self-conscious. 'And I was wondering if you two had time to be my bridesmaids?'

'OOOH! I've never been a bridesmaid,' squeaked Catherine.

'Can we? Can we, Mummy?'

Flora smiled. 'Of course, if that's what Nana wants,' she assured her daughters, who were pink with excitement.

'Can I have a long, frilly dress like a princess?' bright little Marilyn asked.

'We'll see what we can do,' Edna promised. 'But we'll have to be quick about it – you see Malc and I are getting married on Christmas Eve.'

'That's soon,' said Marilyn solemnly.

'Will Father Christmas come to your wedding?' Catherine gasped.

'I think he might be spoken for on Christmas Eve,' Malc explained. 'But it would be nice if you two could be there?'

Marilyn and Catherine, happy beyond words, held hands and danced around the kitchen.

Suddenly anxious that she hadn't first asked Flora's permission, Edna quickly said, 'Is that all right, sweetheart?'

'Of course, Mum,' Flora replied.

Edna's heart skipped a beat every time her daughter called her 'Mum'. She momentarily looked around for somebody else – it would take time to get used to her new precious title.

'I'll take the girls' measurements,' Edna said. 'Then I can pick up some frocks for them in Manchester.'

Flora put an arm around her new mother. 'I'd like to do that with you, Mum. It'll be the first time we go shopping together.'

Fighting back tears of joy, Edna nodded in delight. 'I'd love that, Flora. But what about the girls – shall we take them?' she asked.

'Leave them to me,' Malc announced. 'I'll get one of the lasses at work to babysit for you.'

The lass free to babysit Marilyn and Catherine was in fact Nora, who was so excited she almost fell through Edna's front door when she opened it. 'I can't wait to see them,' Nora gasped, as she rushed into the back room of the chip shop, where she gave a big, gap-toothed grin.

'Hello, I'm Nora!' she announced to the little girls. 'Shall we play a game of Father Christmas and his Potato Elves?' she suggested excitedly.

'Oooh, yes!' squeaked Catherine. 'What do we have to do?'

'You have to fit as many presents into a sack as you can,' Nora explained. 'Here's a sack,' she said as she gave the girls an empty potato sack each.

'Where are the presents?' Marilyn asked.

'Over there, on the table,' Nora laughed as she pointed to a pile of potatoes that she'd removed from Edna's chip bucket.

'POTATOES!' the girls laughed.

'They're not presents,' giggled little Catherine.

'I know, but let's pretend they are for now,' Nora,

318

who was a complete natural with the children, giggled back. 'The one who gets the most potato presents in the sack is the winner!'

'We must dress up,' Marilyn insisted.

Flora gave Edna's arm a tug. 'Come on, Mum, we could be here all day listening to my two – they can play for hours.'

Edna chuckled under her breath. 'So can Nora, from the looks of things!'

Leaving Nora with her charges, the two women caught the bus into Manchester; on the top deck they lit up their cigarettes and smoked as they chatted companionably together.

'Tell me about your husband, Flora,' Edna asked. 'How did you meet him?'

'John and I met at school,' Flora said with a fond smile.

'Just like me and your dad,' Edna recalled.

'Before he got called up, John was a science teacher in Penrith; I was an infant teacher before I had the girls.'

'A teacher!' Edna explained.

'Like I said, my parents gave me a good education,' Flora reminded Edna. 'And I was their only child.'

Edna smiled proudly at her clever daughter. 'Eeh, you've obviously done well for yourself, lovie, not like my bloody feckless family,' she said with a grin.

'You're not feckless!' Flora protested.

'Mi dad was,' Edna replied. 'Spent all his money down the pub.'

'You bought your own shop and built up a successful business all by yourself. I admire any woman who can do that,' Flora said, proud of her independent, successful mother.

'Thanks, lovie. I worked hard, and, like you say, I was on my own, but now suddenly I have a daughter and soon I'll have a husband!' she exclaimed in sheer delight.

Laughing and joking, the two women walked arm in arm into the large Co-operative store in Piccadilly.

Edna said with stars in her eyes, 'I want to dress your little girls as prettily as the two royal princesses when they were children; I remember Elizabeth and Margaret always wore identical clothes, and that's what I want for your two little princesses.'

Flora smiled at her mother, who was flushed with excitement. 'What colours are you wearing?' she asked.

'Royal blue and a big red hat,' Edna replied.

'Wouldn't it be nice if the girls wore matching colours?' Flora suggested. 'Red would be nice and festive, and it would blend in with your outfit too.'

Charmed by the idea, Edna, who had cash and clothes coupons in her purse, and was intent on using both on her grandchildren, began to search the children's racks for girls' red dresses. Eventually, she and Flora found two identical dresses that were the right sizes for Marilyn and Catherine.

'Marilyn's tall for her age, so I might have to let down the hem,' Flora said, holding up the dresses and inspecting them. 'But that's not a problem, not since

John bought me a new Singer sewing machine,' she added happily.

'Before we do anything else . . .' Edna said, after they'd bought the garments.

Flora held up her hands and laughed. 'Don't tell me, you want a fag and a cuppa?'

'Took the words right out of my mouth!' Edna chuckled.

In the Lyons Corner House they both enjoyed a pot of tea and several cigarettes, then they ordered boiled-egg sandwiches – though, as Edna pointed out, the eggs had gone a bit grey in the middle. 'Mustn't grumble,' she said as she tucked in. 'At least it's not dried egg – I detest that stuff!'

After pouring more tea into their empty cups, Edna asked her daughter, 'Were you married when war broke out?'

'We'd been married two years by then,' Flora replied. 'And I had Marilyn very soon after we got married.'

'Strange to think I wasn't at your wedding,' Edna mused.

'But I'll be at yours!' Flora cried joyfully. 'Now, come on, Mum,' she said, briskly dusting crumbs from her skirt, 'we've got more shopping to do before we rescue poor Nora from my girls.'

Edna chuckled, 'Eeeh, lass, you're proper bossy. I don't know who you get that from!'

The rest of the afternoon was spent buying two pairs of black leather shoes with ankle straps, and two little headdresses decorated with artificial flowers.

'That should do it,' said Edna, clambering aboard the Pendleton bus loaded down with bags.

Marilyn and Catherine were ecstatic with their outfits, which they insisted on trying on right away.

'You look lovely,' Edna announced as the girls, holding hands, pretended to be walking down the aisle behind her.

'I can't wait for your wedding day, Nana,' they each said to Edna, who felt a sudden thrill of excitement run through her.

'Neither can I, my sweethearts, but with you two and your mum there, I guarantee it'll be the happiest day of my life!'

Edna hadn't opened her shop that afternoon; nor did she drive up to the Phoenix that night. 'I've got more important things to do,' she told Flora, as they prepared the little girls for bed. 'How often in my life have I had the chance to tell a bedtime story?'

Edna gave her double bed to Flora and the girls, whilst she slept in the single bed in the back room. 'Now, are we all cosy?' she asked as she settled the happy but very tired children under a big lilac eiderdown.

Yawning, the little girls nodded. 'Sing to us, Nana,' Marilyn said, flinging an arm around her sister, who was already half asleep.

Edna smiled: life had come round full circle for her. She'd sung Flora to sleep with the same song she was now singing to her granddaughters.

Golden slumbers kiss your eyes,
Smiles await you when you rise,
Sleep, my darling, do not cry,
And I will sing a lullaby.

By the time she'd finished, they were both asleep. Edna gazed in wonder at their flushed innocent faces in repose. 'Thank you, God,' she said with a heart full of gratitude. 'Thank you for reuniting me with my family.'

It was quiet after Flora and the girls returned to Penrith, promising to be back in good time for the wedding day, but Edna had a lot to do. Before she opened her chip shop for the mill workers' dinner-time rush, she popped into the Black Bull in the market square, which she'd booked for their wedding breakfast. Ted, the landlord, a boy she'd been to school with, had (like Malc!) good contacts on the black market.

'I've done the best I can for you, cock,' Ted told Edna as they both smoked Woodbines at the bar. 'There are no sides of beef or legs of lamb to be had, not even for you.'

'I could've told you that, you daft apeth!' Edna teased. 'So what have you mustered up for mi wedding day?' she asked. 'If you say Lord Woolton pie, I'll throw the bloody thing at you!' she threatened.

'I've got pork from the local allotment,' Ted quickly told her. 'Didn't come cheap,' he added as he stubbed out his cigarette in an ashtray on the beer-stained wooden bar-top.

'Money's Malc's department,' Edna said with a wink. 'What else have you got, or is it just pork butties on offer?'

'Get away with you!' Ted joked. 'If you can let me have half a sack of spuds, I can roast them and serve 'em up with local sprouts, and apple sauce too,' he said with a lick of his lips. 'A feast fit for a king!'

'Sounds good, Ted, thanks for all your help.'

'By the way, Maggie Yates popped in to say she'll supply sherry trifle for the pudding,' Ted added.

Edna's eyes opened wide in amazement. 'Sherry trifle!' she gasped. 'Where's Maggie going to get cream and sherry from?'

Ted winked again as he answered her question. 'A little bird told me there might be some available.'

'Honestly,' Edna sighed. 'If you and Malc carry on buying stuff from under the counter, you'll both be banged up on mi wedding day!'

That evening, as Edna drove her mobile chip shop along the dark winding lanes that led up to the Phoenix, she marvelled at the number of stars that were twinkling in the night sky. The air was clear and frosty, and she felt as excited as a child counting down the days to Christmas.

'Wait till I tell the girls about my two little bridesmaids,' she said out loud as she pulled into the despatch yard and waited for her first customers. 'They'll never believe it,' she murmured. 'And, if the truth be known,' she added with an incredulous smile, 'neither can I!'

29. Arthur's Choice

After Gladys had finished her shift at the Phoenix Infirmary, tired as she was after a night when one of her male patients nearly died as a consequence of a ruptured hernia, Gladys was keen to catch up with her friends – some of whom she felt like she hadn't seen in ages. Cycling down the tarmac road that led from the domestic quarters to the factory, Gladys marvelled at the beauty of the new day unfolding all around her. The sharp frost had turned the moorland vegetation into a filigree of white ice; bracken stood tall and spiky against heather bushes shimmering with icicles. As the sun rose in the sky, the light was so intense Gladys briefly had to close her eyes to protect herself against the sun's golden blinding glare.

When she walked into the canteen, she was thrilled to see Kit at their usual table. Grabbing tea and toast, Gladys rushed to join her friend, who was delighted to see her.

'How are you feeling, Kit?' Gladys immediately asked.

'Wonderful!' Kit replied. 'I could do with more sleep, and my back aches at the end of my shift, but I'm excited about the new baby – so are Ian and Billy too!' she laughed. 'Now tell me your news – Rosa told us you've got a doctor boyfriend,' Kitty said with a teasing smile.

'I think I have!' happy Gladys exclaimed, all her former reserve gone. 'Dr Reggie Lloyd,' she said with a dreamy sigh. 'He's so gorgeous, Kitty,' she added with a proud ring in her voice.

'You've been keeping him a secret, you dark horse,' Kit chided as she wagged a disapproving finger in front of Gladys's radiant face.

Gladys burst out laughing as she poured out the truth to her friend. 'I met him in Naples, then again in London when I was at St Thomas'. It was love at first sight for both of us, but we've encountered so many problems along the way it's a miracle we're even speaking to each other!'

'So you've known him since you went abroad?' Kit asked curiously.

Gladys nodded; she was relieved that she could answer so openly, but she wasn't yet ready to go into detail with Kit just now. She would tell her the full story in time, but for the moment she wanted to enjoy the happiness she felt when she talked about the man she was rapidly falling in love with. 'We met under the Italian stars!' she said.

'Sounds romantic,' Kit sighed.

'Oh, it was,' Gladys assured her, before quickly adding, 'but now that we seem to be back together, our biggest problem is Reggie's in London and I'm up here, so we won't see each other much,' she concluded with a rueful laugh.

'It'll be a test of your love,' Kit said with a knowing smile. 'Oh-oh!' she chuckled as Nora and Maggie approached with thick slices of bread and marg and mugs of steaming hot tea. 'Here comes trouble!'

Maggie and Nora wanted to know all about Gladys's young man, and when Nora heard he worked as a doctor in London her simple trusting face dropped. She hated it when their friendship group was in any way threatened, plus she'd been especially sensitive about losing friends since Myrtle's death. 'You won't go leaving us, will you, our Glad?'

'It would be nice to spend time with Reggie, even though I would miss you, Nora,' Gladys answered gently. 'We've never been together for very long; we could finish up hating each other after a fortnight!' she joked. 'Come on, I'm not going anywhere at the moment – tell me your news,' Gladys urged as she looked from Maggie to Nora. 'Have you heard from our Les?'

'Not recently, and only a couple of letters since he was posted back to the Front,' Maggie answered despondently. 'I don't even know whether he'll be home for Christmas,' she added miserably.

'Mum was wondering the same thing too,' Gladys told her sister-in-law to be. 'She's been living in hope, saving all her ration coupons for a big spread that looks like it won't happen soon – she'll be so disappointed.'

'I'm so sick and tired of this war,' Maggie fumed as she struck a match to light her cigarette. 'It's all about *waiting*: waiting for a letter, waiting to clock on, waiting to clock off, waiting in a queue ... always bloody waiting.' She gave a long weary sigh. 'It's been over four years now. The war they said would be over soon – when will it *ever* be over?'

Gladys, determined to look on the bright side, pointed out the good news. 'It's looking a lot more hopeful since the Bolshies recaptured Kiev in the Ukraine,' she reminded Maggie. 'This time last year they were on the run; now the boot's on the other foot.'

Kit nodded in agreement. 'Gladys is right: just think back to last year, when the Jerries were bombing our beautiful cathedral cities,' she recalled. 'Now we're the ones leading raids on Germany,' she said with a triumphant smile.

'Not to mention the Eighth Army's progress in North Africa,' Gladys added. 'And with the Allies making their way through Italy, nineteen forty-four could be a turning point in the war,' she said with genuine hope in her voice.

Maggie hung her head to hide her tears. 'I just can't keep a stiff upper lip any more, I'm sick of the whole bloody "Keep calm and carry on" routine. I know I'm being pathetic,' she admitted. 'I just miss my Les,' she ended with a feeble sob.

Gladys reached out to give Maggie a hug. 'Come on, sweetheart,' she whispered. 'Les wouldn't like to see you like this.'

Maggie nodded as she wiped away her tears. 'He wouldn't be at all impressed,' she agreed, 'He'd call me a soppy bugger!'

Nora, who was bursting to tell everybody her

wonderful news, blurted out, 'Did you know that Edna's a grandmother!'

Kit, whom Ian had advised to keep Edna's news to herself until Edna broke it publicly, sighed with a mixture of frustration at Nora's lack of discretion, and relief. It would be nice to talk about Edna's news openly; Kit knew everybody would be thrilled for her. If ever a woman deserved trust and devotion, it was their own wonderful Edna.

'I looked after her little granddaughters t'other day,' Nora babbled on. 'They are so cute; they're going to be Edna's bridesmaids! And her daughter's lovely too.'

'That's wonderful news!' murmured Gladys as she wiped a sentimental tear from her eye.

The four friends smiled at each other across the table. 'Looks like we're all happy at the same time, just for once,' Gladys commented.

'Apart from me!' Maggie joked.

'There's usually at least one of us in trouble,' Kit laughed. 'Life wouldn't be the same if we were all happy, would it?' she teased.

'I wouldn't mind being 'appy all't time,' Nora confessed. 'Does 'aving a fella make yer 'appy all't time?' she asked in all innocence.

'In my case it makes me cry a lot,' Maggie laughed.

'Even little Rosa's got a fella,' Nora said, with envy written large in her big blue eyes. 'As usual I'm the only spinster among us,' she groaned.

Maggie gave her a nudge in the ribs. 'Stop bloody moaning!' she said cheerfully.

Nora burst out laughing. 'Eh! Listen to the frying pan calling the pot burnt arse – you were the one that were moaning only five minutes ago!'

'Yeah, well, I've got over it,' Maggie said briskly. 'Anyway, kid, you've got to remember fellas aren't two a penny these days.'

'In my case fellas aren't at all,' Nora responded flatly.

'Shall we fix you up with one?' Maggie asked in all seriousness. 'You know, a blind date?'

Nora's jaw dropped. 'I'm not meeting up with lads I don't know!' she cried indignantly. 'They could be bank robbers – or murderers!'

Luckily, further indignations were drowned out by the factory hooter sounding out.

'Just in time!' Gladys called out, as she saw Rosa come tearing into the canteen, looking like she'd just jumped out of bed.

'I have post,' Rosa gasped breathlessly as she waved one of Roger's postcard sketches in the air. 'And for you too, Glad,' she added as she shoved an envelope into Gladys's hand before dashing off to the changing room, knowing she was already five minutes late for work.

Waving goodbye to her friends, Gladys collected her bike and left the Phoenix. She wheeled it up the cobbled lane to the cowshed, all the time aware of the tantalizing crackle of Reggie's letter tucked safely in her coat pocket. Savouring the pleasure of reading it in bed, Gladys quickly washed and changed into her nightie, then snuggled under her heavy woollen blanket and cosy eiderdown.

My darling,

No words can tell you how much I physically ache to see you. Believe me, I don't stand around moping all day like a love-sick fool – you know how busy the operating theatre is here – but even as I'm removing gunshot from a deep wound or sewing up a tear in a soldier's abdomen, my mind drifts to you . . . I think of your lovely face, your wonderful, sweet-smelling hair, your soft, rosy lips and your eyes, deep-blue and sparkling, and I have to force myself to turn my attention to my patient. So far I've not done any damage, but if I should I will definitely blame you for captivating me with your beauty and your charms.

I've tried every trick in the book to get Christmas leave, but, with the latest wave of wounded rolling in from the casualty stations at the Front, nobody's been granted time off. The daily schedule at St Thomas' is even more demanding than when you were here – sometimes we're working well into the night after an early-morning start, and need I tell you how often the wretched sirens sound out every night? When you see how much these men have suffered, it's wrong to complain, but OH! I WILL MISS YOU! I comfort myself with the knowledge that we will meet in the New Year – the sooner the better.

Write to me, my Gladys, write and tell me of your days on the wards and your long, lonely nights dreaming of me – I hope!

Your loving, all-adoring,
Reggie

After reading the letter three times, Gladys's eyelids began to droop. Tucking the precious letter under her pillow, she closed her eyes and fell instantly asleep with a smile on her lips.

As Gladys slept peacefully well into the afternoon, Arthur made his way to Malc's office, where he was welcomed with a cigarette and a mug of tea. Seeing his friend's face grey with grief, Malc's big heart ached to help him, but he knew better than most what a private, reserved man Arthur was, so he kept his peace and waited. After a few drags on his Pall Mall, Arthur came to the point of his visit.

'There's only one way of saying this, pal,' he started. 'So I'll say it as it is – I've decided to leave the Phoenix and seek work elsewhere.'

If Arthur had hit Malc with a cricket bat, he could not have been more stunned. 'Leave?' he gasped. 'Why?'

'We can't stay here, Malc,' Arthur replied sadly. 'We'd be living nothing but a life of memories. I've given it some thought. In some respects it would be easier to stay at the Phoenix – Stevie and I both know people we love and trust – but I can't do it.' He stubbed out his cigarette in the ashtray on Malc's desk. 'Everywhere I turn I see her: the filling shed, the cordite room, the despatch yard, my allotment' – he choked as he mentioned the place where Violet had finally allowed herself to fall in love with him – 'the house, the town, the moors. It wouldn't be right to bring up Stevie in an environment where he was surrounded by sadness brought on by his mother's death. It's just not working, Malc. I know it's not,' he concluded firmly.

Even though he could see the sense in what Arthur was saying, Malc was panicking about how father and son would survive on their own.

'B-b-but where will you go? How will you manage?'

'Scotland: it's where Violet and I planned to go when we were running away from that evil husband of hers; we would have gone, but after he died she felt safe here and she wanted to stay with her friends, so that's what we did.' He sighed heavily, his expression suggesting he wished they'd moved, then Violet might still be alive. 'I've applied for a job as safety officer in a munitions factory in Dundee. If I get it, we'll leave early in the New Year. I wanted you and the girls to hear it first hand from me, not Mr Featherstone.'

Malc slumped against his chair, where he immediately lit up another cigarette. 'Jesus Christ, Arthur, you've thought it all through,' he gasped.

'I had to,' Arthur confessed. 'It's not like I'm my own man, I have a baby son whom I alone am responsible for; funnily enough, he's the one who's helped me make the decision.'

'How can a five-month-old tell you what to do?' Malc questioned.

'Seeing the place where his mother died, his nursery, made me think that every day, as long as the war lasts, I'll pick up Stevie and instead of swinging him in my arms in joy I'll inevitably, just as I do now, turn to the place where I found Violet and I'll wish I was dead too. That's no way to bring up a child,' he said decisively. 'I'll still be best man at your wedding, Malc,' he said with a shadow of a smile. 'I won't let you down.'

Malc gave a grateful nod, 'Thanks for that, Arthur.'

'You can tell Edna, but I'd as soon tell the girls myself,' Arthur said, as he rose and quietly left the room.

'By Christ, there goes a man with a will of iron,' Malc thought. 'How much easier it would be to stay in Pendleton, supported by his friends, as he is now; but not for Arthur Leadbetter. For the sake of Violet's son, he's going to start anew in order to remove his child from the shadow of his wife's untimely death. That takes guts.'

When Arthur saw Kit, Rosa, Nora and Maggie taking a break together in the canteen, he seized the moment to tell them his plans.

'Hello there,' he started cheerily enough as he sat down at the metal table and handed out cigarettes. 'I was hoping to catch you all together. 'I've got something to tell you . . .'

After he'd finished, Violet's friends sat speechless for several seconds. Kit, who'd known Violet the longest, spoke first. 'I think you're a brave man, Arthur, though I'll miss you and little Stevie. I believe you're doing the right thing for you and your son.'

Arthur's eyes filled with tears as he reached across the table to grip Kit's small hand. 'Thanks, Kit. Knowing you approve helps a lot.'

'How will you manage?' anxious Nora fretted.

'We'll just have to start all over again,' Arthur replied. 'I won't beat about the bush, lass: it'll be hard, making a home and friends on my own, settling Stevie in nursery and trying to live a life without my beloved.' He gulped at the prospect of what lay ahead.

'You will make friends,' said Rosa, who knew more about loneliness and isolation than anybody at the table. 'It take time but you are a very good man and good manager too,' she said with true sincerity. 'And you have Stevie,' she added with an emotional smile. 'He could, how you say, charm anybody?'

Arthur answered with a fond smile. 'He could charm the birds from the trees!'

'Stevie'll make friends wherever he goes,' said Maggie confidently.

Arthur stubbed out his cigarette and rose to his feet. 'He's just like Violet – everybody loved her.'

News quickly got round the factory of the safety manager's decision to leave the Phoenix. Edna, in her mobile chip shop parked up in the despatch yard, heard every point of view going.

'He'd be better off staying put – at least he's got a community to take care of him and the child.'

'I'd go if I were him – no good living in the past.'

'Dundee's a long way away, bloody cold too!'

'Best safety officer I've ever known – he's done a lot for this factory and for the workers in it.'

'He's saved lives too – we'll never get another as conscientious as Arthur Leadbetter.'

'It's a terrible tragedy what's happened to him.'

Edna listened to the workers' comments, then said, 'Everybody has a right to their own opinion but, at the end of the day,' she said as she lit up one of her Woodbines, 'it's Arthur choice. I wish him well, but, my God, I'll miss him.'

30. A Christmas Rush

Oddly enough, just as things were settling down, easy-going Nora put everybody in a flat spin.

'I've been thinking,' she said as they stood in a line clocking on one morning.

'Hold on to your hats, girls!' Maggie chuckled. 'You never know what's coming next when our Nora's had her thinking cap on.'

Rosa, who adored Nora for her sweetness and innocence, said, 'Tell us, mia cara, what are your thoughts?'

'Well,' said Nora as they filed out into the corridor that led to the canteen, 'this time last year Myrtle came up with the idea of having a carol concert in town and raising funds for the war widows,' Nora explained.

'It was lovely!' Kit remembered. 'We had so much fun and we raised a lot of money too.'

They settled down at their favourite table in the canteen and the smokers lit up. 'Why don't we put on another carol service this year, but make it even bigger?'

'Eeh, lovie, you've left it late!' Maggie tittered. 'Christmas is almost upon us and you go and have a brainwave.'

'I only thought about it in bed last night whilst I were saying mi prayers for Myrtle – that's when it dawned on me,' Nora confessed. 'And I had another thought too.'

'Go on, tell us – we should stage a pantomime!' Maggie joked.

'Let the girl speak,' Kit chided as she swotted cheeky Maggie with her hand.

'I thought this year we could donate our takings to a charity that helps refugees,' Nora added, and a deep blush flooded her face.

Rosa stared at Nora incredulously. 'You really are a kind person!' she announced before she flung her arms around Nora and hugged her tightly.

As Nora hugged Rosa back, she said, 'I want to do summat for your friends, lovie. Nobody should be killed or locked up because they're Jewish – it's just not fair,' she added in her characteristically simple and direct way.

Nora's sincere words brought a swell of tears to Kit's eyes, which she wiped away before she said, 'I think it's a wonderful idea. We could involve the children from the Phoenix and the town too,' she suggested. 'We could even ask Malc to dress up as Father Christmas and hand out toys to the children!'

'He'll have only just got married the day before!' Maggie cried. 'He might be on his honeymoon.'

'I'll consult with Edna later,' Kit promised. 'She might know what his plans are.'

'I don't see how Santa, assuming we get one, is going to have a sackful of toys he can hand out,' Maggie added uncertainly.

'I wasn't thinking of BIG toys, just little bits and pieces, wrapped in a twist of tinsel, nothing elaborate,' Kit explained.

Rosa nodded excitedly. 'Like our Hanukkah, we also make little gifts for the children! I could draw pictures of fairies and elves, it would cost nothing.'

Like her sister Emily, Maggie as usual found her thoughts drifting to food. 'We could roast chestnuts,' she said with a smile. 'Thank God you don't need ration coupons for chestnuts!'

'We'll bring our instruments and sing carols round the Christmas tree in the market square, just like we did last year,' Nora said.

'Where possible,' Kit chuckled at the thought of dragging the unwieldy drum kit she used for their band practices all the way down the hill into town. 'I might just manage a snare drum but forget the big bass!' she laughed.

'Let's see what food we can cadge between us to make little festive treats,' Maggie said. 'Everything's rationed, but you never know what hidden tins folks have got stashed away at the back of their cupboards.'

The hooter sounded out, calling the workers around the factory to their different departments – the bomb line didn't stop for anything, not even a carol service in honour of refugees who were victims of war.

Kit made a point of seeing Edna before catching the bus home after her long shift. Luckily, Edna was parking her mobile chip shop in the despatch yard as Kit was leaving.

'Eeh, lovie, how are you?' Edna said gently as she noted Kit's tired face.

'I'm okay, though if truth be told I could sleep for England,' Kit answered frankly. 'How are you?'

'Never happier!' Edna declared with an ecstatic smile. 'I think a lot of my happiness is down to you, young lady. I bet it was your idea to track down my Flora,' she said knowingly.

'Ian did most of the work,' Kit said generously. 'Though, to be honest, we never thought it would happen. It's such a complicated business – there was so little we could do other than scour the ads. Flora's the one who made it easy when she came looking for you, lovely girl that she is.'

'How many times have I wrapped up chips in newspaper and never thought to look in the personal ads!' Edna joked. 'Flora's coming to mi wedding, and the little lasses are going to be my bridesmaids,' Edna added. 'Imagine that, Kit – my granddaughters walking down the aisle behind me on my wedding day. It's the stuff of dreams.'

Kit smiled at Edna's glowing face. 'If anybody deserves joy it's you,' she said lovingly. Taking a deep breath, she continued, 'Actually it's your wedding I want to talk to you about . . . have you got any plans for Christmas Day?'

'We'll be here,' Edna replied. 'Me and Malc thought it weren't fair to go scooting off straight after the wedding breakfast, not with Flora and the little lasses here too. We decided we'd go away on Boxing Day, not that I know whether I'm bound for the Sphinx or the Phoenix!' she joked.

'Phew! That's a relief,' said Kit with a smile.

'Why – what're you girls up to now?' Edna asked with a grin.

'We're planning a big carol service in Pendleton on Christmas Day, and it wouldn't be the same without you,' Kit told her.

'Ooh, I wouldn't miss it for the world,' Edna exclaimed. 'And Marilyn and Catherine will love it too. I could do some cooking, not just chips, maybe apple fritters for a treat – and toffee apples, though God only knows where I'd get the toffee from,' she chuckled.

Before Edna got carried away on alternative festive recipes, Kit rather nervously said, 'Er, Edna . . . do you think your Malc might consider dressing up as Father Christmas?'

Edna looked at her and burst into peals of laughter. 'Oooh!' she gasped. 'I don't think I've ever heard owt so funny in mi life!'

When Edna had got her breath back, Kit explained that Malc, or rather Father Christmas, would hand out gifts to all the children at the carol service. 'That's if we can find any gifts,' she said doubtfully.

'I'm a dab hand at little peg dollies,' Edna said. 'All you need is a wooden peg and a scrap of material – that won't be hard to find.' She gave a little grimace. 'Not that the lads would thank Father Christmas for a doll,' she chuckled. 'They might tell him where to stick it!'

'Do you think Malc will do it?' Kit asked uncertainly. 'You know, dress up in a fake beard and a long red robe?'

Edna winked. 'Don't you fret, cock, he will by the time I've finished with him!'

Gladys was thrilled when she heard from Rosa about the planned Christmas carol service.

'It'll be just like last year,' she cried, then she quickly added, 'We'll have to practise the carols beforehand.'

Rosa, who was busy painting Christmas elves and fairy pictures on scraps of card, looked up in surprise; it was a delight to hear her friend so enthusiastic about their music rehearsals.

'I am happy, mia cara, now you are happy you sing like before, Nora tells me.'

'The bad days are long gone,' Gladys said with a beaming smile that made her eyes sparkle with happiness. 'I'll get mi dad to bring mi alto sax over and maybe his piano accordion too,' she added with a giggle. 'Do you think you could play the accordion instead of the piano?'

Rosa giggled as she twirled round and round as if doing a wild dance, 'Wait till you see me, eh? Gypsy Rosalina on the accordion!'

Everybody threw themselves into Christmas preparations: whether it was making little gifts to go in Santa's sack, devising wartime recipes to make festive treats, or refamiliarizing themselves with their musical instruments after such a long time away from them. With everybody so preoccupied, Kit began to worry about something else.

'Listen,' she said earnestly one lunch-time, 'I know we're all excited about the carol service, but we mustn't let it overshadow Edna's wedding.'

Her friends stared at her with puzzled expressions. 'Course we won't,' Maggie spoke first.

Rosa, more subtle and insightful, turned to Kit and said, 'What makes you say this, Kit?'

'I just worry that with so much going on, Malc and Edna might get sidelined,' Kit admitted.

'Never!' Nora exclaimed.

'I don't mean on purpose, sweetheart,' Kit said quickly, when she saw the hurt look on Nora's face. 'The run-up to Christmas is so frantic – we should be careful to take one day at a time.'

Rosa nodded. 'It make sense,' she said in agreement with Kit. 'First, we have Edna's big day on Christmas Eve, then on Christmas Day we have the children and the carols; then on Boxing Day we have time for ourselves and sleep all day!' Rosa joked.

'You've got it in a nutshell!' Kit laughed. 'At times your English is better than mine, Rosa.'

Gladys was determined to bring Christmas cheer to her patients in the Phoenix Infirmary, especially those who would be hospitalized all through the festive season. She'd asked for Christmas Eve off so she could attend Edna's wedding, but she had to work an early shift Christmas morning, which she didn't mind. She planned to jump on her bike, with her alto sax in her basket, and cycle into Pendleton for the carol service the minute she finished work.

343

After persuading Sister Atkins to let her put up a Christmas tree in the infirmary entrance, Gladys went out one freezing-cold early morning in her mother's posh but rather outdated fur coat and dug up a little fir tree on the moors. Later she planted it in a bucket, which she carefully wrapped in red crêpe paper, then she positioned the tree in pride of place in the infirmary entrance. It did look bare without any decorations, so in desperation Gladys left a notice under the tree saying,

IF YOU HAVE ANY CHRISTMAS DECORATIONS
TO SPARE PLEASE HANG THEM ON OUR HOSPITAL TREE

She was delighted to find that more and more donations of tinsel, baubles, red ribbon and even a star to sit on the topmost branch were added with each visiting hour that passed.

'It's the first time we've ever had a Christmas tree in the infirmary,' Dr Grant remarked with a smile as he passed Gladys in the corridor. 'Thank you for organizing it, Nurse Johnson.'

'A pleasure, Doctor,' Gladys replied with a radiant smile.

'That young woman's too good-looking for her own good,' Dr Grant thought to himself as they went their separate ways. 'But, my God, she cheers the patients up with that sparkling smile of hers.'

The last band rehearsal before the carol service was the evening before Edna's wedding. It had been a frantic rush for all of the girls, who between them and their varying shifts just about managed to find a free hour when they could all meet in the Phoenix chapel, where they'd always held their band practices in the old days.

'Okay,' Gladys said, taking the lead as she'd always done in the past. 'Let's kick off with "Oh, Little Town of Bethlehem", then go straight into "Away in a Manger" – the little kiddies love that. Remember to rock your arms as if you're holding a baby when it comes to the chorus,' Gladys reminded her friends.

'How can I rock mi arms as if I was holding a baby if I'm playing the trombone?' Nora asked.

Gladys smiled as she patiently explained what to everyone else was blindingly obvious. 'You can't pretend to rock a baby and play the trombone at the same time, Nora, and neither can anybody else who's playing a musical instrument,' she added with a giggle.

With Kit on a snare drum, Rosa on the piano accordion, Maggie on trumpet, Nora on trombone and Gladys on her alto sax, it took some time to get in tune with each other, but as they sang the old familiar carols, their musical accompaniment improved and by the end of the session they were all pleased with the outcome.

'Well done – we're almost as good as we used to be,' Gladys said.

'Badly out of practice,' Maggie pointed out.

'Hopefully the children singing at the top of their voices on Christmas Day will drown out any mistakes we might make,' Gladys joked.

Full of thoughts of the past, Maggie reminisced, 'Remember how you used to click your fingers, Gladys: you'd go, "A-1, a-2, a-1, 2, 3, 4", and we'd be off playing beautiful music in unison with one another,' she said in a dreamy, nostalgic voice.

'That was when we were practising nearly every night,' Kit reminded her. 'None of us could begin to think of working that hard now – we all have so many other commitments.'

She stopped short as Nora gave a suppressed sob, rather like a loud hiccup.

'What is it, mia cara?' Rosa asked, as she turned to Nora, who was weeping unashamedly into her grubby hankie.

'I . . . miss . . . Myrtle . . .' she cried as great sobs racked her body. 'And mi mam . . . and our kid who got blown up by the bloody Jerries.'

As Rosa tenderly soothed the weeping girl, Kit, Maggie and Gladys exchanged a knowing glance, 'It's that time of the year,' Kit murmured with a lump in her throat.

Gladys nodded. 'Christmas brings back so many memories,' she said with a catch in her voice.

Kit nodded as her thoughts flew to Violet. 'God alone knows how Arthur's coping.'

In Edna's house, there were no tears that night. As Flora, who'd arrived on the train a few hours earlier with her girls, boiled up milk for cocoa, Edna rolled rags in her granddaughters' hair.

346

'What're you doing, Nana?' Marilyn asked as she wriggled impatiently on the stool that Edna had set by her own chair.

'If you'll stay still, little ferret,' Edna chuckled, 'I'll tell you.'

'Why are you putting bits of old rags in our hair? Mummy uses rollers,' Catherine said knowingly.

'This is how my mam used to curl my hair when I was a kiddie,' Edna explained. 'Not that it needed any curling – always had a headful of frizz,' she joked. 'You take a length of hair like this,' she said, taking a length of Marilyn's silky blonde hair to demonstrate the process. 'Then you carefully wind it round and round the rag, which you knot so it doesn't come undone, and tomorrow, you'll see, you'll have beautiful ringlets, just like a princess.'

Malc, who was as bald as a coot, chuckled, 'You can try that on me later, lass!'

Edna smiled at Malc, who was stoking the fire. Her little back room felt cosy with love and family, and she hugged the sensation to herself like a warm blanket. 'God is good,' she thought gratefully.

After finishing their cocoa, Marilyn and Catherine gave Malc and Edna a big kiss.

'Night, night,' the little girls said.

'Night, night, sleep tight, don't let the bed bugs bite!' Malc joked.

'There's no bed bugs in my clean house,' Edna laughed, as she swatted his arm with a rolled-up newspaper.

*

347

After Flora had taken the little girls upstairs and they were left alone, Edna snuggled up to Malc on the leatherette sofa; watching the coal burning brightly in the fireplace, she smiled contentedly.

'No regrets?' Malc asked as he gently stroked her hair.

'None at all,' she said with a happy sigh.

'Get me to the church on time!' he sang softly.

'It's bad luck to see each other before we're wed in the morning,' she warned him.

'I'll make myself scarce, don't you worry,' he assured her. 'Anyway, I'll have Arthur to keep me on mi toes,' he reminded her.

'Arthur . . .' Just saying his name summoned up a huge lump in Edna's throat.

'Aye, he'll be off before we know it. He made a point of going round personally telling everybody he knew that he'd be leaving in the new year, brave lad that he is,' he told Edna, who, determined to hold on to their happiness, said, 'Who'll be looking after Stevie tomorrow?'

'Ian's taking care of both little lads, God help him,' Malc laughed. 'Kit will be busy being your matron of honour, and the other girls are all playing in the band, so Ian is more than happy to have the boys. Rather him than me!'

'This time tomorrow we'll be wed,' Edna murmured disbelievingly.

'Mr and Mrs Preston,' he said softly.

Malc left shortly afterwards. 'You'll need your beauty

sleep, my sweetheart,' he said thoughtfully. 'See you at the altar – don't be late!'

Edna smiled happily as she waved Malc off. It was only when she closed the door that she realized something was missing. 'He still hasn't given me that bloody bouquet,' she said out loud. 'Daft apeth! I can see me finishing up walking down the aisle with only a bunch of blasted dandelions in mi hands!'

31. Christmas Eve

Christmas Eve dawned frosty cold, bright and beautiful.

'Will it snow, Nana?' Marilyn asked, as Edna unwound the rags from her hair.

'I hope not, chick, I don't want to get my new shoes wet through,' she replied, and with a flourish removed the last rag from Marilyn's hair, then stepped back to admire the full effect.

'What did I tell you!' she exclaimed. 'A headful of ringlets,' she said, holding up the mirror for Marilyn to peer into. 'You look proper bonny,' she added.

Catherine looked anxious. 'Will I always have curly hair now, Nana?'

'No!' Edna assured her with a big hug. 'By the time I'm married to Malc, your hair will be right back to normal.'

Suddenly there was a loud rap on the back door. 'If that's Malc, don't let him in!' superstitious Edna cried.

Flora cautiously opened the door to reveal Kit standing on the doorstep in her smart black barathea two-piece suit.

'Kit!' Flora exclaimed. 'Come in.'

'Thanks, lovie,' Kit said, as she quickly stepped into the back room with her hands behind her back. Smiling mysteriously, she slowly revealed a small but exquisitely beautiful bouquet of red roses, set against a background of green ferns and glossy ivy leaves. 'From your husband-to-be,' Kit said warmly, handing the flowers to Edna, who filled up with tears at the sight of them.

'Well, I never – he managed it in the end!' she gasped. 'I thought I'd be left holding nothing but a bunch of dandelions!'

'He must have spent a pretty penny on that lot,' Flora said knowingly.

'For God's sake, lovie, never ask where they came from,' Edna said with a chuckle.

'There's more,' Kit added as she handed nosegays of red carnations to the little girls and a small spray of roses to Flora. 'Malc's thought of everybody, including me,' she said with a laugh as she pointed to her own spray of red roses, pinned to the lapel of her black suit. 'You're a lucky woman, Edna,' Kit said, as she kissed the bride. 'That man of yours is one in a million.'

Edna nodded. 'I picked a good one,' she said modestly.

Just before eleven, an hour before the midday service, it started to snow: gentle flurries landed on the drab grey church path, covering it like a sparkling white blanket. It drifted on to the lofty church spire, which stood out stark and silvery bright against the blue sky. Freshly fallen snow transformed an ordinary parish churchyard into a twinkling winter wonderland for Edna's wedding to Malc.

When the car, driven by Edna's old school pal, who ran the local garage, arrived for Flora and the brides-maids, Edna's heart began to flutter.

'How do I look?' she said to Kit, when they were alone together.

Seeing her usually confident friend suddenly nervous and uncertain, Kit handed her a tiny glass of brandy, poured from a silver flask that Ian had filled up that morning. 'For emergencies,' he'd said with a knowing wink.

'You look radiant,' Kit said. 'Now drink this – it'll steady your nerves.'

Edna knocked it back. 'That's better,' she said as she licked her lips. 'Give us another one, cock,' she laughed.

As the two friends sipped brandy, Kit assured Edna again that she looked perfect. 'This is your day, sweetheart: you've waited long enough – enjoy every minute of it.'

Moved to tears, the two women hugged each other. Then, seeing the car pulling up outside the chip-shop window, Edna adjusted her red velvet hat and, picking up her fragrant bouquet, held out her arm for Kit to take.

'Lead on, matron of honour!'

The church was packed with Phoenix workers: munitions girls who'd enjoyed her company – and her chips – every night in the despatch yard. Locals who'd known Edna all their lives were there too, and customers from the nearby mill who Edna made dinner for every weekday. All the well-wishers waited expectantly as Rosa, Gladys, Nora and Maggie struck up the music for the opening number, 'Here Comes the Bride'.

When Malc turned to greet Edna, he thought his

heart would burst with joy: this beautiful, strong, loving, generous woman was tying a knot with him that he prayed would hold them strong until the day they died. There wasn't a dry eye in the house as the middle-aged couple exchanged their wedding vows in front of the vicar, who was deeply moved by their faith and the conviction with which they spoke their marriage vows.

'I take thee to my wedded husband, to have and to hold from this day forward, for better for worse, for richer for poorer, in sickness and in health, to love, cherish and to obey, till death us do part, according to God's holy ordinance; and thereto I give thee my troth.'

Another person close by was also deeply moved by the couple's tenderness towards each other: Arthur had to clench his teeth in order to stop his emotions from overwhelming him as he witnessed his best pal make his wedding promises to Edna. As tears blurred his vision, Arthur's own wedding day came back to him as clear as day. His darling Violet, dazzling in her bridal dress, her sky-blue eyes alight with happiness, her delicate face suffused with joy. It had been the hardest struggle of his life to secure Violet's trust, but when she finally gave it to him she gave him her all. After years of pain and marital brutality, she walked into his arms with such hope in her eyes; theirs might have been a short-lived marriage, but, my God, it had been the most powerful, passionate relationship Arthur had ever experienced.

As the bride and groom went off to sign the register with the best man and woman, the congregation were entertained by Gladys, Nora, Rosa and Maggie, who played a cracking rendition of Glenn Miller's 'In the Mood'. It was impossible for some in the pews not to recall their own wedding days, whilst others dreamt of nuptials to come. As Gladys ran her long, slender fingers up and down the valves on her saxophone, she thought of Reggie. Would their new love blossom into a relationship that might lead to marriage? Gladys's skin tingled at the thought of being Reggie Lloyd's wife; she honestly couldn't imagine anything in the world more wonderful than spending the rest of her life with the man who through thick and thin had held out for her.

Rosa's thoughts drifted back to Italy, to weddings she'd celebrated with street parties, the bride and the groom sheltered from the sweltering heat under a white canopy as they enjoyed a banquet of local food and wine with friends and family. Edna's marriage in a stark Northern church on the edge of the Pennines was a world away from her Italian landscape, but it was no less beautiful.

When the bride and groom walked up the aisle, arm in arm with huge, happy smiles on their faces, the congregation clapped and cheered as the band played out Edna's all-time favourite, 'Alexander's Ragtime Band'. Outside, to the newlyweds' delight, a crowd of munitions girls formed a guard of honour all the way down the path from the church porch to the gate. As snow fell and the munitions girls formed an arch for Edna and Malc to walk under, hand in hand and laughing with happiness, they emerged at the end of the line, where guests showered them with confetti that combined with large, floating snowflakes that showered down on their heads.

'Time to throw my bouquet,' Edna announced.

Malc stared at her. 'Throw your bloody bouquet?' he gasped in disbelief. 'It only cost me nearly a week's wages!' he spluttered.

'It's the tradition,' Edna explained. 'Whoever catches it will be the next bride.'

'It seems bloody daft to me,' Malc muttered mutinously. 'Mebbe I'll catch it and flog it on!' he chuckled.

'Can't break with tradition,' Edna said cheerfully. 'It's bad luck.'

'Go on, my lass, bad luck is the last thing we need, chuck it one!' he laughed.

And with that, she whizzed her beautiful red roses up into the air. 'CATCH!' she cried to the guests.

Every single woman rushed forward, but Gladys just happened to be right where the bouquet landed; in fact, if she hadn't moved as quickly as she did, it would have landed on her head!

'Got it!' she cried, as she clutched it tightly.

'Oooh,' said Nora. 'I wish I'd caught it. I need a bit of luck in the wedding department.'

'We can share it, sweetheart,' Gladys said generously. 'It's not like I'm going to be married soon.'

Maggie gave her a cheeky wink. 'Wanna bet on that, our Glad?' she teased.

It was fortunate that the Black Bull was only a five

minute walk from the church, because by the time Arthur (using Malc's old Brownie camera) had taken photographs the snow was falling fast. The pub was warm and welcoming, with a roaring log fire, and the wedding-breakfast tables were prettily set out with white crêpe paper and little bunches of holly arranged along the middle. As guests warmed themselves by the fire, dusting snow and confetti from their coats, Ted, the genial landlord, circulated with trays of sweet sherry and port.

'On the house, so stop fretting,' Ted whispered as he handed husband and wife a large glass apiece. 'Congratulations: it couldn't have happened to a better couple.'

'CHEERS!' cried Malc and Edna as they clinked glasses and sipped the sweet liquid, which quickly warmed them up.

There was a table near the door piled high with presents from guests and friends, who, Edna knew, would have saved all their ration coupons for the specific purpose of buying the newly-weds gifts. A lump rose in Edna's throat; it was without doubt the best day of her life, and she thanked God for it and for her friends' and family's boundless generosity.

Ted was true to his word about the quality of the locally sourced pork: it was roasted to perfection and served with sweet apple sauce, roast potatoes, sprouts and gravy, which was greatly appreciated by the hungry guests, who also marvelled at the sherry trifle that Maggie had provided.

'I don't know where she got her hands on all that

cream,' Edna whispered as she dipped her dessert spoon into the delicious cream and custard topping.

'The less you know about that, sweetheart,' Malc murmured under his breath, 'the better.'

'Can you promise me you won't finish up in the clink before our wedding day's over?' Edna asked nervously.

'If anybody tries locking me up today, I'll have their guts for garters!' Malc chuckled.

Arthur, Malc's best man, delivered his moving speech while gently rocking a sleeping Stevie in his arms. Afterwards, Flora surprised everybody by rising to her feet.

'I'll keep this short,' she said as she spotted Gladys organizing the band in the corner of the pub. 'I know the dancing's going to begin soon, but I just wanted to say, in public, how proud my daughters and I are of their new nana and my new mum.' The clapping and cheering that followed nearly brought the roof down. 'We lost each other for twenty-seven years,' Flora said, holding her mother's gaze. 'But being with you now, believe me, feels as natural as breathing.' Raising her glass of Guinness, she said, 'God bless the happy couple – God bless my mum!'

After keeping her emotions in check all day, Flora's short speech completely undid Edna, who burst into tears. Marilyn and Catherine, concerned that their nana was unwell, rushed to her side.

'Nana, Nana,' they cried as they hugged her.

'Are you not well?' Marilyn asked solemnly.

'I'm very well, sweetheart,' Edna replied, mopping

tears from her face with her best lace hankie. 'In fact, I've never felt better in mi life!'

'Then why are you crying?' Catherine asked, puzzled.

'Because I've found something precious that I thought I'd lost,' Edna replied as she kissed each little girl on the cheek. 'You and your mum!'

The newly-weds took to the floor for the first dance: a waltz to the strains of 'Yours Till the Stars Lose Their Glory', which they danced to while gazing deeply into each other's eyes. As the guests joined in, Edna jolted Malc back to reality with the question that had been foremost in her mind for several weeks.

'Sweetheart, when are you going to tell me where we're going for our honeymoon?' she murmured.

Malc sighed. 'I suppose now's as good a time as any,' he replied. 'First off, we're going to my house tonight – we don't want to be sharing our marriage bed with them granddaughters of yours,' he said with a sly wink. 'Then, on Boxing Day, we'll catch the train with Flora and the girls: they'll get off at Penrith, but we'll stay on,' he added with a mysterious smile.

'For pity's sake, man!' Edna cried as he swung her round the floor to the music. 'Put me out of my misery once and for all.'

'We, my sweetheart, are going to Edinburgh for our honeymoon!' he finally announced triumphantly.

Edna burst out laughing. 'Scotland!' she cried. 'It's lucky I packed mi fur knickers along with the rest of mi trousseau!'

At the end of a wonderful reception, the guests started to drift away, some to clock on for work on Christmas morning.

'Who cares if we're tired – it's been worth it to see our Edna get wed,' they said as they kissed the happy, smiling bride and groom goodnight.

Catherine and Marilyn wanted to carry on dancing in their new party frocks, but Flora told them that Santa was on his way and they needed to be tucked up in Nana's bed before he arrived in Pendleton with his sleigh full of toys.

'Are you coming home to sleep with us, Nana?' the girls asked, while Flora fastened the buttons on their winter coats.

'I bloody hope not!' Malc chortled behind his hand.

'No, sweetheart, I'm sleeping with Malc tonight,' Edna explained.

'Will he keep you warm?' Catherine asked.

Edna exchanged a lusty smile with her husband. 'Don't you worry, chick, Malc will keep me warm all night long.'

Singing 'Jingle Bells', the little girls and Flora, after promising to meet up in the morning, hurried home through the snow.

The only guests left were Gladys, Rosa, Nora and Maggie; Kit, exhausted by the long happy day, had gone home with Ian and Billy, the latter having had the time of his life running round the pub's dance floor all night.

Crowding around Edna, the girls hugged her, then pulled apart to let her go. 'Night, night, sweethearts,'

Edna said, then she left the Black Bull on her husband's arm. 'Wish me luck!' she added with a cheeky grin.

Walking through the falling snow, Edna sighed – she was going home to spend the night with the man she loved. It was to be the perfect end to a very perfect day.

32. Christmas Day

Christmas Day on the wards really shouldn't have been so magical, but for Gladys, somehow it just was.

She woke up when her alarm went off in midwinter darkness. Groping about for her clothes, which she'd carefully left on a chair at the bottom of the bed, she struggled into the bathroom, where, making as little noise as possible, she washed and dressed. Before leaving, she left her Christmas present for Rosa on the sofa; then, closing the door softly behind her, Gladys stepped into drifts of deep, virgin snow. There was no point in even thinking she could ride her bike through the drifts, so she set off determinedly on foot with a smile on her face. 'The world is soooo beautiful,' she thought; here she was in the pre-dawn darkness, watching the stars fade as the sun rose in the east. Slowly, inexorably, the thin slice of light merged into a deep pink as Christmas Day dawned.

'God bless all those brave troops, sailors and pilots; men risking their lives so we can have days like these,' Gladys thought with humbled tears in her eyes. 'What will they be waking up to? Mud-churned fields, gangrenous injuries, nothing to eat and no safe place to keep warm.' She thought of young sailors crossing silver-cold seas deadly with German mines, and pilots flying out on bombing-raids knowing some among their number would never come back.

The waste of life almost caused Gladys physical pain, but she reminded herself that to call it a waste was not honouring those men serving their country with such heroic ferocity, risking their lives for strangers like her, people they would never meet. With such grateful thoughts in her mind, Gladys ploughed on through the icy drifts, even more determined that she would dedicate her nursing career to the wounded troops shipped home from the casualty clearing stations on the Front line.

Arriving at the hospital, she relieved her colleague, who gave her an update on their patients: luckily nobody had suffered any mishaps in the night.

'A young lass had a baby,' her colleague told her with a smile. 'Born on the chimes of midnight to a munitions worker from the filling shed.'

Gladys had the pleasure of bathing the new baby boy, whilst his exhausted mum lay in bed drinking the tea and eating the toast that Gladys had prepared for her.

'I thought of calling him Jesus,' the new mum said without a hint of humour in her voice. 'Not just cos he was born on Christmas Day, but I honest to God thought I was dying having 'im,' she said feebly.

Gladys smothered a smile. 'Jesus might be a bit tricky,' she replied diplomatically.

'Mi husband, who's serving with the Royal Navy on

a mine-sweeper God only knows where, said if it was a lad he should be named George, after the king.'

'That's a nice name,' said Gladys as she lifted the little pink boy from the warm baby bath and gently wrapped him in a soft towel. Holding the precious bundle to her breast, she inhaled the intoxicating smell of a newborn, fresh-as-a-daisy baby.

'Do you think I could get away with George Jesus?' the new mother mused.

'I think you should do what makes you happy,' Gladys said, smothering another smile as she handed the baby – now in a nappy and a little white nightie – back to his mother, who gazed at her son adoringly.

Gladys slipped away so the young mother could nurse her son in private, and with the smell of the baby still in her nostrils dreamily wondered when she might hold her own newborn child in her arms.

'Honestly!' she exclaimed under her breath as she emptied the contents of several bedpans down the sluice. 'Christmas has made me go all broody.'

After taking temperatures and pulses on the men's ward, Gladys wrote up her notes on the charts, and to her astonishment found a little present sitting on the end of every bed.

'What's all this?' she asked as she noticed the gifts, then the smiling faces of her male patients. 'What are you up to?'

'Open them and find out,' an old man called out. 'They're all for you'.

Carefully undoing the wrapping paper so that it

could be reused, Gladys smiled in wonder at the small but thoughtful gifts she'd been given: an orange, a small bar of chocolate, some blue ribbon, a tin of talcum powder and a packet of Woodbines. She was quite overcome, and wondered how on earth they had managed to get hold of these things for her when they were so poorly.

'Sorry, Nurse Johnson, it was me that got you the fags,' a young lad who'd just had his appendix out said with a shy grin, 'Forgot you didn't smoke.'

'Thank you, thank you all of you, for your presents – you've made my day,' Gladys said gratefully.

'The sight of your bonny face, Nurse Johnson,' the young boy said with a gallant smile, 'makes our day – every day. We just wanted to say thank you, Nurse Gladys,' he added cheekily. 'And to wish you a Happy Christmas too.'

Gladys wiped a tell-tale tear from her eye, thanking her patients from the bottom of her heart and feeling more thankful than ever that circumstances had led to this new career of hers, which she so loved. The only thing that could make this day any better would be the sight of Reggie – oh, and maybe Myrtle too, of course – which she knew was absolutely impossible. Reggie had sent her a lovely Christmas card of St Paul's Cathedral, miraculously almost completely unscathed by the Luftwaffe. Inside, he'd written: *With all my love, your devoted Reggie xxx.*

They'd tried to arrange phone calls, but they all fell through: either Sister Atkins was in her office, where the hospital phone was kept, or Reggie couldn't leave the operating theatre at the right time to catch her.

'Never mind,' Gladys said firmly to herself. 'We're not the only sweethearts separated by distance, and, as Reggie said, at least he's not been posted to the Middle East.'

Strangely enough, this single sentence, which she repeated like a mantra to herself as she went about her daily business, gave her great comfort and optimism. London, compared with the Middle East, where terrible atrocities were taking place, was a mere stone's throw away. Separation was bearable; in fact, anything was better than the estranged life they'd lived before Gladys finally dropped her guard with Reggie and told him the truth. Even now, she felt a shudder at the thought of evil Captain Miles, but she took a great deal of satisfaction from the knowledge that he had been court-martialled and shamed before his fine naval colleagues. That justice had been seen to be done gave Gladys immense pleasure; she admired and was grateful to the brave girl in the Admiralty who had blown the whistle on her superior officer.

Back at Yew Tree Farm, Kit lay luxuriously in bed, with Billy beside her rummaging excitedly through his bulging Christmas stocking.

'Happy, darling?' Ian said as he walked into their bedroom bearing two cups of tea and a mug of milk for Billy on a tray.

'Oh, yes,' Kit sighed as she sat upright and fondled

the soft, sage-green silk camisole Ian had bought her. Taking her cup of tea and watching Billy rip his way into a chocolate bar, she said, 'Wasn't Edna's wedding wonderful?'

'It's hard to imagine a happier and more well-suited couple,' Ian answered. 'Well, apart from us,' he said, kissing his wife on the cheek.

'I have to admit,' Kit continued, 'it was hard not to look at Arthur throughout the service. I don't know how he did it – I would have been in bits.'

'He's got to be strong, if only for Stevie,' Ian said softly. 'The more I think about Arthur going away, the more I agree with his decision; only he can know what is right for the two of them, and if he really feels he'll be too haunted by the past, then it's got to be the right thing to move on somewhere new.'

'When you think about it realistically, though,' Kit said sadly, 'we'll probably never see them again.'

'That's a bit dramatic, darling,' he retorted.

'I don't think so. I know we all want to see them, but this feels like the end of a huge chapter in our lives. Violet and her little family will be nothing but memories before we know it,' she finished mournfully.

'Honestly!' Ian cried as he tickled his wife in order to bring a smile to her sad face. 'You and your Irish melancholy!' But he knew in his heart his sensitive wife was probably right, and agreed it was too sad for words.

Newly-weds Malc and Edna were also enjoying an early-morning cup of tea in bed; they both had a dreamy, faraway look, as if the memories of their love-making in the night were still clinging to them.

'How are you this morning, Mrs Preston?'

'Never better,' she answered with a bright smile. 'I think I'd best be making a move; otherwise we'll have the grandchildren out looking for us.'

'One more cuddle, my sweetheart,' said Malc as he drew his wife gently into his arms and kissed her moist, plump lips. 'Thank you for making me the happiest man on earth,' he said with an emotional catch in his voice.

'Thank you, my sweetheart,' she murmured tenderly, then with a giggle she added, 'Now then, we need to check that red robe fits you – and the beard too!'

'Oh, bloody hell!' Malc groaned as he rolled on to his back. 'Is this the end of the honeymoon?'

'You must be joking!' Edna cried. 'We're off to Scotland tomorrow – there'll be no holding me back once we've crossed the border! Now come on, Father Christmas,' she urged. 'Get your finger out!'

As Edna sauntered back to her chip shop with a wide smile on her face, she marvelled at her luck. How could a middle-aged woman going grey and with a definite tummy have snapped up a man as easy-going and generous as her Malc? He was even prepared to dress up as Santa – not many fellas would do that on their honeymoon!

The Christmas tree in the town square looked prettier than ever now that it was draped in a lacy covering of snow. 'Soon the locals will be gathered around it,' thought Edna. 'Singing carols and eating toffee apples.' The thought of hungry people put a skip in Edna's step. 'Better get a move on, kid,' she chided herself. She'd got a lot to do, but the first thing on her mind right now was to kiss her granddaughters and wish them a very merry Christmas.

Over in the Phoenix domestic quarters, Arthur was trying his utmost to treat the day as if it was just another day; he'd had umpteen offers from friends, especially Kit and Ian, who had begged him to spend Christmas with them, but he just couldn't face it. How could he be with other people, laughing and joking, celebrating, when all the time he just wanted to weep? He had no right to spoil others' happiness; the community around him nearly broke their backs working as hard as they did for the war effort, and they deserved every minute of peace and happiness they could snatch – he vowed he'd never get in the way of that. He needed to be home with Stevie, getting through just another day. God! How he needed to leave Pendleton. He was almost counting the days to their departure; it would unquestionably be painful, like ripping open a wound, but the thought of waking up to another view, working with another group of people who knew nothing of his past and starting a new life, just he and Stevie, somehow made the future bearable.

Arthur had got up as soon as Stevie stirred and changed the little chap before spoon-feeding him some warm, watery porridge, which Stevie seemed to relish. After warming up a bottle of formula milk, Arthur cradled his son in one arm whilst he fed him from the bottle; he loved the soft gurgling noises of contentment Stevie made as he hungrily sucked on the rubber teat, and when he stopped feeding to smile at his father Arthur's heart contracted with love.

But there was no doubt he was struggling today, concentrating hard on feeding his son rather than wallowing in despair, Arthur was startled by a sudden knock at the door. Still holding the baby, he made his way to the front door, which he opened before staring in complete amazement at Rosa, standing on the doorstep with presents in her arms.

'Merry Christmas!' she declared in a happy ringing voice. 'Please, can I come in? I know this is a surprise,' she added apologetically. 'But I am alone too! So I come with little gifts for you both.'

'That's very kind of you, Rosa,' Arthur said gratefully. He had grown particularly fond of kind-hearted Rosa and knew he would miss her, and all of the girls, when he moved on, as he knew he must. He gave her a warm smile and handed over Stevie. 'Hold on to the little lad whilst I put the kettle on.'

Waiting for the kettle to boil, Arthur searched around for something to offer Rosa, but his cupboards were bare, with only a slice of stale bread and a tin of baked beans. Feeling rather embarrassed by his lack of Christmas largesse, he returned to the sitting room with mugs of tea for both of them. He was surprised to find Stevie gnawing on a soft woolly teddy bear.

'I knit myself,' Rosa said. 'I got wool from jumble sale,

I wash it well before I knit it,' she assured Arthur. 'The head is too big for body,' she added with a shy smile.

'I can see Stevie already loves it,' Arthur said with delight as he watched his son, clutching his new toy, roll over on to his tummy.

'And this is for you,' said Rosa shyly, as she handed Arthur a large, rather heavy parcel.

Mortified that he hadn't got a thing to give to Rosa, Arthur blushed, touched beyond words by the young girl's thoughtfulness. 'You shouldn't have gone to the trouble,' he mumbled self-consciously.

'No trouble, it was a pleasure,' she replied sincerely.

Arthur removed the crêpe paper, which Stevie grabbed and played with whilst his father stood staring wide-eyed at a framed black-and-white drawing of his wife. Speechless, his eyes drank in the contours of Violet's elegant face, the swoop of her high cheek-bones, the fullness of her lips and her hair falling softly around her slender shoulders.

'It's beautiful,' he said on a long incredulous sigh.

Rosa also gave a sigh; hers was one of relief. 'I copy from a black-and-white photograph of Violet – she was so, so beautiful, we all adore her,' she said with genuine love in her voice.

'Strange,' he mused as he continued to gaze in wonder at the image of his dead wife. 'The fact that it's only black and white somehow accentuates her beauty: she looks almost luminous, like she's not gone, but is just some distance away.'

Rosa's beautiful, dark-brown eyes opened wide; she

certainly hadn't sought to create that illusion, but she was delighted if that's what she'd managed to achieve, and she didn't think she could hope for a better compliment. His words meant more to her than even winning the Salford gallery's prize money. 'I'm glad you like my drawing,' she said softly.

'I LOVE it!' Arthur cried, and before he could stop himself he bent to give the beautiful girl a huge hug. 'I feel awful that I have no gifts for you, no gifts for anybody, if the truth be known,' he added guiltily.

'Don't be daft!' Rosa exclaimed with a definite Northern accent that was at odds with her Mediterranean looks.

'Thank you, Rosa,' Arthur said humbly. 'Thank you from the bottom of my heart.'

Edna, Flora and the little girls were all squashed inside Edna's mobile chip shop.

'Why have you got so many apples, Nana?' Catherine asked.

'For toffee apples, sweetheart,' Edna explained.

'Mum!' Flora cried. 'How are you ever going to find enough sugar in this small town to make toffee?'

'I've been on the scrounge,' Edna said as she knowingly tapped her finger against the side of her snub nose. 'I'm a dab hand at wheedling out Pendleton sugar hoarders. I've cadged just about enough to make a watery toffee dip. The apples were no problem: people store them in cellars and attics, and I knew where to find them,' she said with a sly wink.

She turned around to survey her packed van. 'I'll serve apple fritters, and when they run out I'll make deep-fried potato scallops – they always go down a treat, plenty of scraps too, nobody can ever get enough of scraps.'

'Can me and Marilyn help?' Catherine begged.

'I was hoping you'd say that,' Edna laughed, as she produced two little checked pinafores that she'd made for the girls. 'You'll have to wear these if you're going to help, but you must promise me that you'll not go near the deep-fat fryer,' she added sternly, pointing at the fryer, which was presently stone cold with only a slab of lard sitting in its base. 'When it's hot, it's proper dangerous. Nana does the cooking whilst you two little helpers do the wrapping up and the salt and vinegar.'

With the Christmas celebrations starting at three in the afternoon, there was no time to even think about Christmas dinner, not that there were any chickens or turkeys to be had in Pendleton, but Edna had pre-cooked a rich casserole of scrag end of beef with carrots, onions and swede, which she planned on serving up at some time during the day – or night – with mashed potatoes.

'That's if we ever get a minute to eat!' she laughed as she left Flora and the girls to check out how Malc was getting on.

When she got to his house, the Father Christmas outfit had disappeared, but the sack of toys was still sitting in the middle of the sitting-room floor.

'What the 'ell's going on?' Edna muttered to herself. Had Malc done a runner at the eleventh hour?

Hearing the back gate clang shut, Edna dashed out into the yard, where she saw Malc creeping towards the house like a thief in the night.

'Where've you been?' Edna cried.

'Shssh!' Malc hissed as he nipped indoors clutching a cardboard box.

Intrigued, Edna watched Malc drop the box on to the floor, then breathlessly throw himself on to the sofa. Taking out his cigarettes, he lit one for both of them, then, after deeply inhaling, he told Edna what he'd done.

'When I looked in yon sack you'd left, I saw there were nowt there but lasses' gifts – dollies and pictures of elves and bloody fairies. I thought to myself: what wil't little lads think of me if I give 'em a peg dolly?'

'They wouldn't mind,' Edna protested.

'They bloody would mind!' Malc disagreed. 'And, more to't point, I'd mind.'

Thinking that Malc might have committed an act of burglary, Edna gasped, 'So what did you do?'

'I nipped over to't second-hand shop on Market Street,' Malc confessed with a guilty smile.

'You went to old Ma Barker's on Christmas Day!' Edna cried.

'Aye. I went in the back way and knocked on her window – she nearly had a bloody fit!' Malc chuckled.

'I bet she gave you a gobful?'

'No! She'd had a skinful,' Malc said, and started to

373

laugh. 'She'd been at the gin. I said to her I wanted some little toys for lads; she tottered off and after about ten minutes she staggered back with that lot,' Malc said. He flipped the cardboard lid open so Edna could peer inside the box.

'Toy cars!' she exclaimed in delight. 'Eeh, I bet Ma Barker charged you the earth for them.'

Malc shook his head. 'Nay, lass, she were three sheets gone. She just said, "Here y'are, 'ave em!"' Malc said incredulously. 'So now, thank God, I can look the local lads straight in the eye when I give 'em a gift from Father Christmas.'

Edna wrapped her arms around her grinning husband. 'I love yer,' she murmured as she kissed his lips. 'Yer great big soft apeth!'

33. Christmas Carols

Around three o'clock people started to gather in the market square, drawn by the tantalizing mixture of smells drifting out of Edna's mobile chip shop and the hot, nutty aroma of chestnuts roasting over an open brazier, a task Maggie had delegated to her mother, whilst she played the trumpet in the band.

'This lot are more apple than toffee if the truth be known,' Edna explained to her helpers, as she carefully arranged rows of toffee apples on a metal tray. 'I had to spin out the sugar to make the mixture stretch,' she told Marilyn and Catherine, who were munching their toffee apples without any complaint.

'They're really good, Nana,' was all they could say in between juicy mouthfuls.

One by one, the band girls appeared: Gladys, freshly changed out of her nurse's uniform, had walked down the slippery icy hill into town with Rosa, whose face was prettily flushed by the sharp easterly wind. Ian and Kit had used their precious bit of petrol to drive into town with Kit's drum as well as Billy, all bundled up in a warm coat, a stripy scarf and bobble hat.

'Where's Santa?' the indefatigable little boy cried, hopping out of the car and immediately looking about for his sleigh.

Ian smothered a fond smile as his wife bent down in order to speak to an overexcited Billy.

'Sweetheart,' she murmured, 'Father Christmas will be coming soon, you just have to be patient for a little bit longer.'

'Will he bring Rudolph?' Billy asked.

'Probably not,' Kit replied as she smoothed Billy's dark hair. Seeing her son's big blue eyes register disappointment, she quickly added, 'He had such a busy time last night, galloping all around the world delivering presents, that he's now fast asleep in his stable in Greenland.'

'With my carrot!' Billy added proudly.

Kit nodded as she remembered how Billy had left a carrot for Rudolph on the kitchen table, along with Father Christmas's ration-based mince pie. 'Definitely with your carrot,' she giggled as she kissed her little boy, who as far as she was concerned, grew more wonderful with every passing day.

When she thought how he'd so narrowly escaped death in the nursery garden not so long ago, her heart constricted with fear. She'd heard about her son's near-death encounter from both the matron and Mr Featherstone, and thanked God daily for the matron's quick thinking and immediate action. But for her, all the children would have been blown to kingdom come. It was bad enough that Violet had died in the blast, but the death of innocent babies and children on top of hers would have simply been unbearable. Pushing sad thoughts from her head, Kit focused on joyfully celebrating Christmas Day with her family and friends.

'Help me with the drum, please,' she asked Ian as they lifted it out of the boot and Billy immediately started bashing it. 'I'd better go and find the girls,' Kit said breathlessly.

'Off you go,' Ian said, holding out his hand to Billy. 'Come on, little fella, let's get you a toffee apple from Aunty Edna's big blue van.'

Kit heard Gladys and Rosa before she even saw them: the combination of Rosa's jingling piano accordion and Gladys's syncopated saxophone was unmistakable. Kit hurried towards the centre of the square, where her friends had cleared a space for the band.

'Hello!' she said as she plonked down her drum and gave Rosa and Gladys a big Christmas hug.

'Merry Christmas!' her friends cried as they hugged her back.

'All we need now are the other two,' said Gladys, looking distractedly round the square for Maggie and Nora. 'You don't think they'll have forgotten?' she murmured anxiously.

In answer to her question, Nora and Maggie, walking along arm in arm and laughing their heads off, swung round the corner. 'MERRY CHRISTMAS!' they cried as they rushed to join their friends.

'Eh! Look what I've got,' Maggie shrieked as she flapped an airmail letter before them.

'A letter from our Les!' Gladys said as she recognized her brother's handwriting.

'For some reason or another it went to mi mam's,' Maggie added. 'I've only just picked it up.'

'How is he?' Gladys asked excitedly.

'He's fine – missing us,' Maggie assured her. 'I'll let you read it later – well some of it,' she added with a cheeky wink.

'Isn't this beautiful?' Nora gasped as she surveyed the square, now busy with children jostling excitedly in queues at Edna's van and the hot-chestnut stall.

'Look! Over there!' Rosa cried in astonishment, pointing at the big banner that had been strung between two gas lamp-posts.

Tears came to her eyes as she read the words painted in large capital letters across the banner (which Edna had persuaded Ted, the landlord of the Black Bull, to put up on the basis that he had the longest ladder in town!).

PENDLETON CAROL SERVICE. ALL PROCEEDS
TO REFUGEES, VICTIMS OF WAR
PLEASE GIVE GENEROUSLY

Rosa gulped emotionally: this small town tucked into the folds of a valley high up on the moors was as close to her heart as her own beautiful city of Padua. 'These people,' she thought incredulously. 'They have nothing, but what little they have they share without questions.'

Seeing Rosa filling up as she stared at the flapping banner, Gladys slipped a comforting arm around her shoulder. 'Come on, my darling, sing your heart out for Gabriel, eh?'

'Sì, sì, certo, mia cara,' Rosa responded in Italian, as

she flicked away her tears. 'Where there's life there is hope, as Nora would say,' Rosa quoted with a brave smile.

'Okay, Swing Girls,' Kit called out to her friends. 'Let's tune up.'

'It'll be hard in this bloody weather,' Nora laughed. 'Mi trombone feels like a block of ice.'

'As long as you can squeeze a note out of it, we'll be fine,' Maggie laughed as she hit a high C and frightened the living daylights out of a stray dog snuffling round her feet.

As the band adjusted their instruments, Billy gratefully accepted a toffee apple from Catherine, who leant over the end of Edna's hatch to hand the wide-eyed little boy the first toffee apple of his life.

'That little lad's my godson,' Edna proudly told her granddaughters. 'Hello, my sweetheart!' she called to Billy, who waved back with the free hand that wasn't clutching the precious toffee apple.

'Where's Arthur?' Edna called out to Ian. 'Have you seen him?'

Ian shook his head. 'We stopped by on our way here and offered him a lift, but he said he couldn't face it. He might turn up – you never know.' But as his eyes met Edna's, he knew they were both thinking the same thing: how different the day would have been if Violet was alive.

The band launched into the first number – with a loud crash, bang, wallop from Kit on the drums, followed by the brass section blasting and the accordion joining in. Within minutes, the entire crowd packed in the town square were rocking and swaying back and forth as they sang at the top of their voices:

> We wish you a merry Christmas,
> We wish you a merry Christmas,
> We wish you a merry Christmas,

and then even louder they sang the last verse:

> And a happy new year!

As pennies and small coins, even penny farthings, tinkled into the donations tins, the old favourite carols rolled out: 'Away in a Manger', which all the children knew and loved; 'Oh, Little Town of Bethlehem', 'In the Bleak Midwinter', and then, just as it was going dark and snow started to fall once more, Father Christmas with his sack slung over his shoulder appeared as if by magic under the enormous town council Christmas tree.

'Ho! Ho! Ho!' he bellowed.

Standing by the hatch of her mobile van, Edna had the perfect view of her husband dressed up as Santa. 'Oh, bloody 'ell,' she sniggered to Flora. 'He's seriously getting into the role!'

'He's doing marvellously,' Flora declared as she loudly applauded Malc's heroic efforts.

Ted, dressed in green as one of Santa's helpers, organized an orderly queue of over-excited children, who otherwise might have stampeded Malc, who was perched nervously on a stool by the Christmas tree, looking rather like a man waiting for the guillotine to drop.

'Come along now,' Ted yelled. 'No pushing and shoving – let's make a nice long line for Santa.'

As each child eagerly stepped forward, Malc reached into his sack and drew out one present after another. The delight on the children's little faces touched Malc's tender heart, and when he saw the boys marvelling at their small metal cars he resisted the urge to say, 'Old Ma Barker's got more back in her shop; you could get another free if you nip round now!'

Malc's pulse started to race when he saw Billy standing in front of him. Terrified he might recognize him, Malc spoke in a deep gruff voice, 'Hello little boy!'

'Hello, Father Christmas,' Billy boldly replied. 'Did Rudolph get my carrot last night?'

'Er, well now,' Malc mumbled into his long beard.

Not having a clue what on earth Billy was talking about, Malc wondered how he could bluff his way out of an awkward situation, but luckily he caught sight of Ian standing slightly behind Billy, vigorously nodding his head. Taking the head-nodding as an affirmative, Malc boomed, 'He most certainly did get your carrot, Billy, and he asked me to thank you and to give you this present,' Malc said as he handed Billy a little car wrapped in blue crêpe paper.

'Thank you, Father Christmas,' Billy politely replied. 'Please give Rudolph a kiss from me!'

It was Kit who spotted Arthur pushing Stevie in his pram across the square. 'Thank God he made it,' she said fervently. Waving her hand, she warmly beckoned him over to join the band girls, who were tuning up for the next round of carols.

'Arthur! It's brilliant you've come,' Gladys cried, giving him the biggest hug. 'And Stevie too,' she added as she saw the bright-eyed little lad sitting up against a bank of pillows in his pram.

'As you well know, I hadn't planned on coming down here,' Arthur confessed with a guilty expression. 'I didn't want to be a wet blanket, but the more I thought about it the more I thought how wrong it was to deny Stevie some fun on Christmas Day.'

'Well done,' the girls cried, as they pressed around Arthur and his burbling son. 'We all know how hard this is for you – we miss her dreadfully too and we always will. But I think she'd love it that you're here with us today, I really do,' Kit said with tears in her eyes.

'You are with friends who love you,' Rosa said passionately.

Arthur nodded; he could feel the warmth of their love all around him. 'Thank you,' he said in a choked voice.

Nora, as ever, quite innocently lifted the mood by asking, 'Would your Stevie like an apple fritter? They've cooled down,' she quickly added. 'Edna gave me two.'

'Try him,' said Arthur, and smiled as Stevie grabbed the crispy fritter, which he pressed to his lips and chewed. 'I'd say that was a definite yes,' Arthur chuckled.

'Guess who's Father Christmas?' Maggie whispered mischievously.

Arthur's gaze fell on Santa under the tree, still handing out presents. 'That can't be Malc!' he guffawed.

'Right first time!' Maggie giggled.

'I'll buy him a pint for his troubles later,' Arthur promised.

Whilst Edna and her grandchildren did a roaring trade serving fritters and freshly brewed tea, and Maggie's mum shovelled crispy hot chestnuts into little newspaper cones, Flora and other volunteers wasted no time in working the crowd.

'Eat and drink as much as you like, all free,' Flora called out. 'Donations welcome for refugees, Pendleton's effort to help victims of war, dig deep, ladies and gentlemen – all donations gratefully received.'

As the charity tins continued to fill, the band struck up again, this time with more popular songs, which the crowd sentimentally crooned along to: Bing Crosby's 'I'm Dreaming of a White Christmas', followed by Judy Garland's 'Have Yourself a Merry Little Christmas', then 'Jingle Bells' and other family favourites.

Gladys laid aside her alto sax in order to sing yet another Bing Crosby number, 'I'll be Home for Christmas'. Her sweet but powerful voice echoed around the square, and the audience immediately joined in the singing. How many out there, Gladys mused as she sang her heart out, are yearning for their loved ones, separated from them by land and sea? How many would never ever see their loved ones again in all the years that were to come once the war was over?

The swell of voices filling the square, then floating

383

up into the night sky speckled with falling snow, brought tears to Gladys's eyes, and she could see that her friends, gathered around her singing and playing their instruments, were getting emotional too. As the final verse faded away, Gladys closed her eyes for a few seconds in thought and sighed. And when she opened them again she did a double-take – was she seeing things? Had she had a touch too much of the port last night at Edna's wedding reception? There, right before her eyes, was a large bunch of mistletoe, thick with white berries. A familiar deep voice behind her back said softly, 'Happy Christmas, my darling.'

Gladys whirled round. 'REGGIE!' she all but screamed in surprise and delight. 'REGGIE!' she cried again, as she flung herself into his arms, where she sobbed tears of pure joy.

Still holding the mistletoe high above her head, Reggie whispered, 'A kiss under the mistletoe.'

As their lips met, Gladys felt light-headed and dizzy with the force of Reggie's deep passionate kisses; gold and silver stars exploded in her head as she sank into his embrace. Eventually, short of breath, she had to pull away.

'Oh, Reggie.' She said his name yet again as she slumped against his strong, warm chest in a daze of happiness. 'I can't believe it! I thought you couldn't get off work for a few more days?'

'I wangled it at the last minute,' he told her. 'Swapped my rota and worked through the night.'

'Oh, my love,' she murmured as she traced her fingers tenderly around his tired but still very beautiful eyes.

'Christmas wouldn't be Christmas without you in my arms,' he whispered back.

A cheeky voice behind them made Gladys jump. 'Pleased to meet you!'

Hearing Maggie's giggle brought Gladys down to earth with a bump. Still blinking in disbelief, she introduced her tall, dark, handsome boyfriend to her pals.

'Dr Lloyd,' Rosa said politely. 'I hear so much from Gladys about you.'

Reggie flung his head back and laughed loudly. 'I bet most of it was bad?'

'It got better,' Rosa replied with a diplomatic smile.

The crowd around them weren't going to allow a bit of romance to get in the way of the proceedings. 'Let's have some more sing-song,' they demanded.

Reggie handed Gladys her saxophone. 'Sing for me, my songbird,' he said as his lips curved into a proud smile.

Gladys put the mouthpiece of the instrument she loved to her lips and played out the opening music for 'Silent Night', which the band girls quickly picked up.

> Silent night, holy night,
> All is calm, all is bright,
> Round yon Virgin, mother and child,
> Holy Infant so tender and mild,
> Sleep in heavenly peace,
> Sleep in heavenly peace.

As Edna sang her favourite carol with her strong arms wrapped around her grandchildren, her eyes sought out Arthur in the crowd.

'Soon he'll be gone,' Edna thought as she felt a huge lump rise in her throat. 'To start a new life without any of us here to remind him of Violet. I wish you well, Arthur Leadbetter,' Edna sighed. 'But you'll be sorely missed in Pendleton.'

Feeling like her own cup of happiness had overflowed, Edna lovingly regarded Catherine and Marilyn standing by her side, then her eyes wandered over to Malc, who was still dressed as Father Christmas. 'Poor sod,' she thought as she saw him struggling with the long, itchy beard. 'Never mind – tomorrow when we're on our own in Edinburgh, I'll make it up to him,' she thought with a secret, knowing smile.

Rosa's large brown eyes drifted to the banner waving in the wind. VICTIMS OF WAR, she read and prayed for all of those suffering persecution, torture and starvation as a consequence of Hitler's evil war that had set man against man. Looking up at the stars that were pricking the dark winter sky, she prayed with all her heart, 'Please, sweet God, grant my prayer, let me find my Gabriel soon, please, I beg you, keep him well, keep him alive.'

As the town clock struck seven, the happy crowd started to disperse; calling out season's greetings to one another, they went their separate ways. Edna and her family returned home to the chip shop, where Malc with great relief discarded the Father Christmas costume, then he willingly went with Arthur (who left baby Stevie with Edna and her enraptured grand-daughters) to the Black Bull, where he sank three pints of bitter in rapid succession.

Rosa, out of consideration to Gladys, asked Nora and Maggie if she might accompany them home.

'Why?' asked Nora, who'd never perfected the art of subtlety.

'Shssh!' hissed Rosa as she rolled her eyes towards Gladys and Reggie.

Maggie leant forward to whisper in Nora's ear, 'If she comes home with us, the love-birds can be on their own together, yer daft sod!'

Nora's big blue eyes all but rolled out of her head. 'OOOH!' she gasped as giggling Rosa and Maggie dragged her away before she really could put her foot in it.

Ian bundled exhausted Billy into the car, then, after packing Kit's drum away in the boot, he settled his sleepy wife in the passenger seat.

'Want a lift?' he called over to Gladys and Reggie.

'No, thanks,' Gladys called back, beaming. 'We'll walk.'

As their cries of 'Goodnight' faded away, Gladys slipped her arm through Reggie's. 'Walk me home, sweetheart?' she said with a loving smile.

'First, I've got to give you your Christmas present.'

Gladys blushed – not knowing she'd be seeing Reg-gie so soon, she hadn't got anything to give him. 'Reggie, you shouldn't have,' she said shyly.

'Oh, yes, I should!' he answered robustly as he produced an envelope from his overcoat pocket, which he handed to Gladys. 'Go on, open it,' he urged.

Looking puzzled, Gladys ripped open the envelope, inside of which was a typewritten letter, which she couldn't read because of the darkness and the falling snow. Reggie flicked on his cigarette lighter to cast a glow on to the paper. Squinting, Gladys saw the letter was addressed to her, and read it out loud:

You are asked to report to St Thomas' Hospital, Westminster, London, on 6 January 1944, for a six-month course of advanced post-operative nursing.

Stunned, Gladys gazed into Reggie's sparkling, dark-blue eyes. 'I'm going to London!' she gasped.

'You're coming to London to work with me, my sweet. I've arranged it; I'll be your assigned surgeon and mentor.'

Gladys gaped. 'How did you do that?' she gasped.

Reggie grinned as he gave Gladys a seductive wink. 'I'm a doctor, trust me!' he joked, as he picked her up in his arms and swung her round until she was dizzy. When he finally put her down, he looked at her with some concern. 'I wanted it to be a surprise, so I couldn't actually ask your permission, sweetheart. I know I shouldn't presume that you want to move to be with me. You can think about it – if you want to stay here, and I can see why you would want to be with all these wonderful people, you have only to say the word.'

There was not a single doubt in Gladys's mind; much as she would be sad to leave Pendleton and the community she adored here, her destiny was with Reggie; and her career (she had already determined) was working with the wounded in acute need of post-operative care. 'I don't have to think about it, darling: of course I want to be with you!' she replied as she reached up to kiss him square on the lips. Eventually they drew apart, and, rather dizzy with the ferocity and passion of their kisses, they gazed at each other for several seconds; then Reggie whispered as he twirled a length of her glorious hair around his fingers, 'I thought it would be a good idea for us to get to know each other better before I ask you to be my wife!'

Gladys was so happy she could barely stand up and had to cling on to the man she'd loved from the moment she first saw him that far-off day in the Bay of Naples. In the town she would shortly be leaving for a new life, she gazed up towards the dark outline of the towering hills, where snow fell from a leaden sky; the year would soon turn, and 1944 would dawn, leaving 1943 behind. History would come to view it as the year that changed the course of the war in Europe, but Gladys would remember it till the day she died as the year she lost Violet and Myrtle but found love and a future with Dr Reggie Lloyd.

Acknowledgements

I'd like to thank my wonderful editors at Penguin, Clare Bowron and Donna Poppy, for their attention to detail and their dedication. I have, on one or two occasions, taken a few liberties with historical fact for the sake of the story; I won't be the first author who has done this, nor will I be the last, and I hope, kind reader, you will indulge me in this.

**In the Phoenix Munitions Factory
everyone has their secrets . . .**

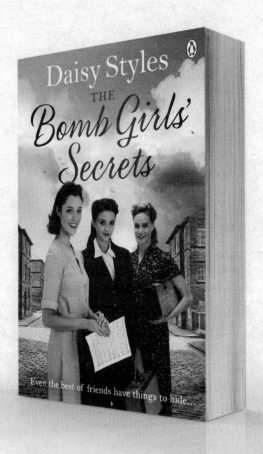

Working hard during the day and playing in the
Bomb Girls' Swing Band by night, Kitty's new life
seems fantastic. But she is keeping a secret from her
friends. And she soon realizes she might need their help
before it's too late . . .

Read on for an extract . . .

1. Kit

On a freezing January night, twenty-four-year-old Kitty Murphy lay in her berth and prayed for death. The biting howling gale whipped around the passenger ship bound for Heysham, sending it tossing and spinning over the churning grey sea. As it plunged and rose like a monstrous sea serpent in the rolling waves, Kit stopped thinking about the possibility of being torpedoed by a German warship or bombed by a German Luftwaffe flying low over the Irish Sea. Instead, she groaned as her stomach went into yet another spasm of dizzying nausea. She'd been sick since the moment of departure from Dublin, and all through the wretched dark night too. In the bunk beds on either side of the cabin that smelt of vomit and cigarettes two other women lay sprawled and groaning on their berths, whilst a third cheerfully sat upright on her bed chain-smoking.

'She must have guts of steel,' thought Kit as sleep mercifully engulfed her.

She suffered tormented dreams of Billy, new born, pink and warm in her arms. The baby she had had to leave behind, only a matter of weeks after a hard birth. Tears rolled unchecked down Kit's thin cheeks; it was less than twenty-four hours since she'd left Billy at home in Chapelizod and it already seemed like a lifetime. Rosie had escorted her sister to the bus stop, where they'd stood in the rain, waiting for the bus that would take Kit to Dublin. Clutching Billy tightly in her arms, she'd inhaled the sweet baby smell of him for the last time, and as the bus loomed up she'd kissed him over and over again, before Rosie had literally wrenched the screaming child from her arms and Kit stumbled on the bus, blinded by tears.

Kit could scarcely remember how she got from the bus station to the Dublin docks. All her instincts had told her this was wrong: she should be walking in the opposite direction. Even her body had protested. Her breasts were sore and engorged with milk, food that Billy, she was quite sure, would be wailing for right now. The thought of him lying in his makeshift crib, a drawer taken from the dresser, crying for food, nearly killed her. Would her younger sister have time to change Billy's nappy and give him the bottle she'd left with instructions on how to sterilize it with boiling water after Billy's feeds? Her womb throbbed from the long walk to the docks; the sensation reminded her so much of when she'd first fed her son. As he caught on the nipple and sucked greedily, she'd felt her womb contract. Just the thought of his birth, the sweet memory of him entering the world, brought a brief barely visible smile to her lips.

Kit's father had refused point-blank to pay out money for a midwife.

'To hell with a feckin' midwife!' he'd announced. 'You'll not find me paying out for your bastard child.'

It was a long hard labour for Kit, who was small and narrow hipped, and Billy, a big bouncing boy, almost tore her apart, but all the pain and fear had been worthwhile.

She cherished the moment of holding Billy for the first time, of putting him to her breast, and worn out by the long labour he slept peacefully in her arms.

As the rain had started to fall and the Dublin docks loomed up in the wet mist that suddenly shrouded the city, Kitty vividly recalled how she'd marvelled at Billy's dask eyelashes fanned out on his soft, pale cheeks. Could this miracle of a child really be the product of Lionel Fitzwilliam?

'He's like an angel, Ma,' she'd whispered to her mother when the labour was over. 'A gift from God.'

After a prolonged spell of coughing, Mrs Murphy had remarked in a frightened whisper, 'Don't be after letting your da hear you talking like that – you've brought shame upon this house.'

When she'd missed her first monthly, Kit wilfully told herself that the shock of Fitzwilliam's brutal attack had upset her body, but when she missed the second and was sick every morning she knew she was pregnant.

'Mi da will kill me,' she whispered to Rosie as they lay together in the single bed they shared, covered with old coats to keep them warm.

'Jesus, Kit! He'll crucify you,' Rosie whispered in a voice full of fear.

Lying in her narrow berth in one of the cheapest cabins, which were close to the engine room, she remembered the long queue of passengers she'd joined the previous day, all poor families hoping for a better life in England. Kit's eyes had instantly picked out the babes in their mothers' arms. She would willingly have sailed around the world and back again if she could only have her baby safe in her arms. She should have known it would end badly after her father's reaction to her pregnancy, which he'd discovered when she started to show in her fifth month. He hadn't crucified her, as Rosie had predicted, but he'd bounced Kit off every wall in the cottage, then hit her repeatedly until stars blazed in her head. The sound of her mother's high-pitched screams finally brought him to a halt. As he stood panting and swearing over his daughter's battered body, Kit tried to tell him what had happened to her.

'It wasn't my fault!' she sobbed.

'WASN'T YOUR FAULT?' he roared like a raging bull. 'It was YOU that opened yer legs, yer filthy little tramp!' he sneered.

'Da, as God's my witness –'

Kit got no further: after giving her a final kick, her father turned away and left the house.

Despite all the terrible things going on in the war-torn world, for Kit the 7th of December 1941 had been the start of a whole new wonderful world; for the first time in her life she felt complete. With her son's arrival the sky was bluer, the grass greener, and the birds sang more sweetly. In a state of blissful infatuation, Kit had no idea that her son's birth date was the fateful day the Japanese bombed Pearl Harbor, an event that, she would later learn, changed the entire course of the war.

When Billy slept in his dresser-drawer cradle, Kit ached to hold him; when he woke, she waited for his blue eyes to open and search out hers. As he grew, his little hands reached for her, and Kit was the first to see his heart-stopping, lop-sided smile. Mrs Murphy, who was weak and breathless after having suffered for two years from tuberculosis, advised her daughter to let Billy cry.

'He can't be having you all of the time,' she chided.

Kit was shocked by her mother's harsh words. 'I don't want to let him cry!' she exclaimed. 'If he's hungry I want to feed him; if he's sad I want to cuddle him.'

'Picking him up and mollycoddling him every five minutes will turn the little lad into a big softie,' her mother warned.

'Ma, he's a few weeks old – what harm can a kiss and a cuddle do?' Kit protested as she scooped Billy out of the drawer and put him to her breast, where he suckled eagerly.

'Mark my words, you'll ruin the boy,' Mrs Murphy said as she shook her head in deep disapproval.

Staring up at the ceiling, trying to stop the waves of nausea overwhelming her, Kit was glad that she had spent those precious first weeks with Billy, responding to his every cry, examining every inch of his soft warm body, kissing his little toes and stroking his rosy cheeks until he drifted off to sleep. As if sensing they would be parted, she had imprinted her baby into her memory: his irresistible smell, his sky-blue eyes, his dimpled chin, the way he sighed when falling asleep, the arch of his small strong back. There was nothing about her son that went unnoticed by his adoring mother.

Only the night before she'd stood at the quayside, standing on Irish soil for as long as she could, clinging to the thought that she and her son were still breathing the same air, still living in the same country.

'All aboard! All aboard!' a sailor had cried, startling Kit, who realized she'd been staring into space, unaware of fellow passengers bustling by.

'Come along, young lady,' the cheerful sailor said as he helped Kit on to the gangplank. 'England awaits!'

'England!' Kit had groaned as she leant over the rails and watched the crew raise the anchor. 'It's Ireland where I should be,' she whispered as the ship's engine powered the massive propeller and they headed her out to sea. As the dark and misty coastline of the land she'd grown up in faded into darkness, Kit wondered if drowning herself in the crashing waves far below would be easier than living without Billy.

And the misery hadn't dissipated. Drifting in and out of a restless sleep, Kit recalled with a shudder how she had come to be on this boat in the first place.

When Billy was almost three weeks old, Mr Murphy had returned rolling drunk from the pub, threatening to send the child away for adoption. Kit, wild and fearless as a tigress guarding her cub, had fought her father with every fibre of her body.

'He's my son!' she protested. 'He belongs to me – I'll never let him go.'

A few days later, and this time stone cold sober and therefore more dangerous, her mercenary father had come up with an alternative plan.

'We'll take care of your bastard in return for five pounds a week.'

Kit's jaw dropped in disbelief.

'That's impossible. You know how much I earn working on the farm: not even half of that!'

'I'm not talking about working on the feckin' farm, yer eejit!' her father snapped. 'It's the Lancashire mills you'll be heading for.'

Kit's incredulity changed to blind panic.

'Lancashire!' she exclaimed. 'My baby's not a month old – I can't leave him.'

Ignoring her words, her father continued. 'There's good money to be had in England.'

'But I want to be with Billy,' Kit said as she started to cry. 'Please don't make me go, Da. *Please, please* let me stay.'

'You've brought disgrace to the family with your dirty little bastard. The only way you can keep him is by going to work in England and sending money home to us to look after him.'

Kit knew full well that any money she sent to her father would disappear down the pub; none of it would go to Billy, who'd be left with her sickly mother whilst her self-seeking father drank himself into oblivion. She bit back the words which, if spoken, would only make her position worse. Through distant relations who'd recently crossed the waters to settle in Manchester, her father had heard of the comparatively high wages paid to workers in the Lancashire cotton mills, and his mind was set on sending Kit there. No matter how much she sobbed and implored, ranted and wept, Mr Murphy's remained resolute, until she slowly realized that leaving home and providing her family with money was really the only way she could keep Billy and avoid his adoption.

After the longest and loneliest night of her life, the ship finally heaved to a halt and Kit, briefly unaware of where she was, thought for a split second that she was back home in bed with Billy.

'Don't cry, my darling,' she said as she reached out to comfort him.

She pictured him gurgling and cooing in her arms, smiling trustingly at his mother, the person who loved him most in the world. Grasping thin air, Kit wept. She had shattered that innocent new-born trust, abandoning him to her mother, who'd be lucky if she lived to see the year out, and her cruel father, who didn't care if the child lived or died. Her only hope was that Rosie would have the time and patience to look out for her precious son.

'Thank Jesus! We've landed,' the chain-smoking girl announced.

Weak and shaky, Kit found a bathroom, where she washed her ashen face and combed her hair. Staring at her reflection, she hardly recognized the girl she'd been a year ago. Her dark hair was still long but it had lost its rich lustre, as had her dark brown eyes. The worry of leaving her son had dramatically reduced her appetite, though she'd still managed to breastfeed Billy until the day she left. Her breasts tingled with the milk seeping from her nipples, sustenance for the baby she'd abandoned, she thought bitterly as she stuffed handkerchiefs into her ragged vest to absorb the liquid. Bone weary, Kit returned to her cabin, where she picked up her cheap, battered suitcase, then she walked down the ship's gangplank and on to English soil with her heart as heavy as lead.

2. Gladys

Gladys Johnson opened her beautiful dark blue eyes wide so she could sweep black mascara on to her long lashes.

'Be sharp now, or you'll miss the bus,' her mum nagged from the back kitchen, where a sheep's head bubbling in a pan on the back burner made the air unpleasantly sickly. Though Gladys knew her mum would later drain the stock off the boiled head and use it to enrich her meat pies, the sight and smell of the sheep's brains always turned her stomach.

'Come on, our Glad,' said Leslie, her handsome young brother, as he flicked her long hair on his way to pick up his coat. 'I'll walk to't bus stop with you.'

'You won't if you keep messing up my hair!' she laughed. 'Gimme a minute to finish mi make-up.'

Les shook his head and smiled fondly as he watched his beautiful big sister apply red lipstick to her full pouting lips, then pull a comb through the rich, glossy brunette ringlets that framed her smiling face.

'Thou art vainest lass in't th'ole of Leeds!' he mocked.

Gladys gave him a cheeky wink. 'You've got to make the most of what you've got, our kid!'

Calling a cheery goodbye to their mother, brother and sister swung down the cobbled terrace street where they'd grown up. With only a couple of years separating them in age, they'd always had a strong bond: they shared the same sense of cheeky humour, they both regularly played in the local Sally Army band along with their dad, and they both had a passion for swing music. They also shared the same good looks: tall and strong, they both had thick curling brunette hair, stunning deep blue eyes, a dimple in the right cheek and a wide smiling mouth.

'Don't mention owt to our mam, but I'm thinking of joining the Yorkshires,' Les said in a whisper. 'I might even get a chance to play my trumpet in the regimental band,' he added excitedly.

Gladys stopped dead in her tracks. 'I knew this was coming!' she exclaimed.

'Come on, Glad,' he reasoned. 'A lot of lads I know joined up as soon as war was declared.'

'Aye!' she said angrily. 'And a lot of them lost their young lives at Dunkirk in 1940.'

'It's my duty, Glad,' he said flatly.

She knew he was right; there were hardly any young men in evidence in Leeds these days, not unless they were briefly home on leave. Of course Les should fight for his country, even though he was her kid brother whom she used to protect from the bullyboys at primary school. As if reading her thoughts, Les added, 'I'm not a kid any more.'

Gladys nodded. 'I know . . .'

Tears filled her eyes at the thought of him going away. The house often rang with his laughter and the sound of his trumpet blasting out of his bedroom. 'God, how I'll miss him,' she thought to herself, but she knew that he was of the age for conscription. Nobody could miss the stern government posters all over the city: BRITAIN NEEDS YOU.

Standing up to kiss Les she gave a brave smiled as she said, 'In that case, I wish you good luck!' She hugged him hard, praying that God would keep him safe. Bravely she swallowed her tears for his sake.

They went their separate ways: Les to the factory where he worked as a welder and Gladys to the Lyons Café on Hudson Road. Lyons employed over a hundred staff to serve food throughout the day and into the evening in a restaurant arranged on four levels. Whilst an orchestra played in the background, Gladys offered hungry customers a dizzying choice of starters, main courses and puddings, followed by coffee, and all for one shilling and sixpence. Wearing a black dress and an immaculately starched and pressed white apron and cap, Gladys glided through the noisy dining room packed with tables, all draped with snowy-white cloths and laid with gleaming cutlery. Skilfully balancing a heavy tray loaded with fish cakes, vegetable hotpot, baked currant pudding and apple turnovers plus a pot of tea, Gladys gracefully circumnavigated boisterous children, impatient old ladies and flustered Nippies to bring food to her expectant customers.

Happy as she was at Lyons, nothing equalled the thrill of her evening job, when she played the alto saxophone in Jimmy Angelo's Swing Band. Gladys had always loved music. From the time they were just tots, she and Les had joined their dad, who played the booming drum for the Salvation Army, in marching through the streets of Leeds, singing hymns and collecting money for the homeless. When his children were still small, Mr Johnson had bought each of them a tiny trumpet, which they proudly tooted as they strode along beside him through the streets of Leeds city centre. In their teens, much influenced by the American swing bands which they both adored, Gladys had moved from the trumpet to the alto sax, whilst Les stuck with his beloved trumpet. Brother and sister loved to play duets: up in their bedrooms they'd take it in turns to pick a dance number and experiment with harmonies until their mother banged on the ceiling with a brush.

'Will you stop that din up there – the neighbours will have us thrown out!' she bellowed.

The Andrews Sisters were their all-time favourites, especially 'Boogie Woogie Bugle Boy of Company B', which they played with wild abandon whenever they could get away with it. Les loved his music and was good at it but his talented sister had bigger ideas; Gladys wanted to take her musical skills to a professional level.

'Perform in public! You must be joking,' Les had laughed when she confessed her burning ambition. 'Our dad'll go crackers!'

'Nothing ventured, nothing gained,' she'd said with a shrug of her pretty shoulders.

When she'd seen an advert in the General Post Office for a dance band saxophonist, Gladys had immediately applied. The dance bandleader, Jimmy Angelo, though born and bred in Leeds, had a Sicilian father and spoke in a thick Northern dialect interspersed with snips of Italian.

'*Eh! Non credo che sia una ragazza!*' he laughed when Gladys turned up to audition.

Not having a clue what he was talking about, Gladys,

in a tight-fitting black crêpe dress with her long dark hair swinging around her shoulders, took her saxophone out of its leather case and played a powerful rendition of 'You are My Sunshine' that took the indulgent smile off Angelo's cocky face. Dropping the Italian, he blurted out, 'Blood 'ell, kid! Who taught you 'ow for't play yon sax?'

'My dad,' she replied proudly. 'There's more,' she added as she launched into 'Oh, Lady Be Good' without any sign of sheet music.

At the end of her performance, Angelo applauded loudly, then blew kisses in the air.

'*Favoloso! Eccellente!* When can you start?'

She was required to play each evening from Friday to Sunday at the Mecca Locarno in the County Arcade in Leeds.

Les had been right when he'd warned Gladys about the family's reaction to her playing in public. Her mother, a born worrier, was appalled by the thought of her twenty-year-old daughter having two jobs.

'You'll kill yourself!' she exclaimed.

But it was her father who was the biggest obstacle. He adored his little girl and wasn't happy about her performing with an all-male band.

'That's not a job for lasses,' he announced as he lit up his pipe and buried his head in the *Yorkshire Evening Post.*

'Lots o' lasses play in the Sally Army band!' Les said in his sister's defence.

Gladys shot him a loving smile. 'Thanks,' she mouthed.

'That's different,' Mr Johnson retorted. 'That's for the Lord.'

Gladys cuddled up to her dad. 'Come on,' she coaxed.

'It's you that taught me music; it's not my fault if I'm good at it – it's a gift from God!'

Mr Johnson finally relented – on condition that he accompanied Gladys to the Locarno and stayed throughout the night to keep an eye on her. He became a regular feature in the ballroom, sitting in a corner drinking warm lemonade and puffing on his pipe. If the truth were known, he loved his nights out watching his dazzling daughter playing the alto sax, which had almost become an extension of her bright, vibrant personality. The complicated melodies that poured out of the instrument when Gladys was playing solo sometimes brought the dancers to a stop; they'd gaze in amazement at the good-looking young girl in her full-length satin ballroom dress embellished with sequins and bows playing the alto saxophone like they'd never heard it played before. Though surrounded by men, Gladys was rarely approached for a date or a dance. Her father's glowering presence frightened off potential suitors, which suited Gladys down to the ground. Her passion was music – men would just get in the way of her secret ambition, which was to lead her own all-female swing band.

Ironically, it wasn't men that got in the way of her dreams: it was female conscription. There was no denying that Gladys, a staunch patriotic Yorkshire lass, wanted to do her bit for the war effort; her only condition was that she wanted to stay in Leeds, where she could continue to play for Jimmy Angelo at the Locarno in between her shifts. So it was with horror that she read her call-up letter, which instructed her to report to a munitions factory in Pendleton, on the other side of the Pennines.

With tears spilling from her lovely blue eyes, she blurted out, 'I don't want to go, Dad!'

Mr Johnson choked back a tear too: not only had his son recently announced he had joined up but he was now losing his daughter. Frightened of betraying his emotions, he replied more brusquely than was necessary. 'Thou's got no choice, our lass.'

'Why can't I do my war work here in Leeds?' she sobbed.

Mr Johnson sighed as he gave her hand a squeeze. 'The government are sending you where you needed, Glad, that's all that's to it.'

On her final night at the Locarno, Gladys played her heart out. After a show-stopping rendition of 'Rhapsody in Blue', she took to the floor with Jimmy, who was a superb ballroom dancer, and, to the strains of 'I Only Have Eyes for You', she leant her head against his shoulder and wept.

'I'll die without my music,' she said as he dabbed away her tears with his red silk handkerchief.

'Come on, amore, it won't be forever,' he assured her. 'The war has to end one day, eh, certo? We'll be waiting for you when you get back.'

Gladys gave a brave smile . . . Little did she know that night in January 1942 that she'd never be coming back.

Emily, Lillian, Alice, Elsie and Agnes.

Five very different young women with very different lives.

But it's 1941 and everyone has to do their bit.

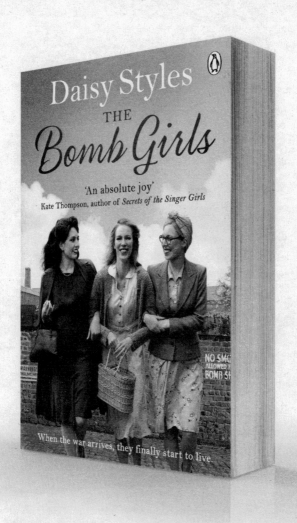

The girls of Walsingham Hall
are determined to unlock the secrets
of a country at war, no matter who
tries to stop them.

He just wanted a decent book to read ...

Not too much to ask, is it? It was in 1935 when Allen Lane, Managing Director of Bodley Head Publishers, stood on a platform at Exeter railway station looking for something good to read on his journey back to London. His choice was limited to popular magazines and poor-quality paperbacks – the same choice faced every day by the vast majority of readers, few of whom could afford hardbacks. Lane's disappointment and subsequent anger at the range of books generally available led him to found a company – and change the world.

'We believed in the existence in this country of a vast reading public for intelligent books at a low price, and staked everything on it'
Sir Allen Lane, 1902–1970, founder of Penguin Books

The quality paperback had arrived – and not just in bookshops. Lane was adamant that his Penguins should appear in chain stores and tobacconists, and should cost no more than a packet of cigarettes.

Reading habits (and cigarette prices) have changed since 1935, but Penguin still believes in publishing the best books for everybody to enjoy. We still believe that good design costs no more than bad design, and we still believe that quality books published passionately and responsibly make the world a better place.

So wherever you see the little bird – whether it's on a piece of prize-winning literary fiction or a celebrity autobiography, political tour de force or historical masterpiece, a serial-killer thriller, reference book, world classic or a piece of pure escapism – you can bet that it represents the very best that the genre has to offer.

Whatever you like to read – trust Penguin.